Frances Brody is the author of seven mysteries featuring Kate
Shackleton as well as many stories and plays for BBC Radio, scripts for
television and four sagas, one of which won the HarperCollins Elizabeth
Elgin Award. Her stage plays have been toured by several theatre
companies and produced at Manchester Library Theatre, the Gate and
Nottingham Playhouse, and *Jehad* was nominated for a *Time Out* Award.
Frances lived in New York for a time before studying at Ruskin
College, Oxford, and reading English Literature and History at
York University. She has taught in colleges, and on
writing courses for the Arvon Foundation.

Visit Frances Brody online:

www.francesbrody.com
www.facebook.com/FrancesBrody
www.twitter.com/FrancesBrody

Praise for Frances Brody:

'This beautifully evoked slice of regional experience offers universal
appeal . . . a colourful network of characters leaps from the pages'
The Guardian

'An exquisite novel . . . fast-moving and compelling [and]
reminiscent of Elizabeth Taylor or Alan Sillitoe'
Big Issue in the North

'Frances Brody has made it to the top rank of crime writers'
Daily Mail

'Brody's winning tale of textile industry shenanigans
is shot through with local colour'
Independent

'An irresistible read . . . full of humour as well as gritty realism'
Jill Hyem, writer of Tenko *and* House of Eliott

'Enriched by a fine array of characters, brought to life with warmth,
compassion and humour . . . thoroughly enjoyable and uplifting'
*David Nobbs, w......'Th.. F.ll......................*Perrin

By Frances Brody:

Sisters on Bread Street
Sixpence in Her Shoe
Halfpenny Dreams

Kate Shackleton Mysteries

Dying in the Wool
A Medal for Murder
Murder in the Afternoon
A Woman Unknown
Murder on a Summer's Day
Death of an Avid Reader
A Death in the Dales

Halfpenny Dreams

FRANCES BRODY

piatkus

PIATKUS

First published in Great Britain in 2007 as *Sisters of Fortune* by Severn House
This edition published in 2016 by Piatkus

1 3 5 7 9 10 8 6 4 2

A CIP catalogue record for this book
is available from the British Library.

ISBN 978-0-349-41073-9

Typeset in Perpetua by M Rules
Printed and bound by CPI Group (UK) Ltd, Croydon, CR0 4YY

Papers used by Piatkus are from well-managed forests
and other responsible sources.

MIX
Paper from
responsible sources
FSC® C104740

Piatkus
An imprint of
Little, Brown Book Group
Carmelite House
50 Victoria Embankment
London EC4Y 0DZ

An Hachette UK Company
www.hachette.co.uk

www.piatkus.co.uk

For George

Author's Note

This book was first published under my Frances McNeil name with the title *Sisters of Fortune*, before I turned to crime. Readers familiar with my Kate Shackleton mystery novels may spot the turning point, leading to darker deeds.

Lydia

I had strict instructions not to dare eat an Easter egg, in case of throwing up in the Registry Office and making a farce of proceedings. But it was very early. The Easter egg from Shelly, Phoebe's understudy, was quite small. And hollow. My wedding day blue taffeta dress and jacket caught the light as I drew back the curtains. Better not put that on yet.

We were on the hotel's second floor. The broadest and most polished of banisters invited me to slither down, holding my Easter egg, looking at the great deep scary drop to marble tiles a mile below.

I was really too old, at going on twelve, to be doing such things, but as the only child in a touring company, I grabbed whatever enjoyment came my way.

The old doorman didn't notice me because he was lifting a guest's portmanteau into the boot of a taxi.

A railway station is always a good place to go and Leeds City Station was bang beside the hotel. The station had its own little picture house, for people to pass the time of day if they were much too early for a train. Photographs of current and coming attractions looked out from a glass frame. Some were pictures of the news, which did not deserve pictures in my opinion because news is dull. More interesting were photographs of a blonde actress in not much of a dress. A man dressed all in black leered over her, staring eyes under bushy dark brows bulging from his bloated face. She was pretty, but not a patch on Phoebe who is dark-haired and dramatic-looking, and plays tragedy and comedy in equally brilliant measure. (A review with those exact words is pasted in our scrapbook.)

I was not the only one gawping.

'Hello, little dark eyes. Do you want to go in?' A clammy hand grabbed my arm. The man's blubbery lips kept smacking after he stopped speaking. His nostrils twitched. 'Do you want to be took in the pictures? I'll pay you in.'

'No thank you.' I pulled away and ran into the station, looking back to make sure he didn't follow me. And he would have too, but the cinema commissionaire stepped forward and said something to him.

Pretending to be part of a family group, I slipped through the barrier, onto the nearest platform, to watch the trains. I liked the sight of people going places, the smell of the steam and the trains' chugger-bugger-chugger-bugger-chugger-bugger.

Sitting on a big wooden trolley, I ate my Easter egg and watched two people say goodbye. When people say goodbye, one of them is always secretly glad. Which of you is glad, and which of you is sorry to your very innards? On a spring day, ladies do not usually dress entirely in black and so it seemed to me that the person going, dabbing a lacy hanky to her eyes, must be setting off for a funeral. The gentleman in the striped suit, saying thoughtful words, must be her husband. Perhaps he didn't like the dead person enough to attend, or else was too busy to go to funerals.

The hand on my shoulder made me jump out of my skin and sent chocolate crumbs scattering.

'Lydia!'

Suddenly everyone on the platform was looking at me, instead of the other way round.

'I guessed you'd be somewhere you shouldn't, and today of all days.'

Ada reached out her hands and took both of mine, pulling me up from the trolley, grabbing me in a big hug. 'You've had me senseless with worry.'

Ada is a tall person, though not so tall as Phoebe. Everything about her is plain and that is the way she likes it. Plain, big-boned looks, salt and pepper braided-up hair, a long black skirt, almost touching the ground, and under it more than one petticoat. To top herself off she has three changes of long-sleeved blouse, over a warm vest: two striped blouses and one paisley. She wore the paisley. Her other item of clothing was not really clothing at all. Fastened between her top petticoat and skirt was a neatly stitched money belt, having a great many press studs at the front and hooks and eyes at the back so that it had to be put on the wrong way round and then turned about.

She liked to say, 'My bank's on my belly, and that's where it stays.'

3

We did not hurry out of the station as fast as Ada expected. She had been made to buy a platform ticket to come and look for me. The inspector demanded to see my ticket, platform or otherwise. He insisted I must have some sort of ticket. Ada blamed him for letting a defenceless child wander through a dangerous station. I cannot now remember how the matter was settled; only that Ada did not pay up.

She kept hold of my hand till we were back in the hotel. There I took off my frock, washed myself – face, neck, arms and legs. She dabbed a flannel at my nose and cheeks saying I'd missed a spot or two of railway cinder. I put on the brand new blue dress with bolero jacket, new white socks and patent-buttoned shoes, polished by Ada to a mirror sheen with petroleum jelly and cotton wool.

No one ever combed and plaited hair as well as Ada, taking short lengths from the bottom, holding the strand firmly with one hand, so as not to tug when she drew down the tortoiseshell comb.

Along the corridor, my mother's hotel room looked like a field of dark tulips. They stood proudly on the dressing table, like soldiers. Some perched on the windowsill, nodding at traffic in City Square. Bedside cabinets sprouted tulips.Ever after that and ever since, when I see tulips, I see my mother, her thick dark hair looped and decorated with oriental combs, her perfect high-cheekboned face and wide mouth, looking at herself in the mirror, dabbing a powder puff to her nose. She wore a new pale turquoise silk dress. A matching coat lay on the bed. I thought my dress a miracle, but hers was magic.

She smiled at me through the mirror and began to apply

lipstick, following the curve of her upper lip with great care, and with that little habit of running her tongue just inside her lower lip and along her even white teeth, as if it helped her concentrate.

I picked up the card that stood between vases on the dressing table. 'To my adored beloved, for whom I have waited too long.'

She had told me his name. Mr Sheldon Thackrey, occupation, banker. He had loved Phoebe since he saw her play Portia when I was just twenty months old, sleeping in a basket in the corner of her dressing room. But Mr Thackrey was married then. She had steadfastly refused to have anything to do with him, other than let him take her to supper and buy her the occasional piece of jewellery, until – according to Ada – the poor man was half mad with desire.

She came to sit beside me on the bed and put a finger under my chin. 'No more living out of a suitcase for you, Lydia.'

Until that morning, the ramifications of Phoebe's marriage to Mr Thackrey did not really begin to sink in. I didn't know it would alter our lives so completely. Perhaps it did not feel real because she had been married so many times on stage.

When she spoke, it was as if she was telling me not about herself but about one of those very characters.

'Lydia, darling, every seven years our bodies change utterly and totally.' (Phoebe once had an admirer who was a professor of medicine.) 'We do not remain the same person. I am in the fourth seven-year cycle of my life.'

'Fifth don't you mean?' Ada said.

Phoebe ignored her. 'Now is the time to take this

5

plunge, for both of our sakes, before the next inexorable change occurs.'

'Tell the kid in words of one syllable,' Ada said. 'Banker's wife is the best part you've been offered.'

We had said goodbye to everyone in the company, except Mr Crampton, our theatre manager, and Ada who was to come with us to the Registry Office.

People turned to look as we walked through the town. Mr Crampton cut a dashing figure in his first-night suit and top hat. He held Phoebe's elbow. Ada and I walked behind, catching the tail end of admiring glances.

Ada said, 'Now don't you worry. Just because you've had an unconventional childhood in the theatre, that doesn't mean you won't fit in.'

As we walked up Park Row, Phoebe said to Mr Crampton, 'Don't look to your right now, Crampy darling, but that's it.'

Mr Crampton immediately looked to his right; so did we. On the other side of the road stood a soot-blackened building with fancy stonework, long flat chimneys and pointy attics.

Mr Crampton whistled.

'I'll say so,' Ada said.

Adults could be very annoying. 'What? Ada, what?'

Ada said, 'Don't stare, but that's Thackreys' Bank, privately owned by your soon-to-be stepfather. It's the last of what they call the country banks. That means a private bank.'

I took another look. I never knew banks had attics.

'Seemingly it's been in his family for generations,' Ada said.

'He must be very rich.'

'Happen so. But banks have crashed before today and will again. Just remember where Ada keeps her few bob.' She tapped her belly. 'Don't go relying on others to see you through life. God helps them that help themselves.'

At the door of the Registry Office, Phoebe turned to me and Ada. 'Time to begin anew. In a short while, Phoebe Bellamy will be no more. Have you got the confetti?'

Ada nodded.

'Be sure to come out ahead of us so that the two of you can shower Mr and Mrs Sheldon Thackrey. Lydia, you better stand on that bit of a wall, and take a good aim. Crampy, you'll snap a picture or two?'

'I will.' Mr Crampton smiled sadly and seemed about to give one of his speeches.

Mostly, I saw their backs as the ceremony took place. Phoebe and Mr Thackrey answered the registrar's questions and said their lines well. Afterwards they signed a big book.

Outside, we threw confetti. Mr Thackrey laughed and brushed the stuff from his shoulders. He insisted that I stand beside them for one of the photographs.

As we strolled back along Park Row, out came all the staff from the bank. They formed a line along the pavement. A small man who wore a monocle hurried along the row, straightening them up. They waved small Union flags, the kind people have for a royal visit.

The monocled man stepped to the edge of the pavement. 'Hip, hip.' Everyone shouted hurray. They sent up three cheers and sang 'For He's a Jolly Good Fellow'. The commissionaire handed me a flag.

Phoebe paused, thanked them so very very much and had to be given Mr Thackrey's handkerchief to dab her eyes.

In a private room, back at the hotel, we sat down to breakfast. Mr Crampton and Mr Broughton, the best man, both toasted the happy couple in champagne. It did a funny bubbly thing to my throat and nose. Mr Crampton whispered to me not to feel obliged. A sip would do the trick, and he polished it off for me.

Mr Thackrey ate a kipper, and I did too. He gave me a pleasant wink and leaned towards me, to help me with the bones. His hair gave off a whiff of lavender which was a peculiar combination of smell to go with kippers. His hands were soft and his nails pink and round and very white at the tops, as if he ran a chalky pencil under them.

I felt fit to bust when Mr Crampton and Mr Broughton took their leave.

When they had gone, Phoebe reached out and ran her fingers from Mr Thackrey's temple to his chin, to his throat that was a little red from the stiffness of his collar. 'Sheldon, my dearest, I hope you won't turn fiercely jealous, but an admiring gentleman has filled my room with tulips.'

He kissed her fingers. 'Admiring and adoring, don't forget the adoring.'

Phoebe smiled her dazzling smile.

He pushed his chair back. 'Am I to be allowed to see these beautiful tulips?'

As Mr Thackrey stood, he reached into his inside pocket and brought out a flat wrapped box. 'For you, Lydia, to remember this day.'

'Thank you.'

Phoebe said, 'Call Mr Thackrey Pa, and call me Ma.

That is what his son will call us. Ma and Pa. We've decided.' She turned to him with a melting glance as if they had decided something else altogether.

Mr Thackrey — Pa — gave Ada an envelope.

I don't think he heard either of us say thank you.

Ada checked the contents of the envelope, thrust her hands under the table, hoisted her skirt and tucked the envelope into her money belt.

I lay the box on the table. A small, sparkling cat gazed up at me.

'It's gold,' Ada said as I placed it against the white cloth. 'Those eyes are sapphires. That's a diamond at the tip of its tail.'

'A real diamond?' My blue-eyed cat smiled with its ruby mouth.

'He's a banker, petal. A diamond to him is like me buying you an ice cream.'

She pinned the brooch on my dress.

'Eh kid!' She and I shared the same space in the revolving door. 'We've a day ahead of us all to ourselves. I should take you round the town, through the market. But to tell you the truth I feel jiggered with it all. These past two nights I haven't slept a wink. I feel fit for nothin'.'

I led her to the newsreel picture house.

Curiosity crept in on me. That bank, with its attics, and its windows like a church. What was it like inside?

'I've forgotten what that bank looked like,' I whispered as a Fifth Avenue Easter Bonnet Parade flickered to life on the newsreel.

'I wouldn't mind a gander at it myself,' Ada said.

*

The commissionaire beamed. He said we were just in time as the bank closed at three, and would we like to be announced? We would not.

Great stone pillars joined the tiled marble floor to a high vaulted ceiling. Across from the entrance, polished wooden counters imprisoned black-clad clerks who wore stiff white shirts and narrow dark ties. In the hushed atmosphere, they did not seem to be the same creatures who, not so long ago, had waved flags and raised cheers. Dotted about the walls were tables and chairs for customers. Each table held a blotter, a pen in a stand, and an inkwell. An old man scraped back a chair and doddered towards the counter.

Great heavy doors led off to other places. One of them, when opened briefly, revealed a sort of iron-barred gate from floor to ceiling.

'The inner sanctum,' Ada whispered.

We did not stay long.

Ada pushed the door. The commissionaire suddenly appeared, a little flustered at not being ready to bow us out. I saw why. He must have been talking to the girl with the light-brown hair and hazel eyes who was about my age, but smaller, yet too big for her clothes. She wore a faded cotton frock and a blue cardigan matted from shrinking in the wash. He had given her a flag, too, because the union flag was stuck in her top buttonhole. When she saw my flag, now tucked behind the cat brooch, she gave me a glare of such rage that if eyeballs were bullets she'd have shot me in the head. I glared back.

Sophie

Us Morans don't like swanks, and that girl was a swank. Stuck-up rich girl. She wore a practically new gabardine with the same paper Union Jack flag as me, only hers was tucked into her coat buttonhole, behind a gold cat pasted with jewels. She kept her coat unbuttoned – to show off her fancy frock.She only eyed me to see if I was looking at her. Swank. Swanky swank. I hate swanks.

I felt like saying to her, 'What are you gawping at, Swank?'

Dad, being the commissionaire, had to practically bow as he opened the door for her and the old woman. They swept off down Park Row, full of themselves.

He told me the girl's mother had that very morning married Mr Thackrey. I thought the old woman must be the girl's mother, but no. Her mother is a glamorous actress. What was that to me? I should cocoa.

I got fed up sometimes with Dad. Catch me sniffing after swanks. Why should we cocoa over them? Dad knew one thing for sure. The pair had wanted to get a good old gander at Thackreys' Bank, and see what the actress had married into. Not that he blamed them.

The grey and gold commissionaire uniform suited my dad, Barney Moran. He looked the part, with his black Irish hair, small moustache, smiling blue eyes and military bearing. It was his war record that got him the job, he liked to say. Mam said different, but we kept quiet over that.

To be a commissionaire at such a bank was a job to be proud of. No one resented his good luck because he was a generous man and would always give a tanner to someone down on their luck, and that was most men round our end. We lived on the Bank – that part of the town beyond the railway, running down to the River Aire, and in the shadow of St Mary's.

The swank and the old woman left the bank a minute before three o'clock. Always, on the dot of three, the big bank door was double locked from the inside. One key turned. The second key turned. From inside came a rap, rap.

Dad gave an answering tap, tap.

That was the signal for him to leave his post for the day, and walk round to the Bond Street door that led into the basement of the bank. He never said much about his other duties, which were mundane and involved a sweeping brush.

'Come on now, Sophie.' He spoke in a whisper. 'You're going to see a sight you won't ever forget.'

He unlocked the bank's Bond Street door and reached for the light switch.

Mam had told me that working for the bank wasn't like

other jobs, where a kid could take her dad his dinner in a pail. The bank worked to strict rules. I hung back, by the low wall.

'I'll wait here, Dad. Mam said I mustn't get you in bother by coming inside.'

'Ah sure, she would say that. What the eye doesn't see and all that. Come on in. I want you to carry home the tale of your dad's little enterprise. Out of a tiny acorn, grows the oak.'

He shut the door behind us. I followed him along a gloomy, echoing passage. Dark barred rooms on our right and left seemed like castle dungeons. I hardly dared look for fear of seeing some half-starved creature clad in sacks, chained to the wall.

'These are the vaults. There'll be no one down here just yet, so don't be worrying yourself.'

At the next flight of stone steps, Dad reached for a torch from a narrow shelf. 'Put your hand on my shoulder. Step careful. They didn't trouble to pipe electricity this deep.'

I stayed close, following the torch beam down to the bowels of the earth, cold as a tomb.

'What's that noise, Dad?'

'The rumbling River Aire, way below ground.'

It gave me the creeps. Our footsteps echoed. The ceiling grew lower, so Dad had to duck. He was forever telling me things, whether I wanted to know or not.

'Leeds is full of passages like this, Sophie. Some lead to the river and some to Kirkstall Abbey – the monks' secret route. There was a tale of a porter set on in the first week the new hotel opened for business. The poor fellow stepped through a plain-as-you-like looking door into a passage such as this and was never seen again.'

13

'Where are we going?'

'To the land of our ancestors. We'll be buying back our rightful inheritance, our ancestral land in Ireland.'

'What does that have to do with this damp tunnel?'

'Out of such humble beginnings, wealth grows. Day-dreams are the seedlings of reality, just remember that.' He raised a latch on a heavy iron-gated door. It creaked open. 'I'll oil that tomorrow.'

His torch lit a trunk-like box filled with earth, smelling like the river bank after rain.

'This is the start of our business, Sophie. Within no time at all, I'll be the one stepping into the bank to make a deposit. Some poor sod will open the door for me.'

'I can't see what it is.'

'Did you fetch the bag?'

'Yes.' I held out the hessian bag.

'Hold it open for me. Now, you can tell your mammy where these came from.'

Torch in one hand, he plucked something and dropped it in the bag, counting one, two, three till he reached thir-teen. 'A baker's dozen! And that's just the start.'

'You've grown thirteen mushrooms?'

'You sound like your mammy. It's not just thirteen mush-rooms. This is where we begin to turn our fortunes around. Mushrooms for ourselves for starters. Before long, I'll be supplying the whole of Leeds market. And that's only the first branch of our enterprise. We'll find an allotment. From there we'll progress to our own house, with grounds back and front. Then it'll be the small-holding. Stepping stones.'

I shivered in my cotton frock and too-tight cardigan that made my arms itch. 'I don't like it down here. I'm cold.'

'Ah you're soft. When I was your age, I'd no coat nor boots to my name.'

We left the vault and walked back into the tunnel.

'Keep this in the family, Sophie. We tell no one till we've made the first thousand.'

'Thousand mushrooms?'

'Thousand pounds.'

I touched the walls, expecting water to drip down.

'When we're rich, we'll find our way back to Ireland, to claim what's ours.'

I never knew why he talked about going back, when both he and Mam were born in Leeds.

'Why should we go there, Dad?' It seemed to me that if people had left in droves, there could be very good reasons for stopping away.

Dad set me right. 'We'll go back because it's the land of your forefathers, the land of saints and scholars, of fiddlers and fairies. And it's where we'll take up our inheritance.'

I had been reading *Treasure Island*. 'Do you have anything written down about this land of ours? Is there a map?'

The beam of the torch wobbled as Dad's fist thumped his heart. 'The map's in here. You wait and see, Sophie. The Thackreys won't be the only ones living out their dream, rattling around in a mansion.'

Lydia

Allerton House
Saturday 26 April 1930
Dear Ada

I wish you could see your 'Little Lydia' now! Here I
am in the Thackrey mansion, sitting in the great
milady's chamber that is my bedroom. I have only been
here a few hours but already am fed up. There is no
one to talk to. Phoebe said not to prattle to the servants
as they will sly quiz me and will gossip. She and Mr
Thackrey have gone to decide something about the
bedroom – along the corridor from me – and have
been gone for ages. They were so lovey-dovey in the
back of the car coming up from the hotel that I had to
stare out of the window the whole time.

Allerton House would stagger and confuse you even
more than that flippin' great hotel. The banister is
wider and more shiny. Phoebe whispered to me that

there is more oak in the entrance and on the stairs here than in the Forest of Arden.

You asked me to tell you all about it. The building is the shape of a capital letter L, but a letter L with a line across the top as well as the bottom. The main entrance to the house is in the long part of the L which faces the front. The other wings are the east and west, the west wing added on as an extension ages ago. That is the part Phoebe likes best because it ends in a round tower with a turret roof. She calls it 'mad Gothic'. The circular room will be her sitting room and the room above it her dressing room. Both rooms catch the afternoon sun. You would expect such a house to be made of stone, but it is solid red brick, and dares you not to like it.

I keep getting lost here. Pa (as I am supposed to call him) showed us round. Through the front door, his study is on the right as you go in. I tried out the big leather chair which suited me very well. Next to the study, going down the wing, is a library and I have never seen so many books that look as if no one ever reads them, though they are not a bit dusty. Then comes a reception room. Along the hall, all the way to the end, is the circular room. Ma (as I am supposed to call her) has great plans for fresh wallpaper and new furniture. On the left of the front door is a large dining room and beyond a small everyday dining room, close to the kitchen and pantries.

It is strange not having you to talk to. I wish you had come with us.

I will send this letter to the Theatre Royal, York,

but you better give me all the dates of the tour again because I lost them.

Love to all
Lydia

PS All I have to do is put this letter in an envelope and set it on the telephone table in the hall and it will be stamped and posted. It is a fine day here and not so foggy and grey as in the town this morning. I am going out to play two-ball on the side wall because Phoebe is still with him being lovey-dovey I suppose and I am fed up being on my own, as I have already said.

PPS In case you cannot follow my description I will draw you a picture of the house on the back of this page.

PPPS Keep my letters in case I want to write the story of my life when I am old.

We ate in the small dining room. Pa said he would take us for a walk after dinner, but Ma had telephone calls to make to a decorator.

While I was waiting for him, I went outside to play two-ball, saying one of my rhymes. I did not hear him coming. He must have been listening a while because he waited for me to get to the end of the alphabet. The game is that you do unders with the ball until the names, and then overs. I was up to, Z my name is Zena, my husband's name is Zachariah, we come from Zanzibar and we sell zinc.

Pa seemed impressed that I could work through the alphabet without hesitation about names, countries or products.

'What a good game. All your characters are so commercially minded. It makes sound business sense that each couple specialises in a single product. People dabble far too much these days.'

He tried two-ball himself but was fingers and thumbs, and not quick enough thinking up names. It seemed strange to me to see a man dressed in a tweed jacket and twill trousers trying to play ball. It made me laugh.

He laughed too. 'I play small ball myself. Hit it with a golf club. You'd be very good at that, too, I'm sure. Fetch one of your balls with you. I expect you can bounce it as we go along.'

We walked along the drive, passing a wood on the right and lawns and flowers on the left. He chatted easily enough, telling me about his son who would be my stepbrother. This boy would normally have been home for the Easter holidays but was staying with Pa's married daughter in Sheffield. She was married to a steel magnet. I snuck a quick look at Pa when he said that, wondering if it was a joke, about the magnet, and also whether the boy was keeping out of the way while Phoebe and I moved into his house.

'What kind of a magnet is she married to?' I imagined a man who spent a lot of time picking up pins.

'My accent!' He smiled. 'You'll grow used to me. I'm Yorkshire through and through. Magnate. Steel magnate.' He spelled it out and explained, without making me feel silly, as if the mistake was his fault.

He took a deep breath. 'I love the weekends, and fresh air. Once upon a time this really was the countryside. Now houses are creeping up from all sides and there's not a thing I can do about it.'

19

We turned right out of the gates, walking along a little cobbled way before coming to a narrow lane overhung with trees. Birds flitted about and it seemed to me magic to look at the sky through the leaves and listen to rowdy birds. A blackbird flew across the churchyard.

'The parson's daughter is about your age.' He waved at the parsonage. 'Penelope. You'll meet her after church tomorrow I expect.'

I stared at the house by the church, half expecting to see her, but there was only an older boy, messing about with a bike.

'Is that still your garden?' I asked when I saw a low gate in the stone wall on our right.

'Yes. We could cut through there on the way back, only I wanted you to see St Stephen's. It was built by one of my ancestors. Not with her bare hands you understand, but commissioned and paid for, which means I have the pleasure of appointing the vicar, and a very sound chap he is too. No long sermons from him.'

We turned into a narrow track, and a great pong smacked my snitch.

'We're coming to the farm. Have you got that ball of yours?'

'Yes.' I threw it in the air and caught it.

'That's the ticket. When we get to the farmyard, throw it high in the air. Lose it well over the fence. Then we'll go look for it.'

'Why?'

He tapped the side of his nose. 'Aha. That's for me to know and you to be in the dark about.'

I threw the ball in the air a couple of times and then hurled it into the farmyard.

'Mum's the word,' he whispered as he opened the five-barred gate. 'Keep looking for it, till I give you the signal.'

'What signal?'

But he didn't explain.

We walked past clucking hens enclosed behind wire mesh. Beyond them, a sheep and her lamb looked at me through their fence. Pa was looking at a brick building with a door whose top half stood open. On the ground inside was a fat pig and wriggling piglets.

A farmer came towards us, wearing wellington boots and an old trilby. 'Have you found that ball yet?' Pa said loudly.

I said I hadn't and went off to look while he spoke to the farmer. The ball had landed in a puddle and a blind man would have found it in the time he left me looking.

Finally, he called over, 'Have one more good look, then we'll give up and leave it for the pigs to find!'

I guessed that was the signal, and after circling the puddle, picked up the ball.

I waved it to him, staying put, not knowing for sure whether I had done the right thing. I dried the ball on a patch of grass.

Pa walked towards me.

'Well done, Lydia. And the farmer knows who you are now, so you can come and see the lambs.'

'What did you look at over there?' I asked. 'Was it the pigs?'

'Ha ha, you're on to me. Getting warm. Guess again.'

'The pigs' house?'

'Just so. I lent Briggs the money to build it. I want to make sure he's put my cash to good use and that I'll have a return.

Doesn't hurt to keep an eye on your investments. But he'd be insulted if he thought I was checking up on him.'

He gave me his handkerchief to wipe the mud from my hands, then suddenly ran backwards, laughing, raising his arms in the air. 'Come on then! Chuck it hither! Let's see if I can catch better than I play two-ball.'

I threw the ball. It sailed past him, over the hawthorn hedge.

Sophie

When someone's ball came flying over the wall. I caught it in one hand, and raised my arm, ready to throw it back.

'Hey up, Sophie!' Dad grabbed my hand in his before I could release the ball. 'Finders keepers, losers weepers. Keep walking.'

'Sure someone'll be looking for it.'

'Let em. The Morans is in luck for once. You're richer by one rubber ball than when you set off from home.'

It had been Dad's idea to take the tram to Chapel Allerton, so that he could show me where the Thackreys lived. We would see whether that manner of set up would suit us, once we made our fortune from the mushrooms. Mam said someone had to go with him, and it was that or helping her in the house.

You could see from the tram window why Dad hankered after such a life. Down our end, the sky hung grey, winter and summer, blown through with smoke from the factories, and a yellow fog that came from I don't know where. You hardly noticed when winter turned to spring. Summer announced itself when the gas tar melted on the cobbles and stuck to the soles of your shoes, with a sharp smell, like liquorice and rubber.

The further the tram trundled away from the town, the more countrified the view from the window. Houses boasted a bit of green in front, with fading daffodils and blowzy tulips. Trees grew along the roadways, their leaves young and green.

The walk from the terminus took us along a cobbled tree-lined road, with big houses on either side. The dwellings fell away as we approached the Thackreys' massive wrought-iron gates.

You couldn't see the whole house from the gates because it lay along a winding drive, with just a glimpse from where we stood. It was big, sturdy and made of solid red bricks.

'Local built, and with Burmantofts bricks.' Dad waved a hand to the left. 'They have their own private wood, see.'

'Come on,' Dad turned from the gates to walk along a cobbled path. 'We might get a better view from another angle.'

From the path we turned into a shady lane. On the right ran a high stone wall, bordering Thackreys' land. On our left stood a solid grey stone Protestant church, a church hall and a parsonage. A lad looked up as we passed. He was cleaning the spokes on a bicycle wheel.

'Who'll come all the way here to church?' I asked. There were no houses nearby.

'Oh they'll flock up from Chapel Allerton. And I expect

24

the Thackreys attend on Sundays. I'm only surprised Mr Thackrey didn't marry Miss Phoebe Bellamy there, instead of in the Registry Office. I thought that was a bit of a poor do myself.'

'If she's a Miss Phoebe Bellamy, how is it she comes with a swanky daughter?'

'She's a widow. And all actresses are called Miss, just like all cooks are called Missis.'

The best part of the day was seeing the farm. A brown cow with great sad eyes came ogling us over the fence. I wanted the lambs to come close enough for me to put my hand through and pat them, but they wouldn't. I wished Mam had come, and brought our Billy. He'd have loved it.

'We'll fetch him another time,' Dad said.

It was by the farm that the rubber ball arced over, right into my hand, a sign of great good luck, according to Dad.

'What's a small-holding?' I asked, as I bounced the ball on the bumpy ground of the lane that led back to the tram terminus. 'That's what you said we'll have when you showed me the mushrooms.'

'It's a decent-sized piece of land, like a farm, but without the trouble of rising early to feed animals.'

'When do you think we'll have one?'

'Ah, it'll be sooner than you know. Only we won't mention it to your mammy yet. She has a way of pooh-poohing such ideas, not having a business head on her shoulders.'

The tram took us back to the terminus in St Peter's Square. As we clambered off, Dad said 'Well here we are, you've had a glimpse of how the other half lives, and now we're almost back to us own midden. Tell your mammy

I'll see her later. I need to know how Flower of Sakara did in the 2.30.'

I trekked along home, back through the narrow streets. By Zion recreation grounds the choirmaster spotted me. So it was too late to escape. Sean Silvester is a great long streak of whitewash. He wears grey trousers, a hand-knitted red pullover, tweed jacket and flat brown cap, winter or summer.

'Sophie Moran!' he sang out to me in his fine baritone voice, his only good attribute.

'Hello.' I felt myself wriggling with discomfort, knowing exactly what was coming. I hated to be put on the spot.

Sean Silvester bends towards you, like a broken lamp post, as if you might not notice his height. 'Your Danny didn't come to choir practice the last two weeks, and he wasn't at High Mass this past Sunday morning.'

I had two choices. I could I feign ignorance, or say that my brother's omissions were sweet bugger all to do with me. It must be a built-in feature of being a person's sister that you ignore the obvious choices and go for making an excuse for them. 'Well, he is working a lot of the time now.'

Being almost fourteen, Danny had to look to his future.

'I'd heard,' Sean Silvester murmured tunefully.

Only he could have loaded two such titchy words with a hundred weight of disapproval. He adjusted his cap. 'For Harry Hescott, if the stories have it right?'

'I haven't seen much of him,' I said evasively. It wasn't up to me to tell tales. Sean Silvester shouldn't think me such a stupid kid that I'd go giving away details of what my family was up to.

I dodged round the choirmaster, stepping into the road

26

to make my escape. 'Only I have to be on my way. I'm on an errand for me mam.'

'Will we see him tomorrow?' he called after me, letting the whole of Leather Street know his business.

'I couldn't be saying!' I called back, without turning round. 'I'll tell him you asked after him.'

I felt pleased with that riposte, for it didn't commit me to passing on the message about choir practice.

When I got home, poor Mam looked frazzled. She was on her own with Billy, who is two years old. He sat on the hearth rug, gnawing at a raw carrot. I teased him a bit, which makes him laugh. He has not yet learned to talk, only make noises that mean much to him and not much to anyone else, except our Rosa who understands every grunt – or so she claims.

Mam does not worry in the least that Billy can't talk. She says that if he's a true Moran male, once he starts to blab he'll never shut up, so we'll make the most of it before he starts giving orders, complaining and taking off into flights of fancy.

Strands of pale red hair trailed from Mam's pinned-up plaits over her pale cheeks. Though Mam and Dad both had Irish parents, hers were from Dublin. She has that fair-skin, light hair and olive green eyes. Dad's family came from the west of Ireland and have the black Spaniard blood in their veins, though Dad managed to wangle himself a pair of bright blue eyes. Danny takes after Dad. Rosa and I favour our Mam. We have all decided that Billy has the best features of Mam and Dad and he alone will rise to perfection in every way. He will be short of nothing. Great disagreements take place as to what grand profession he will follow.

I picked up Billy and twirled him, till he laughed. 'Have you made your mammy cry?' Mam was peeling an onion over a basin of cold water.

Billy shook his head. He dropped the carrot, so it had to be rinsed. I plonked myself on the bed chair, with Billy on my lap, turning him top to tail, so he could see the room upside down.

Mam wanted to know the whole story of where Dad and I had been. She listened, making interested faces, nodding, her eyes lighting up at the descriptions of the house, the trees, the lambs, the catching of the ball and Dad telling me to keep it.

'And where's the man himself now?' She started to peel a potato.

'Gone to see how his horse fared in the 2.30.'

'God help us. You know what's in his mind. He's had you loitering near the Thackreys' place, so he'll believe in his heart and soul some smidgen of their luck and fortune will rub off on him. As if you get rich by the nearness of it.'

'Oh it's not just that. Ouch!' Billy had decided to see whether my hair could be pulled out. 'Dad has plans.'

Billy climbed off my lap to crawl under the table, a favourite spot of his.

'God love him.' Mam shook her head. 'Your dad's always had plans, but it's not marvellous schemes that put food on the table.'

'He says daydreams are the seedlings of reality.'

'Aye. Only daydreams to my mind are the seedlings of bigger daydreams. Now where's my purse. I need you to fetch us a cabbage.'

I took the string bag and set off down the street. And

that's how it always turned out. With Dad, I believed in every plan he painted. The future felt grand, possible and just around the corner. It would be a future lined with luxury. Then Mam would shake her head, take out her long housekeeping tin money box with the different coin slots for rent, coal, candles, the burial club, and I knew that she was right. Watching the pennies day to day, week to week was how we survived, but never prospered.

I got back with the cabbage. Mam stood at the sink, her back to the room.

'Mam, where's Billy?'

He wasn't under the table or behind the chair.

She looked through the window. 'He can't open the door, can he? Surely he didn't try to follow you.'

Mam hurried upstairs, calling his name. Our steps were stone. He might have crawled up safely, but if he tumbled down he would crack his baby skull.

I went down the sixteen steps, into the dim cellar, not calling till I reached the bottom step. One door opened onto the coal hole, where dots of light shone on the small pile of coal through the metal cover that Mr Durkin removed each time he delivered coal. The other door led to the cellar where Mam did her washing. It held the cool box where we kept cheese and milk. A dim light shone through the cellar window.

'Billy? Billy!'

A movement, a small sound came from under the great stone slab table by the far wall.

'Billy! You'll catch your death. Silly boy. Come out.'

Picking up on my anxiety, he started to cry.

'Shhh. It's all right, you daft lad.'

I carried him back upstairs.

Mam took him from me. 'What a fright you gave your mammy. And look at your bonny face, all streaked with muck.'

She held him to the fluted mirror for his own delight. He reached out and touched his reflection.

I damped the corner of the towel and wiped his cheek.

In the mirror, Mam looked suddenly tired. As if she caught my thought, she started to talk ten to the dozen. 'That mirror was a wedding present from my mother. She'd all on to save for it because her tailoring wages was well and truly spoken for, with sons at war, and a wounded husband. But she did it. Even though me and your daddy lived with her at the first, and had no wall of our own to hang a mirror from, she bought it for us. I expect she knew we'd all go on seeing ourselves into the eternity after she died.'

If her words were meant to distract me from her own tired reflection, they did the trick. 'But we haven't always had it. I thought it came from May's shop.'

'Your granny knew, God rest her, that I'd be needing something to pawn from time to time. It's served that purpose. Another time it was looked after by May, when your dad was out of work. We had the shame of drawing the national assistance. They rub your nose in it by coming to see what you've got that might fetch a bob or two. There's no sentiment in them fellers. That's why the mirror hasn't always held its rightful place.' She pushed a strand of hair from her face with the back of her hand.

'You sit down, Mam. I'll get on with the cabbage.'

'I will then, just for a bit. My legs is aching.'

30

She leaned back into the bed chair, Billy in her arms.

I felt torn between how Dad saw the world, and what Mam knew life to be. If only Dad were proved right, and his daydreams became reality. What a fine time we'd have on that day.

'Ah, that mirror.' Mam closed her eyes. 'On the day we married, me and your daddy looked at us selves in it, side by side. We'd no photograph, you see, so pretended we were a portrait of newlyweds. We agreed to keep the picture in our mind's eye forever. Mr and Mrs Moran.'

Lydia

Being part of the Thackrey family could be very confusing. Instead of just my own self and Phoebe, I now had two stepsisters and a stepbrother.

Ma explained to me why she and Pa married in the Registry Office, and not in the church across the lane. Ma insisted on a quiet affair, not wanting to take the shine off the next Thackrey wedding, just four months later. Cecilia's nuptials.

Pa's elder daughter, whom I had not met, married into steel. His younger daughter, Cecilia, was to marry into cement that August. Once I met her, I hoped it would be sticky, wet cement and that I could watch her sink.

Cecilia's door stood open. Clothes lay strewn on the bed. She and Ma had their backs to me, looking at dresses.

'Green is perfect for you, Cecilia. It's your colouring you see. It is so utterly unique in a woman to have light

brown hair that so exactly tones with the shade of the iris.
I would say you are a spring person. Leaves in bud, daffodils in bloom.'

'I do favour those colours . . . '

'You have a natural sense of style. I saw it immediately.
And you see, rather than stop at this wonderful idea of
opening up the two dining rooms, this wedding must be
the event of the Yorkshire year. It'll make such a splash that
even the *Tatler* should despatch a photographer.'

'Well I don't imagine . . . '

Ma took a deep breath and laid a gentle hand on Cecilia's
arm. 'Let me imagine. Marquees on the lawn. Not one, not
two, at least three marquees. An orchestra, under a gazebo
in case of drizzle. You must ask your father to give the bank
staff a day off . . . '

'Well, it will be Saturday.'

'Of course. So much the better. They must all attend. In
years to come, the children and grandchildren of bank staff
will mark that day, just like a royal wedding. People will
remember Cecilia Thackrey's wedding day.'

Phoebe stood up and paced the room. She saw me all
right but was too caught up to acknowledge me. 'I can see
it all. There'll be races for the children, prizes, entertain-
ment, champagne in the top tent.'

'Y-e-s,' Cecilia murmured. 'It does sound rather . . . '

Victory to Phoebe. She had won over the resentful
Cecilia.

I trailed across the landing, running my hand along the
oak rails. I missed Ada. I missed the train journeys, arriving in new towns, being part of the theatre troupe.

In the library were the complete works of Charles

33

Dickens. I chose *David Copperfield* and found a private place, where no one would find me, sitting on the windowsill, behind heavy curtains. It pleased me no end to find, in David Copperfield, a child more miserable than myself.

Mr Clarence Clutterbuck, the monocled chief cashier, took charge of children's activities.Small for a grown man, his trousers were a little on the short side and so were the sleeves of his jacket. It was as if a tailor had thought him even tinier and had cut the material short. Mr Clutterbuck had a sweet, oval face, the shape of a teaspoon. When thinking, he stood with his feet in the first position so that a person could imagine he might at any moment begin a soft-shoe shuffle. He and I had talked about children's prizes in advance, and the choice was left entirely to me.

I wrote down the order of races. Ma had coached me on what to say when handing out prizes, so I felt very confident and glad of something to do when everyone else busied themselves about the wedding.

'Ah!' Mr Clutterbuck beamed. 'Here's young Master Granville. You look splendid, if I may say so.'

My stepbrother was already dressed in his page boy outfit. A year older than me, Granville was tall for his age. He had fair hair and light-blue eyes. Something about the paleness of his eyes made me uneasy. At meal times, when he was busy stuffing his face and taking notice of no one, I would look at him. He hardly ever blinked. Then, if he caught you looking, or felt uneasy about something, he would blink non-stop, as if to prove he was human and could do it. Though he could be charming when he wanted something, there was usually nothing he wanted from me. He would find opportunities to show his superiority, and lord it over me, letting me know that it was a bit of a nuisance to have me in his house.

'Come to help, Master Granville?' Mr Clutterbuck asked. He was about to lift the tablecloth that hid the prizes, to show them off.

Granville scowled. 'Boys will want to play cricket, not run silly races.'

'Perhaps you're right,' Mr Clutterbuck smiled a sad half smile. His monocle slipped onto this chest. 'Then it's a good thing I'm being helped by the girl who's to be the new daughter of the house.'

Granville gave his nasty laugh. 'She'll never be the daughter of the house. Not a Thackrey. Never will be.'

He sauntered off.

Mr Clutterbuck touched my arm. 'Miss Lydia Bellamy. To be Miss Lydia Bellamy is a fine thing. But if I were Mr Thackrey – excuse the presumption – I would want nothing more than to adopt you. If you do not soon become Miss Lydia Thackrey, the chief cashier of Thackreys' Bank, yours truly will eat his monocle in a sandwich.'

And I couldn't even answer. Because he meant it so kindly. It was the kindest thing anyone had ever said to me since Harry, Ma's leading man, guaranteed that his twelve ways of ridding himself of unwanted admirers would be bound to come in handy for me sooner rather than later.

*

I would have to join the family wedding breakfast in the dining room after the ceremony, but would much rather have stayed outside with Mr Clutterbuck, going over the order of races, and waiting for the garden party to begin.

Sophie

Didn't we Morans all have to be entirely spick and span for that garden party. It was madness in our house when any one person was getting ready to step out, never mind all five of us at once. Dad perched on the bedchair, polishing shoes and setting them pair by pair in a row, according to size, across the hearth rug. Billy took this to be a game. He snatched each shoe and searched out a hiding place.

Danny wet the hairbrush and attacked his wild jet-black hair, all the while his bright blue eyes looking at himself with great approval. He was fourteen and had just that summer left school, thinking himself a fine man because he earned a few bob from Harry Hescott. He threw down the brush and picked up a comb. 'I'm too old for this malarkey. And Saturday's our busiest day.'

Dad washed his hands. 'I've had a word with Harry Hescott meself. He's happy for you to go to this garden party. The man's smart enough to know that a do like this is too good an event to miss.'

Mam stopped buttoning Billy's jacket and stood up, her cheeks blazing with a sudden anger. 'Don't either of you dare be chasing people to place bets on the gee-gees, or even mention horse-racing. You'll show me up, not to mention jeopardising your job, Barney.'

'Calm yourself woman.' Dad dried his hands. 'That's not what I meant at all. I'm only saying, you never know who you might bump into at a do like this.' He winked at Danny. 'Someone might know of an opening for a bright lad. You won't want to run for Harry Hescott all your life long. Now what will you sing if you're called on for a turn, Danny?'

Danny rescued his shoes and began to re-thread the one with the broken lace. 'Will it be that kind of do?'

Dad searched the mantelpiece for his collar studs. 'I don't know. But we should have a plan, be prepared for all contingencies. And what would be the point of all them years in the choir if you couldn't give a song at a wedding?'

Danny made no comment about all his years in the choir. Mam's lips tightened. I thought perhaps Sean Silvester had been after her about Danny's non-attendance at choir practice.

Danny thought for a minute. 'How about an Al Jolson? I'll sing "Swanee".'

'Good choice.' Dad pulled open the table drawer and took out his mouth organ. 'Don't let me forget this little feller.'

'And will I do the train?' Danny asked. While Dad knotted his tie for him, Danny started the train. He gave us his brilliant impersonation of a train steaming and hooting its way into a station, hearing the guard's whistle, and steaming out again.

This made it difficult for Mam to keep Billy still. He wriggled and chortled on the table as Mam put on his shoes. No matter how many times Danny did the train, it still made us all laugh, and left you lost in admiration.

'And what will you sing, Rosa?' Dad asked, as Mam fixed his back collar stud.

Rosa sat quietly on the buffet with her back to the wall. Two years younger than me, she looked like a picture book Goldilocks. Her mass of red-gold hair sprang out in a startled way, like coils or curls of copper wire. Even paler than Mam, with the whitest of skin and just a sprinkle of freckles on her nose, her lustrous eyes were the colour of gooseberries.

Rosa would never be outdone. Danny had performed his train, so she would give her party piece. She wore her Mam-made plain green dress with V neck and a swirl to the skirt. Rosa picked up her long fringed scarf to use as a prop, kicked back the hearth rug and began to sing 'Button up your Overcoat', dancing all the actions, flinging her scarf about. The speed of her beginning took Dad by surprise. He grabbed his mouth organ and caught up with her, standing in front of the sink, eyes tight shut. He opened his eyes as she picked up Billy and pirouetted him on the lines, 'Take good care of yourself, you belong to me.'

We all gave her a good clap.

Mam wiped Billy's face with the corner of the towel. 'And what about you, Sophie? Just in case you're asked?'

'Won't two turns from one family be enough?'

39

'Ah don't belittle yourself,' Dad said. 'A recitation will go down a treat. What will it be?'

'Shall I do "The Lake Isle of Innisfree"?'

'That'll be just grand.' Mam sat Billy on his little chamber pot. 'Go on Billy, do it for Mammy. Come on, good boy.'

As Billy obliged, Dad, Danny and Rosa hurried to wait outside.

I tipped the contents of the chamber pot into the slop bucket. 'Will I empty the bucket now, Mam?'

'Ah no, leave it under the sink till we get back.' Mam picked up her bone-handled velvet bag and dampened a tea towel, to take in case of needing to clean up Billy.

The others were already walking along the street. Mam, Billy and I followed on. I'm sure she knew I was going over 'The Lake Isle of Innisfree' in my head, hoping not to be asked.

I needn't have worried. The minute Dad showed our invitation to the man on the gate and we were ushered through, an eejit would have worked out this wouldn't be an occasion for a bit of singing and dancing from the Moran clan.

Mam set Billy on the grass and he began to run like a wild creature. We trod sedately along the drive. Although I'd seen the place from outside, to be in there, listening to the orchestra playing from their platform under a clump of blossomy trees was different again.

Rosa looked round in amazement. 'Do you think this is how film stars live?'

I supposed they probably did.

'Then that's what I shall be,' Rosa said quietly.

It was great to see Billy running free on the grass, as if the door of a cage had been opened.

Mam gazed on the far horizon. 'No wonder your Dad gets fancy ideas, if day in day out he's rubbing up against this lot.'

There were two marquees, one for family and friends, and the other for bank staff.

Between us, Mam and I held Billy's hand and went into the staff tent. Long trestle tables groaned under plates of sandwiches, lettuce leaves, sliced tomatoes. Buns and strawberry tarts spilled off tiered plates. Wobbling jelly sparkled in beams of light that filtered through the marquee. Ladies in white aprons poured lemonade and cream soda from jugs, or cups of tea from urns.

Billy broke free and almost toppled a sedate-looking bank clerk, so Mam said she'd find a spot over by the trees, and I should bring some refreshments across.

We made our picnic under the shade of a tree. Rosa and Danny came over with their plates piled high.

Mam leaned against the tree and shut her eyes. 'This is the life, the life of Riley. Make the most of it, kids.'

Billy wanted to run and run. I picked him up and twirled him.

Mam took him from me. 'Steady! I don't want him sick all over the show.'

As I put him down, I spotted that swanky girl, all dolled up, strolling about on her own with her nose in the air. She wore a white blouse and a maroon silky bolero and matching skirt. Her dark hair bounced in bunches from either side of her hat. She saw me, but looked away. Well, let her. Stuck-up swank.

Danny forgot he was supposed to be grown up. He grabbed the tree's lowest branch and swung, pretending to aim his great feet at Rosa, then missing at the last minute. 'There's races, you two. I'm too old for them but you might have a go and win a prize.'

Mam told him to behave himself. Anyone who looked at him would know whose son he was, so just think on.

Dad led us over to where the races were to take place. He told me in a whisper that the thin, wispy-haired man with the pasty oval face too big for his small body was the chief cashier. The man wore a monocle. It popped from his eye when he tested his starter's whistle.

Dad said, 'Little emperor Clutterbuck. Nothing he likes better than barking orders. He thinks he's the bee's knees because he lives on bank premises.'

'Shhh, Dad. He'll hear you.'

That swanky girl was there too, trying to look as if she was in charge of the prizes.

Lydia

Granville Thackrey made me choke with fury. How dared he muscle in and award prizes, after I had done all the work. Who suggested prizes? Me. Who helped Mr Clutterbuck decide on the types of race and the order in which they should be run? Me.

Granville had just sauntered over when it was time to make the presentations. 'Oh I'd better hand out first and second prizes. Pa will expect it of me. Son of the house and all that, eh Mr Clutterbuck?'

Mr Clutterbuck gave a small bow. He did not meet my look. Of course I began to see why Mr Clutterbuck couldn't stand up for me. Any 'Thackrey' comes before the most exalted employee of the bank, and certainly before me.

But I wouldn't give Granville the satisfaction of letting him know I cared.

The only thing that stopped me from going indoors and

finding a book was the thought that Granville would think he'd defeated me. I wandered towards the woods.

There they were – the show-off Morans who had tried to win every race. They were sitting under a tree, like a game of happy families. Mr Doorman, Mrs Doorman, Master Doorman, the two Misses Doorman and Baby Doorman, trying to totter away from them fast as his skinny little legs would carry him. First-prize-Sophie swooped on him and whirled him round and round. They were all laughing. Master Doorman was making the sound of a train, which I had to admit was pretty good.

Blow me if that bloomin' Granville wasn't on my heels. Probably spying to see where I went. He called out, but not to me.

'I say! Moran! Danny isn't it? Want to give me a hand, set up the cricket?'

I didn't turn round.

The swing, a broad flat seat on thick ropes, hung from the branch of a great chestnut tree. It was close by the stream, away from the summerhouse that Granville made his den and where he kept his cricket stuff. No one could see me, swinging back and forth, looking up through the trees at the bright blue August sky dotted with tiny fast-moving white clouds. My mood changed in a few minutes. It was almost like flying, which has to make you feel on top of the world.

Splashing sounds came from the stream, then a voice.

'Look at that our Sophie. See what your man Clutter-buck did to me.'

'I'd like to do the same back to him. Give him the Chinese burn somewhere he wouldn't forget.'

'Ah why would you stop at that when you could scrape out his eye with the monocle?'

They started to laugh. It was them. The 'winners'. Sophie could barely speak for laughing.

'I know, I know. Will we book our Danny's train to run him down?' She did an imitation of the train coming into the station, but not half as good as her brother.

'Feed him the old mushrooms till he shrinks and keep him in a matchbox.'

'Look at my ankle,' Sophie said. 'The man's a whatnot.'

'What nature of a whatnot?'

'I can't think. But there's a name for it.'

'Bully you mean.'

'No! There's a more elaborate name for it, something to do with a French man, and a bath. Begins with S.'

'Who told you that?'

'The Scholar.'

They were carrying their shoes, paddling upstream. Just let them get within an inch of me and I'd kick their heads as the swing came forwards. That'd teach them to slander poor Mr Clutterbuck.

The swing creaked.

One of them saw me. Silence. They were too far away for me to kick their heads in defence of my own friend, Mr Clutterbuck, the poor man who made his home in the attic of the bank, all alone, and was the longest serving and most trusted employee.

On an upward swing, I called to them. 'Mr Clutterbuck didn't tie your ankles tight on purpose. Everyone in the three-legged race had their ankles tied.'

Sophie stared at me. For a minute I thought she would

turn and disappear. She wouldn't dare talk back. Not Miss Doorman.

Then she said, 'Yes he did.'

The younger one with the mad hair followed suit. 'He's nasty.'

'Mr Clutterbuck wouldn't do such a thing deliberately. He's a gentleman.' I brought the swing to a slow, slow, slow stop.

Without saying another word, they stood side by side and each held up a foot so that I would see the red marks on their ankles.

'Why would he?' I asked.

'Because he doesn't like our dad, and so he didn't want us to win,' Rosa said.

Sophie tugged at her sister's hand. 'Come on. Forget it. What does she know.'

That got me mad. 'I could've beat you any day.'

'Why didn't you take part then?' Sophie turned and stared at me.

I slid off the swing. 'Because I would've won, and prizes are for guests. Even rude guests.'

'Let's see then.' She bounced up and down like a fairground boxer itching for a fight. 'Get yer shoes off and I'll race yer barefoot.'

'Where to?'

'Anywhere you like. Rosa, you can set us off.'

I took off my shoes and pulled off my socks. 'Through the clearing, to the wall. First to get to the wall wins.'

Rosa looked serious. She picked up a broad twig and marked a line on the ground. We took up our positions.

'Are you ready?'

I nodded, not looking at either of them.

'On your marks, get set, go!'

I would show her. I ran fast as I could and was ahead too, till I tripped on a mound. Even then I picked myself up and ran again. She beat me by a fraction.

'Ha ha,' she said.

'I tripped!'

The starter had trotted along behind us, taking her refereeing seriously. 'It's true. She tripped on a fairy house.'

'Well I didn't trip and I won.' Sophie leaned against the wall, catching her breath.

'Best out of three,' I said. 'It's only fair. Then we'll really know.'

'Suit yourself.' Sophie moved away from the wall.

We walked back to the starting line.

'Swap places!' Rosa ordered.

We swapped places. Of course that meant Sophie knew to watch out for bumpy ground.

'Take up your positions!' Rosa was impersonating Mr Clutterbuck. 'On your marks, get set, go!'

We set off on the instant. This time I kept my eyes to the ground, not minding that I trod on primroses and clover. When I glanced up to the wall, to see how far was left to run, I knew I would win. All the same, I put a spurt on, wanting to win well. I reached the wall and almost ran slap into it.

Sophie was a few seconds behind me.

'Race to Lydia!' Rosa called. 'One more race to run. Back to the starting line.'

I put my hand to my chest. Panic. My jewelled cat brooch. It wasn't there.

'What's wrong?' Sophie asked. She looked alarmed, as if she expected me to have a heart attack and blame her.

'My brooch. I've lost my brooch.'

Straight away, the race was forgotten. She said, 'We'll help you look for it. What's it like?'

'It's a cat, with jewels for its eyes and mouth and tail.' Suddenly I felt like a big baby, ready to cry. That cat was the best thing anyone had ever given me. I'd grown to like it more and more. Every night when I wished it sweet dreams, it twinkled its eyes at me. Every morning when I pinned it on – even when Ma said it didn't really suit what I was wearing – I thought it smiled at me.

'When did you last notice it?' Sophie asked.

I shook my head, not able to remember. So much had happened.

The three of us crawled through the grass on our hands and knees, from the wall to the swing.

'What are you playing at?' It was Granville, being superior, carrying a couple of shin pads and a cricket ball.

'Help me look for my brooch!' I felt so desperate I would allow even him to help me search.

Sophie and Rosa combed through the grass near the path.

Granville hissed into my ear. 'Idiot! Can't you see what's what? They've stolen it. You only have to look at them to see what they are.'

'They have not!'

'You know nothing. Just look at them. They're the type every shopkeeper would watch like a hawk.'

'Rubbish.'

'Well I should care.' He started to walk away. 'But I'll

tell you this, if you'd played with Penelope as you're supposed to, you'd still have your brooch. But you can't make proper friends, you're too peculiar.'

'Shut up freak face! What do you know?'

'Vulgarity outs!' he hissed at me as he walked away. 'I knew you'd show yourself up for what you are.'

I wouldn't let him see me cry. Some magpie could have it by now. I looked up to the trees, half hoping to see a curious bird with a flash of jewel held in its beak.

Sophie and Rosa had stopped searching. Perhaps they had heard him. They were standing by a tree, talking quietly. Then Sophie walked away and left Rosa standing there.

'What's the matter with her?' I asked.

'Shhh. Rosa might be able to help you. Sometimes she can.'

Rosa stood still as a statue, pressed against the tree, arms by her sides, her eyes tight shut.

After a few moments, Rosa seemed to sigh. She opened her eyes and walked towards us. Her voice sounded almost sulky.

'I saw your brooch next to a carved wooden box.'

'That's on my dressing table,' I said.

Without waiting to be asked, they walked with me. As we passed their mother and father, they waved. The baby boy began to stumble towards them, and cried out when they didn't offer to pick him up.

'What's he called?' I asked.

'Billy.'

I led them into the house and up the wide staircase, along to the right past Ma and Pa's room to my own mausoleum.

'Ohhh!' Rosa said when we opened the door.

'Is this your room?' Sophie asked.

They had forgotten all about the brooch. I went straight to the dressing table, and there it was. In all the excitement of having to help organise races, and with Ma hurrying me up and Granville making snide remarks about people who had no part to play in the family wedding, I had forgotten to pin on my brooch.

I showed it to them, let them admire it, and pinned it on my bolero.

'I can see why you like it so much,' Sophie said. 'It's very pretty, and a friendly looking cat.'

Ever after that, I thought of them as the canny and the uncanny sisters. Sophie, canny and with a sharp streak. Rosa, uncanny, like some cross between a fairy and a fortune teller.

Sophie said, 'Well I reckon there's plenty of room for three and a cat in here. When shall we move in?'

And for some reason that made us laugh. We just laughed, and laughed and laughed until it hurt, until I cried. I had made friends. So there. I wished they could move in. I wished they were my sisters. When it was time for them to go, I walked them to the gate and waved goodbye.

Sophie

We were almost the last to leave Thackreys' garden party because me and Rosa stayed so long, talking to Lydia.

'Come on!' Mam said. 'We don't want a reputation for outstaying our welcome.' But you could tell she was pleased we'd made a friend of Lydia. 'The poor lass must be lonely, having no sisters or brothers of her own.'

Dad carried Billy on his shoulders to the tram stop.

I sat next to Rosa on the tram. We were clutching our prizes from the races – *Alice's Adventures in Wonderland*, jigsaw puzzle, whip and top, shuttlecock and battledore.

As we got nearer home, Dad sighed and said, 'Ah well, here we are. Almost back in us own midden.'

He and Danny got off the tram before us, to go to the Anglers' Club. They'd catch up on the sports results, and boast about where they'd spent the day.

We got off the tram in Upper Accommodation Road

and turned down Ada View. The streets seemed narrower than ever. It did look different on the Bank, shabbier. The newspaper seller, Skinny Albert, walked ahead of us on Bertha Street, calling out, 'Results! Latest!' He stopped by the presbytery as the priests' housekeeper bought a paper.

'Don't stare so,' Mam said.

But you couldn't help it. It wasn't as if he had the usual kind of bow legs. Skinny Albert was once hit by a car and his legs both bowed in the same direction where he took the blow. Everybody had a trademark, and that was his.

Billy had fallen asleep in Mam's arms. I took him from her to give her a rest. By the time we got home, she was done in. She poured a glass of water, then sat down on the bedchair. Rosa drew out the chair bottom, so Mam could rest her legs.

'Give me the bairn. We'll both have some shut eye. You two take a look in that bag of mine. You'll find a titbit for the Scholar and for your Aunt May. Get yourselves round there before the buns go stale, then you can go on to confession. Me and the boyo here should be fit and fine by the time you're back.'

The Scholar, a pale man, parted his light-coloured hair so far down on the right side of his head that the hair sweeping over looked too thick to be real. A single man, he lived on Musgreaves Fold, worked as a clerk for East Street Mills, and acted as secretary to the local Independent Labour Party branch. All his money went on books. He would lend a book to anyone who wanted to borrow. People went to him for help with forms to complete, or an important letter to write.

52

I tapped on the window, since he had the downstairs room. He drew back the curtain, and motioned us to come in. We didn't. The only thing he could do as well as read and write was talk, so we handed him the sandwich and bun, gave him Mam's greetings, and escaped.

Aunt May kept the second-hand shop on Zion Street. The shop bell rang as Rosa pushed open the door. The place burst at the seams with second-hand clothes and old furniture. Clothes spilled from a heap on the counter. To walk anywhere in May's premises, you had to shift old coats and skirts, step sideways round a tea chest, squeeze between chairs and climb over buffets. Tables wobbled, a tilting chests of drawers missed a leg. In a box was a heap of what she called 'spares': knobs, handles and chair legs. In between coal deliveries, the spares box shrunk, as she threw stuff on the fire. Only May and Rosa could move through the shop without collision and attacks on shins and knees. The shop's prize item, a great stinky armchair, took root because nobody roundabout could fit it in their house. Frayed and faded to mushroom grey, great billows of dust rose as I walked by it to reach the house.

Aunt May, substantial in her print apron, reminded me of a great tea cosy, with a powder-puff face. Her fair hair, done up in a bun, had a lopsided look, as if she had been thinking of something else when pinning it in place.

The best thing about Aunt May's was that she had a piano in her house, sheet music, a gramophone and a pile of records. That was the attraction for Rosa, who made herself at home, chose a record and wound the gramophone.

May poured tea from a big stained pot. 'Tell your mam thank you. Did she send something for the Scholar?'

When I told her yes, she said, 'Ah you should've give it to me, I'd have gone round there after I shut up shop.'

She bit into her sandwich. 'You're a clever lass, Sophie. Help me out. The landlord's finally agreed to paint my shop front, brown and cream. I'm going to have a shop name scribed. What's it to be do you reckon?'

I loved that place, but I hated it as well. The dust made me sneeze. The clothes made me itch. I crushed a flea on my leg. 'I'd call it Mayhem.'

Rosa began to sway and sing in time to 'Putting on the Ritz', stopping mid- verse. 'Call it Anything Goes.'

'Everything Goes would be more like it,' May said. 'Only it doesn't go does it? It just seems to grow in there. If you come one day and you can't see me, you'll know I've gone under.'

As we walked up to church, Rosa said, 'May intends to marry the Scholar.'

'What makes you say that?'

'Well why shouldn't she? They're both on their own. That's why she wanted to take him his sandwich, to give her an excuse to go round there.'

Mam was just waking when we got back from church. She yawned and asked, 'Where's Billy?' Then realised we had only just come in.

She looked under the table and behind the chair. 'Has one of the kids in the street taken him out to play?'

'No. He's not out there.'

'He hasn't crawled upstairs has he?'

Rosa went upstairs. I went down to the cellar. I heard Rosa call that he was nowhere up there.

He wasn't anywhere I could see — not by the set-pot or

under the slab. I turned to go back upstairs. Then suddenly, through the coalhole door, I saw that the mound of coal had grown. Mr Durkin had made a delivery. I pushed the door shut and went back upstairs.

'Not there.'

Sure enough, Mr Durkin's bill was in the letter box. We looked again, under the table, behind the chair, the places we had looked before.

Mam went out into the street, Rosa with her.

Then it struck me. It couldn't be. I must be wrong. But all the same, I went to Rosa and said, 'Go fetch Dad. Tell him he has to come.'

'I'm helping Mam look,' Rosa said.

'Just go, Rosa. Run. Run all the way.'

She opened her mouth to ask me what or why, and then set off. Mam was talking to a neighbour. Little girls in the street loved to make a fuss of Billy. They would come to the door and say, Is Billy playing out?

Something took me back into the cellar. I opened the coalhole door and picked up the shovel, not knowing what to do. Then I saw it, and had to blink because of the dim light, and not knowing if I could believe my eyes. A little foot in a brown lace-up shoe stuck out from beneath the coal, and something white above it. An ankle.

Piece by piece, I shifted the coal. A calf, a leg, an arm. Our Billy. Our sweet Billy, still and cold, white under his shroud of black dust.

What came next seared itself into my mind and body, written into me forever. In life, crying or laughing, wriggling or sulking, he felt so heavy, every ounce of him alive. Carrying him in my arms up the stone steps, he felt like

55

nothing at all, no weight. I felt the same absence in myself, as if some ghost girl might never reach the top step, and take our own boy into the house.

I had him in my arms still, not knowing what to do or say, when Mam came back in, ready to speak, her lips forming a word. Her mouth stayed open. She shook her head. Mam had no colour in her, being so pale, but in that moment her skin turned grey, and never would come back to its own natural pallor.

What came from her was more cry than scream. She took him from me, cradling him in her arms. No, no, no. Billy. Billy.

As if she could bring him back.

That was how she stayed for the longest time, the coal dust on her, the top of Billy's head washed clean with her tears.

What came after did not stay so clear for me. Just as I had sent Rosa for Dad and Danny, I was sent places. Sent to fetch the priest. Sent to fetch the doctor. Rosa went for May.

Somehow Billy was prised from Mam's arms and she was given tea, with extra sugar, to help her shock.

Then someone remembered me.

It was Danny. He made me sit on the buffet and gave me tea saying, 'Here, Sophie. You, too. You found him.'

I shouldn't have stayed so long at May's when we took her the sandwich and cake. If I'd come straight back, I would have seen him wake and kept him from harm.

Dad said, 'I should have put a bolt on this house door, so he couldn't get through.'

Mam said nothing, as if the grief made it too hard to speak. Since Billy was born she made so much of him.

She lay sheets on the table and undressed him. As she washed him so gently in warm water, stroking the dirt from him, all her words came back to me. He was her little lion under the table. He might not have words to say just now, but you only had to look at the little feller to see how much life burst in him, and imagine what he might become.

As she dabbed him dry with the towel, I remembered her hopes for him. With grown up brothers and sisters, nothing would be too good for Billy. We would see to it that he if he showed the least inclination to be a good scholar he would go as far as we could send him. He might become a teacher or a doctor, or a clerk of works.

She pulled on his little nightshirt and kissed him.

When Mam finally spoke, she said, 'I didn't take care of him.'

Dad said, 'Yes, yes you did. It was an accident. He was a little adventurer who ventured too far too soon.' Then he said, 'I shouldn't have gone to the Anglers' Club. You were too tired. I should have come home with you.'

Dad carried Billy up to his little bed in their room, as if he lived and breathed still.

And that was how it went, in circles, round and round, the same things said over and over. Women coming to the door, blessing Billy, sitting with Mam, bringing a pot of soup or a loaf of bread. Some told their own tales of tragedy, as if this somehow made ours less. Mrs McBride's little brother had fallen from a cart and died in the road. Mrs O'Malley's nephew had just the smallest of knocks in the playground that turned into a fatal illness.

Rosa lay beside me in our bed. 'I don't believe it. I can't believe it's true.'

And I wondered at what moment did Mr Durkin throw in the bag of coal that crushed Billy. Was it when Rosa played 'Putting on the Ritz' on May's gramophone? Or when we walked up to church, or waited to go into confession. Why had we done any of those things when the only thing that mattered we had not done. Watched Billy. Kept an eye on Billy. It came to me all the sights Billy would never see. A lamb. Roundhay Park. Inside a schoolroom. He would never read a book, go to a picture house or walk on his own from one end of Tab Street to the other.

Mam wouldn't let him be taken into church the night before his funeral. He was too little to be left alone in such a dark and cavernous place. He came with us on the morning of that day. Dad and Danny carried the small pale coffin to the church, and half the world walked behind us.

May held Mam, with an arm around her waist, and on the other side she was supported by the Scholar. Rosa and I walked side by side behind them. I took her hand. We wouldn't cry. Not in the street.

The mass is different when it is for the dead and so it seemed unfamiliar, and in any case we understood only certain Latin words and single lines that teachers had told us the meaning of. Sanctus, sanctus, sanctus. Holy, holy, holy. Credo. I believe. The resurrection and the life.

Only when Father Connor stepped into the pulpit could we follow his meaning. A big, country Irish man with a weather-beaten face and a shock of grey hair, he paused and looked around the congregation, said an Epistle that I could not remember and a Gospel from Mark. 'They were bringing the children to him that he might touch them; and the disciples rebuked them. But when Jesus saw that, he was indignant. He said to them, Suffer the little children to come unto me, do not hinder them; for to them belongs the kingdom of God.'

He said that we could rest in the knowledge that Billy had entered the kingdom of God and would be in heaven forever more.

He took as his text a verse from Proverbs saying, 'Even a child makes himself known by his acts, whether what he does is pure and right.'

From this he said we should remember his innocence and his joy and carry that with us in our lives.

And I wanted to say that Billy was too little to be known by anything except his laugh and his funny sounds. How I wished I knew what he had tried to say, the times when he turned so vexed at not being understood.

How is it that being empty inside makes you feel so heavy? And yet to see so many hundreds of people packing that church – for us – that made me feel important and proud. We would be marked out forever as the family who suffered the great loss. But it felt to me like a badge of shame.

Mam saw nothing. She saw no one. Dad let one of the altar boys join Danny to carry Billy's coffin out of the church. Dad held Mam, her face grey and streaked with tears. His face was set like a stone statue.

Only then did we part from Billy. His coffin went ahead of us, carried on the hearse, with Father Connor sitting beside the driver. We followed behind, a slow and sedate black horse drawing the carriage, carrying the five of us, and May.

The grave was deep, but oh so narrow and small in length. Father Connor made such tiny movements as he walked about when the coffin was lowered, splashing holy water and muttering words we didn't understand.

When we got back into the carriage, Mam wanted me and Rosa on either side of her. She took our hands.

'I'm sorry your hearts was broke so young.'

But all I could think was how pink his little nails were, and how dark his eyelashes.

Lydia

We were in the Allerton House small dining room at supper when Pa told us about the commissionaire's little boy, and how he died. Neither Ma nor I could eat another moutful after that. It was sad and strange to think that the little boy I had seen running on the grass died in such a tragic way.

Granville kept on chomping. With his mouth full, he said, 'That'll teach the child not to go down the cellar.'

Pa looked at his son so sternly that Granville started to blink.

I excused myself and went to my room. Poor Sophie and Rosa, all of them. They made so much of that little fellow.

About a week later Pa said he would take Granville and me to look round the bank.

It was bright and warm as Granville and I got into the car outside Allerton House for our visit to the bank. The sky turned grey as we drew closer to the town. It seemed always that a pall of smoke floated above the city and turned into a kind of fog, summer or winter.

Barney Moran opened the bank door and touched his hat. I could see from his dull eyes that his little boy had died. The light had gone out of them. It was as if he looked, but could no longer quite see.

Pa strode across the floor. Counter clerks perked to attention, as if they might be asked a hard question and needed to be alert enough to answer.

Mr Clutterbuck made a great fuss of saying good morning to each of us. It seemed silly to me that after being so friendly on the day of the garden party he now turned formal, calling me Miss Lydia, with every other word, just as he called blank eyes Master Granville. From a safe in the wall, Mr Clutterbuck produced a large set of keys and handed them to Pa.

The ancient attendant touched fingers to his forehead and said good day to us all in a respectful manner as we stepped into the lift.

We shuddered down into the bowels of the bank.

'Vaults!' the lift attendant announced. He drew back the concertina door, tottered out and held open the second heavy door, bowing as we stepped into the gloom of a passage way lit by a dim bulb.

Granville bounced into life, turning impatiently, ready to hurry down the passage. 'This is the best part.'

I didn't like it, not one bit. It seemed to me like a tomb.

Pa unlocked a heavy door. It swung open into what seemed a pit of darkness, until he switched on the light.

'Before electric light, customers had to be escorted down here by lantern.'

The shelves were lined with gold, coins and bars. Yet it did not look anything much, just a dull metal. 'It must have looked better by lantern,' I said. 'More glinting.'

Pa laughed. 'Perhaps.'

It made me think of the story of King Midas.

'Don't you want to touch it?' Pa asked.

I stretched out my hand, and touched a piece of gold. 'King Midas wanted everything he touched to turn to gold,' I remembered aloud. 'And that included his daughter, so he lived to regret it.'

'King Midas was a fool,' Granville said. 'He should have framed his wish more carefully.'

'Is this the gold standard room?' I asked. It was something Mr Crampton and Harry talked about a lot, the gold standard.

'What a silly thing to say,' Granville mocked. 'There's no such thing as a gold standard room. It's a vault.'

'Not so silly. Show Lydia how you weigh gold, Granville.'

Granville placed a gold bar on the scale and chose a weight to balance it. 'What a waste to have all this gold hidden away. Just think what it would buy, Pa.'

'It's to prove our worth. Customers know it's here if they demand it.'

'And does that scale tell you how much gold to give in exchange for paper money?' I asked.

'The gold standard's decided by politicians.' Pa held open the door for us to leave. 'And five years ago they made the wrong choice. British business and industry have been paying the price ever since.'

I hoped that would be it and we could go back upstairs into the light.

'One more vault,' Pa said. 'Let's show her the money eh, Granville?'

The notes were set out on shelves in a metal-lined room, like some great coffin for an emperor. Pa was explaining how the room had to be like this, with the most protected vent system for air, because the last thing you would want would be for mice and rats to feast on fivers.

I glanced at Granville while Pa was speaking. He had helped himself to a couple of notes and stealthily shoved them in his pocket. His unblinking eyes stared, daring me to say something. How different life might have turned out if I had spoken at that moment. But something held me back. Perhaps it was the thought of Ma, wanting us to fit in, wanting us not to make enemies of the Thackrey children. Of course it was already too late. It was too late before we had begun.

The lift shuddered us towards the second floor.

'And what's at the very top?' I asked, thinking of the pointy attics.

'Clutterbuck's apartments. Someone has to live above the bank,' Pa said. 'And we couldn't want a more trusted person.'

Pa's office looked out onto Park Row. It smelled of polished wood, leather, cigar smoke and money. The large desk, with just a pen and pencil stand, inkwells and blotter, stood opposite the door, with the window behind. Other chairs were placed near the desk. A Persian carpet that looked magical enough to fly lay in the centre of the room. Pa's portrait hung on the wall, along with portraits of his father, grandfather, great-grandfather and great-great-grandfather.

Granville sat in Pa's chair and swivelled round to face the window.

I thought about Mr Crampton's attaché cases of tour schedules, ledgers, notebooks, cheque stubs and paying in books. 'Where is all the work?'

Pa tapped his head. 'In here.'

'Clerks do the work,' Granville said. 'Don't you know anything? Pa directs Clutterbuck and Clutterbuck directs the clerks. That's why Pa is able to golf as much as he does.'

'Not quite like that.' Pa smiled. 'And never under-estimate how much work takes place on the golf course. Swing improvement, ball-eyeing, considering the hori-zon.'

Pa said, 'Now I'm going to take Granville to meet a clerk who has just passed his banking exams with flying colours. I hope he'll inspire you, Granville.'

Granville began to blink rapidly. He said nothing.

'Can I stay here?' I asked.

'To look out of the window?' Pa asked.

'I'd like to write a letter. The commissionaire's children, I played with them at the garden party. It's very sad for them about their little brother.'

'Excellent idea.' Pa opened a drawer and took out some sheets of plain quarto paper and an envelope. 'Use my pen. And when you've finished, you can wait for us downstairs. Park yourself on one of the chairs.'

After he had gone, I opened the drawer to look for paper with lines, but there was none.

It was hard to know what to write, except to say Dear Sophie and Rosa, I was very sorry to hear about Billy . . .

My pen ran away with me, as pens sometimes do. By the end of the letter I had invited them to come to Allerton House and play. Except I did not say play because it seemed a wrong word for girls of our age, and girls whose brother had died. I believe I asked them to tea.

Sophie

One night, Dad came home from the bank bringing an envelope marked 'Sophie and Rosa Moran'. It was from Lydia Thackrey and was written on good paper, with a sailing ship watermark. She said how sorry she was to hear about Billy's death, and asked if we would visit her, naming the second Saturday in September. That and two other occasions I will describe because they show how a friendship sprung up between us, and then ebbed away.

We nearly didn't go that Saturday. Because after Billy died, Mam seemed constantly to need me beside her. The tasks she normally did alone, she could not manage even the simplest. I wrote the lists for our shopping. We went together, she telling me how to watch that we were not sold mouldy potatoes and rotten cabbage. She showed me how to roast a small joint when we had one, and to make a soup out of bones and not much else when we did not.

She showed me how to bake bread, then said what a waste of time it all seemed. We might just as well buy a loaf.

Dad sometimes took to calling for a drink on his way home. It became my job to go to him at the bank on Fridays and collect his pay. I slid coins into the slots of Mam's housekeeping tin box. Rent, coal, food, burial club, candles.

She showed me which pawn shop we should use, if ever I needed one, and explained how you went about it.

Mam knew every street in Leeds, and every short cut. One day when I had collected Dad's wages, she said she would introduce me to our own bank. I knew from the way she said it she held a grudge now against Thackreys' Bank. Once she said that if it had not been for the garden party, she might not have been so jiggered that day, and Billy might still be alive.

I never before thought that a building could look friendly. This one did. It had a rounded front and its name in big letters above the entrance. The Penny Bank. The interior was tiled in green and brown, and the dark wood counters gleamed.

Mam gave me her passbook and a sixpence to hand across the counter. 'Always save when you can, even small amounts. Take care of the pennies and the pounds will take care of themselves.'

The grey-haired bank clerk looked up and almost smiled. He edged the book closer with the longest little fingernail I had ever seen – at least a couple of inches in length.

He steadied the book with his fingernail, entered and totalled the amount. With the same long fingernail, he pushed the passbook to me. It made me wonder, did all bank clerks grow one long fingernail especially for the purpose of avoiding the touch of poor people's books.

Mam checked the entry. 'This is where your school bank book comes to be totted up. You never know when you're going to need something in an emergency. Your dad doesn't know about this book – though he guesses I have a little something put by.'

I couldn't help but get the giggles, through looking at a framed rhyme on the wall. My shoulders shook. I kept my mouth tight shut, trying not to let the laughter out.

'What is it?' Mam asked. She never used to be far from getting the giggles herself, but hadn't laughed since Billy died.

I pointed to the rhyme. '"If youth knew what age could crave, most surely it would try to save."'

Mam daren't laugh in the bank but she did when we got outside. 'It's a true rhyme right enough,' she said. 'But never mind old age. What about tomorrow, and next month's rainy day.'

She gave me the passbook to carry. 'You're grown up enough to get the hang of how I spin the money.'

I felt proud to be in charge of the bank book.

Mam remembered our day for visiting Lydia and said we must go, and not keep the girl waiting. She insisted that Danny go with us, even though Lydia hadn't included him in her invitation. Danny did not want to go but Mam seemed so fearful something bad might happen. She didn't exactly say she expected the tram car to topple over, but I got that idea.

Lydia was waiting by the gate, bouncing a ball. It was a fine day. We walked up to the paved area around the house above the steps. Lydia had brought out her skipping rope. She and I turned the rope while Rosa skipped, and then Rosa took the rope and I skipped.

Danny sat on a low wall nearby, looking bored. 'I'll come back for you,' he said, and was ready to disappear back to the tram stop when Granville came out. He asked if Danny would like to see his den, and they went off together into the woods.

We played two-ball against the wall. After that, Lydia took us round to the kitchen and collected a picnic basket and a rug. We sat ourselves down by the stream and ate sandwiches, cakes and apples. None of that sounds very much, but it was one of those days that cheered us up no end. We walked by the farm, to look at the sheep and the grown-up lambs. Lydia talked about being made to go to school in Harrogate, and how she dreaded the whole business.

We agreed we would write to each other, and I have one of her letters still.

Dear Sophie,

How I hate this school. All the girls know each other already and have such airs and graces. They ask me where I went to school before, or what sort of governess I had. I am held to be most peculiar because my answers do not fit.

We are in 'houses' and are meant not to let the side down, but I seem to do it all the time. Also, I have no idea how to play hockey and do not care to learn but that is not a choice, it is as essential as A, B, C or $2 + 2 = 22$.

We have an afternoon a week when we can wander into the town and buy sweets but of course we must wear our uniforms and walk straight and tall and not take our hats off or bring disgrace on the school by chomping sweets in the street. To be like you, I went to the Penny Bank and opened an account for myself. At this school they do not do what you do at yours, i.e. take in some money every Monday morning to go in your bank account. I expect that would not suit them. But I like having my name on a bankbook, especially since I opened it before Mr Thackrey adopted me so it is in my own Lydia Bellamy name.

One of the teachers, Miss Drummond, told me about a writer called Thackeray (spelt differently to the bank and Pa). I am reading a story of his, about a clerk who inherits a diamond and it brings him bad luck. If you have been brought up in the theatre you cannot help but be a bit superstitious and so I wish Miss Drummond hadn't told me about him or that I had chosen another story to read. I dreamed about my cat brooch swishing her diamond-tipped tail and meowing.

I hope you and Rosa are well and send my best wishes to your parents and Danny.

Your friend

Lydia Bellamy Thackrey

The next time we saw Lydia, it was because when Rosa was twelve, going on thirteen, she got a job dancing in the pantomime, and wanted Lydia to see her.

The evening came.

Mam, Dad, Danny and me were seated centre front stalls.

The Thackreys took the royal box. I waved to Lydia.

It was the best panto I had ever seen. At the beginning, Rosa and the other Blanchflower Babes were guards on the wall where Humpty-Dumpty sat. They marched and waved swords and shields.

In another scene, the Babes played seahorses, dancing around Father Neptune. While they danced, I truly believed they were under the sea from the way they moved, as if through water. The stage really was the sea, with great coloured bubbles floating around Neptune. A sharp wash-house smell that almost choked you came wafting into the front stalls.

How we all laughed at the Dame, making dumplings for Humpty-Dumpty, shaking his head at Mam and saying he bet she'd never had such trouble with her dumplings. Mam laughed and said no she didn't.

When it came to the 'Me and my Shadow' dance I could barely sit still with the excitement of seeing Rosa there, in her element, shadowing the principal boy who was so glamorous. At the end of the song, the principal boy suddenly spotted Rosa and said, 'Who's this?'

Of course Rosa didn't answer, but the principal boy said. 'Oh I know. This shadow is Mr and Mrs Moran's daughter, Rosa, and there's her mam and dad on the front row, with Danny and Sophie.'

Well, didn't the whole theatre just erupt with applause.

We were beside ourselves with happiness, and Mam had to get out her hanky and blow her nose.

Dad waited outside the stage door with Danny. Mam and I sat inside on the bench. Who should come but Lydia and Mrs Thackrey. The stage doorman practically bowed to Mrs Thackrey and opened the door for them to go through into the theatre. Lydia saw me and said, 'Come on!'

Mrs Thackrey tapped on the dressing-room door and went in.

'Congratulations girls! You were all wonderful.'

She handed a box of sweets to Rosa. 'Well done, Rosa.' She kissed her cheek. 'You reminded me so much of myself at that age.'

Rosa blushed and thanked her.

'Oh don't thank me, darling. I should be thanking all of you, for a most wonderful, magical evening.'

Lydia held a shiny carrier bag. She took out small packets and handed one to each of the girls.

'Just a memento,' Mrs Thackrey said, 'And very good wishes to all of you.'

Lydia and I walked back downstairs slowly. 'Rosa was terrific,' Lydia said. 'You must be proud of her.'

'Oh I am.'

'And what are you doing now?'

'I'm working in a shop.'

'Which shop is it? I'll look out for you.'

I didn't tell her it was May's second-hand shop.

Mrs Thackrey held out her hand to Mam. Mam stood up, and took the hand in a solemn way.

'Congratulations, Mrs Moran. Rosa has such talent. I'm sure she'll go far, and I don't say that lightly.'

'Thank you.'

'I shall follow Rosa's career with interest.'

Then they were gone.

As we all walked home, Mam said, 'The Thackreys might have money, but there's no one in Leeds feels prouder than me and your dad tonight. We're proud of all of you.'

Dad agreed.

Danny said. 'Just wait till you're a real chorus girl, Rosa. Then I'll have something to boast about.'

But Rosa was busy examining her gloves and pulling them on. That was Mrs Thackrey's present to all the Blanchflower Babes, a pair of grey woollen gloves, decorated with sequins.

We walked home, singing 'Me and My Shadow', dancing along the pavements all the way to Tab Street. Dad took Mam in his arms and spun her along, and she couldn't tell him to stop for laughing and coughing.

Every year Mam hoped she would not get bronchitis, and every year along it came, sure as Christmas.

She had fought it off all through December, but in it crept through the fog. She gave in and stayed in bed. I propped pillows behind her, so she could sit up and get her breath. Danny brought up burning coals on a shovel and had to fan the smoke away when it poured back into the room.

'Will I send for the doctor?' Dad asked.

'No, no. Sure, haven't I had this every winter? We know exactly what he'll say.'

Making a poultice is not easy. Rosa helped. She cut neat squares of lint and set them in the oven for a few minutes to warm. I burned myself holding a tablespoon of linseed oil over a steaming pan. I poured linseed oil onto the lint, where it didn't want to stay because I'd dolloped on too much. Then Rosa slapped another piece on top so we made two lint and linseed sandwiches. Rosa helped Mam ease herself forward while I placed a poultice on her back.

She leaned back, too weak to open her nightgown for the second poultice. Rosa undid the buttons.

That night when the others were downstairs, I plaited Mam's hair.

'If anything happens to me, I know you'll take care of Rosa.'

'Mam! Nothing's going to happen to you.'

'Danny will find his way. He's not to worry. Your Dad . . . If he can just keep his feet on the ground. You must see that he does.'

'Shhh. Rest.'

Something drains away when a person is ill. And it never entirely comes back. The scariest thing about seeing Mam ill was that suddenly she looked old, ten years older than on the evening of the pantomime.

Each morning, I ran home from May's shop to give Mam a drop of clear soup at about eleven. At two o'clock every afternoon, I ran home to give her a cup of tea and a slice of bread.

When the wheeze turned into a cough, Mam said I should go to the pharmacy for an expectorant medicine. And the next week, she was up and about again.

'I told you I didn't need no doctor.'

My next memory of our friendship with Lydia was the summer of 1931, which I recall because Danny had bought a bicycle with his horse-racing earnings from Harry

Hescott. This time it was himself, not Mam, that insisted on coming along. He wore herringbone knickerbockers, fawn stockings and soft chestnut-coloured boots.

'I've got my little book with me, in case your friend wants to place a bet.'

'Don't you dare!'

Danny jumped on his bike and pedalled alongside us as Rosa and I walked to the tram stop.

He said, 'Well if she doesn't, I'm sure her brother will. I saw him last night at the fight. He had a front row seat. He's not a bad sport.'

Danny drew the tram conductor's wrath by hanging on the back and being pulled along. At the next stop he overtook us, and in the end, we had to laugh at the way he pulled faces along the tram windows, pretending to be gormless and not see us.

Lydia soon appeared at the gate to let us in.

Her hair was short, soft and full of pretty waves. She wore a high-waisted fine-wool navy crêpe skirt, longer at the back than the front, a cross-over white blouse and a sleeveless jacket that matched her skirt. As she swung the gates back, I saw it was more like trousers than a skirt because it was sewn up the centre.

'Don't you look grand, Lydia.' She was dolled up like a young woman, and we were still scruffy girls, even though we had snaffled the best May's shop had to offer.

When we complimented her on the outfit, Lydia said, 'Oh we've only been messing about on the bikes, that's why I'm wearing this. And . . . ' she looked around and lowered her voice 'trying out the motor car as well, but don't breathe a word.'

Danny came bumping along, ringing his bike bell. 'Am I allowed?' he asked.

'Of course.' She held the gate open until he had cycled through. 'Granville guessed you'd come. Go on round to the courtyard at the back of the house.'

As we turned on the bend in the drive, Lydia suddenly stopped. In a great rush she asked would we like to go over to the woods, straight away, there was something she wanted to show us. She tugged at my arm and I turned to go with her, but a crunching on the gravel made me pause. A huge perambulator rolled into view, pushed by a stiff-looking nurse with a tight bun on her head and two chins held firmly above the sharp white collar of a starched blue dress.

Lydia just said, 'Oh. Oh,' her face the picture of misery.

'What's up?' I asked.

'Not good timing,' she said, as the pram came closer. 'My mother had a baby in March. I didn't tell you because . . . '

In a voice sharp as broken glass, the nurse said, 'Miss Thackrey.'

'Good afternoon, Nurse Dorothea.'

The starched nurse inclined her head disdainfully and left just a moment for us to peer into the pram.

'What's he called?' I asked.

'I call him Baby Bunting,' Lydia said.

A chubby infant took hold of my finger.

'Must be orf!' The nurse set off at a lick, leaving me to run alongside the pram trying to free my finger from the baby's grasp.

When I got back to them, Rosa was looking round as if we had missed something important. 'What was it you wanted to show us in the woods, Lydia?'

'Oh, that . . . ' Lydia shrugged.

We all realised at the same moment. Lydia thought we would look at the baby, remember Billy, and be sad.

I would have said nothing, but that was not Rosa's style. 'Seeing a baby doesn't hurt us. It broke our hearts, especially Mam's, but we don't go round bursting into tears.'

We went to Lydia's room which was even bigger than I remembered, and the wardrobe bursting with clothes. 'Oh Ma insists,' she said. 'If it were up to me there wouldn't be half of that stuff there. Anyway, I'm grown out of most of it. Is there anything you'd like?'

Rosa jumped at the chance. I sat and watched them, because it seemed to me that Lydia would give Rosa anything she wanted, simply because we had the bad timing of seeing the baby brother. So I had to say something.

'Our street heaves with kids, Lydia. If we took a fit or a faint every time we saw a little boy, we'd have to lie in a dark room for the rest of our lives. You don't have to give us half your clothes because you have a little brother.'

After that it was all right between us. We went out, taking it in turns to ride her bike. Danny had already gone home, but Granville let me have a turn on his bike. By the end of the afternoon we got the hang of it.

Granville disappeared while we three girls had tea in a little dining room, with best china and sandwiches with no crusts.

Granville appeared again as we came outside.

'Hey,Lydia! How about we give your friends a lift home on the back of our bikes?'

I said no. It was too far.

'It's a good idea,' Lydia said. She went back inside to

bring the bag of clothes for Rosa. Rosa sat astride Lydia's saddle and I got on behind Granville.

We kept pace with them all along the tram route as far as Gledhow Valley Road. Then Lydia and Rosa kept going and Granville turned off. 'This is quicker. We'll get there before them.'

Halfway along, he pulled into the path by the woods. 'I need a drink from the stream. You can have a pedal after that if you like.'

'Are you getting tired? I can catch the tram.'

'Not a bit, just thought you might like a turn pedalling.'

He drank from the stream, and I did too. As I drank, he came behind me and kissed the back of my neck.

'Hey! What are you doing?'

'Kissing you. Is that all right?' He slid down beside me. 'Has anyone ever kissed you before. Any boy I mean?'

'No. And they're not going to neither.'

He made a quick lurch at me and kissed my lips before I had chance to move. 'There. That wasn't so bad was it?'

'I suppose not.'

'Shall I do it again?'

While I was thinking about it, he did kiss me again, and for longer.

'That's enough.' I stood up and moved back towards the bike. It wouldn't do to let him moon over me. Dad would go mad if he thought his precious Master Granville would be getting himself into bother over me.

Granville began to blink rapidly. 'I like you. I've always liked you, ever since you won the races at the garden party. But I like you more now because you're bigger and you've started to be a woman.'

79

I felt myself turn red.

'It's nothing to be shy about. It's true. I don't like many girls, but I like you.'

'Have you kissed a girl before?' I asked.

'Sit down and I'll tell you.'

'We better go.'

'Give me a rest. Just five minutes.'

I sat down.

He pulled at a blade of grass. 'I have kissed a girl before. But she wasn't as pretty as you, and not so grown up either. There's bluebells further in the wood.'

'I know. I've seen them,' I lied.

'I've kissed a girl, but there's something I haven't done.'

Curiosity got the better of me. 'What?'

'I've never looked at a real girl's bust. Only at pictures. I would like to see your bust if you'll just please open your dress.'

'No!' I'd no intention of letting him look at me, and in any case, what sort of idiot could look at a pinafore dress and think you could just undo it.

'Just lean forward then and let me look down. What harm will that do?'

I began to laugh. He didn't like that. He put his hand in his pocket. 'Half a crown for a look.'

I picked up the half a crown and threw it at him. 'Mucky bugger. Go look at girls round your own end. Don't come bothering me.'

I got up and began to walk back to the road. He caught up with me and grabbed my hand. I kicked his shins and kept walking.

'Ouch! What was that for?' He ran after me. 'I was only asking. Keep your hair on. I wouldn't have asked if I didn't like you. Like you a lot. Oh come on. I'm sorry. Give me another chance. You can ride the bike if you want.'

'All right. I'll give you one more chance. Only I'm not riding the bike because I don't want you and your fast hands behind me. And the only reason I'm giving you another chance is because of Lydia. I feel sorry for her, having you as a brother.'

Once we were back on the bike, he turned his head. 'I suppose you think your brother's a saint?'

'Leave my family out of it.'

He just laughed, as if he knew something about Danny that I didn't.

'Aha!' he yelled, as we wheeled along Tab Street to our house. 'Told you I knew a short cut. We're here first.'

I jumped off. 'Thanks for nothing.'

'Don't mench, wench.' He waited while I opened the door. 'No hard feelings?'

Lydia and Rosa were already inside, with Lydia's bike wheeled indoors. I asked did Lydia want her brother to wait and go back with her.

She shook her head. 'I can find my own way back.'

'Goodbye, Master Granville,' I said sarcastically, and shut the door in his face.

'Where did you get to?' Rosa asked.

'Shortcut.'

Lydia admired everything about the house – the mantelpiece, the mirror.

I told her that the mirror was a wedding present from our grandmother to Mam and Dad.

Rosa looked aggrieved. 'I didn't know that. Nobody told me.'

Lydia admired the cupboards, the range, the rag rug. 'I really like your house. It's cosy. It reminds me ever so much of somewhere, but I can't think where.'

She took a drink of water, and mercifully didn't ask about the lavatory. It was the Grundys turn to clean it, and they never did.

We waved her off as she pedalled out of Tab Street.

Rosa took out the skirts, blouses and dress Lydia had given her. 'She really liked our house.'

'So she said.' I had a strong feeling we would not see her again, or at least not in the same easy way as before. It was not just that the difference between us was so stark, but a kind of uneasiness had crept in.

The summer went by, and the autumn too. The following panto season, Rosa did not mention inviting Lydia to see her in *Aladdin and His Magic Lamp*.

On a bitter January day, Mam and I walked to the Penny Bank, Mam to deposit some of Rosa's earnings, and me carrying May's takings.

'Let's get in out of the wind,' Mam said as we reached the door.

And it was as quick as that. She put her hand to her chest, and her eyes met mine, as if she knew, and then the light was gone from them.

She fell. I caught her.

We were helped into the bank. Two men carried Mam into a back room.

'There's no pulse,' the grey-haired clerk said. He put his hand to Mam's chest. It was the man with the long fingernail, only his nail had broken and was short as anyone's little fingernail.

One of the men closed her eyes. 'I'm sorry, Miss. Your mam has died.'

Another said, 'We've telephoned the hospital.'

I was in a chair, with a cup in my hand and someone saying, 'Drink this.'

And, 'Who shall we send for?'

Someone went for Dad.

And while we waited, I remembered why we had come, and handed the books and money to the clerk.

Because who else could look after such things now? Only me.

Dad came. He agreed that Mam must be taken to the hospital, even though there was no hope.

We were not allowed to go with her, but walked home together. Dad said, 'If a person dies suddenly, it has to be looked into.'

Dad went to Harry Hescott's house, to find out where Danny would be. I met Rosa after school, but daren't tell her till we were in the house because I didn't know how we would walk the rest of the way otherwise.

Mam never had her name in the paper all her life. After her death, she had a newspaper item to herself. I kept the cutting. It said that Agnes Moran collapsed with pneumonia. 'Time and again the coroner had cases of people dropping down dead in the street from no apparent cause, but when a post-mortem examination was made it was shown they were suffering from pneumonia.'

Dad said, 'She never did get over losing Billy.'

The bank let Dad stay off, to make the funeral arrangements. I went with him to see the undertaker, taking the burial club card.

Mr Dudley ushered us into his small office. He waited until we were seated before taking his own place on a captain's chair. He listened, nodding sympathetically while Dad praised Mam. Her loveliness. Thrift. Skill. Intelligence. What a good mother.

I wanted him to just shut up. Just do what had to be done and let us get out of there.

Mr Dudley shook his head sadly. 'It's a great pity there's not more on your burial club card. Because of your previous bereavement, of course.'

Dad said that mustn't stop us giving Mam a fine funeral.

Mr Dudley agreed. 'You have a good position, Mr Moran. People will expect it of you.'

Neighbours on either side, the Hartigans and the Nolans, opened and shut their doors without a sound. At the back, the Grundys seemed no longer to rake their fire.

So long as it hadn't happened, it might not happen.

Rosa climbed over me to get out of bed. I watched her dressing. Soon, I would have to move. The day would begin. Then there would be no going back.

May's voice floated upstairs, saying she had been awake all night.

I levered my legs out of bed, touching my toes against the little peg rug. I sat there, feeling so slowed down, like an old granny.

Downstairs, May tried to make us drink more tea and eat bread and margarine. It stuck in my throat.

May said, 'Everyone in the street has their curtains drawn. They've all scoured their doorsteps, out of respect.'

I wanted the steps to be un-scoured and for it to be a fortnight ago, and Mam still with us, and not this stupid event, like a game we had to play, with no sense and no reality at all.

Dad had ordered a carriage to follow the hearse.

'I'll walk behind,' May said.

Dad took her arm. 'You will not so. You'll sit between Sophie and Rosa.'

Dad and Danny had their backs to the horses and driver.

Tab Street was lined with women who had combed their hair, the ones who could not get to Mass because of skriking bairns. From where I sat, I could not see who walked behind.

There was a frost that morning. My heart went out to the horses, trying to keep a steady footing uphill to the church. It would be too much to bear, if a horse slithered and fell.

At the graveside, May stood beside Danny, holding his arm. Dad took my and Rosa's hands. When the coffin was lowered into the ground, he nearly broke my fingers with the pressure of his grip. Then I knew for sure it was true. I wouldn't see her again. I began to cry. Dad seemed as though he would jump in beside her. He called to her as the coffin touched bottom. 'Agnes love, come back, your bairns are roaring their eyes out for you.'

Afterwards, people I had never met came up and shook my hand.

The funeral breakfast was set out in an upstairs room at the Zion Tavern. Such things as how many people to expect and how they knew to come seemed a mystery to me. Dad must have told them.

People came to say a few words. I could not quite take in what they said. Danny could talk to people. Why couldn't I? He could look at a person he didn't know and pay attention. Did he truly see and hear? I couldn't be sure who was in front of me. Words floated past without sense.

The Scholar was different, because we knew him well. He came to where Rosa and I sat with cups of tea and untouched sandwiches.

'I'm sorry for your loss. To get the time off, I told the boss Agnes was my sister. And that's how I thought of her, though I never realised it until today.'

'It was good of you to come,' Dad said to everyone.

The Scholar said, 'Don't be strangers. Any time you want a book, just knock on my door.'

When we got home, I picked up Mam's borrowed books. One was a medical dictionary in brown calfskin binding. The other was pale blue with dark blue print on the front. *The Home University Library*. In a circle on the bottom right-hand corner, a man leaned forward, scything hay, a glorious sun behind him encircled by great rays.

'Let it fall open. See if it tells us anything,' Rosa said.

I did.

'What does it say?' Rosa asked.

I slid the book across the table to her. 'You do it if you're so fussed.'

She read, 'Wealth is acquired today in over-reaching our neighbours, and spent in insulting them. Establish equality on a firm basis of rational opinion, and you cut off for ever the great occasion of crime, remove the constant spectacle of injustice with all its attendant demoralisation, and liberate genius now immersed in sordid cares.'

Injustice. Sordid cares. Where was the justice in struggling, and all for nothing. Just to watch your mother die. Mam had wanted to make the world a better place, but the world had not wanted her. Cold and mean, it squeezed ice into her veins, fog into her chest and death into her heart.

Rosa opened the book again, this time reading to herself.

'Does it tell you anything?' I asked.

'Just that Mam was cleverer than we thought, if she understood all this stuff.'

*

Danny lay downstairs on his bedchair, singing to himself. 'The Last Rose of Summer'.

I went down for a drink of water and told him to shut up.

'It's not about a flower, that song. It's about a person who dies before her time,' he said.

'Well shut up about it.'

He propped himself on his elbow. 'Will you be all right if I go away from here?'

He held a spill to the dying fire and lit a candle. 'I can move in with Harry Hescott and his wife. I talked to Dad about it.'

That would be one less sad person moping round the house. 'I expect you'll do what you want.'

'You didn't open that letter that came for you.'

'I know.' I picked up Lydia Thackrey's letter and sat at the table. It was kind. It was sympathetic about Mam. I never answered. Couldn't think what to say.

Lydia

It must have been three years after her mother died when I caught a glimpse of Sophie Moran through the car window. She was walking under a gas light, snow falling on her head and shoulders. I almost asked Massey to stop the car, but the moment passed.

Ma and I were in the Riley, on the way home from the railway station after a trip to London. People on the train had been speculating about whether Christmas 1934 would be white.

In London, we had seen a production of *Romeo and Juliet*. One of Ma's old friends was playing the nurse. Ma said, 'You know I have never seen so clearly that Juliet is just a young foolish girl, in her first infatuation. She would have fallen for someone else within a fortnight.'

'That's ridiculous. For heaven's sake, Ma! That's the whole point of Romeo and Juliet. It's a great love story. It's true love and there'd be no shaking it.'

Ma sighed. 'That's exactly why that girl's Juliet seemed to me so fragile and wonderful. She believed totally in her own infatuation.'

I expect when you get as old as Ma you are bound to have a warped view of the world and not see what's under your very nose. If she knew anything about love, she'd know I'm in it, fathoms deep.

For years, I was never really aware of him. He was away at school. In the holidays he was always off doing something else, captaining some team or other, working away in his room or cycling for miles.

We were in church on Sunday morning. Mrs Winterton and Penelope always sat on the left, under the pulpit, looking up at Mr Winterton, giving him silent encouragement for his sermons.

I'd sort of dreamed off during the service. Ma elbowed me to join in the hymn singing, but I couldn't see my book. He was on my right, and singing in the most delicious way that I wondered how I could have lost my concentration for so long. He handed me the book, opened at the page. His hand touched mine and I looked at him, and he looked at me. For what seemed the longest moment, the words on the page wouldn't come into focus. He sang, with such magnificence that if I'd shut my eyes I could have imagined myself at an opera. I finally started to sing, 'Let the fiery, cloudy pillar Lead me all my journey through'. I turned to glance at him, just as he was glancing at me. We both looked away in the instant.

He walked beside me out of the church, towards the parsonage. Mrs Winterton chatted to Ma and Pa. Mr Winterton would come in last, having to take off his surplice, but he always left on his cassock, as if it were his Sunday frock.

When we got to the parsonage gate, he finally spoke.

'In all these years, we've never got to know each other.'

'No.'

He held out his hand. 'I'm Theo.'

'I know.'

'And you're Lydia.'

'Yes.'

No one had ever said my name in quite that way, as if you could go on saying it into eternity.

It was October and the leaves had begun to fall. One spun from a willow tree in the churchyard and blew against his ear, as if it wanted to whisper to him.

He said, 'The leaves will be gone soon. We should walk down the lane before they disappear.'

'Yes.'

And we did, not speaking, not telling anyone. We just let the others go on into the house. We turned our backs on them and walked side by side down the lane.

We reached the narrow turn-off that led to the farm.

He said, 'By Christmas, do you think we'll know each other well enough that I could kiss you under the mistletoe?'

The sheep came towards us. They always think you have something to do with them.

I don't know why I said what I did, perhaps trying to change the subject, but not succeeding. 'There's mistletoe down there, growing by the oak.'

When we reached the oak, we stopped. Our breath made small clouds between us. He said, 'I climbed that tree once.'

'So did I.'

Then his lips touched mine.

The sheep were still waiting and watching.

'Look, if we won't be kissing till Christmas, I mean that's such a long way off.' And he kissed me, again, and I kissed him back.

He said, 'This is love at first sight, isn't it? Tell me it is.'

'It would be, except we've seen each other before. So it's not first sight.'

'But never like today. I saw you for the first time today, and you saw me. It was meant. What age are you, Lydia?'

'Seventeen.'

'I'm nineteen. I'm going to be an architect, only it takes years. I wonder how soon we can be married. I've been told I shouldn't even think of marriage till I'm thirty.'

'I'm going to be married by the time I'm nineteen, at the very latest. So you'd better not kiss me again.'

'Nineteen? I'll be twenty-one. I don't think I can wait that long.' He moved to kiss me again but I moved more quickly, hurrying towards the parsonage.

I wanted the world to fall into place. I wanted to go back into that church there and then and have the bells peal and Mr Winterton put on his surplice and marry us before three o'clock.

But we walked back into the parsonage drawing room, sipped British sherry and sat silently on two straight chairs with a line of electricity between us, while everyone talked. And it seemed to me that although everyone was paying attention to each other, they were really aware of the two of us, sitting in such a powerful silence.

I turned to him. 'What does an architect do? I mean, what kind of architect will you be?'

If I hadn't fallen in love with him ten minutes earlier, I would have fallen in love with him then. You need to know what he looks like to appreciate the passion of his speech.

He is tall and well-built, with fair hair that falls onto his forehead, a tanned look from being outdoors, playing rugger and cricket. When he speaks, the words come from his heart as well as his head.

'Lydia, we were both born during that terrible war. There was a slogan, after the war. Homes fit for heroes. That constituted a promise to the soldiers and their families, as far as I'm concerned. Because the families were heroes too. I want to help keep that promise.'

'You're going to design houses?'

'Yes. Have you seen the kind of houses the poor live in, in this very city?'

'Yes.'

'But have you ever been in one?'

'Yes.'

'Then you're rare, because most privileged people have no idea.'

'It was a nice house, small, clean, a flagged floor, a rag rug.'

'A back-to-back?'

'Yes, in that area, what's it called? – the Bank. Where the Irish live. It was cosy.'

'Cosy! They'll have one lavatory between forty people. Some don't even have a tap in the house but a shared pump. They're damp, rat-infested, the rain pours in. Leeds is the worst place in the country for childhood illness. Tuberculosis, rickets, scarlet fever, diphtheria. It's because of the filth of the place and the lack of air in the houses.'

'The family I know, the family I'm thinking of, they've had more than their fair share of bad luck.'

'In what way?'

'Well, the youngest girl, she had scarlet fever as a child. The boy had diphtheria. The mother died of pneumonia.' I couldn't bring myself, even this long time after, to say how little Billy died.

'That's exactly what I'm saying. Only it's not bad luck, Lydia. It's poverty.'

'But they're not desperately poor. At least I don't think so. The father works at the bank, and the daughters – well, I think of one of them as canny and the other uncanny.'

For a moment I thought he was going to forget where we were and take my hand. 'You have such a good heart. And you're so clever. I don't understand why you didn't go to Oxford with Penelope.'

'I'm not as brainy as your sister, and not cut out for it.'

Mr Winterton said suddenly, 'You must be telling Lydia all about your plans, Theo.'

Theo looked blank. 'Plans?'

'Yes. Your plans for social housing. I'm sure Mr and Mrs Thackrey will be interested to hear.'

Ma, gave that little smile of indulgence that she never used to have.

Mr Winterton said, 'Oh dear, you're standing up. I didn't mean you to give a speech, just you know . . .'

'The thing is,' Theo began, 'I've done some research.' He went into Mr Winterton's study and came back with a sheaf of papers. 'There is not a single civilised country that has the vast tracts of slums that we do. No other country treats its working people, and its poor, with such contempt. The inhabitants of our slums pay with their blood for what our industrialisation has done— early deaths, high infant mortality, poor health. For overcrowding, wretched conditions, noxious air, lack of sanitation – Great Britain takes the prize.'

Mr Winterton topped up the sherry glasses. 'Take them through, Theo. Show them your models.'

Pa put a hand over his glass. He did not like Winterton sherry. Every Christmas he bought Mr Winterton half a dozen bottles of best sherry. By October it had run out.

We trooped into the study. There, on Mr Winterton's sermon-writing table, were tiny pairs of houses, in rows and semi circles, set out on greengrocers' material, meant to look like grass.

'It looks all very fine and grand, Theo,' Pa said patiently. 'What you probably don't realise is that the cost of housing has gone up four-fold since pre-war.'

'Yes I do realise, sir. And that's why we should do it now, before costs rise even further.'

'Some poor taxpayers might say far too much is being done already.'

'Then why do we have tens of thousands of people in every city in the land living in housing that medical officers of health describe as unfit dwellings?'

'Those people . . . ' Pa tapped the table as if the people had already wangled their way into the little model houses. He stood with his back to the window, blocking the light. 'If they had anything about them, they'd filter up to better housing, without a helping hand from you.'

'Theo's right,' I said. 'I've seen how small the rooms are in the houses in that area down by the river, the Bank.'

'When did you see that?' Ma asked.

'It's where . . . some friends of mine . . . I went there once years ago, on my bike.'

I didn't want to mention the Morans in front of Pa. 'It doesn't matter how much people try to keep it clean, when so many people have to share a lavatory, it's unhygienic. And there's nowhere for them to hang washing except across the street. It's dirty as soon as it's put out, because of the smoke from the factories.'

'I suppose you'd rather there weren't any factories,' Pa teased, smiling now. 'I think I know whose house you're talking about, and it's kind of you to be sympathetic. But you see the gentleman in question has had every opportunity to improve his lot. What's that quote m'dear . . . ?' He turned to Ma. '"The fault dear Brutus is not in our stars, but in ourselves."' If a chap has indiscipline in his marrow, a lack of thrift, a sort of inner restlessness that makes him want to reach for the stars, then he won't filter up to a better place in the world, and let his children filter up in turn.'

Theo waited until Pa had finished. 'What's needed – and thank goodness the government and the local councils are beginning to see it this way – is for everyone to have a basic, decent standard of living. It's not impossible to build in a way that suits needs and areas, using local materials. It will boost the economy. Housing has to be done from a rational basis. Just because back-to-back housing once suited the shape of fields, that's not a good enough reason to go on building that way. People need space – a minimum square footage. They want to look out on something green and pleasant. Human beings deserve air and light, and rooms with specific functions. No one should have to bathe in the room where cooking takes place. And people can't filter up in the way you suggest, Mr Thackrey. If you look at the results of the last census, there's been such a rapid rate of new family formation that there simply isn't the housing stock available.'

'I'll say this for you, Theo,' Pa chuckled. 'You orate a touch better than your father sermonises. Perhaps you should have considered holy orders.'

Theo shrugged. Mr and Mrs Winterton laughed. People usually laughed when Pa made a joke. Until that day I had found myself joining in. I wanted to stretch my hand across to Theo's, and let my fingers stroke his, just to tell him I would always be on his side.

'Theo's absolutely right,' I said when they had finished laughing.

Theo's black Labrador sidled up to me and wagged its tail in agreement.

Pa stood up and said to Ma. 'Well there we are, well and truly told by the up and coming generation. Now it must be nearly time for Sunday dinner.'

As I floated back through our wood, Ma and Pa strolling ahead of me, every bird in the world sang. The sky looked bright and clear. A light breeze blew through the leaves that whispered Theo's name as they fell to earth.

Sophie

The mound of old clothes on May's counter had grown. If one more person came in with a hard luck story, trying to flog us a coat, I would scream. We couldn't shift winter coats in April.

He hadn't come to buy or sell. He raised his cap.

'I'm the joiner.' He carried a huge toolbox and wore workmen's overalls.

You would have to go a long way to see such a cheerful face and lively eyes. I had to smile back.

'Mrs Manley won't be back for an hour.'

'I'm here to fix the door.'

'It's that one.' I pointed to the door between the shop and the house. 'It sticks.'

In spite of treading carefully through the shop, he could not avoid hitting a tea chest with his toolbox and knocking against a three-legged stool.

A person who knows what he's doing makes the work look so easy. In no time, he had the door off its hinges, trimming it here and there, smoothing the edges with a file.

He fixed the door back in place. 'Would you like to check it, Miss – sorry, I don't know your name?'

'Sophie.' I shut and opened the door. 'Thank you. That's much better.'

'Don't mench. Mrs Manley spoke to my dad about it, and he said I'd pop round. No charge.' He opened his tool-box and began to lay the screwdriver and file back in their places.

'Then would you like a cup of tea?'

'A drink of water would go down nicely.'

He perched on the three-legged stool while I went through to the house. 'Don't think I'm being cheeky,' he called. 'But what's a girl like you doing working in here? You'd do grand in Lewis's or one of the big town shops.'

That was exactly what I thought myself.

'Being here's handy for home. May doesn't mind, if I've to get a bit of shopping, or go to the wash-house.'

'Where do you live then?'

'Tab Street.'

'We live by East End Park. My dad's the joiner. I'm his apprentice.'

'You did that door very quickly.'

'Doors are easy. Shelves are easy. I could put up a few shelves in here, and a rail or two if you like.'

'You'd have to see Mrs Manley.'

'Tell her I'd put up some shelves on a Saturday after-noon, and just charge her for the materials.'

'Why would you do that?'

He had drunk his water, but held onto the glass. 'I'll do it on condition that I can take you to the pictures tomorrow night.'

'I can't.'

He sighed and handed me back the glass. 'All right. Only asking.'

'I can't because tomorrow night I'm going to see my sister in a play. She's a machinist at Montague Burton's, and she's in the works drama group.'

'What play?' He looked really interested, as if he went to see plays every day of his life.

'It's by Noel Coward. She plays a princess. It's called *The Queen was in the Parlour*.'

'I wouldn't mind seeing that meself.' He gave a big smile. 'Do you think there might be a spare ticket?'

'I could ask.'

'What time does it start?'

'Half seven.'

'I'll be outside the Montague Burton gates at seven, just on the off chance. Is that all right?'

'It's a free country.'

'I'll see you tomorrow then.'

He picked up his toolbox and made for the door.

'I don't know your name.'

He turned that smile on again. 'It's Tony. Tony Wood-house.'

The play made me cry, even though I knew it was only Rosa and Alec Zermansky.

When we got outside, I said, 'Wasn't it so sad?'

Dad blew his nose. 'So sad. Our Rosa looks like a queen,

99

and she's spending her days machining trousers. And you, we had such high hopes, and you're in a bloody flea hole with May Manley.'

'Shhh!' I didn't want Tony to hear. I hadn't realised till then that Dad must have had a drink. He'd taken to eating peppermints, so you couldn't always tell. What gave him away was the moods. One glass of beer and he'd either be happy as a pig in mud or miserable as a porker off to market.

The crowd carried us out onto Hudson Road.

We turned along Stoney Rock. Dad's mood changed in an instant as he got his bearings. 'We're within spitting distance of the Anglers' Club. Do you know it, Tony?'

Tony did know the Anglers' Club. I had visions of finding my way home alone while the two of them drank pints and toasted Rosa.

But we parted company with Dad. Tony said, 'You'll have to show me the nearest way to Tab Street, and I'll walk you home.'

And on Saturday, we went to see Clark Gable at the Gaumont.

On the way back, he told me about some of the other pictures he had seen – which was a lot, and he remembered all the stories in great detail. Whenever we got to a road he held my hand, even if there was no traffic. But then he would let go once we were across.

'Do you ever go to East End Park?' he asked.

I told him yes, because we used to go there with Mam.

'I'm playing there tomorrow in the Boys' Brigade Brass Band. If you're about in the afternoon, give me a wave and I'll play you a tune.'

I asked Rosa the next day, and told her about Tony.

'I'll walk up with you. You don't want to go there on your own or you'll look to be chasing him.'

The boys in the brass band puffed out their cheeks and played in such a jolly way. Tony spotted us and tilted his trumpet in our direction. The conductor flapped his arms as if he were describing the way a bird flies. Then he'd suddenly jerk his arm straight and point to a player to give a little bit of oompah.

When the band stopped playing and Tony came over, Rosa spotted someone she knew on the other side of the park.

Tony put his bandsman's jacket around my shoulders when the breeze blew. 'I'm glad you came today. I'm going to have to give the band a miss now because I've got my carpentry and joinery exams coming up this year and next. It won't leave time for band practice.'

As we walked round the park, he named the trees, oak, elm, sycamore, going up close to them as if they were his great friends. He described how you could tell which was which, from the shape, the bark and the leaves.

'What's your favourite tree?' I asked.

'The oak. Because it grows so grand and it's generous to everything that lives in or near it.'

My favourite was the willow, because it seemed so full of sorrow. When I looked at it, I thought of Billy and Mam, and how the tree seemed brought low with memories. But I didn't tell him that.

'Come under the willow tree,' he said. 'It's like a green tent.'

And that was where he kissed me. His kiss was gentle, like

him. He ran a finger down my cheek. 'You have such soft skin. And I love your hair, your lovely light-brown hair.'

We kissed again.

'Shall you and me go out together?' he asked.

'To the pictures again?'

'I mean, will you be my girl?'

'Yes, I will.'

'Good.'

When we came out from under the willow tree, the sky had turned so much brighter that it took me by surprise.

Every Friday, May paid me. Every Friday, the rent man called. Every Friday, Rosa and I had our bath in front of the fire, and washed our hair over the sink. Dad went to the slipper baths on Fridays and we had the house to ourselves.

We were waiting for the rent man to come.

'That bloody man,' Rosa plonked the tin bath by the cupboard. 'He's getting later and later. I'm sure he does it on purpose.'

'A few minutes doesn't make any difference.' I put the towel over the oven door to warm.

'It might make no difference to you but you know how long my hair takes to dry.'

The rent collector rat-a-tatted on the door. I went to let him in. Mr Enfield was a red-faced man with wavy ginger hair, pale red-rimmed eyes and a Mr Punch nose. 'Hello my favourite girls.'

Rosa ignored him. She was the one whose money was tucked in the rent book and she thought politeness an unnecessary extra.

He brought out a two-ounce bag of pear drops. 'Sweets for the sweet.'

Rosa pushed them back to him in a rude way. 'Save them for the kids at your next call. We're getting a bit old for pear drops.'

When he had gone, Rosa started to fill the bath.

'Bloody man. Who does he think pays the rent?'

'I expect he thinks it's Dad.'

'Well then we should disabuse him and tell him it's me. I don't like him, Sophie. He's gives me the creeps.'

'There's no need to be rude to people.'

'Oh you. You should get yourself out of that shop. All shopworkers are the same. They have to bow and scrape and be nice to people. At least I don't have to do that.'

'I had noticed. I might work in a shop but I'm the one puts food on the table and does all the work in this house.'

'Only because you haven't the guts to go out and do summat different. I don't need your food. I get my dinner in the canteen.'

'Dad needs to eat.'

'Oh does he now? I thought he liked to drink and pick up a bag of chips on his way home.'

There was a knock on the door. Rosa lowered herself into the bath. 'Put the clothes horse by me, with the towel. And if that's that bloody rent collector come back with more sweets, tell him to bugger off.'

'You have got so common since you went to work at Burton's.'

'And so bloody rich.'

'You forget who's the eldest.'

'And you forget who's the smartest.'

I put the shield of the clothes horse next to her, with the

towel, then went through the passage, shutting the house door behind me.

Tony stood on the step. 'Hello.'

'What do you want?'

He looked hurt. 'I've brought you a bag of chips.'

'Oh, right. Well you can't come in. We're washing us hair and that.'

'Oh, sorry.'

I shut the outside door and sat on the steps with him. He looked embarrassed. 'I should've known. Friday night. Only I don't have any sisters.'

'Never mind.'

He handed me a bag of chips. 'I put salt and vinegar on.'

'Thanks.' I hoped Rosa would smell them and be sorry.

But the most annoying part of it all – she was right. The following Friday, I was on my own when the rent man called. Rosa had stayed with a friend from work, just to make a point I felt sure. Dad had gone to the slipper baths. Because I always paid the funeral man on Fridays and cleared the slate with the grocers, I had no money for the rent.

When Mr Enfield knocked, I decided the best thing would be to say it straight out.

He came in, just the same, as if by habit.

'I thought it might come to this, but never mind. Where's your sister?'

'Staying with a friend.'

The rent book was on the table. He opened it and took his pen from his top pocket.

'I don't have it. I said . . . '

He marked it just the same, and initialled the date.

'Why have you done that?'

His Mr Punch nose touched my cheek as he kissed me. 'Because I liked your mother, and I like you. You're a lovely girl and I hate to see you upset.'

And the terrible thing was that if he hadn't stayed so close to me, for just that extra few seconds I might have said nothing. And if Rosa hadn't said, 'He gives me the creeps,' I might have said nothing. And if he hadn't mentioned my mother, I might have said nothing. Because there is something in me I don't like, a not-wanting-to-be-rude, a wanting to give people a chance. But thank God I didn't say nothing. I yelled at him, 'Get out. Get out of here. And don't ever come near me again.'

I went to the door and called after him down the street as loudly as I could.

'Try that again and I'll bash your brains out with the poker.'

He wouldn't have dared try it on with Rosa.

I cried after he had gone. How could a girl of seventeen be more stupid than her fifteen-year-old sister?

More than anything, I wanted my mam.

Lydia

Pa made Sunday dinner a jolly affair. He carved the joint meticulously, giving each person two beautifully neat slices of beef. It was from the farm, so the creature we poured gravy on could well have been staring me in the face a few weeks before.

Over the apple crumble, I asked Ma, 'What does one wear to a May ball?'

Both Ma and Pa were suddenly interested. Who had invited me to a May ball?

'Theo Winterton.'

Pa frowned.

Monday found us loaded with shopping, and taking lunch at the Queen's Hotel, with Ma treating herself to a green cocktail called a Mermaid. She ordered a mixed grill, and I copied.

Ma pushed a gristly piece of black pudding to the side of her plate. 'Theo is a very sweet church mouse and it's jolly that he invited you to the ball. There should be all sorts of interesting young people there and it's good for you to widen your horizons.'

'Why do you call him a church mouse? He was the youngest in his school first eleven.'

'I don't mean physically a mouse, or intellectually, or anything like that. But they haven't two pennies to rub together. He won't qualify as an architect till he's practically middle aged.'

'They can't be so poor, or Penny wouldn't be at Oxford.'

Ma looked pityingly at me, as if I knew nothing. 'There are always odd old relatives in the background, ready to cough up for a child's education. Particularly childless people. They do it to give themselves a stake in the future. The Wintertons aren't fools. They'll have taken great care over the choice of godparents.' She lit a long cigarette and sighed. 'Lydia, dear, you've led a sheltered life since we left the theatre. I don't know how to say this tactfully, but there'll be young men who pursue you not for yourself but for your dowry and expectations.'

'That's ridiculous. Anyway, Theo and I are just friends.'

'Keep your voice down, dear.'

The dress Ma and I chose for the May ball was a fine mixture of silk and linen, with a creamy background and a floral pattern but with flowers and leaves so delicate you could barely see them. Ma said they would catch the light as I danced. It was cut low, and needed a special brassiere, which Ma said would show me to advantage, and I must wear the dress in the house a few times to get used to it or I would be terribly self-conscious about my décolletage and I must be confident and self-assured. We had chosen a cashmere stole in a shade just a little darker than the background of the dress.

Over the next days, Ma gave me tips. Don't let Theo monopolise me. Chat to his friends. Chat to girls, too. Then I would get more invitations. But be careful. There would be people who wanted to know me because of the Thackrey connection. Be vague. Take their cards, and say I'd forgotten mine.

I wore the dress once or twice in the house, with my new shoes, walking along the landing, practising throwing the stole over my shoulder.

Ma said walking downstairs elegantly in heels, however low, took a little getting used to. She stood at the bottom of the stairs and watched me walk down. As she did, Granville slid through the front door. He stared. I ignored him. When I reached the bottom stair, I saw that he was blinking.

Ma turned to him. 'Well, what do you think to your stepsister in her May ball gown?'

He stopped blinking. 'Very nice.'

Ma waited until he walked away. 'Well done, you'll have no difficulties now, not after that audience.'

I didn't ask her what she meant. We always acted as if Granville was exactly what Pa saw him to be. Splendid number one son.

*

I had never seen Theo in evening dress. He looked magnificent, as if he'd stepped off the silver screen. He stood in the hall waiting for me, and his mouth dropped open.

'You look so beautiful.'

In the back of the Riley, we sat far apart, aware of Massey's eyes in his driver's mirror.

Theo would propose to me in the garden that night. Hadley Hall must have a garden. The moon would be full. We would walk away from everyone, the lights and music behind us. I'd shiver a little. He would put his arms around me and say . . .

'Are we picking any other ladies or gentlemen up on the way, Miss Thackrey? Mr Theo?'

'Er, no,' Theo answered the chauffeur as if he had been caught out in some deceit. 'It's just us.'

Just us.

We sat at a great round table with three of Theo's friends, and their partners who were all pretty and friendly. It was so jolly and we all got on just grand, switching partners, trying out dances. We agreed that if one person knew a dance, he or she should take the floor with someone who didn't. So for at least two or three hours, I completely forgot to expect a proposal.

It happened just as I imagined, but not in the way that I imagined. We didn't want to try another mad samba. There was a scent of wallflowers in the garden. We walked along the winding path, here and there seeing couples embracing under the trees.

'Do you want to sit on the bench?'

'No.' I felt sure a proposal should be made in a standing position. Unless he wanted me to sit so that he could go

109

down on one knee. 'Unless you particularly want me to sit on the bench, Theo?'

'No. Not particularly. Only, there's something I have to say, and it's not going to be easy.'

He took off his jacket and placed it on a garden bench. We sat down.

In the moonlight, in his white shirt, he looked as if he belonged in a painting. But no artist could have done him justice.

What was he waiting for? Why didn't he kiss me? Or just pop the question.

He looked away. 'Lydia, I'm not suitable for you. It was wrong for me to . . . for us . . . I told you how long an architect has to study. I have nothing. There are men in there who . . . men whose fathers . . . '

'Theo, stop being silly.'

'It's true. There are other things . . . I wasn't thinking in the lane that day. Or when I asked you to come tonight. I haven't been thinking for months. I see that now.'

I stood up. 'Well, well, if it isn't Harry's method number three.'

He jumped up beside me. 'What? What are you talking about? Who's Harry?'

'Someone I knew a long time ago. A matinee idol in a theatre troupe who had twelve sure-fire ways to rid himself of unwanted admirers.'

'Oh for heaven's sake. Don't make this any harder.'

'Oh sorry. I'm just supposed to hop off and say, well thank you for pretending to be in love with me for seven months and two days. Thank you for pretending it was love at first sight.'

He grabbed my wrists and turned me to him and we were kissing, just like we always kissed but harder and with more passion. He kissed my neck and throat. His hands moved over the straps of my dress and down my back. Then he pulled away, as if he'd burned his fingers.

'Don't you see? Everything. This dress that must have cost . . . I can't imagine. It would keep a poor architect for a year. The Riley. Massey. Mr Thackrey having a quiet word with my father about how we'd get here tonight, and how we'd get home. You're out of reach, Lydia.'

'That's ridiculous!'

'I was mad to dream we could be together.'

'Oh, I see what you're doing. Harry's shake-her-off method number three. Tell her she's out of your reach, and that you're not worthy.'

'Don't you see?'

'I see very well, and your timing stinks.'

I hurried back up the path, wishing there wasn't so far to go to get out of there. He soon caught me up, walking beside me, not speaking. The lights from the hall glowed softly as we came nearer, and the orchestra played a waltz. I kept on going, away from the hall, along the great drive.

He tried to catch my arm. 'Where are you going?'

I shook him off. 'I'm going home.'

'But we're to telephone Massey and tell him to come. Strict instructions.'

'Then go follow your strict instructions. I'm walking.'

'You can't. It's too far. You'll get lost. Those shoes . . .'

I took off my shoes and flung them into the bushes. 'Don't follow me. Go away. I never want to see you again.'

111

'I'll be two minutes. I'm going to phone. I'll catch you up. It's left at the gates when you go out.'

That made me even angrier. He thought I had no sense of direction. But it's true that I would have turned right.

I reached the gates. A dark shape moved towards me, headlights came into view. A window was wound down.

Massey said, 'I thought I might as well wait, Miss Thackrey. Such a fine night.'

I would have kept walking but with his great strides, Theo was almost on top of us.

Massey wound down the window again. 'Mr Theo?'

Theo glared at Massey, ignoring me. 'I'm walking.'

'Very good, sir.'

I couldn't remember breathing on the way home, because I thought if I let my body function as normal, I would scream.

Massey dropped me by the front steps. He jumped from the seat and hurried up ahead of me to open the door.

I heard Ma on the landing, and headed for the kitchen, not wanting to see anyone. I'd get a drink of water and try to calm down.

For a moment I thought the groan came from me, because I certainly felt like groaning. Then I heard a cry. I stopped, suddenly feeling the cold of the floor on my stockinged feet.

The sound came from the pantry. I opened the door, and there was Granville, with Tilly, the cook's assistant. She was against the wall, her skirt around her waist and Granville, with his trousers round his ankles, thrusting himself into her. I closed the door.

In the kitchen, I sat at the table, shaking.

Something. I had to do something to calm down. My mouth felt dry. My temples throbbed. A glass of water.

The water from the tap ran cold, as cold as Theo's heart. I filled the glass and took a sip.

Behind me, the door opened. Granville stepped softly into the kitchen.

'You better keep quiet about what you saw, or else.'

I took my time answering, giving him a look of contempt, taking a small sip of water. 'Or else what?'

He came closer, walking by the side of the deal table, trailing his hand on the scrubbed wood. 'Or else I'll tell – about you and Theo, your slap and tickle in the lane, your secret plans.'

'There's nothing to tell.'

'Oh but there is. Don't think I haven't been watching you two. Did he tell you Pa pays his architect's fees? No. I thought not. All Theo wants is an easy ride through life and he thinks he'll get it with you. Tarts are stupid. All a chap has to do is kiss them hard, and they believe he must be in love with them.' He laughed. 'It's a defect in the female brain.'

I threw what was left of my water in his face and walked out.

He called after me. 'You'll be sorry you did that.'

I did not bother to get up the next day, and for weeks couldn't think what to do with myself. The whole world seemed to me to be dull.

So when I heard the row between Ma and Pa, as I was walking along the landing, I thought it must be about me.

Pa said, 'That's absurd. I have his word. He wouldn't touch her with a barge pole.'

'It wasn't a barge pole got her in that condition.'

'Girls like that try anything. She's after money. She's a cheap little gold digger.'

So it wasn't me then.

And not long after, I saw her through the window. Tilly. Such a tiny, thin figure, with a small bag, her shoulders stooped, looking at the ground.

The following Sunday, it was just the three of us for dinner again, and I was late. Ma and Pa were waiting for me, not wanting to start without me. He was by her chair, with his hands on her shoulders, saying she mustn't fret. He was sorry. He had been hasty. They'd find the girl and give her some money.

I said, 'What girl?'

Ma looked up and said brightly, 'Oh just a girl who came to the gate selling pegs.'

And I said, 'Oh. I thought you meant Tilly.' I took my place and looked round. 'No Granville today?'

Ma gave me a warning look.

Something in Pa's face changed. Ma chatted during the meal, about Baby Bunting, and about where we might go on holiday.

Later, Ma gave Pa her best smile and said she'd follow upstairs shortly.

She came to sit by me. 'I don't believe I've ever told you this, Lydia. Sheldon's first wife, Constance, had a most difficult birth with Granville.'

Huh! Why didn't that surprise me? Poisonous toad.

Ma went on, 'She never properly got her strength back. Perhaps that's why Sheldon bends over backwards to prove to himself that he doesn't hold Granville responsible.'

114

I pushed my cup away. 'He might or might not be responsible for his mother's death. But he was the one grappling with Tilly in the pantry.'

She made the sign of the three wise monkeys. Hear no evil, see no evil, speak no evil. 'Pa's very sensitive over Granville just now. He's failed his banking examination.'

'That's because he's stupid and he doesn't try.'

'Will you help him?'

'Why should I?'

'Like it or not, we're a family, we have to pull together. Do it for me. Please.'

Sophie

Gas tar melted on the cobbles all along the Bank. Tab Street sweltered in August heat.

Just because I asked Rosa if she'd be coming straight home with her wages the next day so I could pay the rent, it turned into a full blazing row.

She thumped the table. 'What's wrong with Dad coughing up for once? I've another payment to make towards the works Bank Holiday day trip to Scarborough. I'll be damned if I'll miss that just because he wants to booze his pay at the Anglers'.'

'He does cough up. Only he'll be in late.'

'Ha ha. Trust you to stick up for him. Well if you're sticking up for him, pay the rent yourself.'

'I'm still paying for Mam's funeral.'

She went very quiet. 'Are you? I didn't know that. You never said.'

'We went mad didn't we? Pairs of horses. A carriage as well as the hearse. A plot that'll give room for Dad. Headstone. Carving.'

'But, what about the burial club money?'

'It was spent up, for Billy.'

'Bloody hell! Why didn't you say?'

'I didn't like to.'

'Do you know, you're turning into a right martyr you.'

'And you're turning into a right common tart with that language you pick up at Montague bloody Burton's.'

She started to laugh, and I couldn't help it, so did I.

'We'll pay off the funeral, Sophie. Get the buggers off our backs. But we have to tackle Dad. I'm going to have it out with him.'

'Let me.' I felt sure that she would only make things worse. 'And I know exactly how much we owe for the funeral.'

'You've got summat in the Penny Bank. Can't we use that?'

'Well maybe, only I wanted it for a rainy day.'

She went to the door and looked out. 'It's that hot, I think we're in for a storm.'

At the funeral director's, paying twelve shillings to clear the debt, I was asked to step into a side room, but refused to budge until I had the receipt in my hand.

Mr Dudley, the skeletal undertaker in his black suit and tie, sat on one side of a small table. I took the chair opposite him. Evergreen leaves poked from a brass vase to his left.

He took a small card from a box on his table and tapped it with a sharp pencil.

'You see the thing is, Miss Moran, we'll need to charge interest because otherwise we're out of pocket. It wasn't foreseen that your moneys would be outstanding so long.'

'You never said anything about interest. I've paid what's owing and that's all I will pay.'

'We shall have to see what your father says.'

My voice came out different this time, older, stronger. 'We've paid what we owed, and cleared our debt. That's all we can afford. You shouldn't have let Dad go for such an expensive funeral.'

Mr Dudley cupped his hands and let his thumbs play against each other.

'I had hoped that under the circumstances of your father leaving the bank, there might be some more substantial payment that would have covered interest. I assume he left for a better job?'

He said this sarcastically, looking for a reaction. He would get no satisfaction from me.

I stood up, putting the receipt in my pocket. At the door I wished him good day in a way that would have made Mam proud. Damn him. Outside, I leaned against the wall, trembling with rage. Bloody man, in his three-piece suit and watch guard. He'd get his hands deeper into your pockets than any cutpurse.

In the middle of washing my hair, Rosa gave a screech. 'I don't believe it. Where've you been?'

'What's up?'

'You've only got nits.'

I ran the nit comb through my hair and examined it.

Suddenly my head began to itch like never before. I grabbed the scissors. 'Cut it off, Rosa.'

'That's a bit drastic.'

'I don't care. Cut it off. Cut it all off. I'll have a bob.'

When Dad came in, my hair was burning in the grate. 'Not your crowning glory. You could have sold it.'

Of course Rosa never wasted any time. 'Have you left your job, Dad?'

He looked startled, caught out like a kid playing truant. Then he was himself again, throwing out his chest. He took a sheaf of papers from the table drawer and smoothed them out.

'This is a business plan. No one ever made money working for a boss. I kept it to meself because I wanted to have something good to say about the new business.'

'What happened?' I asked.

'When did you leave?' Rosa asked.

'Questions, questions. You're not daughters you two, you're a bloody accountant and a damned inquisitor, the pair of you. You're no flesh and blood of mine. At least Danny has a few dreams in his bones. He saw the wisdom of it.'

'Well he would,' Rosa said. 'He doesn't pay the rent here.'

I poked at the last remnants of my hair. It melted and gave off a sharp bitter burned toffee smell. 'I expect the undertaker will fill me in with the details. He was the one who told me.'

So then Dad did tell.

He had been using a bank vault for a little storage, that

119

was all. No one ever went in there, until they decided on that damned inspection of the building. Then Clutterbuck stuck his nose in.

Once we knew, Dad stopped pretending to go to work each day.

He took to lying on his bed, listening for the post to fall through the letter box.

I took Dad a cup of tea, just hoping to get him moving. He took a sip. 'I've a feeling Danny might call round today. He'll have one or two ideas how I can get the business moving.'

'What business, Dad? Why don't you tell us?'

'Because you've no imagination.'

'Is it the mushrooms?'

'You'll find out when the money comes in.'

I went back downstairs. Rosa looked at me. 'What's he say?'

'Oh, he thinks Danny might help him where we don't.'

'Danny ought to be pulling his weight. But when do we see sight or light of Danny?'

'He'll be at York Races tomorrow. I've a mind to go. There's a charabanc going. Tony asked me. Do you want to come?'

'I can't stand gamblers. I hate people who think everything'll fall into their lap tomorrow.'

Rosa went out and slammed the door.

A race course is a most wonderful place. Completely open air almost as far as you can see. A gentle breeze blew against my cheeks, with the scent of grass, horses and expectation.

Danny looked exactly cut out for the job, in his smart

suit. A good suit, too, not one that would turn shiny after a few weeks' wear. My brother might be selfish, but at least he was making something of himself, which was more than the rest of us seemed able to do. Danny had learned tick-tack. We watched him signalling the odds with both hands to someone on another stand a dozen yards down the course. Tick-tack finished, he was taking bets, but saw us and his face lit up.

'You look great, Danny.'

'Thanks, Sophie. You don't look so bad yourself. You suit the hat.'

'I hope you're going to give us a winner,' Tony said.

'It'll be difficult to say today. You could go for the favourite in the second race.'

Danny took another bet from a punter and handed him his slip.

The starter's pistol cracked, and the race began.

'Dad's in one of his black dog moods. I wish you'd come and see him. He keeps talking about you.'

'Yes, sir?' Danny turned to another punter.

Tony waved to me to come to the rail and watch the race. I went to where he stood with Liz Hescott, helping to keep the children from running onto the course.

Beautiful horses flashed by, their colourful riders leaning forwards, urging them on. I turned to see whether Danny watched the races or simply kept his back to them, looking for punters. He was chatting to someone, a familiar figure – a broad back, shock of fair hair. The man turned. It was Granville Thackrey.

'Look who's there.' I nudged Tony. 'Son of Thackreys' Bank no less.'

He turned to look. 'The bad penny.'

'Why do you say that?'

'He's a waster. I've seen him at the boxing matches.'

'He might be a waster, but he's giving Danny and Harry Hescott his business. He could go to anyone on the course.'

'Then why doesn't he?'

The next race started. We yelled for Bookworm who was in the lead, then neck and neck, until Blackjack pipped him at the post.

Tony stayed by the fence. I went to try and get an answer from Danny.

'Will you come home after the races today, for the weekend?'

He must know I wouldn't be asking if it wasn't important. I didn't want to start spewing out family difficulties in the middle of a race course.

He didn't answer straight away.

'What's up, Danny? What's so terrible about coming home? The Hescotts'll be glad of the house to themselves for once.'

He glanced at the betting stand nearest him and said in a low voice, 'It's just that I've got to see someone later.'

'Won't take all night will it?'

'Don't look now, but he's the one I have to see.'

Under the sign 'Back em with Packham' stood a cauli-flower-eared man with a broken nose. His two henchmen looked like a cross between a couple of gangsters and Laurel and Hardy in *Double Whoopee*.

I groaned. He'd got himself into some kind of bother. He saw the question in my eyes and nodded.

'You can still come home. Dad's in low spirits. We're

off back on the train. Come with us. The charabanc lot will be stopping at a pub and take hours.'

The trouble with Danny was that he would agree to anything for a quiet life, and then do exactly what he wanted.

As the race course cleared, the three of us made for Danny's digs on the far side of the course, so that he could collect his suitcase. Tony said he'd wait on the corner and have a smoke, but I wanted to take a nosy in the house.

It had the tiniest of front gardens, with pots of geraniums lined under the bay window. The door opened onto a narrow tiled hall, with a room off to the left. At the far end of the hall a glass panelled door led to a kitchen.

Danny bounded up the stairs. 'Mrs Oates and her kids are at the market. She usually goes at this time on Saturdays.'

His room was neat and clean, with a creamy candlewick bedspread, chest of drawers and hooks on the back of the door.

He slid two clean shirts from a hanger, folded them with the skill of a laundress and put them into the brown suit-case.

He snapped the suitcase shut. 'What's going on with Dad?'

'He's lost his job.'

He sat down heavily on the bed and groaned. 'How are you managing?'

'Badly.'

'How did he lose his job?'

'He's been drinking a lot. I don't know if that's behind it. One of his money-making schemes got him into bother.

I'm guessing he was making free with one of the bank vaults, though he won't say for what.'

'I wonder if they'd reconsider, under the circumstances. The Thackreys I mean.'

'What circumstances?'

'Good and faithful service all them years. A widower. His war record.'

'I don't see it. If a person's sacked, they stay sacked.'

'Maybe, maybe not. I'm on good terms with Granville Thackrey. I'll get him to have a word with his old man.'

He pulled out his wallet and produced a ten-pound note. 'Take it. It's the least I can do. And I'll come round tonight.'

As we went back downstairs, the front door burst open. Danny dropped his case and looked as if he would turn and run back upstairs, then remembered me. He pushed me behind him and said to the two men, 'Look, not now. Not here.'

The first big ugly brute just shook his head, and curled his lips into a cold crooked grin. Not Laurel and Hardy after all. The small wiry one had a cruel, sneering look.

Danny squared up to them, 'Let her out. Let my sister through.'

The big man seemed undecided, but the small man pressed himself back against the wall and said, 'With pleasure. On you go, love, our quarrel's not with you.'

'Wait for me on the corner.' He was telling me to fetch Tony.

The big man said, in a voice that seemed too soft for his frame, 'Do as your big brother says love, we don't hurt women and children.'

I walked down the stairs slowly. Perhaps Tony had already spotted them coming in. Danny stayed where he was. I wondered whether he meant to turn back, lock himself in the bedroom and climb through a window.

The big man let me pass, though the huge size of him, belly tipping over his trousers, made it impossible for me not to brush against him. He had great jowly cheeks, pads of flesh under mean eyes. The thin man gave a slight bow and extended a skeletal hand, as if inviting me to pass in the most sarcastic way he could.

I moved to get by him. Suddenly my arm was up my back as the skeleton croaked at Danny, 'Don't think about disappearing back up them apples and pears.' The strong, bony hand gripped my throat, fingers on my windpipe. I was spun round, and saw Danny's face as he rushed towards me, but was stopped by the sheer size and weight of the big man.

'Just give us all you've got, we can't ask for more, not today,' the big man said in a steady voice, as if ordering a quarter of sweets across the corner shop counter.

'Pay up, Moran,' the skeleton hissed.

I could feel his breath on the back of my neck as I struggled to pull free.

Danny was pushed to the floor. Fatty man kicked at him, but Danny rolled, got up and launched himself at the big man, winding him. The man let out a groan of pain. I managed to kick the skeleton in the shins with my heel, screaming at him at the same time.

Tony burst in, landed a punch on the skeleton and sent him reeling. He grabbed the fat man as Danny jumped to his feet. With two against two, or three against two if you counted me, Laurel and Hardy quietened down.

'Just get outside,' Danny said. 'I'll talk to you there. I wasn't going anywhere.'

When they went out, Tony said, 'I think we should get the police.'

Danny started to cough. He walked to the kitchen. The tap ran. He came back, holding a cup of water, sipping. 'My throat went dry.'

He handed me the cup with a steady hand. Mine shook as I took a drink.

'Thanks,' Danny said to Tony, 'but no cops.'

He took out his wallet then looked at me. 'Sorry, Sophie . . . but that tenner . . . '

I handed it back. 'How much do you owe them?'

'Oh, just a hundred pounds. Ninety now.'

Just a hundred pounds. Any hopes of help from Danny flew from my mind.

We went outside. Danny locked the door and put the key through the letter box.

The men sat in their car, at the end of the street.

'I'll go talk to them,' Danny said. 'Sort it out. You two go on to the station. I'll catch up with you there.'

I didn't want him to be on his own. 'Tony, will you stay with Danny?'

'Course I will. What about you?'

'I'll set off walking to the station.'

As I reached the race course, I looked back at the four of them, still standing on the corner talking.

By the Horse and Jockey, someone called my name. I felt edgy and looked round. Granville Thackrey stood by the pub door. He had just lit a cigarette and slid a lighter back into his pocket. He came towards me.

126

'Hello. Are you all right?'

'Yes.'

'All on your own?'

'I'm meeting the others at the station.'

'You look a bit shaky.'

'It's nothing.'

'Look, I've got my motor there. Let me give you a lift. It's quite a hike.'

I was tempted, but hoped Tony and Danny would soon catch me up.

'Come inside. Sit down for five minutes. You really do look shaken up. Has something happened?' He took my arm. 'Come on. They do pies and sandwiches. You look as if you could use something.'

'I'll miss Danny and Tony.'

'No you won't. I'll get you to the station. Lydia would go mad with me if she thought I'd seen you in this state and let you go wandering off.'

We sat in a corner, under a stained-glass window that shed a soft light on the table. He had ordered roast beef sandwiches, brandy and water.

There was something so sympathetic and charming in his manner, as if he guessed that Danny was in trouble but didn't want to embarrass me.

'Take a sip of brandy, Sophie. Here, let me pour a drop more water in. Is that better?'

'Yes.' And I did feel better, with a roast beef sandwich inside me, and the brandy.

'I owe you an apology, too.'

'What for?'

He looked away, like a little boy caught stealing sweets.

'Oh you know, that day on the bike. I'm sorry. I was very clumsy and stupid. I think it was just that you were the first girl I ever really took a shine to and I thought . . .'

'Forget it. I have.'

'No. I never will. It'll always shame me that I wasn't more gallant, especially to you. For heaven's sake, my sister's friend, the bank commissionaire's daughter. Pa would have had my hide.'

If it hadn't been for the brandy, I wouldn't have said what I did.

'Dad's not commissionaire any more though.'

'Of course he isn't. That was tactless. And I'm afraid none of that was up to me. Clutterbuck tends to rule the roost in those sorts of matters.'

'I don't see how what Dad did was so terrible.'

Granville shook his head sympathetically. 'I agree. That little vault is never used.'

So it *was* the mushrooms. 'Dad looked after them in his own time.'

'Quite. Only Clutterbuck's line was that because they eat paper – your father kept them supplied with shredded newspaper – they were a risk in the bank. Bank notes and all that you know.'

Not the mushrooms, then. I did not want to give him the satisfaction of appearing ignorant. For a moment we sat without speaking. 'Thanks for the sandwich. I'd better get going.'

'No wait.' He took out a gold cigarette case and offered me one.

I shook my head.

'Don't mind if I do? Only it helps me think.' He took a

couple of drags on his cigarette, blew a smoke ring. 'I don't suppose Danny will have mentioned it to you. Not many people know, but I've got an interest in a club. Music, drinks, dancing, that sort of thing. The family wouldn't approve, but it's the sort of place people wouldn't think twice about in London, and they're thin on the ground here. There might be an opening for your father.'

Two men came to sit at the table next to us. I took a quick glance, still uneasy about the Laurel and Hardy characters.

Granville shifted in his seat. 'We can't talk here.' He stood up and offered me his hand. We walked to the doors and into a wide hall and a staircase. 'Somewhere we can talk . . . Follow me.'

I followed him up the stairs. He was talking all the while, about the club and where it was and who Dad should speak to. He would give me a name and address. It was in his room.

I stood by the door while he took a notebook from a drawer and flicked through it. 'I want to help you if I can . . .'

I said I appreciated it, and Danny would too.

'Sophie, the truth is, since the very first time I saw you, I've never forgotten you, and anything I can do to help, I will, really and truly.'

He came towards me, with such a sweet look and drew me to him and began to kiss me. I kissed him back. Just for a moment I thought this was Cinderella and Prince Charming. Just for a moment, I thought he must have fallen in love with me.

'I could take really good care of a girl like you.' His hands were on my breasts. He pinned me to the door, thrusting himself at me. 'Sophie, Sophie, we are going to be so good.'

'Let go of me!'

'Oh no, not this time. You won't be sorry. You know this feels right.'

It was thanks to Fenella Naggs at Montague Burton's that I knew what to do. She told Rosa, and Rosa told me.

I relaxed, let Granville kiss me, drew back and smiled. As he returned my smile, I brought up my knee and crashed it into his privates. While he reeled and held himself, I opened the door and ran along the corridor, down the stairs and out of the pub, shaking. In the doorway I practically knocked a man over, and just kept running.

I didn't know how fast I ran or how much of the road I covered. No one was following. What an idiot I was. Fool, fool, fool.

Rosa was right what she sometimes said about me. I didn't see the world as it was, only as I'd like it to be.

Then I saw him. Tony. Set back from the road was a green, near some alms-houses. A couple of ducks dived and squabbled on the pond in the centre of the green. He waved to me from the bench that faced the neatly trimmed grass.

His smile. His cheerful, unchanging smile. 'Come and sit down.' He patted the bench.

'You had me right worried. Couldn't decide what to do, go on to the station or take a chance on hanging back.'

I couldn't find words. My mind felt blank, scooped out. When you have geared yourself up for a certain course of action and it blows up in your face it leaves you not sure where to go or what to do.

130

Tony took my hand. 'I'm sorry Danny's not with me. Had to see someone about something. I did tell him you really wanted him to come home.'

'Put your arm around me, Tony.'

Something changed between us in those moments. Such a silence held, only the sound of the water as a family of ducks glided by. Then a church clock chimed.

Tony stood up, still holding me. 'We'd better get to the station, love.'

In the station café, Tony ordered two teas and slices of seed cake.

He stirred his tea. 'I've only two years of my apprenticeship to serve. Then I'll be out of my time. I'll be my own man, Sophie, with a trade. Free to go anywhere, do anything. I'm specialising in cabinet making. Some of the lads at night school are happy to work on standard stuff, but I look on it this way. If you're going to spend your life in a trade you want to enjoy it, take a bit of pride. When I get my own house, I'll make all the furniture myself.'

'Where will the house be?'

'In the country I think.'

'I don't like the country. Too quiet.'

'By the sea then. You'd have the sound of the waves.'

'Will you see mermaids from the window?'

'Oh yes. They'll sit on the rocks and sing at midnight. And the foam on the waves will turn into fierce white horses. They'll gallop and take you wherever you want to go.'

'Where do you want to go, Tony?'

'Anywhere where you are.'

Lydia

Every summer the Thackrey family fled to the seaside. Ma and I were just carrying on the tradition.

But what purgatory! To spend four weeks of the summer by the sea, at Sansend, wandering lonely on the beach, looking out at the waves, wanting Theo. I felt dashed to pieces like some helpless baby crab on the rocks.

I sent a postcard to Penelope Winterton, hoping she would show it to Theo. Then he would come one weekend to find me. I combed my hair and sat on the sands under a parasol, reading a book. He didn't come.

In the garden, I lounged in a deck chair, trying to read Sherlock Holmes. The gate would click. He would step across the lawn, calling my name. But the only gate clicker was Nurse Dorothea. The only calls came from Ma and Baby Bunting.

I went home from the seaside with a heavy heart.

Theo did not come into the church on Sundays, at least not while we were there. While Ma and Pa sipped sherry after the service, I took a leaf out of Granville's book, and bolted home.

Theo did not telephone. He did not send a note. So much for his love. As deep as the skin on a rice pudding.

There was nothing for me to do. Mrs Winterton came over to ask if I would like to help with a jumble sale. No. No. No. I refused to be a Good Works Female.

Ma wanted me to shop for baby clothes. No. If I couldn't marry and have babies of my own, I wouldn't shop for hers.

On a weekend in the Lake District with Penelope and her friends, I could not bear to hear about Theo. Theo this, Theo that. All Penelope's friends seemed half in love with him.

And I wandered. Wandered miles, just walking, walking. One day I walked back to Hadley Hall, and sat on the bench in the garden, where he should have proposed to me.

Another day, I walked to Gledhow Valley Woods and looked at the Roman Baths, which is not a Roman Baths at all. Why do we like to fool ourselves, and tell stories that aren't true?

One day I found myself in Thackrey Park, yes there is a Thackrey Park – so influential has that family been for generations.

I made the mistake of leaving the path and then got stuck, sinking into marshy grass, sodden from the night's rain. I turned to look back, to see whether it was best to plod on, or return to the path before it got worse.

A black Labrador came rushing at me, leaping up, kissing my face, making me laugh. At first I didn't recognise her because Labradors are all so similar at a glance.

And then its owner called. 'Here Patience!'

Theo.

I kept walking. He called my name. Cheek of him. Call the dog, call me. He'd be whistling next. I didn't answer, just kept on walking.

He ran after me, calling, asking me to wait.

'Go away. Leave me alone.'

'I want to talk to you. Please, Lydia.'

'If you'd wanted to talk to me, you knew where I was.'

'It wasn't exactly that easy.'

'Oh really? What a shame!'

Patience started to whine.

He was walking sideways, trying to make me look at him.

'Lydia, please listen. I didn't want to see you again until everything could be sorted out between us.'

I had forgotten which way I meant to walk. Both paths were equally far away. I strode towards the path on the left.

'There's nothing to sort out.'

'Your feet are getting wet.'

'They're my feet, nothing to do with you.'

He scooped me up and began to run with me to the shelter.

'Put me down! Let go of me!'

Patience barked and ran in circles round us, thinking it a great game. Suddenly he tripped over the dog and we both went sprawling into the wet muddy grass.

'Sorry, sorry. Have I hurt you?'

He started to help me up. I pushed him away. 'You can't hurt me because I don't give two shakes of sheep's shimmy about you, not any more. And I don't care about this dress, or this coat or anything, because as you know, I don't need to worry.'

'I've never stopped loving you, Lydia, and I never will.'

'Well you've a great way of showing it.'

'Give me another chance. Let me explain. Come and sit down with me for two minutes.'

'No.'

He put his hand in his inside pocket and brought out a small box. He fell to his knees on the grass and said, 'Please, Lydia, will you marry me?'

He opened the box, and there was a ring with a diamond smaller than the one in my cat's tail.

'Where did you get that?'

'I bought it for you.'

'Has somebody else just turned you down?'

'What do I have to say to make you believe me? Try it. Go on.'

Just out of curiosity, I let him put it on my finger. It did fit. 'Just a coincidence.'

'No! Ages ago, when you visited Penelope, I got her to find out your ring size. I had this with me the night of the May ball, but I daren't. I couldn't ask you then.'

'Why not?'

'You know why not. Everything. I wanted to tell you. Mr Thackrey was paying my fees to be an architect. But it wasn't just that. He has the living of St Stephen's.'

'What does that mean?'

'He appointed my father. If he wanted to, he could get

rid of him and find another clergyman. They're twenty to the dozen.'

'He wouldn't do that.'

'No. I think you're right. But you haven't answered me. Will you marry me?'

'What? When you're thirty? When Pa's stopped paying for you?'

'Come and sit down.'

We went into the shelter. Patience flopped onto her belly, as if exhausted from the emotion of it all. She looked at us for a moment as we sat side by side and then shut her eyes, pretending to be asleep.

For a moment, we sat without speaking. Theo spread his hands on his knees.

'This is how things are. I've thought and thought about what to do. I've applied for a job in the local authority housing department, an assistant housing officer. The pay is reasonable, and there'll be prospects. At least I hope there will.'

'Would it mean giving up on the architecture?'

'I could study in the evenings. Once I've worked my trial period, the authority might help me with the architecture course. That way I wouldn't be dependent on Mr Thackrey. I'm grateful for what he's done, but it wouldn't be right to go on taking from him.'

'Do you think you'll get this job?'

'I hope so. I've won an award for one of my designs. That's what made me realise, I can make a go of it on my own, then we don't need anyone's permission.'

'So . . .'

'Let me just say this, before you speak. We wouldn't be

able to live like you're used to. We wouldn't move in the same world. Architects never live in the houses they design. They usually live in better ones. But we could live in one of the new corporation houses, on an estate I've helped design. We'd save up for our own house eventually. But you wouldn't want . . . '

'What wouldn't I want?'

'It would be small. We'd be . . . we'd be ordinary.'

'I hate Allerton House. I hate all houses where when you first go in you can't find your way from your bedroom to where you eat breakfast. I hate all places where you come into a corridor and you don't know whether to turn left or right.'

'That wouldn't be a problem in the houses we're building.'

'I'm eighteen. Do Ma and Pa have to sign a form or something?'

'Is that a yes then?'

'I haven't taken off the ring have I?'

'No. And I'll get you a better one, I promise.'

'No need.'

'I love you, Lydia. I always will. It's true, it was love at first sight and I'll love you till the day I die.'

'I love you.'

We kissed then, like we used to, only better.

I love to make plans. On the way back, we decided that Theo would keep the ring for now. With Ma ready to have another baby, and Theo not sure of whether he would get the job, it would be best to keep our engagement a secret until Christmas.

'You're bound to get the job,' I said, as we held hands

137

and walked back towards the road. 'Any boss would be mad not to want you.'

'If your stepfather thought my getting the job was a prelude to snatching you away, he may put a spoke in the wheel.'

'Do you think so?'

'It's possible. He's a very powerful man, and they don't want us to be together, him and your Ma.'

'It's all right for them. They have each other. They think I'm practically a child still.'

We walked back, hand in hand, and the world held such beauty. Patience found a huge puddle, rolled through it, then shook herself – every drop of water bright as a diamond.

Sophie

I had a strange, uneasy feeling, yet at first, I didn't think anything could be wrong. Dad's note lay in the middle of the table. 'Gone fishing.' He didn't usually put out our breakfast things, but he had set the table. Two cups, two plates, knives. The last slice of bread, cut in half and scraped with dripping. The kettle, hot on the gas ring.

Something was missing from the table. What? I looked around, and opened the drawer. His papers to do with the make-money-from-home scheme were nowhere to be seen. Then I spotted that the neatly laid fire, ready for a match, was not made with balls of newspaper. Rolled and screwed-up notes lay under the chips, Dad's uneven handwriting visible on a jutting out sheet – a few letters, half a word. He had laid the fire with his plans.

Dad kept his fishing tackle in the cellar. I hurried down there to look. Gone. So he had gone fishing, and yet . . .

Upstairs, I shook Rosa awake.

'What is it?'

'Something's wrong. Isn't it? Something's wrong.'

She blinked her sleepy eyes a few times. Nodded.

I pulled on my clothes, in too much of a rush to bother with stockings. Without washing my face or combing my hair, I hurried from the house, not caring who might look out from their window and see me tearing along the street like a mad thing while the day was not yet light.

It must be two miles at least to where he would go, perhaps three. The canal basin.

As I ran, breathless, heart ready to burst, memories came back, like silver fish scuttling from behind a drawer you pulled out suddenly.

Dad saying, 'Something I've been meaning to tell you.'

'What? Meaning to tell me what?'

Mam. Years ago. 'You should tell them. Some day.'

What? What should he tell us some day, one day?

Other things. Going back. Him sitting. Not moving. Day after day, in his chair. Mam sewing at the table, making coats from home for a tailor on North Street.

Dad, out of the chair. Coming up with a good idea, a very good idea. Full of cheer. Jolly. Everyone so happy.

Mam saying, Not so fast!

Then driving the trams during the General Strike, and Mam telling him he ought not to do it, not break the strike. After that, he got the job at the bank.

Mam: 'Your dad's been well for a long time. Let's hope he stays that way.'

Strange, even at the time. Strange, when she was the one who came down with bronchitis every winter.

140

'Look after your dad.' To me.

To Danny: 'Look after your sisters.'

But to me, to look after Dad, and a smile, as if it could be a cruel thing to ask. Had to be tempered with a smile.

Running. Telling myself, Don't get lost this time. Don't take a wrong turning somewhere beyond Call Lane. Run. Faster, faster.

And no one else about. Still too early, even for factory girls and foundry men, even for fishermen.

And he wasn't on the bank. Somewhere else perhaps.

Was I mad? Imagining. But Rosa had said it too.

Something wrong.

Then I saw him. Moving. Through the water. Walking. Out, out. Water to his waist.

Dad! Dad! The voice not coming because no breath, no breath left. Keep running. See his shoes. See his rod and fishing basket. Kick off my shoes. Jump. Jump in. So cold. The stink, but keep him in sight. Don't let him walk another . . .

Dad!

He turns. His mouth open. His arms slightly raised, as if keeping them dry mattered. He shakes his head. No, no. Comes towards me. Tries to. Falls. Slips out of sight. Further in. I can only swim the breadth of York Road baths, not the length. Never got the hang of it. Dad!

He is up again. Towards me. 'Not you, not you,' he says as if I am the one wading in, trying to end it all.

Slowly, slowly, to dry land.

'Your best suit?'

'Only the trousers.'

Now I see. His jacket lays over the basket. All neat. Basket, jacket, rod and line. Shoes.

'Idiot!'

'You should've left me.'

It is too far to go home, through the town, wet to the skin, people going to work now, the clock striking somewhere, a church clock.

He knows a house nearby, from his young days.

Old Grandma Barker. She can be relied on. Knock on her door.

She has no fire but makes one. Lights it. Must remember to send her some coal for this.

Dad sits by the fire, a mug of tea for him, a jam jar of tea for me. Grandma Barker has nothing suitable to lend but a long worn tweed coat in a style from the last century. I wear it to walk home, to fetch Dad's other trousers, a dry shirt.

Rosa has gone to work. Not a thick fog, not six feet of snow, not an earthquake, not an attempt to wade out to watery death will come between Rosa and being in the place she is supposed to be at the time she is supposed to be there. But some concern she shows. Her note says 'Be at Burton's main gate at dinnertime to tell me what is happening.'

I put on a dry skirt, go back, carrying Grandma Barker's coat, and the tin of corned beef, saved for an emergency. Take a couple of coppers to buy an oven bottom cake on the way.

Why did he wear his Sunday suit to die in?

Because he is proud.

And a fool.

I slice the corned beef. He and Grandma Barker tear off a piece of oven bottom cake. He has told some story about a fish. A fall. I do not know what story so say nothing.

Grandma Barker knows. She knows we know. We know she knows. But this is how we do it.

On the way home, I ask him, 'What was it you were meaning to tell me? About that spot.'

No answer.

'What was it Mam said you should tell us one day?'

And then he must speak because the instruction to tell comes from beyond, from before, from her.

He says, 'That was the spot my mother ended her life.'

Spot. Like a beauty spot.

I say, 'Oh.'

So drowning might run in the family. But I do not say that. Only, 'Oh.'

Later, when he is resting (trying to die certainly takes it out of you) I get out the cutting about Mam's death. She was only poorly when she gave out all those instructions about who should take care of whom. So that must have been just in case.

I want to say to Dad, Pull yourself together. Stop being a misery. Do something. Be a man.

I give him tea, saying 'Mam told me to take care of you.'

'You have. But now you'll be best off without me.'

'Didn't she tell you to take care of anyone?'

No answer.

'Don't you see what it would do to us?'

After a long time, he says, 'I know. Because it was done to me.'

'Well then.'

No answer.

I put the mug of tea in his hand, to make him drink. 'You worried me and Rosa sick.'

He took a sip. 'I thought Rosa only had to shut her eyes to know what's happening.'

'Why, Dad?'

He doesn't answer, not for a long time, sipping his tea as if he never expected to drink again. Then, 'I've done my stint on this earth. Time for me to join your mam.'

'Suicide is the sin of despair. You'd go to hell.'

'No. They're wrong love, your priests. The people who fear hell have never been there. I have. It's on this earth, not in the next. But I've known heaven too. I'll join your mam. My fallen comrades.'

'You mustn't think like that.'

He gave his little crooked smile. 'You've hope. So you should have.' He set down his empty mug by the fender. 'Don't worry. I won't scare you again.'

His good trousers never did come right, no matter how much washing, and pressing with brown paper.

It was Rosa's idea that we should go to the Thackreys and ask them to give Dad his job back.

When you are desperate, you'll try anything.

Lydia

It was an Indian summer Saturday in September. Six of us and a dog camped out on the lawn for the afternoon. Ma sat in a deck chair, a voluminous top over her pregnant belly. Penelope would be going back to Oxford on Monday. She tuned up her cello in the gazebo. Theo and Granville lay on the grass, smoking. I played with Baby Bunting and Patience who, is a perfect dog for Bunting to play with, long-suffering, and generous about sharing her ball. Nurse Dorothea had the day off to visit a sick friend – sick being the only kind of friend she seemed to have since we never saw or heard of a well one.

As far as our families were concerned (except Penelope) Theo and I hadn't seen each other since the May Ball. Ma and Pa seemed to think it had all 'blown over'. They didn't know Theo and I were on tenterhooks as to whether he would get the assistant planning officer job, and I was saving every penny of my meagre allowance in the Yorkshire Penny Bank under my old Lydia Bellamy name which I had never troubled to change on the bankbook.

Pa always said to keep the main gates shut. 'You never know who the wind might blow in our direction.'

That Saturday, someone had left the gates wide open.

Two lower-class girls sauntered along the drive, glancing about but heading for the house. Ma caught my eye, telling me to get shot of them. People often came in if the gates were open, looking for work. The last thing we needed in the middle of a lazy afternoon was to be pestered for a job, or to buy lucky heather.

Of course, these city strollers couldn't tell a park from a garden. I called across, pointing out that this was private property, hoping that would do the trick.It didn't. Honestly. Some people! It may not be their fault that they weren't fed properly from birth and it affected their mental capacity. These two were either deaf or stupid.

'I'll go,' I said, not wanting to give Granville the chance to throw his weight about. Their cotton frocks were too short, and with sleeves below the elbow, like asylum inmates might wear. The pair could be escapees from some institution. I'd have the unenviable task of seeing them safely returned to their strait-jackets. That would give me something to talk about on my visit to Oxford.

Then I noticed the younger one's wild hair. It was them. But they were much changed. Sophie looked tired. She had flea bites on her arms. As if she saw how critically I looked at her, she blushed.

'Hello Lydia.'

'Hello, Sophie. Rosa.'

'We'd like to see Mr Thackrey, please,' Sophie said.

'He's not here. He's golfing. Is there anything I can do?'

Sophie shook her head. 'We have to see him. We'll wait.'

'He won't be back for hours.' I couldn't invite them to join us. Ma and Granville would have a fit. 'Let me give him a message. What is it you want?'

Blow the cheek of them. They'd rather not say what they wanted – not to me. Still insisting on speaking to Mr Thackrey, and they hoped I'd persuade him to see them. I so much wanted to deal with this myself – just to show Ma I could. She had started talking about sending me off to be finished in Switzerland. Well bugger that. I was finished enough already, thanks to that damn school in Harrogate. I wouldn't be packed off again. But if her daughter couldn't deal with the lower orders – because that's how Ma would see it – she might insist on finishing school. Then I would have to refuse and it would all come out, about being engaged, and all hell would break loose.

Besides, we'd been friends. Why shouldn't they talk to me?

'Look Sophie, Rosa. You can tell me. What's wrong?'

They were like the needle stuck in the gramophone record. They wanted to wait for Mr Thackrey. They must speak to Mr Thackrey.

It got me angry. All right, we were once close. But that was then and this was now. The truth was it upset me that they wouldn't say. I mustn't let them get the better of me. They wouldn't budge from wanting to see Mr Thackrey, and being willing to wait. Such bloody-minded stubbornness.

I explained again that Pa wasn't at home and perhaps Ma could help, but really she must know what it was they wanted, otherwise she wouldn't spare the time.

Rosa shut her eyes. Sophie ignored me and looked at her with some concern. Rosa opened her eyes and announced that Mr Thackrey *was* at home, reading his newspaper. Like some medium or spiritualist in a stage play, she claimed to see leather, a leather chair, perhaps, or footstool.

Sophie touched her sister's arm. 'Not here, not today.' To me she said, 'It takes it out of her.'

I'd seen Pa leave with his golf clubs. Yet there was Rosa, contradicting me, calling me a liar.

'We've walked all this way to see him,' Sophie said.

Reluctantly, I led them to Ma.

Of course Ma, pretending to be dismayed at one more thing to cope with, was delighted. She loved the drama of being overwrought, and of realising she must deal with everything herself. The words 'Switzerland' and 'Finishing School' seemed to form in a thought bubble above her head.

When Rosa repeated her claim about Pa being in, Ma said that he had indeed come home early, because a golfing partner took a funny turn and he had helped him back to the clubhouse and given him a lift home.

'I didn't know he was at home,' Granville said in a sulky voice, as if he should have hourly reports on Pa's whereabouts.

Ma said that although Mr Thackrey was in his study, he had left strict instructions not to be disturbed.

Rosa burst into tears in a suspiciously fast way. She said, 'Mrs Thackrey, when you came backstage at the

Grand to see me in *Humpty-Dumpty*, and brought all of us Blanchflower Babes a box of sweets and a pair of gloves, that was the best day of my life.'

Ma's eyes grew moist. She put one hand to her breast and the other on the great lump in her belly.

'Oh my dear . . . please don't cry. Lydia, Granville – both of you – take these girls to Mr Thackrey at once. Say I especially want him to hear whatever it is they have to say.'

Granville stubbed out his cigarette on a daisy. 'I know what they have to say and . . .'

'Please, Granville,' Ma said with a pained look, and now both hands on her bump. 'Just do as I ask.'

By the time we were in the hall, and Granville tapping on Pa's study door, Sophie had flushed bright red. Rosa looked near to tears again.

Pa emerged, sheafs of paper in his hands. Sophie made a speech then and there to Pa, asking for her father's job back. She said he was very sorry that he had used a bank vault for breeding bait worms, but hadn't thought it did any harm.

Pa was wonderful. Very kind. He said it was commendable that they called, but their father should not have sent them on such an errand, and they must of course take their tram fare.

They insisted their father knew nothing about their visit. It was their own idea, which I believed. Even a fairly stupid commissionaire could not have imagined for one moment that having been dismissed for misconduct he would be set on again.

When they wouldn't take their tram fare or accept a glass of lemonade, I walked them to the gate. None of us spoke. It felt very awkward, and sad. At the gate, I said goodbye. They didn't answer.

I went back towards the house. Granville had been watching us, sitting on the little wall at the top of the steps.

'What else did they want?' he asked.

I shook my head. 'Nothing.'

'Did they say anything about the bank?' He lit a cigarette. 'No.'

'Or their brother?'

'I wish they had. They didn't say a word. Not even goodbye.'

He gave me an odd look as I went inside and tapped on Pa's door.

Pa called me to enter.

'Is there nothing we can do for the Morans, Pa?'

He put a hand on my shoulder. 'Poor people stay poor because they don't manage their lives well. Those girls would be better doing their homework, and trying for a decent job, instead of coming up here on a wild goose chase.'

Ma sat by the little bed doting, watching Bunting as he afternoon napped. When I went in, she jumped and gave a little cry. 'I wish you wouldn't creep up on me.'

'Just because I don't clump around like an elephant doesn't mean I creep.' I sat on the floor. 'Ma, can't we do something for the Morans? Won't you talk to Pa?'

'Your Pa has other things on his mind.' She lowered her voice. 'Close the door, dear.'

I got up and closed the door.

Could I keep a huge secret, she wanted to know. Even Pa's children hadn't been let in on it.

Sophie

It was the early hours of Wednesday, 9th October. Afterwards, the date became important.

Dad didn't sleep well. He must have heard Danny knocking. Their voices floated up to our bedroom and woke me, though they were talking quietly.

They sat at the kitchen table, drinking tea. Dad's army blanket hung around his shoulders, making him look like a very old man. Danny had rolled one cigarette for Dad and was licking the paper on a second.

It was just like him to turn up after months of our not seeing him and to act as if he owned the place.

'Danny's got some news,' Dad said in a flat voice. 'Good news.'

'Well, sort of.' Danny lit his cigarette and snapped the dead match. 'I'm going away.'

'Where?'

'Working my passage across the Atlantic. Feller I met has got me taken on as a stoker.'

'You, stoking boilers?' He'd spent his whole life trying not to get his hands dirty.

I took Mam's shawl from the back of the door and wrapped it round me. Danny never gives much information in one go. You have to get him to spit it out gobbet by gobbet, questions and answers.

'I go today because I'll be helping load the coal. That has to be done first, before the cleaners go on board.'

'When do you sail?'

'We sail on Saturday, arrive in New York the following Thursday.'

Dad tapped the ash on his cig. 'He wants new opportunities, a chance to show what you can do, eh Danny?'

'I'll make good.' Danny traced the faded pattern on the oil cloth table cover. 'I'll send you something when I'm settled. Who knows? I could be fetching you all over there first class on the self-same liner before you've time to turn around.'

That was a big speech for him.

Dodging Danny's bike at the bottom of the stairs, I went up and shook Rosa awake.

She turned her sleepy face to me. 'What time is it?'

'About three o'clock.'

'Is the house on fire?'

'No.'

'Then bugger off.'

'Danny's here. He's come to say goodbye. He's going to America.'

'I was having a right good dream.'

When we were all at the table, I asked, 'So what's brought this on all of a sudden?'

'I got into a bit of bother.'

Dad put his hand on Danny's arm. 'Are you sure you have to go? If anyone gives you trouble, I'll sort em out. One thing you learn in a war is how to look after your own.'

Unshaven, his hair a mess, Dad didn't appear able to look after himself, much less deal with the kind of people chasing Danny.

In the mirror above the fireplace, I could see the reflection of the top of our heads. 'Danny, I've seen newsreels about America. People are desperate. It looks even worse than here. They queue up for a bowl of soup.'

'Ah but this is different. I've names. Addresses. We've got plans.'

Rosa glanced at me. We both knew what Mam would have said to the word *plans*.

Dad instantly cheered up. 'Oh that's all right then. I'm glad you've got plans. You see they might be on their knees in America, but they'll bounce back. There'll be more scope for a young feller there than here. They appreciate a bit of get up and go.'

'I'll send a postcard from Liverpool, and from New York as soon as I arrive, the minute the ship docks.'

'And your address. We'll want to know where you are.' Dad smiled to keep his mouth from turning down. 'If I'd known you were after going, I'd have got my fob watch out of pawn, for your keepsake.'

'I'm all right, Dad. I need nothing. It's all fixed – lift to Liverpool on a wagon, the job on the liner, someone to meet me at the other end.'

I gave a look at Rosa, and she nodded. I fetched the money tin, taking out what coins there were.

Danny shook his head. 'I'm not taking this. I should have been here with you, not with the Hescotts. You know who's on your side at a time like this.'

Rosa said, 'I'll have overtime this week. It's not a worry if you want it.'

'Everything's dealt with. I'm not that proud that I'd turn down a loan if I needed it.' He got up to go. 'And I've brought my bike round. It's for you two to keep. Don't suppose you'll ride a bike, Dad.'

Dad shook his head. 'Bit late for me to start that game, son.'

I hated to say it, but I had to. 'Danny, if you do find yourself on your uppers, go to the local church, tell them you're Catholic. They'll help you out.'

'Your papers!' Dad said suddenly. 'Find him his papers, Sophie.'

From the Oxo tin, I took Danny's birth certificate and baptismal certificate.

Danny put them in his inside pocket, then picked up his dark overcoat.

'What's the name of the liner?' Dad asked.

'White Star.' Danny buttoned his coat slowly.

Dad frowned. 'That's the shipping line isn't it?'

'Wait a minute!' Rosa ran upstairs. She came back down, carrying a red knitted scarf. 'I did this in my dinner hour at work.' She put it around his neck. 'Keep you warm in the New York winter. It was for Christmas.'

'We'll be like twins,' Dad said. 'She did one for me for my birthday.'

'Thanks, Rosa.' She had not let go of the scarf. He pulled her to him and hugged her.

He turned to me. 'I'm sorry I didn't come back with you that Saturday after York races.'

'Water under the bridge, Danny. Good luck.'

Dad took Danny's hand, then pulled him close. While they were in their clinch, Danny said, 'If anyone's looking for me, you don't know where I am.'

Danny's postcard from Liverpool held pride of place on the mantelpiece, under the mirror. But the mirror wasn't there, only a cleaner stretch of wall where it should have been. Dad had pawned it after a row with Rosa about the rent. I felt caught between the pair of them. Dad had tried to find a job, but no one wanted to take him on. Instead, he went fishing, making much of his catches, trying to sell a fish, or some of his bait worms. He reached an unspoken agreement with the tobacconist on Great George Street where he used to buy his smokes when working at the bank. He would go in when the shop was quiet and trade his catch for a couple of ounces of tobacco.

The week after Danny left, Dad had a good run on his fishing. When I got in from work, he was crouched on his haunches by the range, sleeve pulled over his hand so he could hold the skillet above the fire without burning himself. He gave the handle a little shake so the carp slid about, fixing me with bright dead eyes.

Dad stared back at the carp. 'Well here we are, all set for a slap-up feast on the day Danny will be docking in New York.'

Lately, Dad had taken to eating off his army tin plate. It sat on the table, along with plates for me and Rosa.

I spoke to the back of his bowed head. 'Did you see the billboards – about Thackreys' Bank?'

'No.'

He turned to me, and in that moment I saw him differently. The fire had reddened his cheeks. He needed a shave. His eyes looked dull and without curiosity. All the same, he asked, 'What about Thackreys' bloody bank?'

I showed him the late edition of the evening paper.

'There's been a robbery.'

Lydia

Pa liked to tell me about his prominent ancestors. Crispin Thackrey, Alastair Thackrey and Osbert Thackrey had all served as officers of the Chamber of Commerce and now Pa's stint as president was coming to an end. That evening's dinner dance was to be in his honour.

Ma insisted I go into their room to get myself ready. Since she couldn't attend the function herself, helping me was the next best thing.

'Lydia, darling, you'll look wonderful. Hold the dress against you, let me see.' She lay on the couch in her room, looking enormous, as if about to give birth to a small elephant. 'Come closer.'

She reached out and stroked the taffeta dress as I held it in front of me. 'I had a waist that size once.'

'Will everyone know it's a guinea dress? I just fell in love with it, that's all.'

'It's perfect. Coppery gold. Just the colour for a banker's daughter. There'll be dames in gowns costing ten times as much and they won't be a patch on you.'

Ma lumbered from her lying back position and crossed to her dressing table. 'You'll need a necklace.'

She opened her jewellery box and held up an amber pendant. 'This one? We'll try it when you're ready. I'm so proud of you. Your stepsisters wouldn't be up to this kind of function, even if they were here. They couldn't hold up their end of a conversation with a moulting parrot. Haven't the gift. That's why they went to pudding school and you went to the ladies' college. Has Hilda run your bath yet?'

Hilda had. Suddenly I panicked.

'I'll never be ready in time.'

I crushed Lily of the Valley bath salts into the water and wrapped a towel around my hair, to keep it from being steamed into a mess. Sliding into the bath, I couldn't help a tingle of excitement. Ma and Pa didn't know that Theo had wangled a ticket for the dinner dance. The planning officer at the Town Hall had kindly passed his ticket to his new assistant. Theo.

In a few short hours, we'd be whirling around the floor, and there wouldn't be a thing anyone could do to stop us. We'd dance a waltz, quickstep, perhaps even a tango. No one danced so well, leading me with such a light touch, his hand on the small of my back, gliding and sliding across the floor, drawing me to him, lowering his head to whisper in my ear.

Ma waddled into the bathroom, dispensing advice.

'Now you're going to be danced off your feet tonight,

that's for sure. Your pa and I have a most suitable and eligible young man for you to meet. He'll be at the top table. I'm sure even you will be smitten. So don't be distracted by any fortune hunters and go accepting wildcat invitations.'

I had no intention of accepting invitations from anyone else but my darling Theo.

When she judged my hair to be satisfactory, Ma checked Pa's suit which hung on the wardrobe door, and his shirt and bow tie draped across the bed. 'It's not like Sheldon to be late.' She looked at the little French clock with its enamel floral face. 'But it gives me more time to put the finishing touches to you. Now let's try this.'

We stood in front of her dressing table while she fastened her amber necklace around my throat. 'Perfect. Step into your dress carefully. I'll do you up.'

'Are you tired, Ma?' She hadn't bothered to go downstairs all day.

'A bit fed up with myself, with waiting. But getting you ready takes my mind off things. Bring the chair and set it side-on by the bed, so I can reach your hooks without bending.'

I dabbed Lily of the Valley scent behind my ears and on my wrists.

'Want some, Ma?'

'Go on then. But don't blame me if I drive Pa wild and make you monstrously late.'

'Ma! If you were at boarding school, the mistresses would say you're a disgrace to your sex.'

'Yes, darling, but that's why they're school teachers and I'm married to Sheldon.'

She began to fasten the hooks and eyes on my dress. 'I know. I'm a dreadful old shocker. So don't be in the least

159

like me tonight. Sparkle but be ever so proper. Nothing drives them to distraction more than a lively beautiful gel. It won't hurt your potential suitor to see that you're the belle of the ball. Don't seem too eager, but don't be afraid to hint that you can work up a bit of warmth on the tennis court. And you must remember everything, and tell me all about it. I'll want to know who was there, what they wore, who danced with whom . . . Now do you have your dance card?'

'Ma, hurry up!'

'One more hook and you'll be superb.'

She patted the bed for me to sit beside her. 'Don't you want to know your prospective suitor's name?'

I lied with a smile. 'I'm not ready for all that nonsense. Just want to enjoy myself.'

'Quite right. Now, there may be one or two people who have heard the merest whisper of a rumour about Sheldon's plans for the bank. They'll try and sound you out. You know nothing. *Comprendi*?'

I gave her a wide eyed look. 'Ma! I'm a mere slip of a gel. What could I possibly know about such things? The bank's been in this family for generations. It's inconceivable that there'll be changes.'

'Good girl. I know you can be discreet, we're alike in that. That's why you know and I know, and no one else. Sheldon will decide when to tell Granville.' She raised herself from the bed, picked up my stole from the chair and handed it to me. 'Don't forget your bag. Touch up your lipstick after the meal.'

'About Granville, don't you think he must suspect something's up? There's going to be an audit isn't there?'

'Banks have audits all the time, darling. This one will be

160

a little more thorough that's all. Now stand back. Let me look at you.'

'Will I do?'

'Twirl for me.'

I twirled, then picked up my stole.

'Perfect, but it's not stole weather. You'll need a coat. Take my mink from the wardrobe.'

I hesitated about that. If Theo saw it, he might start all his nonsense about me being out of his reach. All the same, I slid the coat from its hanger.

The car crunched across the gravel. Pa was back.

He stood at the bottom of the stairs. Jack Massey took his overcoat. I started to say something, such as he was cutting it a bit fine, and then a look stopped me. Something was wrong. Massey disappeared down the hall, towards the kitchen.

Pa led me into the drawing room. 'You look lovely, my dear. A picture.'

'What's the matter, Pa?'

He had a little habit, when agitated, of rubbing his fingers in a circular movement on his forehead. 'Now we mustn't worry your Ma with this. There's been an incident at the bank. We've had the police in and out all day.'

'What kind of incident?'

'Yesterday evening, when Clarence Clutterbuck was alone at the bank, there was an entry. He was shot.'

'Shot! Was he . . . ?'

'He was left for dead. Fortunately, the policeman on the beat tried the bank door yesterday evening. I got a call late last night. Didn't tell you or Phoebe, not to be alarmist.'

'How is he?'

'He hasn't regained consciousness. The poor chap looks in a bad way. It's touch and go.'

'That's dreadful!'

'I don't know what to do for the best. If we go to the dinner dance and Clutterbuck dies, it'll look callous. On the other hand . . .'

'The event is in your honour, and it's too late to cancel.'

From somewhere inside me came exactly what we must do. Pa must change into evening dress, and go to the Metropole, even if a little late. While he was dressing, I would go to the infirmary to visit Mr Clutterbuck. I wanted to do it. Of all the bank people, he was the one I got to know well, and the only one I cared about.

Pa began to object, but I insisted, telling him we would both have done our duty. He rubbed his forehead again, and then nodded agreement, saying there was still the matter of whether to bring up the subject at the dinner dance.

'You must judge that at the time, Pa.'

I had read enough detective stories under the bedclothes at school to be able to tell him that in any case he would not be able to comment on the robbery, because of the police investigation.

'If it does seem appropriate to speak on the subject, Pa, you can truthfully say that we have both visited poor, valiant Mr Clutterbuck. And you'll visit him again tomorrow, won't you?'

'Of course.' Pa, unexpectedly, kissed my cheek. 'You're the only child who's not mine, yet you're the one with the hardest head and the most sense of the lot of them.'

Jack Massey flicked an unwelcome speck of dust from the glowing car bonnet before opening the door for me.

'It's a bad business, Miss Thackrey.' Massey looked at me in the rear-view mirror. I never quite knew what to make of him. He had been with Pa for years. Nothing in what he said or did towards me or Ma was out of place, yet I always felt just a little uncomfortable in his presence.

He drew up outside the infirmary, and asked should he wait. I said no, and that he must go straight back for Pa. I could easily find my own way to the Metropole. This was something I must do alone, for dear Mr Clutterbuck, my ally at that very first garden party, and always so kind and respectful.

A policeman stood by the door to the private room. He touched his hat and told me the patient had not regained consciousness.

A nurse appeared in her blue dress and stiffly starched apron. The room was plain, white and sparse. Hardly any light came in through the high window from the dark grey sky. The dish would not run away with my spoon-like Mr Clutterbuck in his present condition. The nurse drew a chair to the bed and suggested I stay just five minutes. She warned that the doctor was already on his evening rounds. As she left the room, the nurse switched on the overhead light, which seemed to me a cruel act, but at least I could see him better. I never knew he had a top set of dentures. Though his jaw had kept its shape, the face above had turned concave. The nurse closed the door on the busy corridor.

The light disturbed dear Mr Clutterbuck, or perhaps he heard me. He opened his eyes and looked at me.

'Mr Clutterbuck. It's Lydia.'

A flicker, the tiniest flicker.

His little tongue moved behind the drawn-in lips. I thought he smiled.

I said something silly, about races, or the garden party, and that I hoped he would soon be better.

He was trying to speak. And the word was so clear, clear enough to annoy me.

'Granville,' he croaked.

He either thought I was Granville, or was asking for Granville. Perhaps his mind was wandering.

'It's Lydia, Mr Clutterbuck. It's Thursday. I'm on my way to the dinner dance at the Metropole. I'm father's partner.'

I didn't say why. To mention Ma's interesting condition didn't seem right.

He seemed to be trying to blame himself for letting the robbery happen, but I couldn't make out his words. Perhaps being deprived of his denture plate made his speech slur. I thought of calling for the nurse, to have her listen. They must be better at catching an invalid's words. But his fluttering hand made me think he was agitated. I leaned closer.

'Doorman,' he said clearly.

'Poor Mr Clutterbuck. Even if there had been a doorman on duty, it could still have happened. Even a doorman could be overpowered by a man with a gun.'

The movement of Mr Clutterbuck's hand became more definite. He made a distinct movement with his finger. He wanted to write. All I had was my dance card and silver-topped pencil. I gave him the pencil, and held the dance card steady, so that he could write on the back. The poor sweet man wrote a shaky letter M.

'Oh Mr Clutterbuck, how thoughtful! It's no trouble at all for me to call in on the way. Don't worry. I won't be late. Anyway, the Metropole can wait.'

He seemed satisfied, and closed his eyes.

I touched his dry white hand with its gnarled blue veins. 'I'll come back tomorrow.'

As I left, I couldn't speak, or I would have blubbed altogether and turned myself into a fright.

Even before I'd handed Ma's coat to the Metropole cloakroom attendant, Granville asked about 'Clutterbuck', as he called him. I knew all that using of surnames was very public school and shouldn't strike me as rude, but it did.

I couldn't resist saying, 'Didn't you go to see him yourself today?'

'You forgot. I was at the Manchester branch till this afternoon. This is the first I've heard about the incident.'

He needn't have added that he hated hospitals. As far as I knew, he'd never set foot in one. Nor had I until that night.

'He looked very poorly.' I refused Granville the satisfaction of saying that Mr Clutterbuck had asked after him.

Theo caught my eye. He sympathised about Mr Clutterbuck. In earshot of Pa, he asked to add his name to my dance card.

Just to stand close to Theo made me want to be in his arms.

After the dinner, Pa was presented with an engraved plate, and a vote of thanks for his contribution to the

Chamber of Commerce, and to trade.He took a sip of water, ready to make his speech. A murmur rippled through the room. People knew. They wondered whether he would say something about events at the bank.

He thanked the Chamber of Commerce for doing him this honour. He believed that in spite of the economic difficulties of recent years, we would pull through. He paused. Not a sound. No one clinked a glass, lit a cigarette, or breathed.

'I was not sure whether I would be here tonight. There cannot be a person in the city who has not now heard of the incident at Thackreys' Bank yesterday evening, when a member of my staff was attacked. I hesitate to use the word shot, because it sounds more like something that would happen in Chicago than in our own fair city. But as we speak, my valued and loyal chief cashier, Mr Clarence Clutterbuck, lies in the infirmary fighting for his life. I sat with him today. My brave daughter, who is deeply fond of the gentle man, has just been to see him, and indeed came here from that visit. Her words give me hope for his recovery. She persuaded me that I must come here this evening. And she was right. During the war, we carried on business as usual. We must not let a vile criminal element prevent us from doing so now.'

A round of applause began, and spread around the room.

Pa held up his hand. 'Thank you for the honour of this occasion, and for the engraved plate, which I shall treasure. My daughter is here tonight in place of her mother who is indisposed. I believe we must now lead you all in the dance.'

The orchestra began to play.

As we began the first waltz, I felt so proud, and properly part of the family for the very first time. Pa smiled at me.

'I'm the envy of every man in the room. I should think you're going to be on your feet all night my dear. And I've someone very special to introduce you to.'

But as the dance ended, a plain clothes policeman was waiting to catch Pa's attention. We were led to a side room that smelled a little dusty and asked to sit at the kind of round table that one expects to be dotted with cocktails.

Pa said, 'Oh dear. You're the bearer of bad news.'

'I'm sorry to say we are. Mr Clutterbuck has passed away.'

I could hardly believe it, having convinced myself he would be better, and that tomorrow I would take him a bottle of lemon barley water and perhaps get cook to bake an individual rice pudding.

I couldn't help but cry, for the pity of it, and how sad that he should die on such a glorious evening of all evenings, my very first dinner dance. Pa gave me his handkerchief.

The policeman pulled a notebook from his pocket.

'I don't like to ask you to give us a statement at a time like this, Miss Thackrey. But did Mr Clutterbuck say anything at all? We believe he did regain consciousness for a short while. You're the only person who witnessed that.'

'Yes. I spoke to him. He recognised me, and I believe seemed pleased to see me. I told him he'd soon be well again – I truly thought he would . . .'

'There, there,' Pa patted my arm.

'Anything else?' the policeman prompted.

'He seemed to think if there had been a doorman there, it wouldn't have happened.'

'What were his exact words, Miss?'

'Doorman.'

'Anything else?'

'I told him about coming to the Metropole tonight, which of course he knew about. He didn't want me to be late.'

'Is that what he said?'

'He indicated that he wanted to write. I gave him my dance card. He wrote an M for Metropole, meaning to get myself off to the dinner dance.'

'May I see the card?'

Suddenly I was all fingers and thumbs, fumbling in my bag for the card. There was the new lipstick. Ma told me to repair my lipstick after the meal. She would ask if I'd done it, and I'd have to say no.

The policeman looked at my dance card.

'Do you have a doorman at the bank, sir?'

'No. We haven't for some time. I'm afraid our customers are left to deal with the door themselves these days.'

The policeman looked interested. 'So you did have a doorman?'

'We employed a commissionaire. Barney Moran. After he left we decided against replacing him.'

'May I keep the dance card Miss Thackrey?' The policeman asked.

I nodded, and hated my treachery towards Mr Clutterbuck, for in that moment I thought of Theo. I wanted to ask for the dance card back, so that if I couldn't dance with him, I could at least look at his name.

Pa stood. He placed a hand on my shoulder. 'My daughter was very fond of Mr Clutterbuck. We shall go home now.'

He wrote a note to Granville, to tell him Mr Clutter-buck had died, and to ask him to stay on, keep up appearances and say nothing of the news that would interfere with the evening's enjoyment.

Massey drove us in the Rolls with the detective. We stopped outside the bank, which had a police guard on the door. A bit late for that.

The officer asked if Mr Thackrey would kindly enter the bank with him, and direct him to the filing cabinet where staff records were kept.

I half expected Pa to disclaim knowledge of such a mundane piece of information, but he agreed. They disappeared into the bank. For once, I was glad to have Massey there, even though he had nothing to say. The building itself looked different somehow, more ominous and threatening.

'What will happen now?' I asked Pa as we were driven home.

'Our former commissionaire will be paid a visit by His Majesty's constabulary. And by heaven, Lydia, if Moran did it, I'm willing to hang the blighter myself.'

Sophie

Motor vehicles never came along Tab Street. I moved the blind to take a look. The big van stopped by our house. Doors opened, and slammed shut.

A thump, thump at the door, loud enough to burst your eardrums.

'Police! Open up!'

Rosa slept peacefully.

A pock-faced man in a long light gabardine coat and bowler hat pulled something like a tiny wallet from his inside pocket. 'Detective Sergeant Wallis, Leeds City Police.'

Behind him stood a uniformed policeman, tall and black as a crow with black buttons and a black badge.

Wallis said, 'Where's Barney Moran, and who are you?'

'He's sleeping. I'm his daughter, Sophie.'

Dad wouldn't be sleeping. A sigh could wake him he slept so lightly. I thought I heard a movement from his room.

Wallis nodded to the uniformed man. 'Go get him.'

The uniformed man pushed past me and went upstairs. He barked something at Dad.

'Who else is in the house?' Wallis asked.

'My sister. What's going on?'

'I'll ask the questions.' He said something to the doorway and another policeman went upstairs.

Rosa screamed. I moved to go to her. Wallis barred my way. 'Sit down.'

I heard movements above, and voices. Moments later, Dad was being brought down the stairs. I called to him.

'Quiet!' Wallis ordered as he marched to the door, pulling out his identity card, flipping it open, holding it for Dad to see. 'I'm Detective Sergeant Wallis of Leeds City Police. You are Barney Moran?'

'Yes.'

'Barney Moran, you are being arrested on suspicion of having robbed a bank and committed murder in the process of that robbery.'

I ran to the doorway, trying to push my way past the detective. Dad's mouth opened. No words came. He shook his head. I heard myself say no. No.

'What were you wearing yesterday, Moran?' the detective asked.

'What I'm wearing now.'

'No topcoat?'

'No.'

'Scarf?'

171

'Yes.'

Dad had draped his scarf on the hook behind the door. The uniformed constable picked it up. 'This one?'

Dad nodded.

Wallis said, 'Take him into the van.'

With the scarf draped over his arm, the constable handcuffed Dad.

Dad turned back to look at me and said softly, 'This breaks my dream.'

'No talking!' the constable barked as he marched Dad to the van.

The second constable brought Rosa downstairs. He was telling her to be quiet, but she wouldn't. 'What's going on? This is ridiculous. I have to be at work in a few hours.'

Wallis said to me, 'You've five minutes to go upstairs and put some clothes on.'

He followed me upstairs and stood in the doorway with his back to me. My hands were shaking as I pulled on my clothes.

In the van, we weren't allowed to speak or look at each other. Dad sat opposite me. I reached out my foot and touched his toe. He tapped his toe and touched mine.

'None of that,' the sergeant said.

The only window was in the back of the van. It was too dark to see out.

Eventually, we came to a stop. Dad was led away first, then Rosa. A few moments later, it was my turn. Nothing felt real. I never knew there was a warren of passages underneath the town hall, and that they smelled like a dark forbidding cave.

*

When you are in bare cell, anxious, waiting, there is sweet bugger all you can do. That is the worst feeling. Helplessness. Helplessness for myself, for my dad, and for my sister.

A great weight lumped itself everywhere, in my chest, head, shoulders, pressing in until it hurt, making it hard to breathe, hard to see. There were white tiles on the walls, like a public lavatory, a badly plastered ceiling and an uneven stone floor. I sat on a hard wooden bench. They had taken my shawl at the desk, the laces from my boots and the handkerchief from my pocket. I wanted my shawl. Poor Dad, poor Rosa. They'd be so cold.

I was glad to be taken into another room, given the chance to speak. Soon they would realise their mistake. We could all go home again. I felt myself blush at the shame of it. Everyone in the street would know we'd been hauled off like criminals.

It was the same man, Detective Sergeant Wallis with the pock-marked face. He had taken off his raincoat and wore a dark suit. He smiled at me, as if we were old friends. 'Do sit down. We'll wait for my colleague.'

The door burst open and slammed shut. The man who stomped into the room looked more chimpanzee than human. His broad face and low forehead seemed pulled outwards by great ears. His sharp eyes bore down on me suspiciously, then darted about as if I might have concealed something from him. He was so like a chimp that for a moment I thought he would start scratching his armpits. His mouth curled in a snarl, showing a row of flat yellow teeth.

Cold numbed my brain. Don't let them see me shiver. They'll think I'm afraid. Guilty.

'Name?' the chimp asked.

They knew my name already. I said it again, and my address, age, occupation – shop assistant.

'Tell us everything you've done since getting up on Wednesday morning,' Wallis demanded. 'In your own time, in your own words.'

I didn't see how I could tell them in anyone else's words. There was not much to tell. Work on Wednesday. Home to a supper of bread and margarine and a cup of tea.

Chimp wrote down my answers.

'Tell us more about Wednesday evening,' Wallis said.

This was where I could clear up their mistake.

'I got home from work about six. Dad was already there. He'd been out looking for work and had no success. He was in all evening. We had a go at playing chess, but I'm not very good at it.'

'Where was your sister?'

'At a workmate's house.'

'Workmate's name?'

'Fenella Naggs.'

'And Thursday?' Wallis asked. 'How did your father spend Thursday?'

I told them he probably did what he always did. Got up after we left the house, saw to the bait worms in the cellar, went to look for work, walked about, went fishing.

'He caught a couple of carp on Thursday. We had them for tea.'

The chimp left off writing. He thumped the table so hard it should have cracked. I heard myself gasp. He looked as if he would thump me too, reaching over the table to snarl. 'You're not taking this serious. We can keep you here till kingdom come, till you come up with the truth.'

Wallis made a small sound and touched his arm, as if to restrain him. Then he smiled at me. 'Better tell him the truth. It'll make it easier.'

'I am telling the truth.'

Chimp flung the chair against the far wall. 'The truth? How do you work out the truth of what your father does? He's in bed when you leave in the morning, and hogging the fire when you get in at night. Here is a man who believes the world owes him a living . . .'

'No!'

' . . . and he's got you as his alibi. Well it won't wash, girl.'

He stuck his face next to mine, the tobacco of his breath blowing into my mouth before he turned his back and spat.

'Take her back to the bloody cell and throw away the key.'

He marched out, slamming the door behind him. My breath came fast and shallow. What use would I be to Dad if I couldn't make them believe me?

'He has a point,' smiling Wallis said gently. 'Though he doesn't put it over with great finesse you might say. It comes of dealing with hardened criminals.'

I couldn't speak to say we were not criminals, hardened or otherwise.

'You had Thursday's evening paper in the house,' Wallis said. 'What did your father say when he read about the bank robbery?'

'Not much.'

'What was that not much?'

I didn't know how to answer. If I repeated Dad's words,

they'd twist what I said. 'I can't really remember. He didn't want to burn the fish. He said he'd read it later.'

'And when he read it later?'

'He tossed it aside. The bank's a sore point with him since he hasn't found another job.'

Straight away I realised that might not have been a good thing to admit.

'Tell you what.' Wallis pulled a small notebook from his inside pocket and found a pencil behind his ear. His ears were small and neat and looked hardly big enough to hold a pencil. 'You can't be expected to be an objective judge of your father's character. But others can. Tell me the names and addresses of everyone he has dealings with. When you say he goes looking for work, who does he go to? If he has the brass to buy a pint, where does he sup?'

At last I could do something. There wasn't a soul on earth who, knowing Dad, could suspect him to be a killer.

In the cell, I sat on the hard bench, back to the wall. Stay awake, just stay awake. They wouldn't keep me much longer now. But my eyes started to shut. Count the tiles on the wall. I would count the tiles going up. I got halfway and had to start again. Bigger tiles would be easier. Count in twos.

I didn't know whether I fell asleep for a few minutes or an hour. The door clanked open. The policeman who stood over me saying, 'Come on lass,' had silver buttons on his coat. It must be morning. Daytime buttons. As we walked the tunnel, he towered over me, solid, well fed. If Dad had been a policeman instead of a commissionaire we wouldn't be in this mess.

*

It was the same room, the same two men, Wallis and chimp. Chimp has found out some bad thing about me. I see it in his eyes.

One of them was speaking. I didn't get it straight away. Being cold put the blocks on words. The sound but not the meaning came through.

Wallis spoke, a sighing friendly sadness to his words. 'You're cold, but not as cold as poor dead Mr Clutterbuck.'

Chimp pushed back his chair. 'Happen you'd like to see him, the dead cashier? Look at his deep wound where the bullet entered.'

'No.'

'Thought not.'

He threw a letter on the table. 'Look at that then. Tell me what you make of the epistle according to Barney Moran.'

It was the unfinished letter Dad had been writing to Danny, a putting-on-a-brave-face-letter.

Dear Danny

I hope this finds you well after the voyage. Even though we do not yet know what your address will be, this is ready to send to you the moment we hear. So each day, I shall write a little more, and hope we hear from you before this epistle reaches epic proportions.

Danny, you must make the most of this great chance in life. Do not worry about us or spend your time looking back. Things go well with us.

You would be surprised how many fish have bitten

for me these last days. Although nothing has come up as regards a job, I have some plans. An old angler I gave worms to rents a house near allotments. He and his wife have three lodgers, two young machine operatives from Kershaws and an old porter from the hospital. I have a plan to do the same. With my fishing, the produce of an allotment, rent coming in, not to mention Rosa's wages and Sophie's, we will all manage more than well enough. We will live the life of Riley. Who knows but in a year or so we could be crossing the Atlantic ourselves.

The latest news – and what a shocker. There has been a robbery at Thackreys' Bank no less, and the shooting of chief cashier Clutterbuck. You will remember he held sway at the garden party children's races, and is the same fellow as got me sacked, God forgive him.

The chimp said, 'You all hated Clutterbuck, didn't you? Your father especially.'
'No.'
'You hated him for what he'd done.'
'No. I never gave him a thought.'
'How was your father going to pay the rent on a bigger house in a good area, near an allotment?'
'That's just his way. He likes to plan. Nothing comes of it.'
'And an allotment no less. How would he manage that?'
'It's pipe dreams with Dad. He likes to imagine how our lives will get better, he always has.'

'Where does he go fishing?'

'The canal basin.'

'Where else?'

'The river.'

'Do you recognise this scarf?'

I nodded. It was Dad's red knitted scarf.

'Where does he keep his gun?'

'He has no gun.'

The chimp did not believe me. Soldiers brought guns back from the war, and kitbags and anything they could lay their thieving hands on, he told me. Our house had been searched. We had army blankets, a soldier's tin plate and mug. Was it a pistol that Dad brought back? Did he keep it under the bed? Or a revolver, at the back of a cupboard, on the top shelf, in the cellar behind a brick? Where was the gun? Did it look like this picture? Or this?

'He had no gun.'

'How could you know for sure?'

'Mam wouldn't have had a gun in the house.'

'So there was a row about it?'

'No. I never saw a gun, never heard talk of a gun.'

'But he shot people in the war. Killing's not new to him, he's a dab hand at shooting men.'

The red scarf lies across the table like a splash of blood.

'He expected you all to be setting sail for America in a year or so. That'd cost. Is that why he robbed a bank?'

'He expected Danny to do well and send for us.'

'That's not what he says. You're lying!' Chimp leaped to my side of the table, thumping his fist. 'You're not telling a proper tale. You're holding back. You'll sit there till you get your story straight.' He flung the rent book on the table, his nicotine-stained fingers turning page after page where we paid something on account or held the rent over. 'And you tell me that a house by an allotment is going to come out of thin air, and three passages to America from a young feller who hasn't been there five minutes. I'm not coming back in here until you get your story straight.'

At the door he turned to Detective Sergeant Wallis. 'Call me when she's ready to talk.'

The chair began to slide and the room to spin. I leaned forward to catch myself on the table, spinning, spinning, going to be sick, then everything went black.

I was back in the cell, a blanket around my shoulders. Policeman in black, sitting beside me on the bench, black uniform, black night time buttons. 'Drink this.'

Poison. They're going to kill me.

'It's tea. Dunk the bread in it. That's what people do when it's too dry.' The policeman didn't look at me but at his shoes.

A smell. There was vomit on my skirt.

Old men dunked bread in tea. I took a drink from the tin cup. I wouldn't dunk bread. I wouldn't touch their mouldy bread.

Was it the third time in the room with Wallis and the chimp, or the fourth or the hundredth?

Had the policeman who marched me along the corridor worn daytime silver buttons or nighttime black? I didn't know. Maybe indoors they sometimes wore silver buttons at night to confuse. Maybe they wore black on the beat in the day because a man had died.

True to his word, the chimp had not come back —
because I did not tell a proper tale, a tale to his liking.

The dunk bread policeman told me the superintendent
would see me. Wallis sat with the superintendent, and you
could see who was boss. Carefully, Wallis set out three
pawn tickets on the table, as if he would have liked to show
me a card trick. I had to blink to get my tired eyes to see.

Part of the trick involved explaining that on three
consecutive Thursdays, Barney Moran visited the pawn
shop.

'Tell us something about what he pawned.'

This was too easy. A trick question? Each ticket named
an item. Ticket one. He pawned the mirror, their wedding
present. That mirror Mam prized had been more off the
wall than on. I saw it suddenly in my mind's eye, Mam and
Dad, long ago, looking into it, pretending to be a portrait.
So silly.

Ticket two. Wedding ring. That I didn't know. Two
weeks ago he pawned her ring.

Ticket three. Coat.

This Thursday gone, yesterday or the day before? I lost
track of time.

But he didn't have a coat. How could he pawn a coat he
didn't own?

Wallis wants me to agree with him that Dad pawned the
coat because he was seen wearing it, spotted near the bank,
cap pulled down, long dark coat, red scarf wound around
his throat and mouth. After he robbed the bank, he pawned
the coat.

'Dad doesn't have a topcoat.'

Wrong answer.

The only time he had a coat was when he borrowed Danny's. I did not say that, too weary to say more. Besides something in my brain said, Don't mention Danny's name. One Moran at least is free of blame, don't breathe him into this place with his long coat, his pulled-down cap, his red scarf.

Back to the cell.

Sitting. How many tiles. Up. Across. And if they were doing this to me, what of Dad. And Rosa? Time passed. The spy hole opened, to see if I was sleeping. I looked back. Damn you, let us go.

Footsteps. I'm to be questioned again.

Chimp speaks. He was no longer angry. So politely, he asked me to sit down. The superintendent came into the room.

'Your father has confessed. You'll be let out on bail, just as soon as you've made a full statement. It'll go better with you all if you tell us where the money is.'

I followed a tall constable along the tiled corridor, through two sets of doors that he unlocked and locked again. Was it day or night? I couldn't tell.

'You've been bailed. Sign here!' He pointed to a ledger, daintily dipped a pen in the inkwell and handed it to me.

I signed for our shawls and Rosa's boot laces.

'Where's my sister?'

'She's waiting for you, through there.'

'What about Dad?'

He held the door for me. 'Just sling yer hook. Unless you like it in here and want to stay on.'

I walked through to the waiting area. Rosa sat still as a

statue on the bench, next to May. Rosa had something that she used to do when she was little, almost like bringing a curtain down between herself and the world. She would radiate quietness that Mam called Rosa's trance. May looked at me, with such anguish, but stayed in the silence, with Rosa.

Tony was by the wall. He came to me, saying my name. He took my shawl, placed it around my shoulders and drew me to him for just a moment.

'Come and sit down. I'll see to Rosa's boots.'

Rosa seemed unable to move. May leaned her forward while I put the shawl around her, and then squeezed her hand. I wanted to ask, did she do that in the questioning, go into her trance? If so, all the shouting in the world wouldn't reach her.

Tony knelt on one knee to lace her boots. 'Would you like straight-laced, or crossed?'

Rosa didn't answer.

He laced carefully, tying a knot and a bow.

'What day is it?' I asked.

May stood. 'Sunday. Sunday night, going on nine. I've a bit of dinner waiting for you.'

I remained standing, while I still had the strength. Heart pounding, I went to the desk.

'Officer.'

He looked surprised.

'I'd like to see my father. Mr Moran.'

'Would you now? We're talking murder here you realise?'

'Can I see him?'

'Get out of here before I call the superintendent.'

'When can I see my dad?'

'You'll see him in court if you've a mind. And if you don't want to be in the dock alongside him, hop it!' He looked past me to May who came over and edged me away from the desk.

Rosa spoke for the first time. 'He's gone from here.'

Tony took my hand. 'Rosa's right. He's not here. They've remanded him in custody at Armley Gaol. We saw him taken out earlier.'

A moan of pain came from somewhere deep inside me. Why hadn't I seen him? Dad. I wanted my dad.

Sunday night, factories closed, the sky spread above us clear as a kid's drawing, with a bright painted-on moon. The town hall clock struck nine. I wanted Dad to be outside with us, to look at the moon and feel the air on his cheeks.

Tony seemed to be steering me by the arms like some wheelbarrow. I pulled free of him wondering which way was Armley? If we could go to the gaol I might see him.

'There's nothing you can do, Sophie. Your dad confessed.' Tony began to walk faster.

'He didn't do it.'

'He says different.'

'Hold your horses, Tony,' May called. 'We can't keep up.'

I said, 'They must have browbeaten him into it.'

Everything in the world seemed distant to me, as if we were no longer part of it. Cut off. Set drifting in some other world. It struck me as so strange. We must look like anyone else. We walked down the Headrow, past Lewis's great windows with ghost mannequins displaying the latest fashion behind the great plate-glass windows, past the Three Legs with drunks shouting the odds on the pavement.

'Come on, girls,' May said. 'Let's get you warmed up and a night's sleep. It's what your dad would want.'

I stopped. My legs wouldn't move. 'He didn't do it. He didn't do it.'

May hurried me along. 'Don't worry. It won't stand up. The damn crooks must know they need evidence. It'll get thrown out, you'll see.'

Tony said, 'Come on. Left right. You can do it.'

We were moving again.

I wanted something from Tony, some reassurance, some faith. I said, 'You don't know what it's like in there. They twist your words.'

'They couldn't get to your dad that easy. Not a man like him.'

I pulled my arm free. 'What do you know about him? You've only met him once.'

'It didn't stop the police coming to our house, and our workshop,' Tony said. 'They've searched the whole place, turned it upside down. Mam went mental.'

May's shop stood in darkness. She put the key in the lock and said to Tony, 'We'll be all right now, lad. You get yourself home.'

'If you're sure?'

'I'm sure.'

'Goodnight, Sophie.' He kissed my cheek. 'Goodnight, Rosa. I'll let you get some rest.'

Even in the dark, I could tell the difference – something

about the feel of the shop, and the smell – disturbed muck and dust.

As we felt our way through the furniture and boxes, May said, 'They took the place apart, searching for stolen money.'

I held onto a chair to steady myself. 'That was my fault. I gave everyone's name, thinking they'd speak for Dad. I didn't know . . .'

Rosa spoke for the first time. 'I did too. The same thing.'

May lit the gas mantle, then built up the fire.

'Have a bite to eat.' She lifted plates from the oven with her apron and placed them on the table. A potato each, dark cabbage, a small curling slice of brown meat. She took a third plate and divided its contents between us. 'Get it down you,' she ordered, pouring gravy from the pan that had sat on the hob, a film of soot covering its surface.

'It's sooty,' I said.

'There's nowt bad in a speck of soot. You'll eat a peck of muck afore you die.'

And instead of being with us, eating dried-up food doused in dirty gravy, Dad languished in Armley Gaol. Armley Gaol, a place I had heard of but never seen. The very name filled me with dread. Picking up knife and fork seemed strange, as if only other people did such normal things.

Rosa shivered and shook. She couldn't hold her knife and fork. May led her to the fire, to the big saggy fireside chair that was covered with a counterpane. She put a blanket around Rosa's legs, and a tray on her lap. 'You eat your dinner here. Get warm.'

Rosa shuffled in the chair.

'I know it can't be that comfy. Coppers ripped its innards. I shoved the stuffing back best I could. This chair's had it. Same as the other upholstered stuff.'

'How do you mean?' I asked.

'They ripped everything apart in the searches. Mattresses included. I've made you up a bed of coats and suchlike.'

When we had eaten, I asked to borrow her torch, to go home and see the worst.

She wouldn't give it to me. 'Nay, lass. Tomorrow's soon enough. Rest. Get out of that mucky skirt. Stop here. Get your strength back. You'll need it.'

She picked up the plates and put them down by the fire for her cats to lick the gravy.

There was nothing for it then but to climb the stairs to May's attic, the two of us, lying on bedsprings overlaid with old blankets and coats, covered with more blankets and a big eiderdown. I wondered how the eiderdown had survived police enquiries. Perhaps they just checked all its feathers by feel. The room stank of sour, dusty old flocks from the split mattress.

Through the rattling window, I could just make out the moon, bright and high.

'What are we going to do?' Rosa asked.

'I don't know. I can't sort it out in my head.' The springs creaked as I turned towards her.

Rosa said, 'They went on at me about the pawn tickets. They seemed to think Dad must have run out of stuff to pawn, and so he robbed a bank. They're mad, Sophie.'

'And how could he have pawned a black coat? He didn't have a coat.'

'May gave him one. She told them that.'

'I wish she'd told me. I felt a fool not knowing. They thought I was lying.'

Below, May walked about in her bedroom. She went downstairs again.

A few minutes later, she came up, carrying two cups. 'I should've given you this sooner. It'll shut your eyes.'

'What is it?'

'Nighter.'

It smelled sweet and bitter at the same time, but not unpleasant. I took a sip.

'That's it. Drink it down.' She sat on the end of the creaking bed. 'Bloody hell it's freezing in here. Wouldn't be surprised if we don't have a frost tonight.'

The cup warmed my hands. 'May, why did they make a beeline for Dad? Why did they treat us all as guilty when they knew nothing. When we'd done nothing?'

For a moment, May didn't answer. 'Well, I have a clue on that. One of my customers cleans at the Town Hall. Seemingly, Clutterbuck came round in the infirmary. He named your dad.'

'Clutterbuck? Why would he do that?'

'That's what I asked meself,' May sighed. 'The only conclusion I reached was that he must have been delirious.'

'So he said that to the police, or one of the nurses?'

'No. To one of the Thackrey family. Now lay down. Get some sleep. You'll do no good if you're exhausted.'

She took the cups from us. 'Goodnight, loves. Sleep as best you can.'

'What are we going to do?' I asked Rosa.

'I don't know. I think I have to go to work as usual, to prove to people we're not guilty. We've nothing to hide.'

'You won't be able to concentrate.'

'I'll have to. I'm gonna show them, Sophie. We don't need stolen money. We Morans earn our own living.'

After Rosa went to work, I began to clear up May's shop. I straightened the furniture, picked up clothes, hung up coats and skirts and trousers, folded shirts, blouses and jumpers and placed them on the shelves Tony had fitted.

Tony. He had not said it in so many words, but I knew he thought Dad guilty. Let him. I was finished with him if that was his view.

Some stuff would have to be thrown out, broken ornaments. Having to sort through everything made me ruthless. 'I'm putting rubbish in this tea chest for the rag and bone man, May.'

Usually, she would have objected, gone through it item by item. She just nodded.

In the middle of the morning, I told May I would go look at our house, and see the damage.

'Don't go yet. I can't leave the shop. Wait till Rosa comes home, then I'll come with you.'

'It'll be dark then.' I pulled on my coat.

'Believe me, it's best seen in the dark, the state they've left it.'

'I have to go, May. I need clean underwear. We've papers there, our birth certificates. I can't just leave it.'

'All right, all right, if you must.' She gave me some bags and sacks, to pack what I wanted to bring back. 'You won't want to live there again.'

May stood in the shop doorway. At the corner, I turned to wave to her. A man in a long raincoat emerged from the recreation ground. He followed me onto Church Road. I slipped into St Mary's, intending to go out by a side door and shake him off. As I lit a candle and said a prayer for Dad, I heard footsteps. A heavy man, trying to tread lightly.

Well, let him follow me. Did he think we'd hidden bank notes in with the church candles?

A policeman stood outside our door on Tab Street. My heart missed a beat. Everyone in the street would know. Curtains moved aside. Mrs Molloy peered at me, caught my eye, and turned away.

The policeman was young, with small red-rimmed eyes. 'You can't go in there.'

'I've come to get some of our clothes.'

'Ah. You're . . . '

'Sophie Moran.'

He stepped aside and said in a quiet voice, 'I'll need to check what you take out, Sophie.' He opened the door. 'Be careful in there, if you go upstairs.'

The cupboard doors hung from their hinges, contents on the floor. Even the oven door stood open, as if it had been expected we would cook the money for our dinner. Mam's money box tin with its slots stood empty. I held it in my hand and went to the door. 'There was money in this. Do you know where it's gone?'

He shook his head. 'Some stuff will have been taken for evidence.'

The contents of the bureau were strewn around the stone floor. I pick up our birth certificates, Mam and Dad's marriage certificate, holy pictures, mass cards, sealing wax and string. A couple of books lent to us by the Scholar had their spines broken.

A sick feeling came into my gut. I had told them about the Scholar, imagining him speaking up for Dad. A sudden picture of the Scholar's only room – library, bedroom and kitchen combined – came into my mind. If they had done this to our books, and the same to his, his life's collection, his life's achievement would be reduced to strewn torn pages.

The Oxo tin on the stairs with Mam's recipes had been tipped out. I stepped over it and went to our bedroom. Then I saw what he meant about being careful. The floor-boards had been ripped up. My nightgown lay on the joists. I picked it up and stepped gingerly, taking this and that – underwear, a blouse turned filthy during the search. In Dad's room I picked up some of his clothes and folded them, put them in the bag.

At the bottom of the stairs, I left the bag and went into the cellar. In the dim light, I found Dad's fishing rods and basket. Then I stepped on something soft. His bait. The tin of maggots lay untouched, but the worms he bred so care-fully had been tipped out onto the floor. One of them was hopelessly trying to burrow its way through hard stone. I couldn't bear to watch it. Nothing for it but to rescue them.

I hated worms, the slimy touch of them, but what was that against everything that had happened.

I scooped them up and put them in the sack. It must have taken me a long time, because the policeman called down. When I didn't answer he came to see.

'It's Dad's bait. He'll need it when he goes fishing. He's looked after these worms a long time.'

He sounded disappointed, as if he expected I had been

stuffing my pockets with treasure. 'I shouldn't worry about that. He won't be going fishing for some considerable while.'

He carried the fishing basket and rods upstairs. I heard him open the basket and rummage through.

When I came upstairs, carrying the bait, I realised there was almost too much to carry. The sack, the rods, basket, bag of clothes.

Somehow, I managed it, sack over my back held with the same hand as the bag of clothes, the basket in my other hand, and rods over my shoulder, like a rifle.

'Is that it?' The policeman said.

I nodded. It wasn't much to show for our life.

'You might want to see what you can get for the furniture,' he said. So at least he didn't believe that we had a secret store of cash somewhere.

I didn't trust myself to speak, but walked away.

I was not very far along, when Mrs Hartigan's door opened. She called to the police officer in that fog horn voice of hers. 'I expect it's all right if I offer the girl a hand. Not that we ever had anything to do with them,' she added quickly.

She caught up with me. 'Here, give me summat to carry.'

'What about the kids?' I asked.

'They'll be all right for ten minutes. I told them to stop under the table, away from the fire.'

She took the fishing basket and rods from me. 'We're sorry for your trouble, lass.'

'Thanks.'

'I wish my man had it in him to rob a bank, though I

wouldn't wish him caught or to have blood on his hands. That must have been an accident I'm sure.'

I stopped. 'You think Dad did it?'

'Oh no, not I, for sure not I. But people are saying . . .'

I grabbed the rods and basket from her. 'I don't need help, Mrs Hartigan, not from someone who thinks my Dad's guilty.'

I walked away, leaving her standing there, for once speechless. How would we get at the truth? Only one other family had it in their interest to know what really happened at Thackreys' Bank, and that was the Thackreys themselves.

I would see Lydia. She would know who spoke to Mr Clutterbuck. Who got the wrong end of the stick so securely that they pointed a finger at Dad. Lydia would help, I felt sure.

Lydia

From my spot in the window seat of my room, I looked out across the bleak garden. The horrible business at the bank made it so hard to concentrate. Poor Clarence Clutterbuck. Now that he was dead, I always thought of him under his full name. The 'mister' slipped away. Death turned him into an equal, a friend. Having seen him in the hospital, lying there helpless and small against the bright white linen, it was even possible to think of him as a baby. Baby Clarence, apple of his parents' eyes.

The season matched my mood. When I was a child, I loved Autumn. 'My favourite season', I wrote at school. Turning leaves. Apples gathered in. Harvest moons and misty mornings. Looking forward to Bonfire Night and woodsmoke. Now Autumn seemed to hold the world still with dread.

Ma was in the nursing home well ahead of her time,

ordered to rest. Pa went round the house either snapping or preoccupied, worrying about Ma and the unborn baby. Pa's first wife died after giving birth to Granville. What if that happened again? And the worst of it was, they didn't want me to go and see her. The nursing home wouldn't allow it, as if I were a child, too young to set foot in a maternity home.

My life seemed a permanent full stop. Theo and I kept our engagement secret still. Pa occasionally remembered to sing praises of the chap they had in mind for me. Mercifully, the interruption of the dinner dance had saved me from having to do more than shake hands with the puny paragon of all virtues, heir to wondrous fortunes. Ma's absence allowed me a breathing space.

Whenever I was with Theo, snatching some time together away from prying eyes, I saw the sense in biding our time, choosing the right moment. When we were apart, like now, it seemed madness.

I wanted to shout out loud. Theo and Lydia. Lydia and Theo, true love for ever and ever. I wished we'd fallen in love as children so we could have carved our initials on every tree, with hearts and arrows.

Looking out across the garden, I could just see the top of the big gates. One gate opened, then the other. Perhaps Pa was coming home early, which could mean there was news from the nursing home about Ma.

A small Morris Minor drew up at a polite distance from the front of the house. The policeman, who seemed to be specially appointed to talk to me, got out. He was young-ish, with rosy cheeks, looking and sounding as if he had moved into town from the countryside.

What could he want this time? I'd gone over my account of seeing poor Clarence Clutterbuck. There was nothing more to tell.

The policeman stood by the drawing-room window. 'Good afternoon, Sergeant.'

He turned to face me. 'Good afternoon Miss Thackrey.' Such a friendly, open smile, as if he'd come to talk about a cow that had skipped its field and escaped into the road.

'Do sit down.'

Almost as soon as we sat down, Enid arrived with tea. 'Cook put on a few buns, Miss.' She spoke to me but looked at him, blushing and with a little smile.

I stirred the pot, and poured. It comes to something when you have seen a policeman enough times to know he takes two lumps of sugar.

He waited until Enid closed the door behind her. 'There've been developments. We wanted to keep you informed.'

My tea threatened to go down the wrong way. Perhaps Moran had escaped, was on the run, gunning for me.

Sergeant Dickinson must have seen the alarm on my face because he said quickly, 'The situation now is that Moran confessed. There'll be committal proceedings before a magistrate. Your statement will form part of those proceedings. A date will be set for a hearing.'

He said it as if I should be relieved. I felt uncomfortable, and stupid for not knowing what he was talking about.

'Will I have to give evidence?'

'Unlikely. With the accused entering a guilty plea, witnesses won't be called.'

In my mind's eye, I pictured Moran standing outside the bank in his uniform, as Ma and I came out from seeing Pa one rainy day. We had laughed afterwards, at how he tried to touch his hat and unfurl the umbrella at the same time.

'What about his daughters?'

'We don't suspect their involvement, but they're under surveillance, just in case.'

'But if they weren't involved . . . ?'

'We have to keep an open mind. Someone may try to contact them.'

'You haven't found the money?'

'Moran hasn't come clean on that, not yet. We'll keep going back to him. Prison has a way of loosening a man's tongue.'

Not until I walked him into the hall did I think to ask, 'How soon will it be brought to a conclusion?'

We stood by the front door. 'Things will move pretty quickly now. It'll all be over by Christmas. You'll be able to put the whole business behind you and enjoy the festive season.'

I walked back through the house, to the spot in the kitchen where Ma kept her secateurs, then out into the garden. It suddenly struck me what he meant by saying it would all be over by Christmas. Sophie and Rosa's father would swing on the end of a rope. How could it be that a man who once held an umbrella to keep the rain off you could come to such an end? Never again comb his hair, put on his coat, look at the sky for rain clouds.

I walked towards the woods. The hebe shrub scattered rain drops as I began to clip.

The sudden movement startled me. I thought it must

be a fox come in from the field down at the back of the house.

Sophie looked dishevelled, desperate. 'Please! I only want to talk.'

'How did you get in?'

'Climbed the wall. Didn't notice there was broken glass cemented on top.' She held out bleeding hands.

'I saw the police car leaving. Then someone shut the gates.'

'Why are you here?'

She seemed not to focus, but to go on with her explanation of how she got in, as if that gave her some rights.

'The summerhouse has a tap. You better rinse your hands. There could be glass.'

'I don't care.'

But she followed me anyway.

I tried the door. Locked. The set of keys hung at my waist. I was in charge of all I surveyed in Ma's absence. But there was no key for the summerhouse. Granville used not to lock it. I tried under the stone by the door. No key.

We walked to the fast-flowing stream. She dipped her hands in the water, her blood washing over the pebbles.

'You'd better leave. I'll open the gate.'

'No!' She jumped up from the stream and grabbed my wrist. 'I have to talk to you.'

I shook her off. 'I'm not allowed to talk to you. It's against the law for me to talk to you. I'm a witness.'

'You?' Her look, her words accused me. 'It was you Clutterbuck spoke to?'

'Yes.'

'Then one of you is lying. Dad had nothing to do with it.

He was at home all the time, with me. I swear it. I've told the police.'

'If you don't want to be in more trouble, get out of here.'

'How can we be in more trouble? Why did you say that about my dad when it's not true? He'd never shoot at a man. He'd never rob a bank.'

'Mr Clutterbuck named him. I shouldn't be telling you this. You shouldn't be here.'

'And did Mr Clutterbuck say, "Barney Moran shot me."? Because if he did say that, he told a damn lie. I know you shouldn't speak ill of the dead, but if he said that, he'll rot in hell for eternity.'

'He named him.'

'Named him? If he did, he was regretting on his deathbed that he'd done him a bad turn.' The absurd thing to have come out was that Dad had kept his bait worms in an empty vault space. That was why he was sacked.

'Mr Clutterbuck said, "Doorman", as clearly as I'm speaking to you.'

'Doorman? Doorman, doorman. What does that prove? He could have been saying the killer came to the door. The man at the door.'

'He wrote a letter M.'

'That could mean anything.'

'Your father has confessed his guilt.'

'You don't know what it's like to be held in a cell hour after hour, freezing cold, not allowed to sleep, denied a drink of water until someone's inclined to give you one. If a person isn't strong, they'd plead guilty to twenty murders in the hope of ending the torment. Dad's not strong.

He was wounded in the war. He never tells anyone, and won't have it spoken of, but he has a plate in his head.'

'No one would admit murder and bank robbery if it wasn't true.'

'If he stole your precious money, why would we sit there, waiting for the police to come? We've no house now, no furniture, no money, no food, no hope. Do you think if my dad had robbed a bank he would have waited to be arrested, left us to starve? We're living in a flea pit of a second-hand shop on the Bank, with a grand view of Zion Recreation Park. We're watched and followed. Do you know why? Because the police believe that if I'm desperate I'll go dig up the treasure. Well the coppers are telling themselves a fairy tale, and you started it.'

'He has an accomplice. Just because you don't know about it . . .'

Sophie flung herself at me, knocking me off balance, shoving me against a tree. 'You're a liar. You're all liars. You want my dad to hang. Whoever got in had a key.'

I was bigger than Sophie but couldn't match her fury. I tried to reason with her. 'He worked for the bank for years. He knew it inside out. He could have stolen a key.'

'He didn't, he didn't.'

Sophie's eyes looked mad. She started to hit me. 'Liar, bloody liar.'

I hit her back, and only when I brought the secateurs to her throat did she stop. Her arms fell to her sides. I had never seen anyone look so soaked in misery. But something about her scared me.

'Get the hell out of our garden or I'll have you thrown out.'

I was trembling. Sophie was too. The fight had entirely gone out of her. She followed me to the side gate.

'He didn't do it,' Sophie said one final time as I shut the gate behind her.

'Stay away from us.' It didn't seem a strong enough thing to say. I felt afraid of her, and afraid for her. I don't know where the words came from, but I yelled after her. 'If I see you once more, you'll be up on a charge of trespass and attempted murder.'

For a long time, I stood by the wall, shaking. Of all the girls I'd met in all my life, why did I have to make such good friends of those two? Horror. Her blood was on me, on my hands, on the sleeves and front of Ma's gardening jacket.

Bobbing down by the swollen stream, I washed my hands and splashed my face and throat. I'd lost Ma's favourite secateurs.

I set the greenery on the hall table, feeling too drained of energy to bother with a vase. Let someone else see to it. I locked the front door and walked slowly up to my room, shutting the door behind me.

My hair was full of twigs and leaves. I sat brushing it, wondering should I report Sophie to the police. I didn't have the heart.

From somewhere, for the first time, a nagging doubt crept into my mind.

What if I was right in my very first thought that evening in the infirmary? What if Clarence Clutterbuck was not accusing the commissionaire but saying that if there had been a doorman, the break in would not have taken place.

I couldn't say that to Pa. He'd pooh-pooh the idea straight away.

Theo. I must talk to Theo. He would know what to do.

I waited in the lane, keeping close to the wall. Light shone from the Wintertons' dining-room window. Mrs Winterton set something on the table. The lane smelled of damp leaves. A drop of rain fell on the back of my neck.

Theo would come up from town on the tram, but I daren't go to meet him at the terminus, for fear of being caught in the car headlights as Jack Massey drove Pa and Granville home from the office.

It seemed an age before I heard Theo's jaunty footsteps on the cobbles. He walked briskly, like a man who had far to go.

Suddenly, I felt silly, like some schoolgirl hanging about on a corner. I moved away from the wall just as he came into view.

'Boo!'

He laughed, pretending to be scared, then took me in his arms. 'Lydia, darling, what are you doing in the lane in this chill? You'll catch a cold.'

'Then hold me.' A shudder ran through me, thinking of Sophie's hands – how cold they were, and of her desperation.

'What is it?'

'I've had a beastly day.'

'What darling? Not your ma . . . ?'

'No. We've had no news of her yet. It was the police, Sergeant Dickinson. Moran has pleaded guilty.'

'Yes, I heard. We get the gossip, being in the Town

Hall. But I'm just glad you won't have to go to court. That'd be horrid.'

The car lamps made a blaze of light. Theo took my hand. 'Come on. I'll walk you back.'

'It's not just that. Theo, I have to talk to someone. That Moran girl came today. Sophie.'

'I hope you told the sergeant.'

'No. Theo, she says I'm wrong. That he didn't do it.'

'She's bound to say that. Who could bear it, a murderer for a father.'

'But what if she's right and I was wrong?'

'Naturally you're upset. But all you did was tell the police what poor Clutterbuck said. They did the rest. You've nothing to reproach yourself with.'

'Are you sure?'

'Positive.' He hugged me close.

'I'll be glad when this is all over.'

'So will I, for your sake.'

'I'd better go, Theo. That was Pa's car.'

'I know. Look, I get off work early tomorrow. Shall I come round?'

'Meet me in the summerhouse. I don't want Pa getting all het up again. He's impossible just now, with Ma in the nursing home.'

'All right. I'll be there about half four. That'll give us at least half an hour before Mr Thackrey gets home.'

'Don't walk me back. But I'd better go now. Pa will be sending out search parties.'

I tried to go in quietly but he called to me the moment I stepped into the hall.

'Lydia!'

'Yes, Pa?'

He stood by the fireplace. 'So it was you, in the lane, canoodling with Winterton.'

'We weren't canoodling.'

'We caught you in the headlights. Is that what you do, wait for him by the wall?'

'I needed to talk to him.'

'Talk? That's not what we called it in my day.'

I wanted to shout at him that he'd no business catching us in his headlights. My cheeks burned with rage.

'We had your word. You told your Ma it was all over between you.'

'It was.'

'Was? Was?' He came towards me, his face filled with rage. For a moment I thought he would strike me. 'Don't you think I have enough on my plate? Fears for your Ma. Clutterbuck's funeral to arrange. The bank's reputation to rescue. And now you. We've found you a perfect match and the minute your mother's out of the house you're running wild.'

'I'm not running wild. Theo and I . . .'

'Stop right there! Forget Theo. Theo is not in a position to marry, and I'm disappointed that after giving me his word he has so little backbone that all you have to do is chase after him and he lets himself be dragged in.'

I started to protest, but he held up his hand. 'Enough!' He poured himself a whisky. 'Lydia, Lydia. You're in a fragile state. Theo Winterton's the last person you should be confiding in, just because he's nearby.' He took a sip from the glass. 'We can't upset your mother with this.'

'We were talking, that's all.'

The telephone rang. Both of us moved to answer it at the same moment, but it stopped.

In the hall, Granville gave the number, then paused and said, 'Yes I'll get him.'

He came into the study. 'Pa! It's the call you've been waiting for.'

Pa put down his glass and hurried to the phone.

Granville picked up the glass and drank it down. He poured another whisky saying, 'Well isn't your Ma clever, Lydia. She's had another boy.'

But the baby wasn't due. I felt a shiver of dread and ran into the hall just as Pa put down the phone.

He said, 'I'm going across to the nursing home.'

'Can I come?'

'No. And you don't leave this house until I give permission. Not for any reason whatsoever.'

'How is she?'

'Not well. So I won't be telling her about your capers. I don't want to upset her.'

He was gone.

I slumped in Pa's chair. It was too bad. When would I get to see Ma and the baby? What if she never came home?

Granville smirked. 'Well, well, now you know. Now you know how it feels to be out of favour.' He poured another whisky and drank it down. 'Want a tot?'

'No.'

'Of course, Lydia my dear, you won't stay out of favour quite as long as I do. Your oh so fertile dam will squirm you back in.'

'Don't you dare speak about my mother like that.'

'No offence meant. Only she does seem determined to swizzle me out of my inheritance by supplying a new line of male offspring.'

'Granville, why are you always so nasty?'

'Am I? That's a pity. Because you are not nasty. You look quite lovely, even though you've had a telling-off. And I can't say I'm sorry it's ended in tears between you and the parson's son. He wasn't a good match.'

I wouldn't rise to the bait. 'If you say so.'

'Oh, I do.'

He came so close I could smell the whisky on his breath. 'How about you and I join forces?' He chuckled.

'What do you mean?'

'No need to look like that. I'm not talking in *that* way — though we're not related, there'd be no bar on it.'

'You've never shown any sign of wanting to join forces with me before. You were horrible to me from the moment I came into this house.'

'That's not true. We had our moments. Though we did get off to a bad start. Think about it from my point of view. I got a letter at school to say Pa was getting married and I'd have a new sister. But that's ancient history. We could put it all behind us.'

He went back to the drinks cabinet and poured himself another whisky. 'You can't refuse to toast our new little brother. Sherry?'

'I'll have a brandy, please.'

'My, my, you do take your tellings-off to heart.'

'It's not just that. It's the whole business, my statement and all that. The sergeant was here again today.'

'I know,' he said, sympathetically. 'It's a bad business.

I bet you wish you'd never gone to see Clutterbuck that night.'

He turned on the Tiffany lamp, and switched off Pa's reading light. 'Sounds as if you could have done with a brandy a few hours ago. Top up?'

I shook my head. 'Steady on. Pa will notice.'

'He might notice the whisky, not the brandy. So he won't blame you. It'll be me in the dog house again. I think that's why he sometimes leaves me out.'

'Out of what?'

'That's just it. Something's going on. You probably know more than I do.'

'Me? I know nothing.'

'But you could if you wanted. Ma must know. Something's going on at the bank.'

'The bank will be the last thing on Ma's mind just now.'

He pulled his chair closer to mine. 'You never told me. What did Clutterbuck say that night? His exact words.'

Suddenly, I was back in the room. The nurse had switched on the light. Such a harsh light. I sat by the bedside. Mr Clutterbuck opened his eyes.

'He said your name. Granville.'

For a moment neither of us spoke. The fire crackled.

'Did you tell the police that he said my name?'

'No.'

'Thanks.' He spoke softly.

'What do you mean, thanks? It slipped my mind. I'd assumed he thought you were with me, or something like that.'

'That's probably exactly it. What else did he say?'

I told him.

'Poor Lydia. It's been a real strain for you.'

'Yes.'

'Lydia, Lydia.' He was out of his chair and kneeling in front of me. 'Poor, sweet Lydia. You've been in the woods. You smell of leaves and autumn and . . .'

His head was in my lap. 'Dear Lydia. We'd be a good pair, you and me. With your brains and my flair, we could reinvigorate the dynasty in more ways than one.'

Pa's chair is on casters. I pushed it back. Granville sprawled on the carpet, spilling his whisky.

I left him there and went upstairs.

Sophie

If the police were as sure of Dad's guilt as they pretended, they wouldn't have made an appeal for witnesses. We sat by May's fire. Rosa read from the evening paper.

'Police wish to speak to any person or persons who found themselves in the vicinity of Park Lane or Bond Street, Leeds on the evening of Wednesday 16th October. In particular, they appeal for contact from persons who may have seen a man of middle height in the vicinity of Thackreys' Bank at about seven p.m. The man was thought to be wearing a dark topcoat, cap, and knitted scarf.'

May pushed her feet closer to the fire, big toes thrusting through holes in her plaid slippers. She gave a scornful grunt. 'Man of middle height! Could be anyone. Topcoat! Who wouldn't wear a topcoat at this time of year, if he possessed one. Knitted scarf. That only accounts for about half the population.'

Rosa lowered the newspaper. In that moment, she and I exchanged a look. We each knew what the other thought.

Dad had confessed because he had somehow got it into his head that Danny robbed the bank and shot Clutterbuck, safe in his cast-iron alibi of having gone to Liverpool and set off for New York days before it happened. Somehow, Dad had convinced himself that Danny had not sailed.

Only when we were safely out of May's hearing, lying in the junk-filled attic room, could we speak of it. We lay side by side, each of us with one foot on the bed warmer.

Rosa said, 'That would explain why Dad took the blame. To protect Danny.'

Every time either of us breathed too deeply, the bed creaked. I said, 'But why? Why would he have jumped to the conclusion that Danny hadn't left the country?

Her foot tapped the bed warmer, making a tune on the springs. 'I'm trying to think. Something about Danny's last visit. He seemed so sure. Do you remember? Said he'd send for us within the year.'

I switched feet on the bed warmer. 'That was just his bravado.'

We tried to remember every detail of that night, piecing it together. Rosa remembered that Dad warned Danny against doing anything silly. I recalled one of us asking Danny what ship he would work on. Danny had answered 'White Star.'

We inched the bed warmer up to unfreeze our legs.

Rosa said, 'Dad knew White Star wasn't a ship, but a shipping company. Because when the postcard arrived he said, "Now he tells us what ship." Was it odd that Danny didn't know what ship to name until he got to Liverpool, or is that what happens when someone signs on as a stoker?'

I said, 'It might or might not be odd, but if that's what Dad thinks . . .'

Rosa sighed. 'If, say, for instance, Danny *didn't* sail that Saturday, then the police could be after *him*.'

'But if he did sail, and Dad knew that for sure, then he'd take back his confession. We have to go to Liverpool Rosa, to the White Star line. Find out whether Danny sailed.'

'Will they tell us? And how do we do that? I'm followed to and from Montague Burton's. You're spied on when you light candles in church.'

As soon as the Penny Bank opened the next morning, I was through the door. I'm sorry, Mam, I said in my head as I signed the withdrawal form.

The clerk remembered me. He spoke quietly. 'Won't you just leave threepence in?' His long little fingernail had grown again. 'Keep your account open for better days.'

'No thank you.' I couldn't imagine better days. Couldn't imagine beyond that day.

He counted out the balance, rubber stamped the account book closed and passed it back to me.

Outside, the raincoat man who followed me watched from across the street. I walked back to Zion Street and through the shop door. No doubt Mr Raincoat would be in the bank, asking the clerk whether Sophie Moran had deposited the proceeds of a robbery. Even so, I took no chances. Someone else could be watching.

May's side window opened onto the passage that led to the yard at the back, and the lavatories. I climbed through, followed by Rosa. Once in the yard, I hitched myself up by the lavatory drain pipe, onto the roof and over the wall into the yard at the back, across the next wall into Zion Square, and through the passage onto Cavalier Street. Rosa followed, muttering about the filth.

The train drew out of the station, away from the town. Through the train window, the sight of Armley Gaol on its high hill gave us an unexpected shock, like a snowball down your back. It looked for all the world like a fortress. I imagined Dad in his lonely cell. For his sake, we must do this right. If we could prove to him that Danny had sailed on the appointed day, at the appointed time, Dad would give up his mad notion of taking the blame.

In spite of everything, the sight of the smoky towns and tall chimneys gave me hope. Names that were so familiar of places we had never seen took shape on railway platforms. Bradford. Hebden Bridge. Halifax. Todmorden. Places to escape to, once we'd helped clear Dad's name. We would begin again somewhere else, find work in mills or a factory. Muck, steam, smoke and clatter screeched of work and a new way to earn a living. Life went on everywhere. It would start afresh for me, Rosa and Dad. After we came through the nightmare, nothing would ever again seem terrible.

Rosa sat on the opposite seat, her back to the engine, looking out of the window. Her frown deepened. She was dressed in a dark skirt and green cape with tiny matching hat. The only sign of her climb over lavatories and walls was a scuff on her shoe.

We had agreed that she would do the talking at the shipping office. I felt sure if she played this part as well as she played Princess Nadya in the works drama group, we would have no difficulty finding out what we needed to know. We neared Liverpool.

As we got off the train in the cavernous station, she said, 'The thing about being in a play is you know what the other characters will say. Real life is different. What if no one wants to tell us anything? That's what people are like.'

The size of the buildings by the docks overwhelmed us. It was how we'd imagined the pyramids or Houses of Parliament. It wasn't just the size, but that there were so many huge buildings, all in a row, shouting their own importance.

A crooked old man with a walking stick directed us to the White Star building, raising his stick and pointing when we couldn't make out a word he said.

As we walked through the door, Rosa drew herself up to her great height of five feet two inches and glided towards the youngest clerk. He was a pale-faced young man with dark hair and Irish eyes.

We took the chairs opposite him, and he thought we had come to book a passage on a liner. I wished!

Rosa explained that our brother, always a worry to his mother, had signed on as a stoker with the *Britannic*, bound for New York. Though we'd received a postcard from Liverpool, since then – not a word. She took out her hanky and lowered her lashes. Although rebellious, our brother was such a reliable fellow in other ways, always true to his word. We feared some accident had befallen him, and perhaps he had not sailed after all, or not returned with the ship.

The clerk looked about him. 'I'm really only here to take bookings, but I'll see what I can do. I'm on a late dinner hour, and it will be in five minutes. If you wait outside . . . Let me take a note of his name and the sailing date.'

We waited by the broad stone steps for ten or fifteen minutes.

He came out smiling, confirming that Danny had sailed. 'And don't take it amiss that he didn't come back on the return voyage. Fellers jump ship, for a bit of adventure in New York. He'll be back. Tell your mam not to fret.'

'You daft bats,' May said, when we told her where we had been. 'You wasted good brass going all the way to Liverpool to find out summat we knew already. How much did that set you back?'

I left Rosa to explain, as I wrote to Dad. It took a long time to get the words right.

Dear Dad,

How are you feeling? We hope we will see you soon and that we will all be together again before very long. It was shocking to be in the Bridewell but even more shocking for you not to come out at the same time as we did. When the police find the person who really committed the crime they will let you go. We have talked about what to do then, and we think it a good idea to go somewhere else and have a fresh start. If you agree, that will be something to look forward to. Rosa and I went on the train to Liverpool and passed a few towns that look busy. It could be worth thinking about a new place where we might all find work.

Why did we go on a train? you ask. We wanted to see whether Danny arrived safely in New York, and whether we could find an address for him. We went to the White Star shipping company. A helpful young clerk there told us that Danny was on board the *Britannic* as a stoker when it sailed from Liverpool on Saturday 12th October, arriving in New York the following Thursday, and he did not come back on that ship. So we will just have to wait for a postcard or letter from him.

In the meantime we imagine him doffing his cap to the Statue of Liberty, and admiring the Empire State Building.

Dad, we know you didn't do that crime. It says in the paper that the police are looking for the stolen money. We feel sure once they find the money they will find the true culprit and you will be set free.

With lots of love from your daughters

PS As you will see from the address, we have moved in with May so do not worry about us. I go every day to Tab Street to see if Danny has written.

It started to rain before we got to City Square, and didn't let up all the way along Wellington Street. We walked arm in arm, under our one umbrella. It was further than we expected. Our feet, legs, the hems of our skirts were wet through. Either us or the rain kept changing direction and great gusts of it caught us out and sprayed our faces.

The prison dominated the horizon, rising through mist

and drizzle like a castle from a horror story. Silence hung so thickly around the building, I felt almost able to touch it.

I rang the bell on the gate.

After what seemed a long time, a man in dark trousers, jacket and cap emerged from the gatehouse. He walked slowly towards us.

'We're here with a letter for my father, Barney Moran. And we'd like to see him, please.'

The man held out his hand for the letter. 'I'll pass it on.'

'And can we see him, please sir?' Politeness seemed in order. It might work.

'No. There's a visiting day, and a pass is issued — requested by the prisoner.'

'Then could we come on the visiting day? I'm sure my dad . . . '

'He's in for murder and bank robbery. There won't be any visits for him. Not for . . . ' He shifted his weight. 'He's newly in. It's sometimes weeks or months before a person gets a visit.'

The man retreated into his gatehouse and closed the door.

Rosa tugged at my sleeve. 'Come on. No use stopping here.'

'How can they? It's not fair. What can we do?'

'I should've told you,' Rosa said. 'The Scholar went to the police station to ask about seeing him, and talked to someone he knows on the council. There's nothing anyone can do.'

'But there must be. And why didn't you tell me? Why didn't anybody tell me?'

'Because . . . because you don't listen. You always think we can make things right.'

'We can. We must.'

Rosa sighed. 'Let's walk round the prison. Who knows, he could be looking from a window and see us. At least then he'd know we were here, that we care.'

We walked the perimeter of the prison, trying to see, but the walls were too high.

The rain had stopped. Rosa shook the umbrella, and we began the long walk back. A thought struck me. 'If we find the money, then we find the person who did it.'

'And how are we supposed to do that?'

'You'll find it. You can find lost things.'

She sighed. 'If the person who lost a thing asks me, then I can concentrate, and see in my mind's eye where they lost it, and how, and if it's still there. But who can ask me about the bank money? It wasn't lost. It was thieved.'

'I'm asking you.'

'Sophie! I'm trying to tell you . . . that's not . . . I can't . . .'

'Well I wish you would tell me.'

A tram car came trundling up behind. 'Have we got enough to take us to the terminus from here?' Rosa asked.

'Yes. Just.'

We climbed on the tram. I paid for our tickets while Rosa found a seat at the back.

'I'll try to tell you,' Rosa said. 'Only don't interrupt.'

'All right.'

'You see. You've interrupted already.'

I said nothing.

After a long time, Rosa spoke. 'Do you remember when

217

I was little and got scarlet fever? They took me into the fever hospital. I always knew when Mam or Dad came to see me. No one was allowed in, because we were contagious. The mothers would come and stand outside. Children would go to the window. I wasn't allowed out of bed because of being too poorly. When Mam came, the picture of her would come into my mind. I knew whether she wore a coat, or a shawl. I knew if she carried a basket.'

'How did you know you were right? Sorry, sorry. I didn't mean to interrupt.'

'I just knew. Then, as I got better, I would see her first in my mind's eye, before going to the window. There she would be, exactly as I saw her. That was how it began. I thought everyone could do it.'

'But the finding of things?'

'One day, Mam was telling me something, through the window. That she'd lost her tram fare. I saw her shape the words, lost my fare. And I knew she had a hole in her pocket and the money had slipped into the lining of her coat. She'd already checked but I pointed, and made her do it again, and there it was – slid round to the back of the lining.'

I waited until I was sure she didn't want to say more. 'Rosa, we have to find that money and clear Dad's name.'

'How? I can't get any pictures about it, none at all.'

'Then we'll go to the bank. We'll stand by Thackreys' Bank. That damn building is alive. I've always known it from the first time I saw it. The bank'll want its money back. The bank will ask you to find the money.'

Lydia

At breakfast, Pa was stony.

I poured myself a cup of tea. 'What time shall I visit Ma?'

He got up from the table, which was a signal for Granville to bolt his last slice of toast. Pa marched into the hall, calling back to me, 'She doesn't want to see you. Poor Phoebe is so sensitive she'll know at once what you've been up to. You'll need to earn back our respect by behaving yourself.'

How dare he. Sometimes I wish she'd never married him. He didn't care who heard him either. Granville took the opportunity to look superior. I swear Nurse Dorothea was listening from the landing.

I didn't give him the satisfaction of an answer.

Not only was I suffering because of loving the 'wrong' man, but now the canny and uncanny sisters had decided to plague me.

Fortunately, the letter from Rosa came by second post and I saw it first. I took it to my room after breakfast and sat on the window seat.

Dear Lydia

Please excuse me writing to you, so soon after Sophie called to see you. She is sorry if she alarmed you but we are deeply upset that our dad is falsely accused. He had his arm twisted into confessing.

Do you remember the time I found your brooch? Also my knowing Mr Thackrey was in his study when you thought he was golfing. I have some ability in that line. As a rule we do not speak of it outside the family. Mam never liked me to do it as she said it diddled St Anthony out of a job. I would not let on to anyone at Montague Burton's where I worked as a machinist. My workmates would have plagued the life out of me to tell fortunes and suchlike.

Things are very bad for us. I tried going back to my job. I put up with stares and whispers. I am not one to mind being stared at. People always stare because of my hair. Also I was stared at because of starring in the factory amateur dramatics. This was different. Girls from the factory and the offices, and the cutters and pressers too – everybody rubber-necked me. I could not bear it. Some came to talk to me and I know it was so they could say they know me and boast about speaking to the killer's daughter. I could not bear to go back.

Sophie nattered me to see if I could locate the missing money. I did not feel able to do it. Usually I find

something a person has asked me to find, or I am close
to it. The bank's money was not lost but stolen. No
one knows the thief. Sophie said the bank itself might
help. So I stood outside and in the porch. I got a few
funny looks but fortunately no one turned me away.

A picture came into my mind of a hand holding an
attaché case, just that picture. Another picture came
into my mind of the grounds of your house and a hut
not far from the stream. I do not remember seeing
that hut on our visit for the garden party, or when we
came to ask for Dad's job back, but I can tell you that
in my picture, it was shaped like a giant threepenny
bit. I saw a trap door on the floor of that place. That is
all I can say.

We went to the Bridewell and told what I had seen
to the sergeant on the desk. He said we were
slandering the Thackreys by hinting that they robbed
their own bank, which we did not say. If I am right
that the money is on your premises, that may lead to
the true culprit.

Please help us if you can. We do not know who
else to ask. No one will listen.

Yours sincerely

Rosa Moran

I screwed up the letter and flung it across the room. Why
shouldn't she see an octagonal hut? Sophie would have told
her I tried to open the summerhouse door to get to the tap
after she cut her hands climbing the wall.

*

The summerhouse smelled of cricket pads and old football boots. Granville mustn't have been there for ages. It wasn't the most salubrious place to be trysting with Theo, but it would have to do. I wouldn't unlock the side gate until nearer our meeting time. One of those mad girls might decide to turn up.

Propping the door open, I let in some air. I brought a cover from the house, to lay over the mouldy cushions, along with plenty of candles. Of course it was cold, but who cared about that? Then I spotted the paraffin heater. Why not try it? It looked simple enough. I struck a match, and burned my fingers trying to touch the match to the right spot. On a second try, the heater stunk into life. I could see the attraction the hut had held for Granville, a secret place, a private place, not seen from the house.

I shut the summerhouse door and left the heater to warm the place. There would be time for a bath, and to change, and to make myself beautiful.

When I climbed from the bath, wrapped in towels, some devil got into me. I went to Ma's room, telling myself I'd use her dressing table. Ma has gorgeous silk lingerie, bought in Paris, a slinky camisole and cami knickers. The matching suspender belt was more than a little on the large side, but I could make it fit with a discreet safety pin in the back. I certainly didn't want the corsets. Silk stockings. Never worn. Well I would wear them.

The mirror liked me. No wonder Theo wanted me, as I wanted him. I touched myself in the places his hands had strayed. But always he had touched me outside my dress. One day all that would change and there'd be no holding back.

Of course the only thing to wear was an everyday skirt and sweater. Anything else would set the dread Dorothea's antennae twitching, ready to tittle-tattle to Pa. *Didn't Lydia look a treat earlier? I wonder where she was going?*

A less romantic place would have been hard to find. The hut was stifling, and stunk of paraffin. I re-lit the candles, turned down the heater and by the time I went to the gate, there he was. Great, beautiful Theo, kissing me the moment the gate shut behind him, holding hands as we walked along the path.

He slid the ring on my finger and for a few minutes, all we did was kiss.

Then it all came out. Pa being horrible. My doubts. How Clarence Clutterbuck said Granville's name. About Rosa's letter.

Of course Theo had to be maddeningly reasonable. He saw Pa's point. What a lot he had on his mind and so on. 'Let's not rush, Lydia darling. We know we're going to be together. Don't let's give them the ammunition of being able to say you're too young. And as for that letter from the Moran girl, well if there is a hidden trap door, let's find it!'

He made me laugh, going round on his hands on knees feeling at the strips of carpet that had been flung down at different times to keep the place warm. 'No! No trap door.' He came to sit beside me. 'Try to stop worrying, darling. Those girls shouldn't be pestering you. Who wouldn't feel sorry for them? But it's not your fault.'

And one of us must have made the first move – the kiss, the touch, that took us farther into our love-making than we had ever strayed. Our clothes just seemed to get in the way. My shoes, sweater, skirt lay in a pile, along with his jacket and trousers. Finally, he lay on top of me, moving, sighing, and I drew him close to me.

'You drive me mad, Lydia. I can't tell you how much I want you.'

'How will we ever wait, Theo? It's so unfair. There's Ma having babies and I'm supposed to behave like some virtuous young schoolgirl.'

We lay side by side.

'The time'll soon pass.' He ruffled my hair. 'It won't be so very long till we don't have to hold back. Around Easter, I'll have my six months' trial period behind me. I know my pay's nothing by Thackrey standards, but it's enough for ordinary mortals. That's when we'll stake our claim to a future.'

I snuggled close, feeling so happy, knowing our lives would be perfect.

Reluctantly, he stood up and began to dress, pulling on his trousers.

The door flew.

'Excuse me!' It was Granville. He closed the door quickly.

'Oh no!' Theo groaned. 'I'm sorry, I'm so sorry, Lydia.'

I stood up quickly and pulled on my skirt. 'What does he want?'

'He probably saw the candlelight.'

'You can't see the hut from the house.'

'Perhaps he was looking for you. It is getting late. Let me walk you back to the house. Let's speak to your pa now.'

'No. He's probably at the nursing home anyway. And I don't believe Granville will give us away.' I tried to sound more sure than I felt.

The paraffin heater had conked out. Theo put the cloak

around my shoulders and hugged me. 'I love you. I'd marry you tomorrow, or yesterday.'

'I know. Go now. Give me five minutes to gather my wits.'

One of my earrings was missing.

I shook the cover from the cushions and the lost earring rolled under the paraffin heater. I pushed the heater away, bent down and clipped the earring back. There was a protrusion under the carpet, shaped like a ring. I turned back the floor covering. It gave me a strange sensation to see the trap door in the floor.

'Theo!' I called from the doorway, but he was gone.He'd be halfway up the lane.

The ring of the trap door felt cool and light as I pulled it open. Something lay inside. A brown attaché case.

I half fell, half sat back on the cushions, as if I'd been jolted by an electric current. Could Rosa have been right? Or had the Morans hidden it there – as the last place anyone would look – then took fright and tried to shift the blame. What better place to hide something than in the grounds of its owner?

But perhaps this was nothing. Granville used to save cigarette cards as a boy.

The catches flicked open at a touch.

Bundles of notes, fastened with strips of brown paper glued at the edges, seem to spring to life like a Jack-in-the-box. It was not just money. I brought a candle closer, to take a good look. There were promissory notes on legal paper, signed by Granville, and other signatures, not legible. He must have made loans on his own authority. Yet he hadn't the authority to make loans.

The door opened.

'Theo! Thank God you're . . .'

It was Granville, staring, unblinking. I snapped the case shut.

He strode towards me. His face told it all. He began to blink rapidly. I could hear my breathing, with a kind of panic to it, coming faster and faster.

'It was you. When Mr Clutterbuck said "Granville", he was telling me who robbed the bank, who shot him.'

'That's ridiculous. Why would I need to break in?'

'It was someone with a key. It was you.'

'He named Moran,' Granville snapped.

'He named you. You've lent money you'd no right to lend. It was about that wasn't it? You didn't want to be found out before the audit.'

'Oh the audit. So now you know there's going to be an audit. Aren't you the clever one? When was I to be told? Eh?'

A spluttering candle burned suddenly brighter in its pool of wax, lighting up his contorted face. And I knew.

'You killed Clarence Clutterbuck.'

'No, no I swear I didn't.'

'Pa has to know.'

'Don't threaten me.'

'I'm not threatening. The truth will have to come out.'

'Will it? Which truth? The truth that you set up a little love nest in a garden shed? Pa will love that.'

'We're engaged. We love each other.'

'The truth that Theo was giving you a good seeing to.' He was looming over me, his face close to mine. 'Enjoy it did you?'

He made a grab for me. I dodged and made for the door, but stumbled over the attaché case. He was at the door before me, blocking my way.

'Think about it, Lydia. There's too much at stake, too much to lose.'

'For you.'

'For you. Mr Sherry Face Reverend Winterton will be kicked out of his living if it comes out that his only begotten son is ravishing the lovely Lydia.'

'Get out of my way.'

'Too much to lose altogether.' He had my wrist, twisting my arm. 'Listen to me before you go blabbing. Don't think I can't do some blabbing of my own. Your mother was a whore. A high class whore, granted. Don't tell me you hadn't worked that out. Why do you think your father never gets a mention? He could've been any visitor to her salon. I've found out things about your mother that would make Pa divorce her tomorrow.'

'Liar!'

In a sudden jerking movement he twisted my arm up my back, shoving my face into the door, his body against me, pinning me so I couldn't move, could only kick at his shins.

'Like mother, like daughter.' His free hand was up my skirt, tearing at the silk, his fist pounding into me. I screamed as he tried to get his fist inside me.

'Granville let go of me! Stop it! Don't.'

He thrust his fingers inside me. 'What's one more slice off a loaf? Don't tell me you don't like it. You love it. Admit it.'

He was fiddling with his clothes. That was my moment. I pulled free and shoved him, but not hard enough. He regained his balance, grabbed me and flung me backwards. My head struck the corner of the paraffin heater with a blow that made me so dizzy I couldn't see. When I struggled to get up, he was on top of me. I screamed for Theo.

'Theo can't help you.'

The cushion on my face stopped my breath. I was going to die, die with his fingers inside me. 'Oh yes you're ready all right. Thank you Theo Winterton!'

I must have passed out, unable to breathe. When I came to he was thrusting himself into me. 'Just like your mother with my Pa, always giving the come on. Admit it, admit your mother's a whore.'

He had let go of the pillow. I fought for breath.

'Say I'm better than him, say I'm a better man than Theo.'

No words would come, but I shook my head.

'Say it, my lovely, say it! I won't stop until you do.' His hands were on my throat. He kept on and on, pumping into me, trying his hardest to hurt me.

Theo had forgotten to take back the engagement ring. My thumb touched the ring on my left finger. If I could just go on touching that ring, I might live. It gave me the strength to try and push him off, to tear into his arm and try to get my nails into his face. He grabbed both arms, holding me down. When I tried to resist with my head, to bite at him, he brought his forehead sharply onto my nose, so that my eyes watered with pain, then everything turned black.

Only as he gave a cry, and then rolled off, did the dim hut come back into some kind of focus.

'God but you look a mess.' He straightened his clothes.

I lay as if paralysed.

He picked up the attaché case and left.

I wanted to scream or cry, but no sound would come. The last candle spluttered and died. After what seemed an age, I got up, felt for my cloak and pulled it around me. A shoe was missing. Couldn't find it. Gave up.

Through the gate, I saw the light in the Wintertons' house. Theo, why didn't you come?

Branches tearing at me, hard ground hurting, I stumbled back towards the house. Please God let no one see me come in. Let the door be unlocked. Don't let Pa be waiting, his study door open, to call me in and say, What time do you call this? Because I didn't know the time, or the day, or why or how this terrible thing had happened.

I slowly pushed the front door open. No sound. No light from the study. Hurry, make the stairs, bedroom, shut the door. After tonight I wouldn't stay here. I'd go away. Go to Penelope in Oxford, that would do. Penelope would find me somewhere. Get a job. Waitress. Shop girl. Anything. Until Theo and I could marry.

But Theo wouldn't want me now. Ma warned against taking the gilt off the gingerbread. Well, no gilt. No gingerbread. I ran the bath, wanting no bath salts, no Lily of the Valley, just water, hot as it could be.

I heard the car on the drive. Pa home. It was too late for him to come looking for me. At least he wouldn't see me. Anyone who looked at me would know my shame.

Ma, why did you have to pick now to go off having a baby, and what if you never come home? This damn Thackrey family would have done for both of us.

Wearing just my bathrobe, I climbed into bed, beyond

misery, feeling a kind of terror in case Granville came back. I propped pillows behind me and sat up, staring into darkness.

A tap on the door. I didn't answer. They would think me asleep and go away. Another tap. The door opened.

'Lydia?' Pa's voice, stern, concerned.

'What?'

'You're awake.'

'Yes.' As I feared, Ma had died. 'Is it Ma?' My heart stopped beating.

'No. Your Ma . . . there's no change. She's going to be all right.'

The door opened wider, but it wasn't Pa. In came Dorothea.

Light flooded the room. Too bright. I covered my eyes. Dorothea stood there, in her dressing gown, as if she had been summoned from her room.

'Mr Thackrey has asked me to speak to you.' Her icily polite voice cut me to the heart.

There was no sound from Pa, but I knew he was one the other side of the door.

'Go away. Leave me alone.'

'I'm afraid Mr Thackrey insists.' She came across to the bed. 'Something bad has happened to you, I think. An awkward thing to talk about.'

'Get out!'

'We need to know whether to call a doctor.'

'Leave me.'

'If you'll let me . . . I am a nurse.'

Quickly, she pulled back the covers. 'You have a bruise.'

I snatched the covers back. 'Don't you dare touch me.'

'I've seen enough. I can guess the rest. Don't blame yourself. You were foolish that's all. Men have urges that they can't control. Just because Theodore Winterton is a neighbour and . . .'

'Theo? You think Theo did this to me.'

'Your brother has told us. There's no point in denying it. Rest. I'll bring something to give you a good night's sleep. No steps will be taken till morning.'

'You're mad! Get out of my room! Get out!'

When the woman had gone, I slid from the bed and ran down the stairs to Pa's study. He sat by the fire, a tumbler half full of whisky in his hand.

'It wasn't Theo did this to me. It was Granville. Ask him.'

Pa was looking at me as if at any moment he might be sick. He took my left hand in his. 'And Granville gave you this ring I suppose? From a Christmas cracker.'

'I'm engaged to Theo.'

'Granville told me. Everything.'

'Did he tell you who robbed the bank? Ask him about the attaché case of cash and promissory notes. It was in the hut, under the trap door.'

Pa looked at me coldly. 'You're overwrought. Yes, there was an attaché case. Granville told me. Old cigarette cards. And I've seen the Wintertons. They're as shocked as I am at your carrying on. Theo has owned up.'

'Owned up to what?'

'You won't be seeing him again. As soon as your mother comes home, we'll arrange for you to go to Switzerland.'

Dorothea knocked on the door, 'Mr Thackrey. Is Miss Thackrey with you? I have the night draught.'

231

He took it from her. 'That'll be all, nurse. Thank you.'

My hands shook as I pushed away the steaming cup. 'No!'

'Then I shall call the doctor. And the police. If I do that, Theo Winterton's career is over before it's begun. Now take off that silly ring and give it to me.'

I took off the ring but slid it into my pocket. 'If Theo had been there this wouldn't have happened to me.'

'Granville saw you both in a state of undress.'

'Granville's a thief, a murderer, a liar, and he attacked me.'

'Drink this for God's sake, and calm down.'

If I drank, if I spoke calmly, he'd listen. The drink smelled sweet and bitter, like gin and almonds.

As he watched me drink, he said, 'You've disgraced this house.'

'Me? Me? It's your son. It was Granville did this to me.'

It was as if I talked to a statue. Granville was the one he believed. I was the liar. Nothing made sense. I didn't want to imagine what Pa had said to Theo. Dorothea was in the room again, helping me back up the stairs. Dizziness swept over me, as if I floated outside my own body, as if part of my brain had shrunk and rattled about in my head.

My head touched the pillow with a sinking sensation, as if I would slip into another world. But I made myself reach for the alarm clock. Made myself wind it. So hard to wind. He would not get away with it. In the morning I'd . . .

The alarm came from some faraway place. I reached out and clumsily knocked the clock to the floor. It stopped. Somewhere in the room was a movement. I couldn't look.

232

Head too heavy, unable to lift itself from the pillow. I lay there, eyes tight shut, trying to force my eyelids to move. The dim room came into focus, and out. The door clicked open, closed.

Must move, and could not remember why, not until I turned my head and grey light pierced the gap in the curtains. I hurt. Throat hurt, arms hurt, down there hurt. Then I remembered.

Theo. Must see Theo.

My clothes would not cooperate. The stocking toes didn't match my toes, the stocking heel in the wrong place. Boots. If I wore boots, no one would see drunken stockings. Picked long tweedy skirt and dark red sweater, no not red. It burned my hand. Picked brown, brown like the earth. A hat, pulled down and no need to comb my hair. The coat had change in the pocket. That would do. Just get to the tram stop.

My bedroom door was locked.

Sophie

The image of Dad standing in the dock comes back to me as I write. Until my dying day I will see his face and form, as clearly as my own reflection in a glass.

His dark hair looked as thick and wavy as ever. I had half expected it would have turned white. He wore a dark suit, the jacket hanging loosely on his shoulders. Dad stood erect, taller than the warders on either side of him. He glanced about. His face looked gaunt and drawn, but he gave a small sad smile that lit his eyes. He raised his hand just a fraction.

I raised mine. I hope I smiled.

It was the first time we had seen him since that Friday night when we were all taken to the Bridewell and he touched my toe with his across the floor of the paddy wagon.

A voice barked, 'The court will rise.'

We all stood. In walked the judge, in a flowing red robe and a white wig. He took his seat behind a heavy oak bench.

Dad remained standing when the rest of us sat down.

The same voice barked at him, 'Prisoner at the bar, how do you plead?'

He gave the wrong answer, missing off the first word. He said, 'Guilty.'

Before I had a chance to speak, May grabbed my arm and whispered. 'Shhh. They'll throw you out.'

The judge called on the counsel for the prosecution.

A short, portly man in black robe and white wig stood and bowed. He settled a pair of spectacles on his nose, and took his time with a sheaf of papers. When he spoke, his voice had a mean, hard edge.

'M'lud, I shall be brief. The case against the accused was outlined at committal proceedings and his statement is before your lordship. Therefore my remarks will be confined to an outline of events, the accused's motivation and opportunity, and new evidence which has come to light since committal proceedings.

'At about 7 p.m. on the evening of Wednesday 16th October, the accused, a former bank servant, went to Thackreys' Bank armed with a pistol, intending to commit a robbery. He knew the habits of the chief cashier, Mr Clarence Clutterbuck. He knew that Mr Clutterbuck would leave the bank at a little after 7 p.m. to attend his Masonic meeting. The accused forced Mr Clutterbuck back inside the bank and demanded money. He then shot him, leaving him for dead. The patrolling constable tried the door of the bank premises at 8.15 pm and found it to be unlocked. He called for assistance. An ambulance transported Mr Clutterbuck to the infirmary, where he died of his wounds the following day.

'In the matter of evidence, I present to your honour the coat worn by Mr Clutterbuck which still bears strands of the red knitted scarf owned by the accused and worn on the day of the crime – Deceased's coat, exhibit A; Accused's scarf, exhibit B.

'Since committal proceedings, new evidence has come to light, namely a canvas bag of the type used by soldiers. It contains four hundred pounds in used notes and was recovered from the grounds of the Anglers' Club, Burmantofts, where the accused was a member for six years. He has admitted hiding the money there. Additional money remains unrecovered. The accused insists he acted alone, although it is thought he is protecting an accomplice. I rest the prosecution's case, your lordship.'

My mouth felt dry. A great feeling of weakness clutched me, and a nausea. Let me not be sick.

Dad wouldn't look at me. He stared straight ahead. What had they done to him to make him agree to this pack of lies?

The judge called for the defence counsel to speak. I wanted to leap up myself, jump the bench, go to the front of the court and denounce them all. But at least someone was going to speak up for him.

Another man in black, white wig perched on his head, rose to his feet. For a moment I thought it was the same man, they looked so alike. But this one did not wear spectacles, and he spoke more softly.

'Your lordship, I speak for the defence. Barney Moran is a man previously of good character who served his country in the West Yorkshire Regiment during the Great War and was awarded the Silver War Badge. Following his dismissal from the bank, for a misdemeanour not involving dishonesty, he suffered hardship. He acted when driven to the edge of despair by his inability to provide for his family, namely his daughters, and by the emotional upset of seeing his only son depart these shores for America. His desire to follow that young man and to provide passage for himself and his daughters drove him to this desperate act. He is unable to account for the whereabouts of the remaining stolen money, but strongly denies having an accomplice. He expresses deep regret for his actions.'

Was I the only one who had come to see wrongs put right, to see him set free? I looked around. Rosa sat still as a statue, gazing at Dad, as if committing him to memory, like a part she had to learn. May was crying, tears flowing down her cheeks. People were writing in notebooks, there was a kind of excitement. I wanted to throw buckets of water on them, let in some sense.

I stood up and shouted, 'It's all made up. None of it's true. He didn't do it!'

The judge called for silence. An usher had his hands on my shoulders, waiting to see whether the judge would have me thrown me out.

May said, 'Shhh. It's no good.'

The judge called for silence.

My mouth was too dry to let more words come. Every inch of me strained to be nearer Dad, to touch him. If I could only be beside him, make him say he didn't do it.

237

The judge lowered his head and seemed to fumble for something. Even then, I hoped it would be a piece of last-minute evidence, to turn the verdict round. He placed a black cap on his head.

'Bernard Moran, you have pleaded guilty to murder. Taking into consideration the evidence against you, and the gravity of your crime, the sentence of this court is that you be taken from this place to a lawful prison, and thence to a place of execution and that you be there hanged by the neck until you be dead. Do you have anything to say?'

Dad moved his lips. No sound came. He tried again. 'I have nothing to say, your lordship.'

'May the Lord have mercy on your soul. Take the prisoner down.'

Dad gave us a last look. He raised his hand and attempted a brave smile. Then he was gone.

'The court will rise.'

I could not move. I didn't rise.

The judge was gone. People began to talk in low excited voices, and to walk from the court room, in a hurry to be somewhere.

Only we three stayed, without strength or purpose, until everyone else had gone.

Rosa said, 'They didn't give him your letter. He still thinks Danny did it.'

I jumped up. 'Come on! If we hurry, we might catch sight of him being taken back to the gaol.'

Three days after the trial, the letter came. My hands shook as I tore open the envelope, I hoped. And feared. I hoped it would tell me that the terrible mistake had come to light. There would be an appeal against Dad's conviction.

One glance at the sheet of paper dashed my hopes. A great heaviness filled me, except just below my ribs where I felt hollowed out, and the hole in the centre of me filled with loss, with hurt.

The prison name was printed starkly at the top of the page, with official printing on the back of the sheet. Dad had written in a minute hand, to fit as much as he could on the page.

My dear children, Sophie, Rosa – and Danny too, when he sees this letter, which may be some long time into the future, for I want you to put it in his hands personally, Sophie, and not let him have harsh tidings by post. Do not be upset for me. Try not to grieve too much. All of us must leave this world sometime and my time has come, far later than so many of my fallen comrades who made the sacrifice for those they loved. If what your mam believed is true, she will be waiting for me in heaven. Probably with a frying pan in her hand to bash me on the napper and say I was an idiot.

   Look to the future. Believe me, there was nothing I could do in the path of the steamroller that is the Leeds City Police, the judiciary and the gaolers that now take such good care of me night and day so that I might meet my fate in one piece.

(Here there were crossings out in a black pen)

I do not want you to visit me, but maybe that is selfish, because daft as I am there may be something you want to ask me or say to me and it would not be fair for me to deny that. Sophie, you are the one who could come and if you write back to me and say you want to come, then I will put in a request for a visit. But this is the truth, I would rather you remember me as I was.

Rosa, when you were in the hospital with Scarlet Fever, we were beside ourselves and every day one of us would go, your mam or me, and will you to be better, looking up at the window. But I expect it was your own strength brought you through because you were always so determined. Hold onto that determination. I will not see you again because you are too young to come into the prison and I would not want you to. But you are in my heart and if love can reach through prison walls, take my love.

Sophie, you are such a good girl, so strong and practical and were a great support and friend to your Mam. It grieves me that in so short a time you have lost your lovely mam and now your daft dad who you tried your best to keep on the right path. If it was not for your and your mam's sense, we would all have been in worse shape. I know you have it in you to come through whatever life throws at you after this. It cheers me to think of the time we went fishing together.

Danny, my first born, you did not always go the way we hoped but you are a lad full of life and so hold onto that. I see a lot of myself in you and it gives me

comfort to know you are out there in the wide world
and will make a much better fist of it than I ever did.
Do your best for your sisters. Make the most of the
chances you have. No one is perfect and I know for
sure there is more good in you than bad. Whatever
anyone says to the contrary, life is not too short to
improve your chess!

With love and blessings. Have no regrets my
treasured ones. Live well.

Your loving Dad

Of course I wanted to go see him. How could I not?

Lydia

If there'd been anywhere else for me to go, I wouldn't have knocked on that shop door. Sophie glared at me with contempt. Rosa looked as if she were thinking up some evil spell to cast.

The mouldy smell of second-hand clothes and shabby portable property took me back to childhood expeditions with Ada. She used to take me out and about with her, searching out props and costumes. It had seemed so glamorous then. The reality was different. The place was damp, dirty, jumping with fleas.

When Sophie and Rosa treated me with fury, I could stand that. It became unbearable when they looked to me as the person who might bring some last-minute reprieve to their father.

I would not have escaped from my room but Ma had asked to see me. Massey kept the car doors locked as we drove to the maternity home, as if I might jump out as the car slowed down on some street corner.

Ma looked so pale and ill, having lost a lot of blood.

'Don't look so worried, Lydia. I've come through worse than this. No intention of croaking just yet.'

So Pa had not told her anything of what had happened. I didn't say that Massey was waiting for me by the door of the nursing home, to take me back to Allerton House like some prisoner under guard.

She asked me to brush her hair. 'I'm so worn out, I can hardly raise my arms.'

As I brushed her hair gently, she said, 'Pa tells me you'll go to Switzerland after all. I'm so glad.'

When I kissed her goodbye, I went to peep at my new baby stepbrother, left by the back door and hitched a ride on a wagon going into Leeds. If Pa wouldn't believe me about Granville's guilt, Sergeant Dickinson would.

The desk sergeant at Millgarth Police Station asked me to wait. I was taken into a cramped room and sat at a wooden table across from a constable who licked his stubby pencil in between writing down my words. I explained about the trap door in the summerhouse, the attaché case, the money, the documents and Granville's fury at being found out.

'You mean he actually attacked you? Knocked you down?'

'Yes.'

He looked doubtful. Something in his voice, and the way he breathed like a tired horse, making a whistling sound through his nostrils, made it plain that he didn't believe me.

'Where is Sergeant Dickinson? I always see Sergeant Dickinson.'

'He's not on duty today, Miss. But if you'll just wait one moment.'

The man who came back with him wore plain clothes. His face was pockmarked as if he must have suffered from disease as a child.

'Miss, if you choose to withdraw your statement, and accuse a third party, that is up to you – though it's a serious matter. It will make no difference to the case against Moran. He's pleaded guilty. The evidence is strongly against him. All that matters in a court of law is evidence.'

'But the attaché case is evidence. I saw it.'

He cleared his throat and hesitated before he spoke. 'Are you sure that what you saw in that case wasn't just, well, a collection of cigarette cards.'

I felt as if I'd been hit in the chest. Pa had spoken to them before me. He would believe Granville at all costs. That made me a liar. And it made Theo the worst kind of violent abuser.

After that, there was nowhere for me to go, except the shop where I knew Sophie and Rosa lived. On the Bank, opposite the recreation ground.

They listened to what I had to say. For a long time, neither of them spoke. Rosa folded her arms and shut her eyes.

Sophie's voice came out like a whisper. 'They don't believe you for the same reasons they didn't believe me. They want Dad to be guilty. Nothing a girl says will make a difference, not unless it's what they want to hear.'

'Then they'll listen to Theo. I'll write to Theo.'

While I scribbled a note, May called a trusted urchin into

244

the shop and gave him instructions about where the letter should be delivered. To Theodore Winterton Esquire, Planning Office, Town Hall. And he must wait for a reply.

When the boy came back, May grabbed him and pulled him into the shop.

'Now you didn't give away where you've come from?'

He stood shivering with cold. 'No Mrs Manley.'

'And you never will?'

'No, Mrs Manley.'

'Then here's a threepenny bit. And you might just find a pair of boots in that there box that'll fit you, and a pair of socks an all.'

'Thank you, Mrs Manley.'

'Say it again, what the gentleman told you.'

'Miss Thackrey must meet him in the parish church today at four o'clock.'

The hand on the parish church clock crept towards four.

Theo would know what to do about the mistake made in my statement, about Granville and the money. The police and the solicitors would listen to him.

He'd know where I could hide and how we'd live, from that day forwards.

Sophie had come with me. She said. 'I'll make myself scarce. You won't want me in on it.'

The heavy rain of that morning turned the graveyard clay to squelching mud. I hated to walk across graves, not knowing who lay beneath my feet. Carefully as I could, I picked my way to the path and towards the church porch.

A new kind of panic rose inside me. I felt so different, didn't like myself at all, so why should he?

The church was deserted. It was good to be inside, out of the wind. Such a peaceful feeling came over me as I waited. For the first time, I knew for sure that everything would be all right once Theo came.

The church door opened and footsteps struck the flags. I turned to look.

Into the church came Jack Massey and Dorothea, walking towards me.

In an instant I rushed from the pew and made for the side door. Sophie stood by a gravestone. She called to me. I raced towards her. She grabbed my hand and we ran, ran through the graveyard, and the gate. We did not stop running until we reached the crowded market.

Sophie

Afterwards, I remembered in snatches that visit to Armley Gaol.Ringing the bell, producing the card authorising Sophie Moran to visit Bernard Moran. The long silent walk through prison grounds felt like moving through a tunnel into another world. Gates and doors were unlocked and locked behind me. With each step along the next corridor, my own footsteps ratcheted through me. Something in my head seemed to loosen and float away, leaving me powerless.

In a white tiled room, I sat at a small scrubbed table. The warder stood a few paces behind me. Footsteps. In walked Dad, flanked by two warders, only one of them coming into the room with him.

Dad. His eyebrows shot up in greeting, a sudden brightness lit his eyes. A small smile, and a wink.

'You look grand, Sophie lass. But this is no place for you.'

'Nor you neither, Dad.'

'Ah well.'

For a moment we said nothing, just looked at each other. The warders had stepped back and were either not listening, or pretending not to listen. One stood behind Dad, the other behind me.

I reached out to Dad across the table. He took my hands.

'No touching,' the warder's flat voice hit the back of my neck.

Slowly, our fingers untangled.

'Dad . . . I know you didn't do it. It's not too late . . .'

'Shhh. Talk about summat else.'

'We went to Liverpool, to see if Danny's ship had sailed on time.'

He gave me a warning glare.

So I was right. He had confessed because he thought Danny had robbed the bank. 'Did you get my letter, telling you Danny had sailed as planned?'

He shook his head. 'I suppose they choose what I get given and what I don't. It's all out of my hands now.' He turned up his palms and looked at them, as if he might see his fortune.

The relief I expected to see, the change in him I'd hoped for, didn't happen. Very calmly, he said. 'Well that's good that he sailed as he should. Don't tell him how things are. Not yet.'

'We wouldn't know where to get in touch with him.'

'You will. Trust Danny. He'll look after you. Danny's got the interests of the family at heart. I want you to promise you'll go to him, and tell him in person what's happened to me, not write the news in a letter.'

How the hell did he expect me to get to America? Dad in dreamland. Again.

'Promise me.'

'I will. I'll find him.'

I had not meant to be talking about Danny. Danny, Danny, Danny. Always the same, even in prison. As if he read my thoughts, he said, 'How's Rosa?'

'Sends her love and a kiss, Dad. '

He nodded. 'Same back.'

'Lydia Thackrey's written to the chief constable, to say she made a mistake. They won't listen. Her brother did the robbery.'

A flicker of understanding came into Dad's eyes. I expected him to tell me. *I'm innocent. I didn't do it.*

The warder behind Dad cleared his throat. 'I shall have to conclude the visit if you discuss the case or the findings or the sentence of the court.'

Dad said again, 'How's Rosa?'

The irritation squeezed my voice into a whine. 'Floored. Same as me. We keep expecting to wake up from all this.'

'I know, love.' He swallowed, as if his throat had gone dry, then flexed his fingers. 'I expect May's looked out for you?'

I nodded. Why wouldn't he protest?

'I knew May would come up trumps for you. I daresay you'll repay her, some day.'

I lowered my voice to a whisper. 'Dad, tell them you didn't do it. You didn't do it, did you? You didn't rob the bank. You didn't kill that man.'

He reached over and squeezed my hands. This time the warders did not intervene.

'When I knew you were set on coming, I thought what to say to you. It'll go from me if I don't spit it out. So bear with me, Sophie, let me collect meself.' He shut his eyes. 'So much of our life is dull, full of sameness. Even the sun doesn't shine on Tab Street. But we had one day, our family, a glorious day, blue sky, white clouds, green grass, butter-cups and daisies, a red squirrel. There was a smell of fruit cake and cheese, fresh bread for the sandwiches, and that lemonade – I didn't taste your lemonade but I took a sniff of Danny's. I thought what it must be to have a childhood where someone makes you lemonade in a glass jug. I wanted that for you. I wanted so much for you, all of you. Go on being bonny and bright. Don't let this bring you down.'

'What day? What day was that?'

'The day your mam sat under the tree and said this was the life, the life of Riley. You sat under the tree with her, you, Rosa and Billy. All except Danny who swung from the branch, like the king of the jungle. I should have just sat with you, instead of wandering around marquees, but there we are.'

'The garden party?'

'That was it. The day of the garden party, the day of a wedding.'

I felt confused. Was this some message, about the Thackreys? He'd always had that mad idea that Mr Thack-rey was on his side, the great god Mr Thackrey. Did he think he owed them something? Did he know about Granville Thackrey and expect him to give us some reward for Dad's silence? I couldn't bear the thought.

250

The warder behind Dad was listening. Perhaps he also wondered whether this was some coded message about where the money lay. I imagined him reporting back. *The prisoner mentioned a tree in a garden.*

'Was there anything you want to ask me, Sophie?'

What was the point? He was stubborn as ever, adamant as ever. A fool.

'Rosa wants to know where her name comes from. Was she named after someone in your family, or Mam's?'

'Oh no. She came into the world looking like a rosebud. We both thought so.'

He seemed to think this would please Rosa. Surely this isn't how you were supposed to talk on what might be the last time you would see your foolish, stubborn dad. Did he want to die? Perhaps I should have left him in the canal, anything better than this.

'They're not leaving me alone now,' he said. 'Every minute of the day there's someone with me, playing blackjack, chess, chatting. Not bad chaps. I don't suppose it's an easy job, to be a minder to someone in my situation.' He leaned close, 'I shall hold my breath the night before. Don't you worry. I'll go peaceful to meet your mam. They won't put a rope around my neck.'

I couldn't speak.

'I'm sorry I pawned everything. If you can manage to redeem the pledges, your mam'd be glad to think you and Rosa had her mirror back. One of you have the mirror, the other your mammy's ring. Give my watch to Danny when you see him. Will you do that for me?'

I nodded.

'I was a bit of a pawn in this life, Sophie. Don't you be.

251

You look like a queen, sitting there in your fine dress and beads. Remember how your mam always held her head high. You do that, you and Rosa. Don't forget. Remember the good times.'

I remember nothing else about that day, only that Rosa and May met me outside and, somehow, we got home.

Lydia

The only funerals I ever witnessed were on stage, when Ma was still Phoebe Bellamy, dabbing at her tears with a lace hanky, or keening as she tore her hair. I had never in my life been to a real funeral.

Now I was to go to an execution. A hanging. The word itself hung over us for days. Hang. He will hang by the neck until dead. We were ten days off Christmas, and Barney Moran would not see it. Barring some miracle, he would not see another day.

Sophie and Rosa did not want to go to bed. They sat till the early hours of the morning, looking into the fire that May banked up. She said that this was no time to spare coal. The pictures in the fire filled me with horror. I saw a noose, demons, a gallows, hell itself. Sophie looked away, perhaps seeing the same frightening images.

At about one o'clock, Rosa jumped up and took her coat from the hook at the back of the door.

'I'm going to walk to the prison. Someone should keep watch outside.'

I believed I should offer to go with her, because if I hadn't pointed the finger, Barney Moran might not at that moment have been in the death cell, passing his last night on earth. I stood up and reached for the tram conductor cape May had given me.

'Sit down, both of you,' May ordered. 'Rosa, you'd do no good, for your dad or yourself.' May took the coat from her and led her back to the fire. 'We'll be keeping watch there soon enough.'

She gave Rosa a toasting fork and told Sophie to cut slices of bread.

'And you,' she tapped my shoulder 'just come in the shop and shine a light. I've a second toasting fork somewhere.'

I followed her into the shop. In spite of the shambles of the place, she found the toasting fork straight away, on top of a box of assorted cutlery, bottle tops, pen knives and string. She spoke quietly. 'Now give over thinking on them lines. There's no point going on blaming thissen. If it hadn't been you pointed the finger, someone else would. Them two know it and so does Barney. The guilt came from his own mouth.'

All night, May made pots of tea, and poured a drop of rum into every cup. At about two o'clock in the morning, when my eyes started to shut more than they stayed open, I took a candle and lit myself to bed.

Now that I wanted to sleep, sleep fled.

Inches from the bed, rain dripped through the ceiling, plop-plopping into the enamel bucket set to catch the leak. Near the window, rain dripped into an earthenware dish. I got it into my head that the dish was about to overflow and got up to see.

It was not ready to overflow, but all the same, I opened the window and threw out the contents. When I got back into bed, my feet would not get warm. My toes pointed to the ceiling. Morbid thoughts overwhelmed me so that I almost thought myself a corpse, lying like those figures you see on top of tombs in old churches.

My neck hurt, as if it thought of another neck, Mr Moran's. I remembered the garden party when I first saw them all, and thought I imagined that little boy, Billy, hanging on his father's neck. His neck was buttoned up then, a neat collar encircling it.

I must, finally, have fallen asleep and they must, finally, have come to bed. In the early light I woke and felt two pairs of feet, one pair on either side of my cold shoulders. This meant I would be trapped until they moved, and my bladder grew near to bursting from last night's tea and rum.

I did not have to wait long. Sophie swung herself from the bed with a sigh, and got to the chamber pot before me.

I almost lost my nerve for going to the prison, wondering whether someone would turn up to snatch me and take me home. May found me a different cape, this one blue-black, with a hood. 'Hide thissen in that,' she said. 'And if someone tries to grab thee, they'll have me to deal with, and others besides.'

We took the tram car to Swinegate, and from Swinegate to Armley.

Tony, who seems to be Sophie's chap, paid the fares on the first tram. He carried an instrument case.

A hank of wire kind of man who clerks at East Street Mills paid the fares for the second tram. They called him the Scholar, but introduced him by his full name. Jack Scoular. The pallor of his complexion made it appear that he never spent much time outdoors. When I looked at his light hazel eyes as he sat opposite me on the tram, I imagined that they may have started out as dark brown or bright green and he had worn out the colour from reading.

The rain had stopped but the air felt soaked with it still. Armley Gaol loomed through the damp foggy day like a medieval fortress. We arrived at half past seven, though the execution was set for nine. Sophie trusted no one. She said, they may change the time, to confuse us. Executions used to be held at eight, the Scholar said, but now it was nine.

May was one of those people who sighed without knowing it. She stood in what she thought was silence. As the time ticked by, I believe she heaved a great sigh every two or three minutes.

Tony stood close to Sophie. Once I saw him reach to take her hand, but she shoved her hands in her pockets. He took a trumpet from his case.

Just before nine o'clock, a bell tolled. May put her arm around Rosa.

Sophie looked at the ground as Tony brought the trumpet to his lips and began to play the last post. Then Sophie straightened up like a soldier and called in a voice that should have brought down the thickest of prison walls.

'Dad! Dad! We're here! Dad!'

Tony kept on playing, the trumpet glued to his mouth, and tilted towards heaven.

At last, the Scholar touched Tony's arm. 'Stop now, lad. It's done.'

But Tony seemed to have forgotten how to put his trumpet back in its case. He couldn't make it fit, or click the lid shut.

I felt up my sleeve for a hanky that wasn't there, and so wiped my eyes on the hem of the rough old cape.

When I turned away, I saw that behind us stood three old men, carrying fishing rods over their shoulders like rifles. One by one, they went to Sophie and Rosa and shook hands. Until the last one shook her hand, Sophie stood still, showing no emotion. The moment she moved, she began sobbing as though she would break, the Scholar and Tony on either side of her, supporting her. Rosa's face streamed with silent tears. She held herself erect, with May's arm around her.

The gate of the prison opened and a man in cap and uniform stepped out. In his hands he held a small bundle.

'Personal effects.' He offered them to no one of us in particular. 'To be signed for.'

Sophie stepped forward and took the bundle from him, clutching it to her. He held out a ledger and a pen. She couldn't make her hand stop shaking but wouldn't let go of the pen for someone else to sign. I took the bundle from her. With her left hand, she held her right wrist steady, to keep it from trembling. And then she signed for Barney Moran's worldly goods.

It was over.

Overhead, the pub sign creaked in the wind. Though it was early morning, May said, 'The landlord's expecting us.'

She pushed open the brass-handled door and led us into the stone-flagged passageway, calling out to the landlord as she did so.

We were shown into a small room, the snug. Flames of a blazing coal fire licked the black chimney back with such ferocity I expected the soot to catch light.

Sophie had turned into a stone statue. Rosa began to shake. They were bustled to chairs on either side of the fire.

Tony guided me into a chair beside Sophie. He seated himself opposite, leaving a space by Rosa for May. The Scholar sat beside me, so we made a kind of horseshoe, at the top of which the silent landlord placed a round brass-topped table.

From the counter he brought hot sweet red drinks, some kind of fortified wine.

I passed the first glass along to Sophie. She held it in both hands, as if it might warm her.

When we were all provided for, the Scholar raised his glass. 'To Barney Moran. He may have gone from this world in an untimely and cruel fashion, but he's left us with his hopes and dreams. God knows we need dreams. And in some future time, may Sophie and Rosa, and Danny on his far flung shore, fulfil their father's dreams.'

We raised our glasses and drank.

Sophie seemed to speak into her glass. 'Dad, you were a fool.'

And the words came from somewhere but stayed rolling round my head. *And my poor fool is hang'd. No, no, no life! Never, never, never, never, never.*

'Why do you say he was a fool?' I asked her.

'Because he thought he was protecting someone.'

'Granville?' I asked.

She shook her head.

The landlord was arranging food on the table. Pork pie, cheese, bread, pickles.

The Scholar raised his glass again. 'To the lasses our friend leaves behind. May they go on to better times than we old ones have ever known, and if their mam and dad look on from some other place, let them look with pride.'

I handed Sophie some bread and cheese on a plate.

'I can't eat.' She held the glass in both hands so tightly I thought it would break.

'They can do him no more harm,' May said. 'They've done their worst. You must eat. Just a bit of bread and cheese.'

On the tram from Armley, we got a strange look from the conductor, so many people piling on together, and not at an hour to be on the way to work.

The Scholar said, 'Upstairs!' He bought the tickets as we clambered up to the top deck of the swaying tram, walking towards the back away from the few passengers near the top of the stairs.

Cigarette smoke choked the air and made me cough. Tab ends lay flattened on the wooden floor. Had they given Mr Moran a smoke this morning, to calm his nerves?

Tony sat beside Sophie, absent-mindedly patting and stroking his trumpet case.

The Scholar sat beside me, looking at the tickets in his hand as if they represented some kind of difficult riddle he could never solve.

The tram would stop at the terminus. We would change trams. The next tram would stop at another terminus. Endings. Everything seemed to be ending. My life with Phoebe at Allerton House. Dreams of living happily ever after with Theo. Most of all, Mr Moran's life, and Sophie and Rosa's happiness. What would become of me, I wondered. I could see no future, no tomorrow even.

The tram swayed. Sparks flew from the overhead cable. The taste of fortified wine came up into the back of my throat.

Sophie jumped up.

'I have to get off!'

Tony let her out of the seat, then hurried after her down the stairs, the two of them jumping off as the tram slowed for the next stop.

I looked out of the window. Sophie was vomiting into the gutter.

Sophie

Red bitter vomit spewed from me into the gutter.

'There's no shame, Sophie,' Tony said. 'Better out than in.'

He drew a corked bottle of water from his inside pocket. 'Here. Rinse your mouth. Take a sip or two.'

We sat down on a low factory wall.

As I dabbed at my mouth with his handkerchief, Tony said, 'You've no need to run away, either you or Rosa. Stop where you know people, and where people care for you.'

'Who said we're going away?'

'My mam said you're bound to. Listen to me, I've less than two years before I'm out of my time. I want you to come and meet my mam. Will you come with me?'

I didn't want to speak, couldn't take in his words. Just shook my head to say not now. He didn't stop.

'Don't worry about Rosa. She's your sister, and I'll treat her like mine.'

'You think Dad was guilty, don't you?'

'It's you I'm thinking of. Your dad would want you to gerron with your life.'

The factory hooter sounded. I stood up, not wanting to be trampled by hordes pouring out for the dinner break. Tony took my hand as we walked towards town.

'Sorry. Sorry, Sophie. I know it's too soon. And until I'm out of my time, I'm not my own man. All the same, I wanted to get in first, before you do anything silly, before you and Rosa go rushing off somewhere.'

I pushed my hands deep into the pockets my coat. 'Rush off where? We haven't a farthing to our name. I suppose you think Dad tipped me off where he stashed the money?'

'I know you had nowt to do with it.'

'But you believe Dad did.'

'I'm trying to be straight with you. Everything points to it. But I don't know. What's wrong with saying I don't know?'

'Because it's another way of saying he did it.'

He put his arm around my shoulders. 'No it's not. And I want to look after you. A joiner needn't ever be out of work if he's any good. People always die and want a coffin. And once I'm out of my time, I'd go anywhere you want. The other end of the country, the other side of the globe.'

He was looking at me, waiting for an answer, as if he must have it there and then. A lorry passed by sending a splash of puddle onto his trousers.

'Tony, I can't think about any of that now.'

We reached a tram stop. 'There's one coming,' Tony said. 'Let's get on. You're frozen through.'

On the tram he said, 'Come and see my mam. I said I'd fetch you round.'

I felt too weary to argue.

Tony's mother was kneading dough, her arms and face dusty with white flour. She smiled at me, that same cheerful, captivating smile that Tony had but without the teeth. 'Sit the girl down in your dad's chair, Tony love. We'll have a good chat.'

I wanted to run from the room, expecting a grilling. She would use me as gossip tomorrow. *Oh that poor girl, looked so pale, and still believing in her dad. Shame.*

She said to Tony, 'Leave Sophie with me. You get off to work. Your dad needs you.'

He went upstairs and came back down in his overalls.

'Take that tin to your dad, Tony. He forgot his dinner.'

Tony glanced from me to his mam, as if imagining a calm and rosy future.

Mrs Woodhouse set the bowl of bread dough on the hearth and covered it with a starched white cloth. 'I'm sorry for your trouble, love. You Morans have had the worst of times these past years.'

She had mashed a pot of tea and handed me a cup. 'That lad of mine is a diamond. There's nothing he can't do. Make and mend. Play in the band. The bandmaster's begging him not to leave off. Do his sums at night school for all the measuring. You get a lad like that once in a blue moon.'

She perched on a stool at the table, looking down at me. 'Naturally you're quiet today. Naturally you haven't much to say.'

'No.'

'My lad can't go marrying before he's out of his time. You'll know that.'

I nodded.

'Then we understand each other. He thinks the world of you, but he's too young to know his own mind. Put him off. Both of you give yourselves a chance to see what's what.'

I got up and tipped the tea down the sink. 'Tony might need time to see what's what . . . '

Her smiling mask slipped.

' . . . but I already know. To save him the bother of coming round again, you can tell him I've no intention of marrying.'

'I'm sure that's the wisest way.'

'And you can tell him, and your husband, and yourself, and anybody else with an ear to listen, Barney Moran is innocent.'

When I left Tony's house, I set off back to May's by way of St Mary's. In the church, I met up with Rosa. She was kneeling at the small bench, watching candles flicker in front of the statue of Our Lady.

She looked up at me. 'Light a candle. Light two.'

'I don't have any money.'

'Our Lady won't mind.'

'Father Connor might.'

He was the priest who thought nothing on a Sunday of stepping into the pulpit and saying, 'There's so many buttons in this week's collection plate that I'm surprised any one of you has a stitch of clothing on your back. I'm sending round the plate again.'

I chose three candles, lit them and set them in the holders, one for Mam, one for Dad, one for Billy. I knelt on the bench and asked Our Lady to take care of them, and see them into heaven soon. Though I knew Dad didn't believe, and if you don't believe, how could you go there?

I watched the candles flickering, lighting up the polished brass, the dust in the air above. The church smelled of stale incense and cold air. How many times Mam must have watched the candles flicker in just the same way. She would never have lit an unpaid for candle. I wondered what thoughts she had as she watched candles flicker. She must have thought our lives together would go on forever. Once she said, 'Whenever I dream of you, you're always young, always my babies.' Not until she was dead did I dream of her. Dad must have dreamed in his cell. Too late to ask what he dreamed. Sometimes he had nightmares that Danny said were of the war, of dead soldiers, blown to pieces.

Danny. Dad talked to him more than to me. He taught him to play chess. I didn't want to learn, couldn't be bothered. Too much to do.

Rosa had gone to sit in one of the pews. I went to join her.

'What are we going to do?'

She didn't look at me. 'You tell me.'

'Dad asked me to find Danny.'

'It would be easier for Danny to find us, if he wanted to.'

'What do you think we should do then?'

'Earn some money. We're living free at May's. She won't chuck us out, but it's not on, especially with Lydia there as well.'

'You're right. There's four pawn tickets to redeem – the mirror, Mam's ring, Dad's watch and coat. Dad said . . . '

'You told me what he said. Stop rubbing it in that you saw him and I didn't. I don't want to hear, not any of it. What use is that mirror? What use is the ring? What good did it ever do Mam? Everything's finished.'

I didn't answer. Rosa could reckon not to care if she wanted. Later she'd be glad. We should hang onto something of our old life. Anyway, Dad didn't ask her, he asked me.

The church had grown dark.

'We can't sit here forever.'

She didn't budge, just looked straight ahead, as if waiting for a sign. After a long time, she said, 'When one of the priests comes in, I'm going to ask for a mass to be said for Dad. If he wants money, or says Dad's a Protestant, I'll never cross a church threshold again.'

'Let's hope it's not Father Connor then.'

I left her sitting there and walked slowly out of the church. There seemed to be nowhere to go, nothing to do, nothing that mattered any more.

As I walked down the hill, the Scholar strode towards me.

'I thought I'd find you, if I looked long enough.'

He crooked his arm for me to link it. We walked back down the hill to the recreation ground.

'Is it too cold for you to sit down?' he asked.

'No.'

We sat on a bench. 'I've a book for you. It's Yeats's poetry. Your dad said you recited "The Lake Isle of Innisfree" like a good un.'

'Thank you.' The book smelled of glue.

'The smell will fade. Only the police went to town on

my books, thinking to find bank notes in the pages. Anyhow, something good came of it. I've taught myself bookbinding and I'll rest my eyes from reading for the rest of the winter while I repair what volumes I can.'

On the recreation ground, a few half-starved lads jumped on the pork pie roundabout and pushed themselves round and round.

'I'm sorry they ransacked your place.'

'It's nothing. Nothing to what they've done to you, and Barney.'

'I don't know why he pleaded guilty, except . . .' I couldn't say it. If Dad kept silence, I must do the same.

The Scholar sighed. 'I guessed it myself. Barney thought he was protecting someone.'

'It's the only explanation. But he went on and on sticking to it beyond any need.'

The lads left the pork pie roundabout and made for the swings.

'Sophie, I'm not a religious man. I don't go to church or follow any creed. Don't take it amiss what I'm going to say. In my mind, people who subscribe to a religion, they do it, at bottom, because they're afraid of hell. But there's another kind of belief, that's mine and I think it was your dad's. It's as spiritual in its way, maybe even more so because it's hard won. Hell holds no fear if you've already been there. I have, and so had your dad. He won't be afraid of what comes next. But one thing I'm sure, there'll be the spirits of old comrades on the other side to meet him, and lead him to your mam.'

'How do you know?'

'Because I see them every night in my dreams. They

come to talk to me, walk through my door, pick up a book, give a wry smile at all my nonsense.'

He walked with me back to May's, then shook my hand at her door.

Rosa came back shortly after me. I looked at her to see whether she would tell me if a mass was to be said for Dad. She said nothing, but went upstairs to bed. Lydia, looking exhausted and ill, followed her, perhaps to keep her company.

May began to roll a cigarette. 'You two keep out of the shop tomorrow. I've a feeling we might have a few gawpers, rubber-necking you because of what's happened.'

'I know. That's why Rosa's not going back to Burton's.'

'Something'll turn up, you'll see.'

I nodded. 'Suppose so.'

'I thought that chap of yours would have been here.'

'Tony's not my chap.'

May lit her cigarette. 'He'd like to be.'

'Yes.'

'You could do worse.'

'His mam doesn't like me.'

'It wouldn't be his mam you'd be marrying.'

'As good as. He's two years to go on his apprenticeship. And I don't want to get wed. You haven't, May, and you're well enough set up. Besides, how could I even think of it just now?'

'It'd move you on.'

'We'll move on. We'll be out of your hair soon.'

'That's not it and you know it. And since you mention it, I did marry. I was a wife for a week.'

'I didn't know.'

'No reason why you should.'

'What was he like?'

She flicked ash into the fire. 'Sometimes I forget his face. We had a lovely week, and then he was off to the front. We should have had our photo took, but we thought there'd be time. We both felt sure there'd be a future for us. And since you ask what he was like – like your Tony. He was Tony's uncle. That's why his dad'll do a few jobs for me for nowt. All I'm saying is, don't be hasty. Tony's steady as a rock. He has a good heart. You'd go a long way to find a steadier, better-natured young feller.'

I looked across at her and tried to think what she must have been like when she was young. Her legs were mottled with burn marks from sitting too close to the fire. Two fingers on her right hand were brown to the roots from holding cigarettes. She liked to powder her face and some of the powder had spilled onto her jumper. She got up and stretched. 'Ah well. All that was before you were born, but to me, it's like yesterday.'

That night as we three lay on the bed like sardines in a tin, Rosa said, 'We none of us know what to do next. So Sophie and Lydia, when you go to sleep, dream an answer. Dream of what we should do tomorrow, and the next day, and the day after.'

Icicles decorated the inside of our attic window. A white carpet of frost lay across the recreation ground. I dressed as quickly as I could. Rosa and Lydia had already gone downstairs.

Lydia, who had a sore throat and a headache, was gargling at the sink in an alarming way, making elaborate noises in her throat. She changed the water, adding more salt to a drop of water from the kettle, cooling it, and gargling again.

The teapot was still warm. I poured myself a cup.

'Well?' Rosa asked as she sorted through a pile of old clothes. 'Did you dream anything useful?'

'I was disguised as a cabin boy, on a voyage to America. Dad was on deck. He asked me if I'd got his fob watch for Danny, and was it keeping good time.'

She did not look impressed. 'Right then. Lydia hasn't dreamed nowt neither. We go with what I say.'

Lydia stopped gargling, and turned to listen.

Rosa's plan was for us to make rag dolls and stuffed animals, to sell in the shop, and on the streets, for Christmas presents. She had already decided on patterns, cut out and made the first doll, the first walrus and the first seal. From her original patterns, I was to cut out and she would sew, leaving space for filling the bodies with flocks from the ripped up mattresses.

Since no one else had a better idea, we got May to agree that we could use some of the old clothes, cleared the table, and began.

I cut. Rosa sewed, adding button eyes and red felt lips. Lydia stuffed with flocks.

We worked all day and into the night, long after May went to bed. When every surface was filled with dolls, seals, walruses and creatures less easily identifiable, we stopped.

Rosa picked up one of her very first efforts, a doll with a crooked mouth. She held it by her face and said, 'Oh dear, what a poor specimen am I. Who will take care of me?'

In that moment Rosa, my poor little sister, so much reminded me of Mam. I picked up a gruff-voiced walrus who said, 'I will take care of you. Ride on my back into the crested waves.'

Rosa's doll said, 'No, no, not the crested waves!'

Lydia held up a morose-looking boy doll made of green velvet. 'I will take care of you.'

Her doll voice was scarcely more than a whisper. It seemed to startle her, and perhaps hurt her throat because she straight away went to the sink for a glass of water.

When Lydia came back to the table, she took up her boy doll in one hand and Rosa's lopsided lips doll in the other. Lopsided lips said, 'What is to be done?' The green velvet boy replied, 'Lydia will visit her ma, and not come back empty-handed.'

Lydia

That damn hellhole of a second-hand shop was making me ill. Headaches. Sore throats. Flea bites. And an aching heart, because of Theo's betrayal. Everything in my life had gone entirely wrong and it was because of my own stupidity. I'd misunderstood poor Clarence Clutterbuck as he breathed out the last words of his life. I'd thought Pa had some regard for me – enough to believe when I told him nothing but the plain ugly truth.Most of all, I had fooled myself into thinking Theo loved me, when for once my evil stepbrother spoke the truth. Theo wanted to weasel his way into the Thackrey family and was prepared to betray me to do it. Till my dying day I would never rid myself of the sound of Dorothea and Massey clattering into the parish church, and the sight of them bearing down on me when I had expected to be rescued by Theo.

I missed Ma. One miserable postcard, that's all I'd sent her, to say I was all right and not to worry.

In the week coming up to Christmas, it was time to act.

It was time to act, but what must I do?

My attributes: I had the education and writing hand to be a clerk. I had the good taste and refined voice for a shop assistant in a select store. The Scholar offered to write me excellent references, as coming from a former boss. He had a small printing set on which to produce letter headings, and an elegant and effusive turn of phrase that would satisfy the most fastidious would-be employer.

Well then, if I must say goodbye to the old life and start again, I'd need my bank book, jewellery, clothes. I liked to think that Ma would want to know for sure that I was well.

I set out to arrive in Chapel Allerton about two o'clock in the afternoon when Dorothea would be out with the little ones, and Pa and Granville at work. Phoebe should be in her cosy circular room, which I would approach, unseen, from the fields at the back of the house.

The slate-blue sky hung low as I got off the tram a stop too soon, so as to come at the house by a roundabout way, avoiding the lane that led to Allerton House and the parsonage.

My feet sank into the muddy field so I soon gave up trying to step carefully. Between field and Thackrey land, the hawthorn hedge stood bare and sharp with twigs. The most plump and lovely robin looked at me in such a friendly and familiar way that I wanted to reach out and touch it.

I looked for the gap in the hedge – not so wide as it once

was – and squeezed through, catching my cape and tearing yet more threads. Before going further I looked round and glanced at the windows from which I could be seen.

The church clock chimed two. If Phoebe ran true to form, she would be snuggled in her wing chair, close to the drawing-room fire, reading a novel.

The fire burned brightly, wing chair turned towards it. She must be there or the fire wouldn't be banked so high. Heart pounding, I tapped on the window, with a sudden dread that Sheldon may have taken time off from the bank in the approach to Christmas. If he loomed from the other chair, hidden just out of my view, I would turn and run. No response. I tapped again.

Phoebe rose from her chair. The sight of the familiar head, chignon at the nape of her neck, elegant wrap sliding from her shoulders as she stood, gave me a stab of love. I wanted it to be just the two of us again, with Ada, years ago, before Sheldon Thackrey came into our lives. She laid her book on the chair arm and hurried towards the window, as if I might suddenly disappear, her face alive with joy and astonishment. She turned as if she would go to the door, to come out and meet me.

I tapped again. 'Open the window!'

She was there in an instant and snapped back the catch. I was already pushing at the sash window from below.

Phoebe started to laugh and cry at the same time as I climbed in, half dragged by her. She gripped my arm tightly, as if I might suddenly bolt, making the getting in more difficult.

'Where on earth have you been? You've had me delirious with worry.'

I put a finger to my lips but don't think she noticed. She pulled me to her in a hug as though she'd never let me go.

My muddy footprints marked the polished floor. I slipped off the shoes.

'I've been worried sick. Where have you been?'

'With friends.'

'Friends? Where? I've had a useless enquiry agent on the prowl. He's supposed to have left no stone unturned. And look at the state of you. The sooner you get a bath . . . ' She propelled me towards the fire.

'I'm not coming back. It's not safe for me here. I know too much.'

'Oh my God, Sheldon was right. The balance of your mind . . . The murder case and so on. Don't worry, dear. I've read about such things. Or perhaps it's a sort of sympathetic ailment. Certain women turn peculiar after giving birth. You were worrying about me – along with everything else – and infected yourself with anxiety. Sit in my chair.'

She shoved me backwards, sending me sprawling into the chair.

'Oh stop it Ma! Take notice of what's under your nose.'

'I'll ask Molly to put on another cup.' Her hand reached for the push button bell.

I had to be quick to grab her arm. 'You're not listening. I won't live under this roof. Granville was involved with the robbery at the bank. Did Sheldon tell you that?'

Phoebe's mouth fell open. I spoke quickly, knowing I had to make her believe me. 'I saw. In his summerhouse, the attaché case with notes and bonds. And don't you tell

275

me it was cigarette cards. I know money when I see it, smell it, touch it.'

She believed me. No daughter of hers would confuse cigarette cards and hard cash. I rushed to get my words out before she had chance to interrupt. 'Granville must have made loans without proper security. He had to conceal the evidence. *He* attacked me. Not Theo, though Theo's not worth a light.'

She gave a kind of gasp, and put her hand to her chest. 'Sheldon didn't . . . no one told me about an attack.'

From the hall came the sound of footsteps and the rattle of a tray. I dashed back to the window and hid behind the curtain until Molly had put down the tea tray and left the room.

We sat side by side on the sofa. Ma asked, 'What were you doing in the summerhouse?'

'I met Theo there.'

'So that much was true. Sheldon told me you and Theo were secretly engaged.'

'More fool me.'

Ma stirred the tea in the pot and began to pour. 'We'll just have to share a cup, since you're being so cloak and dagger about everything. But don't worry. Your mother's here now. I'll speak to Sheldon. We'll sort this out. You must come home. This is ridiculous. You've lost weight. What are you living on?'

'Nothing.' I pulled two toy creatures from my pockets and put them on the low table. 'I made these. For Bunting, and the new little chap.'

'How sweet.' She made no move to touch them. Now that I saw them there, in such grand surroundings, they looked just what they were. Badly stuffed men's socks. I didn't bother to say that one was meant to be a caterpillar, and the other a seal.

'How are they, Bunting and the new boy?'

'Bunting's fine. And Hugo, he's very well, a rosy little fellow. The dragon's out with the pair of them now.' Phoebe sighed. 'I knew you hadn't gone mad. You're too steady to be rocked by giving a statement to the police.'

'Is that what Sheldon said?' I took a drink of tea and handed the cup back to her.

She nodded. 'He said that started it all off. What a pickle. But this Granville business, you should have spoken to me first. If he was involved with Moran in the robbery, that would explain a few questions that popped up for me. I know it sounds heartless, but it's a pity you let on.'

'How could I not speak out about something like that?'

'Sometimes it's best to say nothing. Moran held his silence.'

'Ma! How could I?' It was the fury made me cry, and the fact that she refused to see why I had to speak out.

She put her arms around me, holding me, rocking me, saying, 'Shhh. My poor little girl. I blame that school and the damn Girl Guides.'

I pulled away. 'What on earth has it got to do with the Girl Guides?'

'Oh you know, all that honour and duty stuff. It's no good for an impressionable gel. We have to know which side our bread's buttered. But look, let me talk to Sheldon. Tell him you'll keep what you know – what you suspected – to yourself. Say you were mistaken even.'

'No! And, I'm not coming back. Not ever.'

'I have an idea. We're all spending Christmas with the cement mixers, Cecilia and Marmaduke and all the little rubbles. If you go to Stoneycroft ahead of us . . .'

'Oh no . . .'

'Don't be hasty. Think about it. You'll be on neutral ground there. We might find some kind of accommodation between you and Sheldon.'

'And Granville?' I heard the bitterness in my voice and did not bother to add that I saw nothing neutral about Stoneycroft.

'Then where will you go, darling?'

'I'll get a job.'

She gave me such a forlorn look. 'I've done my best by you. Just think, you could be on your way home for the holidays, from a finishing school in Switzerland.'

I stood up. 'I'm going.'

'Lydia, you are not leaving this house . . .'

'Try and stop me.'

' . . . Not until I know your plans.'

'I have friends. Someone's found me a job in Oxford. I'll see Penelope. She'll let you have news of me.'

She nodded, believing what I said, or pretending to.

'Wait!' She got up, ready to leave the room.

I put a hand on her arm. 'Don't tell anyone I'm here.'

'I have a little cash upstairs, and you need something decent on your feet.'

When she came back, carrying my tapestry carpet bag, she had been crying.

'Don't worry, Ma. I'll be all right.'

She kissed me. 'You must at least tell me where you are. I'll visit you.'

'Best not, Ma. Not just yet. We'll let the dust settle, eh?' I kissed her cheek and she clutched at me again. I broke free and pushed up the window.

Not until I was on the tram did I look to see what she had stuffed in the bag. A skirt and top, underwear, shoes, my purse with coins and a couple of notes, and in a small velvet bag, my gold bracelet and cat brooch. She hadn't included my bank book, or the rest of my jewellery.

That evening, I sat talking with Sophie. The plan began to take hold, almost as if it sprang to life on the hearth between us – with a shape and a life of its own.

Sophie

It was the day before Christmas Eve. The two of us were on our own, sitting by May's fire under the soft splutter of the gas light, sharing a Woodbine. Lydia held her cat brooch in the palm of her hand, as if trying to hypnotise herself with it. It made me angry to see her. She didn't want to be at May's any more than we did.

'Just go home Lydia. Forget about us. You've somewhere to go. We haven't.'

She reached for the cig. 'I can't go back.'

That's when she told me the gory details of what Granville had done to her, and how her stepfather took his side.

So she truly did have as much reason to want to get away as we did.

She pinned the brooch on her jumper. 'I've a bankbook in my room at Allerton House. I opened it when I was at school in Harrogate, copying you, Sophie. You had a Penny Bank account, so I wanted one. It's not a huge amount, but it would get us to another town.'

Suddenly, I felt fed up with myself at being the only one of the three of us not to come up with a single idea.

I stood up. 'Come on then, let's go and get it.'

Lydia didn't budge. 'Ma's not there. The house is locked up. I told you, they've all gone to the cement mixers for Christmas.'

'So much the better. We'll open a window and get in. There's bound to be one window we can get through, I'll take a knife to slip the catch.'

Lydia said, 'Yes, why not? It's my bankbook. My money.'

Half an hour later, I was pedalling my legs off, heart bursting. It would have been far enough with one person on Danny's heavy bike, let alone two. My numb fingers froze to the handlebars. When I ran out of puff, we changed places.

The blue light of the police station shone through the gloomy evening as we turned right. 'I'm going round the back,' Lydia called. 'Can't bear to go by the front and risk seeing Theo. He sometimes walks Patience in the lane around this time.'

Something in the way she said Theo's name expressed such loss and hurt. I tried Tony's name in my head, to see whether it had the same ring. It did. Perhaps May was right, and he would be the one for me.

At the end of a narrow lane, Lydia brought the bike to a stop. She leaned it against a prickly hedge. 'Through this gate.'

My feet sank in mud. Nearby, a cow gave a menacing moo.

'We'll be all right,' Lydia said. 'As long as there isn't a bull loose.'

'And if there is?'

'Then turn off the flashlight, hope he doesn't see us.'

Taking no chances, I switched off the flashlight and tagged along behind her as she followed the line of the hedge.

She stumbled along the furrowed field, muttering that the gap in the hedge was somewhere here, not far, just along a bit.

'Call that a gap?' I asked as she got stuck halfway.

A spiky hawthorn branch clawed into her as if it had been specially instructed to do so by Mr Thackrey.

I followed her through.

The downstairs rooms were shuttered and dark, but we had come prepared. Lydia, being taller than me, slid the knife into the window latch, releasing it. Between us, we raised the sash window. Lydia slotted the blade into the shutter hook. It clicked free. She climbed on the window-sill and propelled herself inside. In a moment, our muddy shoes were marking the polished wooden floor of what Lydia said was her mother's drawing room. The fire was neatly laid, ready to be lit. On the small table by the wing chair lay a book, opened at one page and with a book-mark in another.

'I didn't see any lights, but keep your fingers crossed there's no one lurking.'

I stopped. 'You said the house would be empty.'

'Well the family's away, obviously. But they may have

left one or two of the maids behind to keep an eye on things. I suppose if we'd thought about it, we could have done a reccy round the outside first, to check for lights.'

Before I had time to say that's exactly what we should do, she was at the door that led to the hall.

She tried the handle, once, twice. It didn't budge. 'Damn them,' she said loudly. 'They've locked the doors from the outside. For heaven's sake, did they expect burglars or something?'

It was not a moment to call attention to ourselves by making a noise, but I couldn't help laughing.

'Shut up!'

I couldn't stop. The laughter shook me as I tried to get out the words, 'But we are, we are burglars!'

'Speak for yourself, Sophie Moran. All I want is my own bankbook.'

Lydia picked up her mother's book. 'She's reading *The Child's Guide to Knowledge*.' That made us laugh.

'What page is she at?' I asked when I could get the words out.

Lydia shone the torch. 'It's questions and answers. She's on "Steel". Question, "What does the hardness of steel render it capable of?" Answer, "Receiving a very sharp edge, which makes it particularly useful for the blades of all instruments for cutting."'

Fortunately, we didn't find that too hilarious and so stopped laughing.

She turned to the book marked page. 'This is "Cement". Ma's been swotting up, ready to make polite Christmas dinner conversation with the steel magnate and the cement mixer.'

I shone the torch on our muddy footprints. Lydia planted her right foot on a small Persian rug and skated across the polished floor, wiping out the marks.

Five minutes later, we were out of the drawing room, shutters pulled to but not fastened behind us, window closed but not locked.

'Someone'll get into bother, for not checking the windows,' Lydia said with satisfaction.

I wasn't so sure, especially since she had left a great muddy footprint on the Persian rug. I asked, 'Which is your room? Is there a drainpipe?'

'Round there,' she waved to the left. 'And no drainpipe. But let's try another way in.'

As we walked round to the front of the building, she said, 'Ma's so thoughtless. She could have at least have left her door open. For all she knows, I might have needed a warm coat.'

At the front of the house, the windowsill stood higher. Lydia gave me a peg up so that I could work the knife under the catch, release it, and flick the latch.

Once we were inside, Lydia closed the window. 'Better be quiet. If there are servants, they'll be across the other side of the house and shouldn't hear, but you never know. They might decide to wander around, use Ma's bath or something.'

She tried the door from the study into the hall. As I'd guessed, that was also locked.

'All right,' Lydia said, 'if I can't have my bankbook, Mr Sheldon Thackrey will just have to spare me a few guineas.' She crossed the room. By the fireplace, she moved a leather buffet and revealed a low safe in the wall.

'Shine the torch!' she ordered as she bent to the safe, selecting numbers, turning the knob and handle. 'Blow me, he's changed the ruddy combination. How low and deceitful. Especially from someone who owes me – owes me compensation.'

It occurred to me that Rosa and I were owed a little compensation too.

'So what do we do now?' I sat in the big leather chair, wishing Dad could see me, or be there himself, to sit in that chair, smoke his pipe and know that he'd turned the corner.

'Give me the flashlight.' Lydia was at the desk. 'Would you believe it? The desk is locked. He's so careful, or thinks he is.' From the tobacco box on the mantelpiece, she took out a small key. 'This opens the desk. He thinks he's clever, but he can't remember two numbers together, always has to write them down.' She opened the desk drawer. 'This is where he writes them, on his pad. And he writes them backwards. The only person he confuses is himself.'

She went back to the safe, clicked the new numbers. The safe door swung open. 'Come and take a look.'

There was a cash box, locked, a jewellery box, locked, and a bunch of keys.

'Would one of the keys unlock this room door?' I asked. 'If the coast's clear, you could nip upstairs for your bank book.'

'No.' She stood up. 'Those keys are no use. They're the keys to Thackreys' Bank.'

We stood very still, side by side, looking at the keys.

'What shall we do?' I asked.

She answered slowly. 'I don't know. What do you think we should do?'

I thought for a moment. My life, Rosa's life, Lydia's, had been turned upside down and inside out. Dad and Clarence Clutterbuck had lost their lives.

'There's only one thing we can do.'

'What's that?' Lydia asked quietly.

It seemed so obvious. 'Rob the bank.'

Slowly, Lydia took the keys from the safe, and closed the door.

We waited, listening to the house, listening for movements.

She said, 'If they have left any maids here, they must be out, or haven't heard us.'

'Then let's go.' I switched off the flashlight, slid out of the window first, and dropped to the ground. Lydia followed, pulling the inner shutters closed as best she could, and lowering the window.

Ten minutes later, I was pedalling back the way we had come.

'Shall we go straight there, to the bank I mean?' Lydia asked. 'Before we lose our nerve.'

'No. We need to plan it, go about it careful like.' Dad had taken the blame for robbing a bank when he had done nothing. I needed to reverse that — rob a bank in such a flawless fashion that we would never be found out.

'How do you propose to do that?' Lydia shouted as we overtook a tram at its stop.

'With military precision.'

On Christmas Eve, the town teemed with office workers, factory hands, foundry men and market people, small and large groups of revellers heading to and from the pubs for their Christmas fuddles, shouting, laughing and determined to have a good time. The two of us wove in and out of them like any other last-minute shoppers, carrying our baskets.

No merry-makers ventured onto Park Row. After seven o'clock, it was quiet, with only a solitary person at the tram stop and a man carrying a rolled umbrella walking towards the railway station. In evidence against Dad, the prosecutor said that the beat policeman tried the bank door at 8.15 p.m. and found it unlocked. That gave us an hour to do our work and scarper, as long as Christmas Eve meant no change to the police patrol timetable.

The coast clear, we dodged into the bank porch.

'Thanks, Gilbert,' Lydia said.

'Who's Gilbert?'

'George Gilbert Scott designed the bank. He specially put on a porch so that we'd be able to hide in it while I fiddled with keys.' There were two locks. Lydia tried a key. It didn't fit. She tried another. It dawned on me – they were the wrong keys.

'Shut up,' she said. 'You're putting me off.'

'I didn't say a word.'

'No but you're thinking loudly.'

She tried another key. The lock turned. She chose another key for the second lock. Success.

Once inside, Lydia locked the door behind us. 'The door to the vaults is behind the counter. Shine the torch! Keep it low.'

I had never been in that part of the bank, only through the side door with Dad, on the day he took me to see his mushrooms growing. I shone the torch all around the tiled floor.

Through high windows, street lamps cast a shadowy light on the walls and vaulted ceiling. It was for all the world like a great cathedral, dim, cool, echoey. I had worn soft shoes. Lydia's footsteps rang out as she crossed the floor. My mouth felt dry. I could feel my heart, trying to burst.

Suddenly, Lydia tapped her feet on the floor. 'What was that song -Rosa's solo in the panto?' She tapped in a great circle in the middle of the bank floor, singing, 'Me and my shadow, walking down the avenue. Me and my shadow, rob a bank and don't feel blue.'

I didn't move. 'Go on, be brave, Sophie. How many times will you get a chance to do a soft-shoe shuffle in the last of the country banks?'

I did a few steps, swaying, shuffling my feet. 'Me and my shadow, walking down the avenue. Me and my shadow, watch me Dad, rob the bank for you!'

She gave me an encouraging little pat on the back. 'That's it. We've no need to fret. No beat bobby will imagine lightning would strike in the same place twice. Come and look at this painting.'

'Lydia!'

'No, just take one look, because you may never see it again.' She took the torch from me and directed it at an oil painting.

'Yes, I can see.' I couldn't see. My eyes wouldn't focus. I felt ghosts crowding in on me from behind.

'It's called *Park Row by Moonlight*. There's the bank, in the foreground.'

'Right. Well can we rob it now, please, or are you getting cold feet?'

'No, but what's the rush. It's not every day you rob a

bank. I think we should make the most of it, write an account for our grandchildren.' She sighed. 'If either of us ever have any. I'm sure you will.'

'Now's not the time. You'll meet someone else. Theo wasn't worth it.'

'You're right. Now where did I put the keys?'

'Lydia!'

'Only joking.'

As we descended the stone stairway into the vaults, the chill scent of earth and money seemed to rise to meet us. I shivered. This felt like the prison, going through locked doors to the heart of hell.

'How will you know which vault?' I asked.

'I don't, I can't remember.'

The first vault contained locked, numbered boxes. The second vault was lined from floor to ceiling with shelves of gold bars. For a moment, I was tempted to take just one and drop it in my basket. But best stick to the plan.

The door to the third vault swung open. I felt a dizzy sensation and had a sudden inkling that there would be some trap, ready to be sprung.

Lydia must have felt the same, because she held the door, as if it might suddenly shut on us, lock of its own accord and leave us in the cold, black, airless room. She said, 'I'll hold the door.'

I lifted bundles of white five-pound notes, large green one-pound notes, tenners, twenties, fifties. As the money belt under my skirt filled, I stopped looking to see what denomination the notes were and just stuffed them in. I filled my pockets, and the shopping basket, taking care to set the blue cloth bag aside to go back on top.

'Your turn.' I held the door, while Lydia scooped up notes.

When she could fit no more into her money belt and pockets, she said, 'Your turn again. Last part of the plan.'

'Last but one,' I said. 'The last part is to get away with it.'

We swapped places. Gently I picked up the blue cloth bag, full of Dad's wriggling worms. 'You never tasted bank notes,' I told them as I tipped them out onto the remaining notes. 'Dad lost his job because he bred you lot in this bank, and you were a terrible danger to paper money. Well here's your chance. Everything we can't carry, you can munch.'

The last of the shining, shifting tangle of worms slithered onto the notes.

Lydia locked the vault door behind us. Once again, we climbed the stairs. I wouldn't breathe freely until we got out of there, away from the morgue. Poor worms. I hated leaving them there.

Back on the ground floor, Lydia dropped the keys on her foot. 'Damn!' She retrieved them, feeling for the right key. 'I'm going to open the door and go out first. If it's clear, I'll tap twice for you to come out. If I tap once, let me back in.'

'Do it the other way round. If you tap once to come in, I might not be quick enough. I'll be waiting for the second tap.'

'Right. Once for you to come out, twice to let me back.'

She tapped once. When I came out, she locked the door behind me.

The street was deserted. We cut round into Bond Street and onto Briggate, heading back to the Ham Shank by the most direct route.

'Wouldn't it be terrible,' Lydia said, 'if there was a hole in your money belt and you were leaving a trail of five-pound notes all the way to May's shop.'

Lydia

Sophie laughed nervously when I made my joke about leaving a trail of notes all the way to May's shop.

As we passed the parish church, I felt a pang of sorrow. Theo had betrayed me so completely. As if she read my thoughts, Sophie squeezed my hand and tried to force some gaiety into her voice. 'You're best off without him. The world's our oyster now.'

Who wants to live in an oyster? Not I.

As we reached the well-lit tramways terminus, we linked arms. Sophie barely moved her lips. 'Stick close. We'll cut through by the mills to keep off the coppers' beat, just in case.'

On the last lap towards Zion Street, I thought over what we'd done. It was one thing to grab the money, but we could hardly deposit hundreds of notes in the Penny Bank without drawing attention. And it was way too much to stick in a money box. From the recreation ground, I saw the light was left on for us in the shop.

'Under the bed then?' I asked Sophie. My mouth felt dry.

'Yes. I'll take mine up first. You talk to Rosa and May.'

'What if they stare at me with this great money belt under my skirt?'

'Keep your cloak on. Say you're chilly.'

The shop the door was locked. Rosa let us in, trying to get a look at the basket to see how many dolls and creatures we'd sold. Sophie swung the basket away and made straight for the stairs.

Rosa gave me a quick curious glance, as if she knew we'd been up to something, then went back to arranging May's hair.

The house looked transformed. A log crackled and sparked on the banked-up fire. A fir tree decked with candles stood in the corner.

Tony stood by the Christmas tree, a great grinning creature with a box of matches in his hand. 'I'll light the candles when Sophie comes down. Oh and I got you that paper you wanted, Lydia, from W H Smith.'

He passed me a copy of *The Stage*.

'Thank you.'

Such an obliging fellow, but I wished him gone.

I sat at the table, tucking myself close in so as no to show the bump of money belt. I turned the pages of *The Stage*. Phoebe used to ask Ada to read the interesting items to her, by which she usually meant reviews and features about herself. We would cut out and save them for the scrap book. At this time of year, the paper gave details of all the pantos.

'Aren't you hot?' May demanded to know.

My face burned red, sweat trickled down my temples. My breast and underarms felt sticky. 'No, no.'

'You look it.'

'It's windy. I'm windblown.'

To distract attention from myself, I read out the names of the pantos playing in Leeds.

Tony said, in that eager voice of his, 'Would you all like to go to a pantomime?'

Rosa sighed. 'Tony! I know it's supposed to be Christmas and all that, but are you mad? Do you honestly think we'll feel like going to a panto. Apart from respect for Dad, would we ever want to be more stared at than Cinderella and the ugly sisters. "Oh there's Moran's lasses, sitting in the balcony, laughing their hard-hearted heads off."'

'Sorry,' Tony said, twirling a match, listening for Sophie.

Rosa curled strands of May's hair around her fingers and pinned the curls on top of her head, like lots of tiny sausages. May looked at herself in her favourite mirror, the one that made her look young. The sight must have cheered her, reminded her that she was the mistress of all she surveyed. She waved a slender hand towards the woodlouse-ridden sideboard. I had bought bottles of brandy and fortified wine, paid for with the proceeds of the gold bracelet.

'Pour us all a festive glass, Lydia. You'll join us in a drink, Tony?'

'If you're all having one.'

I took the small wine glasses from the cupboard.

'Not them!' May got up herself, brought out bright blue and gold glasses that looked like fairground prizes. Blowing the dust off, she set them on the sideboard. 'And take your cape off, Lydia lass. Look as if you're stoppin.'

I began to pour.

'Only a thimbleful for me,' May ordered. 'Just to be sociable.'

I stopped pouring.

'Nay lass, a person's thimbleful, not a fairy's. Keep pouring. Only I shall be supping when I'm out and don't want to overdo it. Keep going. I'll say when.'

When the glass would hold no more, she said when.

May beamed at Tony. 'Me and the Scholar's going out to his club.'

Sophie appeared, free of her coat, basket and money belt. She picked up her wine.

Tony raised his glass. 'Here's to ones who aren't with us anymore. May we have Christmas for them as well as usselves.'

I did sometimes feel sorry for the poor chump. He tried so hard. But at least Sophie had a faithful swain, unlike me.

He lit candle after candle on the Christmas tree.

May reached for her coat. She said to Tony. 'You can walk me to the end of Cavalier Street, if you've a mind.'

He hesitated. 'I will, yes. But I came to ask you summat, Sophie. Me mam always does a shepherd's pie on Christmas Eve. We wondered if you'd come round and join us for a bite. Rosa and Lydia too, if they're inclined.'

Rosa polished off her drink. 'I wouldn't say no to a bit of shepherd's pie.'

Tony didn't manage to hide his disappointment when Sophie refused.

Left alone, we bolted the shop door. Sophie brought down the money and we spread it on the table, in piles of twenty pounds. We were neither of us slouches at sums but had a few false starts before agreeing a total of £3,125.

Sophie picked up a handful of notes. 'Bejasus, we've broken the bank.'

'If it was a branch of the Penny Bank, no doubt. But not the head office of Thackreys. It would take a bit bigger robbery to break that bank.'

There was a sudden bang, like a knocking. I jumped, ready to scoop up the money. But it was only next door, someone making a racket.

'Pay no heed,' Sophie picked a stray fiver from the floor. 'They're always shifting some damn item hither and thither. They think if the sideboard and the table change places, the twelve of them will fit in better.'

She started to put the money back in the belt bags, wanting it packed away, out of sight. 'Wouldn't it be terrible if the police came back?'

'I expect they'll have better things to do on Christmas Eve.'

'I hope so. You don't know them, not like I do. That night they came for us . . . The way they just tore everything apart.' She leaned forward, her elbows on the table. 'And they won't give up on us Morans. You've never seen inside a prison cell have you?'

'No.'

'And I don't suppose you ever will. If it comes to being caught, your family would ride to the rescue. I'll be the one to cop it if this lot's discovered.'

'That's why I want you to leave it to me, Sophie. Tomorrow, I'll return the keys to the safe. On the day after Boxing Day, I'll go to Manchester.'

'Why Manchester?'

I opened *The Stage* at the article about our old theatre company. They were performing *Jack and the Beanstalk* at the Palace Theatre.

'And then what?' Sophie asked.

'I'm not sure. But it'll come clear. And when it's safe, you and Rosa come and join me there. We'll arrange a day and time to meet. Come to the stage door of the theatre. Only you'll have to make sure you're not followed.'

'That still doesn't tell us what to do with the money now.' Sophie ran her hands through her hair. 'Dad told me about someone in the market who hid a diamond ring in a cabbage, then couldn't remember which cabbage and had to chop them all up till he found it.'

'We'd need a field of cabbages to hid this lot. But if I'm to take it to Manchester, I'll need to have it sewn in my clothes, so we could do that now.'

'If the police come, they'll rip everything apart. But you're right. I'll do the sewing.' She reached for a wicker sewing basket and pulled out needle and thread.

We agreed I would wear two money belts, one at the back, one at my front. The rest of the money would be sewn into the lining of the tram inspector cape.

When the cape lining was undone and re-sewn, Sophie wrapped it and the two money belts in a sack.

'You'll have to do the next bit. Go in the cellar. Take some coal from the bottom of the heap. Put the sack there, then pile it up again.'

After the job was done, we unbolted the shop door.

Sitting by the fire, we sipped port and nibbled on pork pie. I felt exhausted.

'What do you think of Tony?' Sophie asked.

'He's steady. He'd never let you down.'

'No. I don't think he ever would. He's been very good, to me and to Rosa.'

'You won't tell him about the money?'

'What kind of eejit do you take me for?' She took another sip of wine.

'Will you marry him?'

'His mam won't let him, and he hasn't asked me.'

'He will. What then?'

'I don't know. There's something I have to do, you see. Something I promised Dad.'

She stared into the fire, as if trying to see her future.

Sophie

Mirror. Wedding ring. Coat. Watch. Rosa was right about me always hoping for the best. Even as I thought about getting stuff out of pawn, I hoped to find something in the coat pocket. A note. A sweet. Something. Something I could hold onto, that would shift the way things were.

I stood looking out of the attic window at the recreation ground, sparkling frost topped a light covering of snow. The springs groaned as Lydia clambered off the bed.

'Any of our detective friends out there?' she asked.

'Can't see anyone.' I moved away from the window and picked up my clothes, to dress downstairs. 'They won't have stayed out all night in this weather. If you get a move on soon, you shouldn't be followed to the station.'

Rosa opened her eyes. She grunted her annoyance at me. 'Do you think the coppers'll give up that easy? They'll have found a window to watch from – paid some slime bug a few bob to let them spy on us from the warmth of an attic, a great fire burning night and day. Bet on it.'

At the door of the attic, I called back to Rosa. 'We need to give Lydia a clear run to the station. You and me should go out first. Then if anyone's to be followed, it'll be us.'

Rosa turned over and pulled the blanket up to her nose.

I went downstairs, leaving it to Lydia to persuade Rosa to get up.

After Lydia had got well away, that would be soon enough to tell my sister about the money. If Lydia was caught, Rosa at least would be in the clear.

There was no sound from May's room.

Shivering in front of the dead kitchen fire, I dressed quickly.

With the tongs I lifted half-burned cinders from the fire grate and set them aside to burn again, poking the ash so that it dropped through to the already full pan below. Screwing sheets of newspaper into twists gave me time to think. If Lydia was caught, then what? The stepdaughter of Thackreys' Bank would hardly end up in the clink. I would.

Being in the second-hand line, May had two of everything. Her oak coal cabinet held chips of wood. She used the cast-iron scuttle for coal. I lay the wood chips in a careful pattern, as Dad used to. On top of that came the cinders. Then coal.

Even laying the fire spoke to me of Dad. In my mind's eye, he was still there, full of life.

Opening the shop door, I scattered ashes on the icy

pavement, asking myself how it was that a person could go on doing such normal things.

A mother and daughter grinned at me on their way to East Street Mills. I was not the only person who had thrown out ash. The two of them stepped carefully, avoiding the slippery parts of the pavement. Two boys were sliding along the street, back and forth on the same strip of ground, trying to make a slide. Watching them, watching the women retreat, I looked all around. Perhaps Rosa was right and some policeman, or a pair of them, sat at a window. Watching. Waiting.

I touched a match to the newspaper in the grate. Reluctantly, the flames took hold. Burn. Burn. Don't make me start again, I told the fire. Don't make me hold a shovel and a newspaper to you, begging you to blaze.

Even such a long time after Billy's death, going down into a coal cellar still gave me a light-headed feeling, so that I feared I would slip or fall. With the coal scuttle in my right hand, I steadied myself with the other hand against the damp, distempered wall.

Lydia had not done the best of jobs in hiding her sack. I could see the corner of it coming up between the coals. Taking the shovel, I filled the scuttle, then tugged at the sack.

It was a relief to hear Lydia call to me from the top of the cellar steps.

'Here.' Halfway up the steps, I handed her the blackened sack that held money belts and cape.

She said nothing, just nodded and hurried back, to dress in front of the struggling fire.

As I set the coal scuttle on the hearth, I knew another

reason why I hadn't confided in Rosa. Rosa trusted no one fully. She would say, 'You're letting Lady Lydia sling her hook to Manchester with all that brass?'

Lydia wore a full skirt, a striped shirt and a baggy cardigan. The looseness of her clothing disguised the bulk of the money belts. Her hair straggled across her high cheekbones. It struck me that she could wear any old thing and still look good.

'I need money to redeem Dad's pledges,' I said.

Someone else was up, and coming down the stairs. May. She had a slow, heavy tread, like a person who has far to go and in her heart doesn't believe she'll arrive.

Lydia lifted her skirt. 'How much?' Without waiting for an answer, she slid her hand into the money belt and peeled off pound notes.

I scrunched them up and pushed them in my pocket.

'The stage door of the Palace Theatre,' she said quickly. 'Noon, or sooner, on the sixth of January.'

May came yawning into the room, scratching her neck. 'That fire needs a shovel at it.'

Rosa didn't see the point of the two of us leaving the shop separately, and setting off in different directions. 'Where am I supposed to go?'

'Wherever you like. Go to some firm as if you're looking for a job. That'll throw them off the scent.'

'I'm tired. I'm cold. I thought we were going to get out of Leeds, not go tramping around.'

'Go to the market then. Buy something.'

'What?'

'Food.'

'What with?'

I fingered the notes in my pocket, wishing we'd we found the bank's piles of shillings and tanners. Reluctantly I produced a note.

Her eyes widened. 'Where'd you get that?'

'Lydia.'

'Did she sell her cat brooch?'

'Something like that.'

She took the note, looking at me with a sudden flash of knowing, but not knowing what.

'Don't ask me, Rosa. You'll know soon enough.'

Rosa put the note in her shoe.

Moments later, I was on my way to York Road, to the pawn shop, hurrying, cutting through the streets and alleys, looking back to see whether I was followed.

Only as I joined the line of waiting women did it strike me that to be redeeming and not pawning after Christmas would seem suspicious enough.

The pawnbroker wore his black apron, a green shade on his forehead. His eyeglass sat on the counter. A customer shuffled towards the door, coins in her hand.

There were two more women ahead of me.

His next customer had holes the size of potatoes in her stockings, and wore slippers whose backs had given way. She pointed at the eyeglass. 'Expecting jewellery are you, Henry?'

The pawnbroker angrily snatched up his eyeglass and set it under the counter as he glanced at her bundle.

'Tenpence!' he announced.

'Tenpence? Tenpence? You've gotta be kidding. I want me usual.'

He pawed the bundle. 'It's getting old and shabby. I can't go to a shilling this week.'

'Then I'll tek it somwhere else.'

'Go on then. They'll tell you the same.'

'I must have me usual or I can't manage.'

'Take it or leave it. Try along the road, but he's got his own customers same as me.'

'Well then I'll just stand here, and I'll tell you this. I see Mrs Macarthur's big black coat hanging up over there. She bought it out of the insurance money when her hubby died, God rest him. Two pounds you're asking for it and you lent her five bob.'

'Yer talking out the back of yer neck, woman. Eleven pence and that's me last offer.'

'Five bob Mrs Mac got off you. And interest you charged her. She'd no hope, no hope, what with that lad out of work. And another thing, that ring in the centre of your window. I know who that came from and how much she got from you.'

'Henry!' the woman's voice came from the house. The pawnbroker turned to his wife who stood in the doorway between house and shop. She whispered something to him. He sighed.

Back at the counter, he slapped down money. 'Right. For once, you win.'

The woman picked up her shilling.

He called after her. 'Friday night, six o'clock, on the dot, with your one and threepence!'

She swaggered out with her shilling, smiling at me, and the queue behind me. 'He hates it when you let on you know his business.'

It was my turn. I lay the pawn tickets on the counter in a row.

He looked at them, looked at me, and blinked. 'I didn't expect . . . '

Please God, don't let him start to talk about Dad. Not here. Not with a queue behind me. I put a pound note on the counter. Straight away, I wanted to snatch it back. Too late. He held it. Perhaps the bank notes were numbered. By the time I got back to May's, the police would be at the door.

He left the tickets on the counter, and walked into the house. My heart hurt. Perhaps he had the mirror on his own wall. After what seemed a long time, he came back. First, he handed me Mam's ring. I slid it on the middle finger of my left hand. My hands trembled. I held one hand with the other, to try and keep them still. He lifted the mirror onto the counter, pointing to one of its four clips. In a low voice he said, 'That clip'll need replacing but it's not down to me. It were damaged by you know who. I can't be held responsible.'

The bulky coat looked huge. It and the mirror would be awkward to carry. I leaned the mirror on my side of the counter while I took the coat. Its lining had been split.

The woman behind me in the queue had kept a polite distance up till then. She stepped forward, picked up the coat and held it for me. 'It's big, but put it on, love. Thah'll frame better.'

The sleeves fell way below my hands. The bottom just missed trailing the floor.

There was nothing in the pockets, except a hole.

I picked up the mirror, and left.

Rosa stood outside the shop. 'Trust you to come for the mirror on the iciest, slipperiest day of the year.'

'I thought you'd gone to the market.'

'Yes well, you know what happened to thought.' She took one end of the mirror. 'We'll manage it best between us. And if you're slipping, slip. Leave the mirror to me. I'll do the same. If it smashes we might earn seven years' bad luck, then where would we be?'

We trod on the ashes people had spread on the pavements, clutching the mirror for dear life. I thought of Dad. His little saying. 'If it wasn't for bad luck, I'd have no luck at all'.

By the corner we stopped. Rosa pulled her sleeves over her palms to keep the edge of the mirror from cutting into her hands. 'Lydia didn't sell her cat brooch did she?'

'No.'

'Sophie, what's going on between you and Lydia?'

'You'll know soon enough.'

When we got back to May's, Lydia had gone.

May took the mirror from us. 'Get warmed up, kids. You're frozen through.' Rosa's face was so white, not a freckle showed. The dampness in her hair looked sprinkled on, like icy dew. She went into the house to warm herself by the fire.

I stayed in the shop with May. The black overcoat had kept me warm. Reluctantly, I took it off. Dad had not worn it long enough for it to seem like his. I hung it on a shop hanger and placed it on the rail.

May glanced at the ring on my finger. 'So you've redeemed the lot?'

I nodded.

'Courtesy of Lydia?' May asked.

'Yes.'

'Then if you're asked, you best say I stumped up the money, and leave her out of it. The police were here.'

'What did they want?'

'To talk to you, and to anyone else I might have staying. Oh don't worry, I told em nowt.'

Rosa was listening. When we went through to the house, she asked. 'What else did they say, May?'

'They asked was there a third girl stopping here. I said no.'

My hands had started to shake. I gripped the mug of tea, trying to keep steady. The police would come back, I felt sure. We'd be dragged to the Bridewell. Hauled into cells. Questioned.

Rosa gulped down her tea. 'I'm off out, and I'm gonna borrow that black coat.' She stood up.

'Nay lass, stay put. It's like the North Pole out there,' May said.

Rosa put her cup in the sink.

'Where are you going?' I asked.

'You told me to go to the market. I always do as I'm bid.'

May tut-tutted after her. 'If you must brave the elements, put on a bonnet. Cover your ears.'

When May went back into the shop, I climbed the stairs, to our attic. From under the bed, I took the bundle given to me outside the prison. Until that moment, I couldn't bear to look at it. Perhaps it was the disappointment of not finding anything in the pockets of the big black coat that made me want to see what else Dad may have left. I undid the bundle. Took out Dad's old tweed jacket. It smelled of Sweet Briar tobacco, and dried rain. It felt rough and smooth against my cheek, depending how I touched the nap of the cloth against my skin. There were the letters I had written to him, and letters from the Scholar, from Rosa, and in a hand I didn't know. Some other time I would look at them. Not now.

I sat with my back against the bedhead, a blanket drawn over my knees. Outside, the day grew dark.

Come on, I said to the police in my head. Come on, do your worst, see if I could care.

As if I'd willed them, someone came. The shop bell sounded different when he entered. Something in the house changed. May called up the stairs.

Slowly, I threw the blanket off my legs, pulled Dad's jacket tightly round me and went down. At least Rosa had not come back. She would avoid their questions.

As I walked down the stairs, I wondered what they knew now. Perhaps Lydia had been picked up at the station. The Thackrey stepdaughter. She was a familiar face, and a missing person. I smiled at the thought of all that money. We'd done it. Even if they caught up with us now, we'd done it.

He stood to one side of the fire, his back to me. His black shoes were wet. His dark snow-sprinkled coat lay across the back of a chair, snowflakes melting. As he turned, I saw by the stripes on his sleeve he was a sergeant.

I slid further into Dad's jacket. If he was arresting me, I would keep it with me, for warmth in the cell. I tried sending a silent message to Rosa. *Don't come home.*

He had a face like a farmer from a child's picture book, his bushy eyebrows still wet from sleet or snow. 'I'm Sergeant Dickinson. I'd like to ask you a few questions.'

I slid my hands into the pockets of the jacket. In the right pocket were tiny flakes of tobacco and a match. I touched them between my finger and thumb.

'Do sit down,' he said, taking the big chair himself.

I turned a straight chair from the table and faced him. Suddenly I felt cold all over. I wanted someone to hold me, make me warm.

'You're Sophie Moran,' he said. 'The eldest?'

'Yes.'

'Your sister not here?'

'She went to the market.'

'You redeemed some pledges today.'

'Yes.'

'Where did you get the money to do that?'

I crossed my fingers in the jacket pockets. 'From May. The coat Dad pawned was hers. She only lent him it.'

I didn't say that she had 'only lent it' so that Dad *wouldn't* pawn it. And then he did.

'What was the hurry to get these particular items back?'

I took my left hand from the pocket and held it towards him. It didn't look like my hand at all. 'I wanted my mother's ring.'

'There are reports of a third girl staying here. What do you have to say about that?'

The shop bell rang, and Rosa came in, talking, and another voice with her. For a moment, I thought it must be Lydia, but the accent was wrong. They burst into the room. Though May must surely have tipped her off that the sergeant was there, Rosa came in saying something to me, and looked surprised to see him.

He remembered her at once. People always did remember Rosa. He stood up. No other policeman had been so polite as to stand. Straight away I knew he had expected to see Lydia.

The girl with Rosa gave us all a smile. 'Am I in the way, officer?'

'And you are?' he asked.

'Fenella Naggs. Rosa and me worked together in the tailoring before she got driven from the place by rubber-neckers and curiosity gazers.' She took out her purse and put some coins on the table. 'I was selling some of Sophie and Rosa's soft toys to my workmates. Here's the rest of your cash, girls.'

'You've been here before?' the sergeant asked.

'Oh aye,' Fenella said. 'Rosa and me are best friends. And you need your friends at a time like this.'

The sergeant turned to me. 'The reports of a third girl staying here.'

Rosa caught my eye, then looked away. She and Fenella sat side by side on high stools, legs dangling.

I didn't blink or flinch. 'Like Fen says, you need pals in hard times. I'm glad Rosa has Fen to stick by her.'

'You were friends with Lydia Thackrey once,' the sergeant said. 'Has she stayed here?'

It wasn't hard to tell him that I hated her for what she had said about Dad. And that the thought of Miss Lydia Thackrey staying in a second-hand shop on the Bank would be funny, if it wasn't so daft. 'I'm sure May won't mind if you want to search the house.'

He didn't.

When he had gone, Rosa picked up the coins Fenella had stacked on the table. 'I've never had a such a great need of a bag of chips. What do you say, Fen?'

Of all the nights to go to the fish and chip shop, we had to pick the night and the time when Tony stood in the queue.

The moment he saw me, he gave up his place to Rosa and Fenella and caught me by the hand.

We stood under the street light, the warmth of the fish shop just beyond us. 'I'm that glad I've seen you.'

'You'd no need to lose your place, Tony.'

'What's a place in the queue to me? I've had a rotten Christmas, worrying about you, wondering how you are.'

'How do you think I am?'

He put his arm around me and drew me close. 'I want to look after you. I want you to marry me, Sophie. I know this isn't the most romantic place to propose. Just walk with me a bit.'

We walked. By the rec, he took my hand. The frost-covered path crunched underfoot. Moonlight played through bare branches and lit the snow-covered grass. Single blades stood white and upright as if in a state of shock.

'I've talked to my dad. We can live above the joinery workshop. I'll make it grand, a little palace for you. Rosa too, if she has a mind to come.'

A bolt hole. A new place to be. A new me. He put his arms around me and drew me close. Kissed me. I kissed him back. For the first time that day, I felt warm. But it didn't go deep enough. For me to stay, my feelings would have to be so strong that I wouldn't care about being stared

311

at, pointed out as from that family who had such bad luck over their little lad, and to cap it all, their dad got topped for murder.

Tony was kind, good, reliable. He'd be steady, and a good provider. A man with a trade.

My hands slid away, into the pockets of the old jacket, to the strands of tobacco and the solitary match. 'I can't. I'm sorry.'

'Why not?'

'I don't have the right feelings.'

'Sophie! I don't expect you to. Not after what you've been through. But you will. I know you will. We'll get to the other side of all your troubles.'

I shook my head. 'No. It'll be best if I go away. I have to go away.'

'Then I will too. Where shall we go?'

'Go back to the fish and chip shop, Tony. I'm off to May's. I won't be changing my mind.'

And I broke free and ran, not turning back.

I couldn't tell him where I was going. Dad had asked me to find Danny and tell him in person what had happened. That's what I had to do. That was my mission.

Lydia

Pushing open the stage door of the Palace Theatre after all those years, catching a whiff of tobacco, and the smell of a paraffin heater, I felt twelve years old again, Phoebe Bellamy's daughter, and ready for anything.

Long-lost feelings bubbled up from somewhere deep inside. I wondered how our lives might have turned out if Phoebe hadn't married Sheldon Thackrey.

The stage doorkeeper looked up from his crossword puzzle.

'Hello, Sid.' I smiled at him. 'You don't remember me?'

'Something about you . . .'

'I'm Lydia, Phoebe Bellamy's daughter.'

The crossword page fell to the floor as he pushed his chair back. 'Lydia! Little Lydia! Let me shake you by the hand.' He stepped out to greet me. 'I remember you right enough, throwing your balls against that there wall.'

'I hope I wasn't a great pest.'

'As long as I could hear you, I knew you was all right. How's your mam?'

'She's well thanks. Has two little boys.'

'Well I'm right glad for her, and for you. You look a treat.'

'You haven't changed a bit, Sid.'

'Get away with you!' He took off his cap, showing a shining bald head. 'You'll be stopping to see the panto?'

'I wouldn't miss it.'

Ada liked to wear a long white pinafore in the dressing rooms, to protect her striped shirts against face powder. When I tapped on the door, she came into the corridor. In the dim light, she looked at me, and looked, then threw the pinafore over her face, and brought it down again, staring at me as if expecting I would have disappeared.

'Lydia!' She grabbed me and gave me a kiss. 'What a lovely surprise. And is Phoebe with you?'

'No, just me.'

'Well come along, come and see . . . ' She led me along the narrow corridor towards the little office where Mr Crampton camped out with his cash box, ledgers and theatre programmes. 'It'll do him good to see you. Take his mind off things.'

'Poor box office?'

'No, not that. The box office for the panto is always fine.' She stopped and turned to me. 'It's lovely to see you at any time, and I'm going to take you into the show. Starts in fifteen minutes. It's just that there's a bit of a palaver on at the moment.'

I laughed. 'When isn't there a palaver?'

'Harry's back from America. He agreed to be the villain in the panto but he's after Mr Crampton stumping up for a Noel Coward musical in London that will let him shine.'

Ada left me with a smiling Mr Crampton. He asked after Phoebe. Things had never been the same since she left. Fingering his moustache, he reminded me of her triumph in this very theatre.

I didn't want to hear about Ma's triumphs. 'Ada says the panto's going well.'

'Couldn't be better. You come out there with me in five minutes and I won't be asking you to count the occupied seats, but the unoccupied. You'll only need the one hand.'

Mr Crampton had tramlines on his forehead. The hollows from his nose to his lips had deepened. His hair looked too black.

He tilted his head to one side and bit his lip. 'You know me, Lydia. Not one to beat around the bush. You're not dressed like a banker's daughter, and you've turned up out the blue. Something's up. Am I right?'

'Everything's fine.'

'You've put a bit of weight on.'

I smiled. He thought I was pregnant and thrown out, and he was ready to help me.

'Have you and Phoebe and the banker . . . Is something amiss?'

Ada tapped on the door, saving me from telling a lie. 'Come on m'dear. You don't want to miss the overture.'

We took our seats on the back row of the stalls. Ada squeezed my hand. 'It's that lovely to see you. Just grand.'

*

If it hadn't been for Harry cheering me up with tales of playing Chicago; Dayton, Ohio; Cleveland and Boston, I might have gone to bed in the room next to Ada's and turned my face to the wall during the whole of that horrible New Year nonsense. I could see no future for myself in 1936, or ever after. What was the use of having a small fortune in used notes strapped to my body yet with nothing to do and nowhere to go. I even hesitated to walk around too much, in case I was knocked down by a tram car and had my fortune surgically removed.

I ventured into Mr Crampton's office and helped him with the accounts.

Harry popped his head round now and again, to cheer me up, reminding me that this was a leap year and he was open to proposals. That only made me feel worse, knowing how badly Theo had betrayed me. Never would I trust any man again, as long as I lived. Sometimes, out of nowhere, came the horrible memory of Granville, shoving me, hurting me. Raping me. Perhaps it was best to look at men from a distance, from a theatre seat as they pretended to be heroes and villains.

Even the damn calendar had let me down. The sixth of January was a Monday and so the theatre would be closed on the day I had told Sophie and Rosa to meet me at the stage door. I would have to hang about outside in the freezing cold. The thought of standing alone for hours terrified me.

Sid agreed to open up the stage door on the morning of the sixth, though he insisted he would have to sit in and ensure I was protected.

At half an hour before noon, the stage door opened and in they came.

'I told you she'd be here!' Sophie said to Rosa.

I could see they had been arguing. When Rosa went to the ladies' room, Sophie said. 'She's lost faith in everything. I went to the seven o'clock Mass at the cathedral this morning. She won't go any more. She didn't think you'd be here. I don't know what to do.'

'Then it's a good thing I have a few ideas.'

*

The three of us shopped for clothes, shoes, handbags and boots. Not only that, but we wore them from the shop, carrying as much as we could and arranging to have the rest delivered to our digs.

Sophie needed at least a couple of evening dresses to wear on board ship when she set off for New York to find her brother. Rosa had no trouble finding outfits to suit. For myself, I could not imagine where I might go, or what I might want to wear. I had a sudden horror vision of turning into Ada – advising other people on how to look their best. I had even chosen a striped blouse that looked as if it could belong to Ada. Well then, it would be hers – my present to her.

Finally, I chose a beige wool coat with astrakhan collar. Everything in my pile seemed to have a no-colour colour that matched the blankness of my feelings.

We took a taxi back to our lodgings. Rosa and I got out as Sophie settled with the driver.

'Lydia.' No one ever spoke my name as Theo did. He seemed to give it an extra syllable and a coat of velvet.

Suddenly he was there, helping with the load, taking a hat box and shopping bags from my arms, depositing them in the hallway, then coming back to me.

'Theo.'

I stood on the pavement, unable to move. Sophie and Rosa disappeared inside, though I called them not to.

I looked round, half expecting to see the Thackrey car, or a policeman.

He took my hands and I was glad to have kid gloves between my skin and his because I would not be brought round by his melting look and his soft words.

I pulled away.

'I've looked for you everywhere, darling.'

'Why?'

'Why? Because I love you.'

'You fooled me once, not again.'

'What is it you think I've done, or not done? I tried to find you.'

'You know very well. If you wanted to find me, why did you send a message telling me to meet you in the parish church, and then have Massey and Dorothea come to grab me.'

'Your Ma told me about that. I wasn't in work that day. I swear I've never stopped loving you. If I'd had your note, a word even, I'd have been with you like a shot.'

I couldn't move from the spot. 'Why didn't you find me sooner then?'

'I searched. Penelope swore you hadn't gone to Oxford, which was my first thought. She suggested Harrogate — mentioned one of the teachers at your school that you all got on with. So I went to Harrogate and tried to find you there. People go to London to lose themselves. I went there — walked everywhere, every park, every gallery. Madness. Finally, I went to Mrs Thackrey. She'd asked

Sergeant Dickinson to look for you. He thought he'd tracked you down to a second-hand shop on the Bank with the Moran girls, but no luck. Then she mentioned her old theatre company — just as a last ditch possibility. I saw Ada . . .'

'She shouldn't have told you where I was.'

'Darling, everyone but you can see that I adore you.'

I stepped back as he moved to embrace me. A sudden memory, a fear of what he might do shivered through me.

As if he guessed my thoughts, his arms dropped to his side. When he looked at me, I knew he was as different from Granville as day from night.

'You do believe me, don't you?'

I nodded.

'Thank God.'

'Theo, darling. I was so afraid. I thought everyone was against me, including you.'

I lifted my face to him, not wanting to wait another minute before his lips touched mine.

'I'll never let you go again, Lydia. We're going back together. We'll face your stepfather together. I know Mrs Thackrey will be on our side. She's been frantic with worry.'

I wanted him to stop talking, and kiss me again.

The landlady glared from the window. Let her.

'Get your things, Lydia. We're leaving. How long will it take you to pack?'

'I can't go back today. I have something to do here, on Saturday.'

'What's so important? I've looked for you long enough.'

'Then come with me on Saturday. Or do you have to be back at work?'

'I have a little bit of freedom. Tomorrow's Friday. I could telephone my boss from Manchester Corporation offices this afternoon. Tell him I'm looking at housing plans over here.'

We began to walk, away from the prying eyes of the landlady. 'Then do it. Stay here till Saturday. Come and wave Sophie goodbye. She's sailing for New York on the *Britannic*.'

'Alone?'

'Yes. I tried to make her wait, or think it through a bit more, but she won't. She believes she'll just go there and find her brother.'

'What about Rosa?'

'If you want to go to the panto tonight, you'll see her on the chorus line.'

Sophie

The ship rocked gently. I moved along the deck, trying to keep my own little farewell party in view, holding on to the last glimpse. Rosa's hair. Her red coat. Lydia's black-gloved hand. Then they were gone, turned into specks on the horizon. My last connection to the past cracked loose and blew across the waves.

I'd promised Dad. As simple as that. Or so it seemed until the ship rocked its way across the Irish sea. Liverpool disappeared. England disappeared. There were hundreds of people on the ship, but I was alone. Perhaps it was the departure that brought my party piece to mind. The words spoke themselves in my head, and I would have sworn didn't make it to my lips. *I will arise and go now, and go to Innisfree, And a small cabin build there, of clay and wattles made; Nine bean-rows will I have there, a hive for the honey-bee, And live alone in the bee-loud glade.*

Never so alone as in that moment. But it was New York where I was headed, not some bee-loud glade. When I finally turned away from watching the departing shore, a smartly dressed young steward walked along the deck, carrying a tray.

'Beef tea, Miss? If you sit yourself down in a deck chair . . .'

I sat down and took the tea. 'Thank you.'

With one hand, he steadied the tray and with another picked up a blanket from a nearby chair and expertly draped it across my knees. As I sipped my tea, my party poem went on reciting itself in my head. Just for a moment, I thought it was Dad, answering me from somewhere in the sea or sky, or inbetween. Like when the words of a song went through my head, and then Rosa would start to sing it aloud from the very point I'd reached. But the words were real, spoken in a Yankee twang, and came from the man lowering himself into the deck chair beside me, stretching out his long legs.

'*And I shall have some peace there, for peace comes dropping slow, Dropping from the veils of the morning to where the cricket sings, There midnight's all a-glimmer, and noon a purple glow, and evenings full of the linnet's wings.*'

The man looked at me, with a sheepish apologetic smile, and I realised I must have spoken the words aloud, like some mad woman, as I stood by the ship's rail.

For a long time neither of us spoke. Then he held out his hand.

'I'm Fergal Corey, returning to New York.'

He had black wavy hair and grey smiling eyes flecked with green. Instead of telling him my own name, I started to say something about not realising I'd said the words of the poem aloud.

'And you spoke it well.' He still had my hand in his. 'I went to hear the man himself give a reading, in London. He says it's a young man's poem, and if he was to write it now, he would leave out the *Arise and go*.'

'But I like the arise and go. The arise and go is what draws me in.'

'Then Yeats himself is wrong and you are right. Sure he's an old man now. What does he know?'

'What else did he say?'

'He talked about the purple heather on the island. Of course, I was there at the wrong time of year for seeing it.'

'You've been to Isle of Innisfree?' Until that moment I never knew there was such a place. I thought it was as invented as Dad's claim to a piece of land. Perhaps Innisfree was imaginary, and this Fergal Corey was one of the men Ada had warned me about. Fast men on ships, ready to ply a girl with gin or pull out a syringe brimming with opium. Before you knew it, you'd be imprisoned in some harem. I hadn't believed her. Now here I was, not twenty miles into the journey, and the feller was after me.

Keep calm, I told myself as I sipped the beef tea and listened as he told me about Lough Gill, Sligo, and how Innisfree meant heather island. He had studied literature at university and wanted to see places from the poems he had studied. In London he had suits made and walked London Bridge, reciting from 'The Waste Land'.

He contemplated the toe caps of his shiny shoes. 'I think you and I are among the few travelling alone.'

That was my cue to speak back to him, but I had no conversation about the geography of poems and did not want to talk about myself. The steward collected beef tea empties. I slid from the deck chair.

'I'm arising and going to my cabin now.'

'Your name, you didn't tell me your name,' he called after me.

I pretended not to hear. Though I was willing to say my first name, I wouldn't say Moran. He may have read the papers. Everyone likes to read about a murder, and a hanging.

My cabin mate was a well-made American woman in her forties. She had a floury dough face, curling grey hair and a way of taking up the whole space just by being there. She sat on the only chair and poured herself a glass of gin. 'It steadies the digestive system against the rocking of the boat. Will you take a drop, honey?'

'No thank you.'

'I expect your digestion is good enough. I'll take the top bunk. The higher I am, the less likely to throw up. Now, tell me all about yourself. You're going out to join relatives, am I right?'

Now it would start. Questions. Your name, your history, your future. My name carried shame, my history pain, and my future took the shape of a shifting fog.

'My brother,' I said, and found an excuse to leave the cabin again, seeking fresh air on the deck. That's when I saw the stairs with the chain across, the door with a painted sign forbidding passengers to enter. This was the door I would watch. The door to the engine room. Perhaps one of the stokers might come up from the depths to cool himself and I could ask, Did you work with my brother? Did you meet my brother Danny?

Nearby was a deck chair and blanket. I waited.

No one came.

A hooter sounded for the evening meal.

The ingeniousness of the dining room amazed me. Ledges edged the tables so that plates and dishes wouldn't slide away as the ship rocked. And so much food. Soup. Meat and veg. Semolina pudding. Cups of tea and coffee.

After the meal, I took up my post again, by the forbidden door.

No one came.

In the blackness of that night, the sky seemed closer than it had ever been, with hundreds of silvery stars. Crashing waves mocked me, rising and falling with a relentless, cruel rhythm. Danny, they jeered. No-Dan. No-Dad. No-Mam. All I could see in the darkness was the waves' white crests. The ocean cared nothing for us. Why should it, how could it? Hearts could break, men, women and children die in a thousand ways over a thousand years and it matters not a jot. Only to me.

What madness had possessed me to think I would ever find Danny? And if I could hardly bear to pass a night alone on deck, there would be no hope for me in a strange city. As the waves crashed and broke, something inside me crashed and broke also. Great sobs welled up and shook me so that I could not stay still. Battered by the wind, I struggled to the ship's rail and looked into the dark deep, seeing nothing, sobbing, half wishing to fall over and be washed away forever, not to have to go on.

By the time that 'Crew Only' door opened, towards dawn, I missed the moment. The door slammed. A thin shadow moved away with silent steps.

The foolishness of my journey to find Danny struck me with gale force. May had said it. Lydia's Mr Crampton and Ada had warned me. Theo said, 'Make sure you have a return ticket, and enough money.'

I didn't listen, except to the return ticket part.

Now I knew for sure, I would never find Danny. And perhaps that would be for the best. Why find him to break his heart? Because. Because I had promised Dad.

The next day, I ducked under the chain and opened the 'Crew Only' door. Down, down I went so that the ship's engine deafened me and the heat made it hard to breathe. I must be near, near to the furnaces that fired the engine. If I found someone, would I make myself heard, or hear a reply? In my head, I tried out the words. *Did you work with Danny Moran? He was a stoker on this ship last October.*

Behind the great iron doors – that must be the place I would find the stokers. Heat rolled off them. Then a hand on my shoulder. I turned. An officer, by his cap and jacket. He took my arm and led me away. For a moment I thought of telling him that I wanted to speak to a stoker. But his look was so strange that I couldn't ask. We walked back along corridors and up winding stairs, he saying it was dangerous down there, and please keep to the passenger areas.

The door opened onto the morning light.

And there he was again, Fergal Corey, the reciter of my poem, just strolling by as the officer lifted the forbidding link chain that separated passengers from crew, and plonked the chain back in place as he left me on the other side.

'Oh there you are,' said Fergal, as if he had been expecting me. 'I wondered where you'd got to. I forgot to say what it was prompted Yeats to write about Innisfree.'

'I don't want to know.' Defeat spread from my scalp to my toes. If I couldn't even speak to a stoker, how would I find Danny in a great city like New York?

Fergal fell into step with me, matching his stride to mine. He wore polished brogues, a dark brown suit and a long smooth scarf, the colour of buttercups.

We walked once round the deck, not speaking.

He turned to me, taking the scarf from his throat. 'Would you say this canary job is a man's colour?'

'I don't know.'

'I'd say not.' He placed the scarf around my neck. 'Which way would you like to wear it?'

'I don't know.'

'There are so many ways to wear a scarf. You can sort of sling it round, as if daring a breeze to steal it. Or tie it, like this, so you'll never lose it.'

It was soft to the touch. The label said cashmere, and the name of a London shop.

His hands still held the scarf. 'Will you accept it, Sophie Moran?'

'How do you know my name?'

'I heard your sister call you Sophie, when you kissed goodbye.'

'How do you know she's my sister?'

'Do you always interrogate admirers?' He set off walking round the deck. I stayed put. 'Come on. It's one of the ways to keep warm.' I didn't budge. He took my hand and slid my arm through his. 'All right, I'll tell you. I knew she was your sister because the connection was in the air between you, and there's a likeness, too. Does that satisfy?'

'Are you a detective? Rosa didn't say our last name.'

'You got me in one. I've looked at the evidence – the passenger list. And I also know that you disappear like Cinderella after the ball, without even going to the ball. There was a dance last night, you know? And boxing. Would you like to go to the top deck and watch the wooden horses race?'

'No.'

'Then neither would I.'

He had the kind of eyes and the joking voice that made me smile.

'Ah so you do smile. And will you come to the dance tonight?'

'I might.'

'Good. I like certainty. Then I'll walk you back to your cabin, so I'll know where to hunt you out if you stand me up.'

Ada had said I should expect to dance. From her costume box she found me a deep purple mid-calf length dress with a yoke neck, a low back and smooth sleeves that ruched just above the wrists. It looked as if it belonged to an old lady, until she made me try it, then it looked perfect.

And dance we did. Fergal knew all the steps. He was light on his feet, almost like a man on castors, and in his arms I felt I couldn't put a foot wrong.

For the first time in months, I felt a kind of lightness in my being, not entirely a forgetfulness of loss, but as if the heaviness lifted, like a fog can clear just for a few yards so you could almost imagine yourself through it. But fog had a way of hovering, ready to envelop you again.

In the ship's ballroom, the lights glowed soft and warm. We seemed to float on the music. If we could dance there forever, holding that moment, then all the pain and hurt might disappear.

He had a way of singing the words into my ear as we danced.

'You must have been a choir boy.'

'I was too. How did you know?'

'My brother was a choir boy. He said any lad who came in on the right notes six times out of ten had no chance of escape.'

He laughed. 'He was dead right. Except in my case it was five times out of ten.'

'Liar. You can sing.'

'If I could truly sing, how would I know half of Yeats's output by heart? I'm like you. The recitations were my party pieces. Now, after this dance, we have to try a cocktail, choosing it by the glory of its name.'

I tried out a Mermaid cocktail that tasted like peppermints.

Fergal told me that he had been to Ireland to meet his dying great-grandfather, for the first and last time, and to clear the mortgage on the family's patch of land in Sligo.

'Are you going back to live there then?' I thought of Dad, and his dreams of a piece of land in Ireland.

'No. The farm is for the cousins over there, not for us. We're settled in the States now, with fingers in a few pies.'

'What kind of pies?'

He brought out his card that said Corey & Sons, building contractors.

'So you're a builder?'

'No. My older brothers took to the business. I was meant to be the priest or the doctor, but instead I'm the professor.'

'Really a professor?'

'According to the mammy. Though I'm still studying. I have a term's teaching lined up after Easter, to undergraduates at NYU. If any one of them can recite Yeats with your yearning, I'll be well pleased.'

I shook my head. 'You've lost me. I don't know what NYU is, or an undergraduate, or why you should expect them to recite. And I certainly can't imagine why you're still studying at your age. I left school at fourteen.'

He spluttered into his drink. 'Please don't say that. You sound like my dad. Only he left school at eleven, and worked from the age of, I don't know, before he could crawl if you believed him.'

Then we were dancing again. 'My dad will like you, so will the mammy. You'll meet them.'

'Why should I meet them?'

He snapped his fingers. 'Just like me to forget the important part. Because we're going to marry. I knew that the moment I saw you on the quayside. I don't hold it against you for not noticing me then, but notice me now.'

He stopped, right in the centre of the dance floor, under the mirror globe. Other dancers circled and spun, leaving

330

that space to us. For a long moment, I thought the music stopped. Something about him made me feel I'd always known him. There was kindness and intelligence in his eyes, and he looked like a man who would take care of you, but also like a little boy, ready to laugh.

'Well?'

'I've noticed you.'

'And?'

I nodded.

'Good.'

The music started again, the dance floor came back into motion. We didn't speak another word through the next dance, or the one after, or the one after that.

When we sat down and the waiter brought us more cocktails, Fergal said, 'You looked so brave on the quay-side. So determined. And I just knew. When you waved to your sister, it broke my heart. I said to myself, once we're together, we'll never part. Because I couldn't bear for you to wave me goodbye.'

We touched glasses.

I felt that I had fallen into some shapeless dream, and didn't want to wake.

Later, when the dance ended, we found a blanket on the deck. Wrapped in the blanket, we stood at the stern of the ship, waiting for the sun to rise. It came up from the horizon so quietly, like the hush in a promise.

That was when I told him that I was going to New York to find Danny, and that I had no idea where to look.

'I'll help you. When did he come? What does he do?'

'He came in October. At home he worked as a book-maker's clerk.'

'Does he know anyone stateside?'

The only person I could think of was the choirmaster's brother who had joined some monastery, not in New York City, but somewhere further north, in New York State, the choirmaster had said.

'I'll find him for you. And until I do, you can stay with my parents.'

'How can I? They don't know me.'

'I've cabled them to meet us, and told them about you. They're delighted that I'm going to marry an Irish girl.'

'I'm not Irish. I'm English!'

'Same difference. And no English person has a name like Moran.'

The Moran clan, Dad had called us. Dad. How could I ever tell anyone the truth about what happened to him? No one would marry the daughter of a hanged man.

I heard myself give a sigh that would have outdone May at her dreariest.

'What's that about?' Fergal asked.

'Who said anything about getting married?'

'Sorry, I thought I'd mentioned that.'

The sun rose a little higher, but gently as if testing whether it was worth its while to stay in the world.

'You don't know anything about me, Fergal.'

'And I'm not going to yet, am I? Not until after you've seen your brother.'

'What makes you say that?'

'You're coming to tell him something, and until you have, you won't tell me.'

It gave me a shiver to think that he had guessed, or half guessed.

'You're cold.' He drew me closer under the blanket.

'You're right that I've something to tell him. That our dad died, and how he died.'

'I'm sorry.'

In that moment, I wanted to pull away, before it was too late. Before he said he was sorry that he had made his rash promise of marriage, which of course he would withdraw when he knew.

'I know we Americans gas a lot more than you do, but sometimes it's best to talk. You could try it out on me. Tell me how your dad died, if it's so painful.'

'It is, and I can't.'

'OK. OK.'

He walked me back to my cabin, the blanket from the deck still round my shoulders. I was about to slip it off and give it to him, to return it. He took its edges and pulled it, drawing me towards him. With his arms around me, he kissed my forehead. The blanket fell to the floor. He kissed my neck, my eyelids, and then my lips. It was like the magic in the ballroom, lifting me into a different world.

'Sleep tight, Sophie my love. I'll see you at lunch or beef tea time if you're awake.'

I opened my cabin door and sleep-walked to the chair, catching my breath. After a few moments, I took off my dress, dropped it onto the back of the chair and climbed into the bunk.

Above me, my cabin mate stirred in her bunk. 'Everyone falls in love on a ship. It lasts until you dock.'

But I knew. Something had happened between me and Fergal. That was why I had said no to Tony. This was what

I had waited for. It was like feeling consigned to hell, and then the gates of heaven opened.

It was a tall house in Brooklyn Heights, its woodwork painted green and cream. Within half an hour of meeting Mr and Mrs Corey, I'd learned that they'd hoped Fergal would marry his second cousin from Sligo and fetch her back.

'Was that why you pounced on me?' I asked him. We were holding hands, looking out across the river towards Manhattan. The sun set dramatically, falling like a great ball of fire, into the East River beyond. 'So you wouldn't come back empty-handed.'

'That's about the size of it. Besides, marrying your second cousin could lead to inbreeding. And she couldn't stay awake long enough to watch the sun rise.'

He stood behind me and cradled me in his arms. It had been three weeks, and sometimes I could forget for hours on end why I had come to New York. He kissed my hair. 'Sophie.'

'Mmm?'

I expected him to whisper again that he loved me.

'I've found him. Don't look now, but he's walking over the bridge. The bench just behind us, you sit there. Danny will come to you. Then wait for me.'

Then Fergal was gone.

Soon it would be over. I would tell Danny how Dad died, and why. Then I would have to tell Fergal. Only I wouldn't. I couldn't bear to see the look on his face, the disappointment, the shame, the refusal, the back-tracking of his love.

Danny walked across the bridge, looking behind him once or twice, as if half expecting to be followed.

334

His face filled with joy to see me as I ran to meet him. We hugged. 'Daft lass. You'd no need to come after me. I'd have written.'

'When?' We sat side by side on the bench.

'Did you think I wouldn't manage?' he asked.

'If you had, you'd have written to boast about it.' I took out Dad's fob watch and gave it to him.

He seemed to weigh it in his hand. 'Is that the time?'

'Yes. I've kept it wound.'

'What's happened, Sophie?'

I told him about the bank robbery and murder, our arrest and Dad being charged. I explained that I felt sure Dad believed Danny was involved and that he was protecting him, even though Rosa and I had gone to Liverpool and checked with the shipping line to make sure Danny had sailed. Finally, I told him how Dad died.

Danny folded his arms across his chest and rocked.

I took out Dad's letter.

The tears flowed down Danny's cheeks. 'I can't read it. Read it to me.'

Though I knew the letter by heart, I read it by the soft glow that came from a nearby lamp at the bottom of a garden. When I had read it once, I said again the message that Dad had written for him.

Danny, my first born, you did not always go the way we hoped but you are a lad full of life and so hold onto that. I see a lot of myself in you and it gives me comfort to know you are out there in the wide world and will make a much better fist of it than I ever did. Do your best for your sisters. Make the most of the chances you have. No one is perfect and I know for sure there is more good in you than bad. Whatever anyone says to the contrary, life is not too short to improve your chess!

With love and blessings. Have no regrets my treasured ones. Live well.

Your loving Dad

I thought Danny would never stop crying. 'I've made a bloody awful fist of it.'

After a long while, he said, 'He was right. But I didn't shoot the old man. That was Granville. It was his idea. I was only there to make it look like an outside job.'

'But, I don't understand. How could you have been there? Your name was on the ship's list. Stoker. You'd sailed when it happened. On the *Britannic*.'

'No. That was my alibi. Someone else sailed with my name, a chap both me and Granville knew. After the robbery, I laid low in Liverpool for a couple of days and sailed after – a different ship.'

'Then Dad was right.'

Danny nodded. 'I killed him, Sophie. I killed our dad.'

There was barely a trace of the sun now, just a blotch of red in the sky where it had been.

'So Dad wasn't a fool. He was a hero.'

'He was a bloody martyr. For me. What can I ever do now, Sophie?'

'I don't know. He said to live well.'

'There's blood on my hands. No wonder, no wonder nothing goes right.'

336

'Dad wanted me to find you. He didn't say what any of us should do. He thought you'd be well set up, and I suppose he was glad of that since nothing much ever seemed to work out the way he wanted.'

'I feel cursed now. I used to think my life was just around the corner. Now I know it's not. It ended when Granville pulled the trigger. He didn't just kill the cashier, it was Dad, me, you, all of us.'

'We'll have to go on, that's all. Life doesn't just stop.'

A tug boat in the river sounded a hooter. Its lights glowed brightly on the dark water. 'For Dad's sake, we'll just have to do what we can, do our best and . . .'

'I've made such a pig's ear of things.'

'How much money did you rob?'

'Don't ask.'

'What are you doing with yourself now?'

He shook his head. 'You've to speculate to accumulate. I thought I was onto a good thing. I met this feller in a bar and he . . . It all backfired. I've made some enemies.'

'Where are you living? What are you doing?'

'I won't tell you. That way it'll keep you out of it.' He stood up. 'I'm gonna go now, Sophie.'

'I can help you.'

'This is something I've to sort out myself. But at least it's a bit of good luck you finding such a clever feller. Fergal Corey. It's a family to be reckoned with. About time one of us had some luck.'

I didn't tell him that the clever feller might cool towards me once he knew more about us. I took a notebook from my pocket. 'I want an address, Danny. I might need it, need you.'

He stood up. 'Walk with me to the bridge.'

I had to hurry to keep up. 'Where do I come to find you?'

'You don't. I'm not gonna drag you down.'

Wanting to shake him, I grabbed his sleeve and tugged at him to stop. 'Will you listen to me? I might need to find you.'

'Not with the Corey family behind you you won't.'

'They might not stay behind me.'

He pulled free. 'I'll find you when there's something good to report. It'll be soon.' He touched my arm lightly. 'So long, kiddo.'

I called after him as he strode across the bridge. 'Danny, stay in touch with me! And with Rosa, through May.'

'I will. I will, I promise.'

Twice, he turned to wave, then the gloomy evening swallowed him.

Slowly, heavy and reluctant, I turned back towards the look-out point across the river, where Fergal waited for me on the bench. He patted it for me to sit beside him, and then took my hand.

I pulled away. 'I better just say what I have to say. If you don't want to stick with me, then that's all right by me.' It wasn't of course, but I had my pride.

He took my hand again, 'Let me just say this first . . . '

'No! Bigmouth! You listen to me for once.'

But he didn't. 'Sophie, a family doesn't get to where ours has reached by keeping their hands scrupulously clean, that's all. Your turn.'

'My father was hanged for a murder he didn't commit.'

He let out some low curse and thumped our hands on

338

the wooden slats of the bench. 'How can even my big mouth know what to say to that?'

'Then don't say anything. I can leave in the morning. I have a return ticket to Liverpool.'

'And what would be the point of that? I can't have a wedding without a bride.'

'Then send for your cousin.'

'Too late. My mother's fixed on you now, and so am I. You can't back out.'

'Don't you want to know any more, about the murderous Morans?'

'Some day maybe, when you want to tell me.'

Would being a bank robber be an impediment to marriage? Could some member of the congregation, still feeling hard done by at the loss of the Sligo cousin, stand up and shout about me in the church?

As we walked back to his house, Fergal said, 'Mom will ask you to go shopping tomorrow. Put her off. There's somewhere I want you to see.'

After an early breakfast, we walked across the bridge and up through Manhattan, past tall buildings that made me dizzy, through streets filled with grocery shops and children playing in gutters. Mothers called out in Italian and Chinese.

'Amazing huh?'

'It feels like being in a film. It's what you see when you go to the pictures.'

We passed a soup kitchen, a row of beaten-looking men, shuffling along in a straggly queue. I looked for Danny in the line.

Fergal pointed to a cobbled street where washing hung

from upstairs windows. 'We lived along there when Granddad first came over, and Dad was a boy.'

'Is that what we've come to see? Where your family started from?'

'And where we're going, you and me.'

It was a grey stone building, with wide steps leading to wood and glass doors with long brass handles. He pushed the door for me to step inside. 'This is NYU. It's where I'm going to teach, and where you can join the class. I'll need one friendly face at least.'

'I can't go to university.'

'That's where you're wrong. Here anyone can, if they can pay.'

'I'm not clever enough. I told you, I left school . . .'

'. . . and at fourteen and you were a shop assistant. That was then, this is now. Anyway, that's not what Danny said.'

'What did he say?'

'That he was fly, and had a good line in impersonations, that Rosa could sing and dance, and that you were smart and kept everyone in line.'

We walked around the building. It seemed to me some of the students were much older than I was. Why shouldn't I have an easy life, reading books, learning to talk up a storm.

'Writing as well. You'll be good at that, Sophie.'

'All right, then, if they'll have me. I don't know what else to do.'

We filled in forms, and I was handed a book list, with titles of novels and poetry by people I'd never heard of. I'd already missed so much of what the other students had begun to read.

'I'll be able to pay for myself,' I told him as we left the

building to head for a bookshop, 'once my bank account is sorted out.'

Fergal has a little sideways twist of the head and a raising of an eyebrow when he thinks a person is being fly. 'You did well then, for a shop assistant.'

I felt myself blush. Then I thought of Mam and her Penny Bank account. Now I would have my own account, with the New York City Bank. Once Lydia had transferred money to me, my account would be a little larger than most, that's all.

We walked all the way up Manhattan, past the public library, on up to Central Park. From the warmth of the cafè, we watched ice skaters gliding.

I sipped my hot chocolate. 'I'd like to try that.'

Fergal shook his head. 'Not yet. I don't want my bride to hobble into the church on crutches.'

Danny put in one more appearance, to walk me down the aisle in my white satin dress. I wished Rosa could be there beside me, but I would write to her every last detail of the ceremony, the way the Corey family filled both sides of the church and how I couldn't possibly tell her about them all because they were too many.

At the reception, Danny gave a speech, and raised a glass to us, and said all the right things, though afterwards I couldn't remember a word. No one did because he went straight into his party piece of the train coming into and out of the station, and while everyone clutched their bellies and laughed, he chugged around to me and gave a last whisper in my ear, leaving me astonished as to where he had decided to go. Continuing his steam train, he chugged away from the reception, and out of our lives.

Lydia

I hoped Theo and I would have the railway carriage to ourselves all the way to Leeds, so we could kiss, hold and touch each other.

Theo lifted my new suitcases onto the rack, and squeezed the hat boxes beside them.

'We could well have this carriage to ourselves. If anyone sees the amount of luggage you have, they'll believe we're expecting another three people.'

'Don't be impertinent, Mr Winterton, or I shall be cross with you. I might just have to slap your legs.'

He bent over me and tilted my face to his. 'Kiss me instead.'

When we kissed, I almost melted inside, thinking that in just a few months we would be together properly, and could do exactly as we pleased, loving each other, and nothing and no one to get in the way.

'I do love you, Lydia.'

'And I love you. I've missed you. My life felt empty without you.'

'If we keep on kissing,' he whispered, 'no one else will dare come in this carriage. We'll be too outrageous for them.'

And no one did.

He took my hand. 'Darling Lydia, at last, we're together, without Moran girls crowding in.'

'But you like them don't you?'

'Of course I do, they're your friends. Who am I to say that Rosa's full of herself and Sophie's mad, going all that way across the Atlantic on her own. Anyway, I'm not interested in them. Only you.'

The train pulled out of the station. One of my hat boxes shuffled along above us. He stood up to push it more firmly onto the rack. 'A chap could be a bit curious about how you three girls managed to tog yourselves out with copious items of fashion when you came from a sleazy second-hand shop, wearing what you described as jumble sale rejects.'

'That's easy,' I said, pulling at his hand, making him sit back down beside me. 'Kiss me and I'll tell you.'

He kissed me and put his hand on my waist. 'Let me guess. Some elderly gentleman admirer saw the three of you feeding pigeons in St Peter's Square and insisted on becoming your patron.'

There should be no secrets when two people love each other as Theo and I do, when they intend to spend the rest of their lives together.

'No, silly! I robbed a bank.'

'Oh good.' He kissed me again. 'I'm glad I'll be marrying a girl with a bit of spunk. What bank, may I ask?'

'We robbed Thackreys' Bank, just before Christmas.'

'It's not really funny, after what happened. But I suppose the three of you had to find a way of dealing with it all.'

'Yes. It was their compensation for what happened to their father, and mine for what Granville . . .'

'Poor Lydia. Don't even think about Granville. I haven't seen him for weeks. But when I do I won't answer for the consequences. I've got a feeling Mr Thackrey has banished him to some other branch of the bank.'

'I don't ever want to see him again.'

'Then I'll make sure you don't. And don't ever imagine because he acted as he did that I would ever hurt you. I'll cherish you, Lydia, I promise.'

He took both my hands in his, raising them to his lips, kissing the palms, and each finger turn by turn.

'And why not rob the bank on your own doorstep? Silly to travel great distances. Did the three of you wear masks?'

'It was just me and Sophie.'

He laughed. 'You're mad sometimes. You're going to drive me wild.'

So he couldn't say I hadn't told him.

There should be no secrets, when two people love each other.

Darkness had fallen as the train crossed the Pennines. Lights glinted from the cottages by the railway lines. Soon we would have a place of our own, snug and cosy together on a Saturday night, with a fire glowing.

'What are you thinking?' Theo asked, running his finger down the back of my neck.

'Shameless thoughts, about how once we're married we'll be together every night, and do exactly as we please, like true lovers.'

He sighed. 'I can't wait. Show me, show me how you'll kiss me.'

So I did. The journey was like being outside of time and space, in a world all our own.

At Leeds Station, the taxi driver loaded our luggage into the boot while Theo opened the car door for me. We drove past the bank. I was closest to it and tried not to look. Sophie always thought the bank malevolent, but I had never experienced it in that way before. Yet I knew what she meant. As we went by, I could almost feel the bank, smouldering with malice.

'It's all right,' Theo whispered. 'Don't worry, Lydia darling. You're coming to our house. You don't have to even think about seeing your mother and stepfather until tomorrow.'

'It's not Ma that worries me.'

'No one can hurt you. Not now that we're together.'

I snuggled up to him, trying to feel brave.

Theo directed the driver along the lane that led to the parsonage. When it stopped, he said, 'You go on. Mother's expecting you.'

He had telephoned from the station.

Mrs Winterton heard the car. She stood in the doorway, framed by a glow of light.

'Lydia, dear, how lovely to see you!' She spoke with lightness in her tone, as if I trotted up her garden path every Saturday night, clutching a hat box. 'Come inside and get warm.'

Theo followed me up the drive, carrying the cases.

Thankfully, his mother asked me no questions, just led us both into the dining room where a fire blazed.

'You two sit yourselves by the fire. Have you eaten? There are sandwiches, and I'll make some cocoa.'

I sat in the tapestry-covered chair. 'Thank you.'

'Your father's putting the finishing touches to his sermon, Theo. You can have a word with him later.'

When she had gone, Theo drew my chair nearer the fire. 'You see. I told you everything would be all right.'

'I wish we could just run away to Gretna Green.'

'We'll do this properly, Lydia. Tomorrow, after the service, I shall make it quite clear that we want to marry and wish to have permission. But that we'll marry in any case as soon as you're of age.'

Mrs Winterton came back with two mugs of cocoa. 'Here we are. This should warm you up and help you get a good night's sleep.'

I was thankful she didn't ask me a hundred questions about where I had been and why.

'I'm putting you in Penelope's room, Lydia.'

'Thank you.'

'And tomorrow morning, before the service, I'll go across and speak to Mrs Thackrey and tell her you're here. I don't want her to just walk into the church and see you there. In fact, I wonder whether it's too late to go over there now.'

'Yes it is,' I said quickly. 'Please don't, Mrs Winterton.'

'Lydia's gone through a lot, Mother,' Theo said quietly. 'I'm sure she needs her rest tonight, and no excitement.'

His mischievous eyes caught mine as he said that. I

looked away, so as not to smile. I would have loved some excitement that night, but not the kind involving Ma and Sheldon Thackrey.

For what seemed hours, I couldn't sleep. When finally sleep came, it brought mad dreams. Sophie's ship was sinking and I had to warn her, but someone or something put obstacles in my way as I stumbled along the deck in darkness, bumping into old furniture. Granville was laughing. He was the one who had set the obstacles. I needed to find Theo, but he was locked in a cabin. Mountainous waves crashed over the side of the ship. One hit me in the chest, knocked me to the deck. I floundered and struggled to free myself. My heart pounded. In the darkness, I slipped and was washed overboard, falling, falling.

I woke to find Mrs Winterton standing over me in her plain white nightgown, candle in hand, long plait over her right shoulder. Theo stood in the doorway behind her. 'It's all right, Theo. You go back to bed,' Mrs Winterton said to him.

But he came to me as she lowered herself onto my bed, placing her candle holder on the bedside table.

Theo took my hand. 'It's only a bad dream. You're safe.'

'Thank you, dear,' Mrs Winterton said firmly.

'Good night then, dearest.' Reluctantly, Theo let my hand fall back on the counterpane, and turned to go.

I heard him stub his toe on the door frame and let out a quiet groan and curse.

Mrs Winterton tut-tutted. 'I put cheese in the sandwiches because I expected you sooner. It was far too near bedtime for cheese. No wonder you've had a nightmare.'

347

Cheese. She put it down to cheese. I'd wrongly pointed the finger at an innocent man. I'd been raped, feared myself betrayed by the only person who truly loved me, gone into hiding, robbed a bank, fled the city, waved my best friend off on an uncertain voyage, and tomorrow needed to face my mother and stepfather, and perhaps even evil Granville. Sheldon Thackrey might have guessed who robbed his bank, might try and have me locked up.

Mrs. Winterton said, 'Wensleydale is such a reliable cheese, but not after seven o'clock I always think.'

'I'm all right now, thank you.'

'Goodnight then, dear.' Mrs Winterton sighed and left the room.

At breakfast, dishes on the sideboard held porridge, toast and bacon. It was lovely to be alone with Theo.

Mr Winterton had already left the house for the early service, and Mrs Winterton with him.

When I poured tea for myself and Theo, I could pretend it was our house, and we were starting our lives together. This was how it would be, chatting over breakfast.

He thought that, too. I could tell by the way he smiled and lifted a rasher of bacon onto my plate.

'You look pale, Lydia. Are you still worried?'

Before I had time to answer, I heard Ma's voice in the hall as she pushed past the Wintertons' servant and came marching into the dining room.

'Lydia!' Ma rushed at me and almost upset my chair as she grabbed me. 'You devil! You've had me beside myself with worry. And look at you, cool as a cucumber, helping yourself to . . . '

'A hearty breakfast, like the condemned man is said to have?'

'Oh do stop harping. When you're a mother yourself you'll know what agonies you've put me through. Good morning, Theo.'

'Good morning, Mrs Thackrey.'

Although he sounded a little like a schoolboy, greeting the teacher, he stood up and pulled out a chair for Ma. 'Can I get you a cup of something? Tea?'

She shook her head. 'This is all I want. To see my delin- quent daughter.'

'Me delinquent? Me?'

'Whatever possessed you to disappear like that? Crampton and Ada had no business keeping it from me that you were with them. Wait until I see them!'

I told her it was no use her blaming them. Somebody had to be on my side and she should be glad of it. Of course she never could let a person have the last word.

'And don't imagine Sheldon will be trotting over to the church service this morning, and that everything will be nicely sorted out over a glass of sherry. We want you home. Sheldon wants to talk to you. Pronto.'

Theo had stopped buttering his toast, but seemed to forget he held the knife in his hand. 'Mrs Thackrey, I want to ask for Lydia's hand in marriage. We love each other and we'd like to marry as soon as possible. So I shall come back with you.' He put down the knife.

Ma took a deep breath. 'I can't say I'm surprised. I'm grateful to you for bringing Lydia home but . . . for heaven's sake let Lydia have her breakfast and let her talk to her stepfather as he asks.'

Theo held onto the back of my chair. His hands slid onto my shoulders. 'I want to come with you, and ask properly – yourself and Mr Thackrey. We love each other. I have a job in the town hall, a job with prospects. I know I couldn't keep Lydia in the style to which . . .'

Ma waved her hand, 'Not now Theo, darling. As far as I'm concerned it's yes. You seem to be the only one who holds any sway over her, I'm sure I don't.'

I jumped up. Between us, Theo and I managed to knock over the chair as we embraced.

Then I flung my arms around Phoebe. 'Thanks, Ma!'

'Don't thank me yet. We've Sheldon to talk to first.'

'He's not my father.'

'As good as. Anyway, he insists on talking to you, Lydia. Unfinished business, he says. So get on with that rasher of bacon and come home. I'll go back and smooth the way. You can't imagine the strain of being pig in the . . .'

'I won't talk to him without Theo beside me.'

' . . . pig in the middle. So for heaven's sake let's restore a little peace.' She got up to go, then turned back and said, 'You look very smart. Who took you shopping?'

'No one took me. I went with my friends, the Moran sisters.'

She raised an eyebrow but said nothing.

I wanted to tell her that if she still thought Mr Moran robbed the bank, she was wrong. But she left before I had chance to frame my words, which was perhaps just as well. It seemed not such a good idea to talk about bank robberies and weddings all at once.

The church bells chimed for the mid-morning service as

Theo and I walked through the side gate and along the path towards Allerton House.

I stopped. 'Let's make them wait. We intended to go to the service, so why change our plans just because Sheldon Thackrey snaps his fingers. If we don't go, perhaps he will come over and then I won't run the risk of seeing Granville.'

Theo hesitated. 'I just want to have it all sorted out between us, and get permission.'

'I want to go to the service. After all, we should be in the congregation since we intend to be married there.'

'You're right.'

I had quite a lot of prayers to say that day, all of them serious requests. That Sophie would be safe, and find her brother. That Sheldon Thackrey would not connect me with the second bank robbery. That Theo and I would be married in double-quick time. And if God granted me those requests, I swore I would never rob another bank as long as I lived, or at least not without very good cause.

After the service, there was no more delaying.

We walked to Allerton House, up the front steps and opened the unlocked door. Ma must have been watching from the dining-room window. She appeared in the hall. There wasn't a servant in sight so I guessed they had all been banished to quarters, so as not to earwig.

'Pa's waiting for you, Lydia,' she said wearily. 'Theo, come and join me for coffee. Sheldon needs to speak to Lydia privately. They'll join us shortly.'

The thought of stepping back into that house had terrified me. But with Ma acting so normally, and asking Theo for coffee, my fears slipped away. I opened the study door without knocking.

He was sitting in his chair by the fire, the newspaper on his lap. Some of the pages had fallen to the floor. I would not call him Pa. I would not call him anything.

'You wanted to see me?'

He gave a start, and began to scramble the papers together, picking up stray sheets from the floor, trying to re-assemble the newspaper and making a hash of it. 'Lydia, yes, yes. Come and sit down.'

He looked older, and somehow distracted. I wanted to help him with the newspaper, but didn't. The last time I had been in that room with him, I had begged him to believe that Granville had attacked me. He chose not to. My fists clenched. 'I'll stand. If you've something to say to me . . .'

He put the newspaper on the table by the window. As he moved, I saw that the door to his safe in the wall stood open.

When he walked towards me, I rooted myself so tightly to the spot that I felt I must be swaying. My shoulders, arms and legs hurt from the effort to stand firm.

'I owe you an apology,' he said quietly, taking my clenched fist in his hand. 'Now will you come and sit down?'

Even as I walked across the room to the chair he had placed opposite his, I listened for footsteps. Dorothea. Massey. Granville.

'My God, what have I done,' he said, half to himself. 'What have I done to you, to make you so wary?'

He was not going to sit down till I did. I perched on the edge of the chair.

'Where do I begin?' He reached out to the safe beside him, taking out a journal and some papers.

352

Perhaps we sat for half an hour, perhaps longer. He told me that it was not until after Christmas that he went through Mr Clutterbuck's papers, kept in the safe in his apartment above the bank. My poor dear Clarence Clutterbuck had uncovered Granville's shady deals, his unsecured loans to cronies, loans which would never be repaid. Mr Clutterbuck had arranged a meeting with Pa for ten o'clock on a Friday morning. They never kept that arrangement because by then, the cashier was dead.

Pa looked grey. He would have let me see the papers and journal, but I did not need to. The story of Granville's deceits and bad dealings told itself.

'I wanted to see the best in Granville, for his mother's sake. The truth is, he was never cut out for a banker's life. You once almost told me as much, after you'd coached him for the exams. I didn't listen. Yet you and my dear Phoebe never found a fault with him . . . '

Not to your face, I wanted to say.

'When I challenged him with what Clutterbuck had found out, Granville admitted his scheming. I saw the guilt in his face. You were right. He robbed the bank. He pulled the trigger.'

'He admitted it?'

Pa waved his hand, as if not wanting to go into details. 'I did what I should have done years ago. I beat it out of him. I'm not proud of that, or having to do it. But it's not the worst thing I did. The worst thing was letting an innocent man go to the gallows.'

I shut my eyes, thinking of Sophie, and Rosa. 'They knew it. His daughters knew he was innocent. They guessed why he pleaded guilty.'

353

'Yes. He took on the sins of his son. Danny was Granville's accomplice. But it was Granville who pulled the trigger. With my gun. Afterwards he threw it in the River Aire. For that and what he did to you . . .' For a long time he seemed unable to speak. 'If there were some way . . . I owe those girls. The man's daughters.'

'They won't want anything from you.' I suppressed the sudden urge to tell him they had some small compensation.

'That's a pity,' Pa said. 'And do you know, the strangest thing . . . what made me begin to re-think my certainties . . . He was a fisherman you know, Mr Moran.'

'I know.'

'Kept worms, maggots, that sort of thing.'

'Did he?' I shifted in my chair, remembering the bag of worms we had tipped onto the remaining bank notes.

'He bred them. That was what led to his dismissal – using a bank vault for his own little business of breeding bait for anglers.'

'Oh.'

'After Christmas, by some bizarre fluke or . . . I'm glad I'm not a superstitious man or I would say it was a hand from beyond the grave.'

'What?'

'One of the vaults was crawling with worms. They'd gorged themselves on paper currency.'

'Good heavens.'

'The worms must somehow have found their way through the ventilation system, or through cracks in the walls or floor. God knows how. It was a judgement on me. That very day, I went up to Clutterbuck's apartment. The police had gone through the place, but of course they didn't look in the safe, and I wasn't about to invite the constabulary to check whatever private papers he kept there. That was up to me. If I'd done it sooner . . . but with your mother and the baby . . . and then . . . '

He still held the papers in his hand. 'I was going to show you . . . Clutterbuck's journal, his notes, but you don't want to see them?'

I shook my head.

He shut the safe door.

So had he reported Granville to the police, I wondered, but could not bring myself to say my stepbrother's name.

As if he read my thoughts, Pa said, 'There's someone else owes you an apology besides me.'

He rang the bell.

Perhaps he meant Dorothea, or Massey. But when Emma came to the door in answer to his ring, he asked her to request Master Granville to come to the study.

'I don't want to see him. Not ever. He should be arrested.'

'I can't do that. I can't have more blood on my hands, and the scandal . . . This will be the last time. He must beg your pardon.'

'I won't give it. Don't make me see him.'

'I've told him he must. I can't go back on that.' Pa rose from his chair and placed himself between me and the door.

Granville tapped and walked in. 'You wanted to see me, Pa?'

'Don't call me by that name. You know what you must do. Do it, then be gone.'

Granville stared at his feet, and then raised his eyes towards me. All his arrogance had fled. I remembered the

355

evening when he poured himself a whisky and knelt before me. As I thought of it, the stench of his breath seemed to make a cloud around me, even though he was too far away. His left cheek bore a pale yellow stain, as though from a fading bruise.

'I'm very sorry for what I did, Lydia. I beg your pardon.'

He did not look as though he expected a reply, and I could think of none to give, not even a curse.

Silence hung in the room.

Pa rang the bell. After a few moments, Emma appeared again.

'Telephone the lodge, Emma. Tell Massey we'll have the motor now. Master Granville is leaving.'

Granville turned and walked away. At the door, he turned back. 'Father!'

Pa averted his eyes. 'Just go. Go now.'

When the door closed, we waited. Pa went back to his chair. He sighed. The fire crackled. The front door opened, and closed. Moments later, tyres crunched over gravel.

Pa went to the sideboard, poured himself a brandy and drank it down in one great gulp. 'Come, I believe your Ma has ordered coffee.'

'Theo is with her.'

'Yes.'

Pa's thoughts seemed to be elsewhere as Ma gave him coffee. But he listened gravely while Theo made his speech about our being in love and wanting to marry, explaining his post with prospects at the Town Hall.

Ma took Pa's arm. She kissed his cheek, then stroked the back of his neck. 'Well darling, they're waiting for you to say yes. I already have, you see.'

'Then who am I to say anything but congratulations?'

He shook Theo's hand. I grabbed Pa and kissed him.

Ma unhooked me. 'Now, Theo, I suggest you go back to the parsonage and ask your parents to join us for Sunday dinner. And Sheldon, darling, why don't you take a walk across with Theo. The air will do you good and I'm sure Mr Winterton will have missed having sherry with you.'

Theo took both my hands in his. We wanted to jump for joy, and I did.

'Theo dear, take Mr Thackrey to have a word with your parents, and say I warmly invite them to lunch. Let me have a few moments with my daughter. And I shall need to make the arrangements for three extra places.'

She waited until they had gone.

'Shall I ring the bell?' I asked.

'No, no. I made the arrangements earlier. I just thought we needed a little chat.'

'About the wedding?'

'Possibly. And about . . . Well, how do I put this in a delicate fashion? Am I to take it, from your clothing, and the understanding that your friend Sophie Moran has set sail from these shores, that you have somehow . . . shall we say, come in to your legacy from your natural father?'

'But . . .'

'Think!' she said. 'I know we have never spoken of a legacy . . .'

'No..' We'd never spoken of a natural father either.

'No matter. But obviously you've got money from somewhere and I for one don't believe it came from the generosity or shallow purse of Mr Crampton or Ada. So it must have been your legacy?' She gazed out across the

357

garden, to where Pa and Theo walked side by side towards the side gate that led to the parsonage.

Very slowly, I cottoned on. 'I suppose so. It must have been my legacy.'

'Good. That's settled then. Now about Granville . . .'

'I don't want to know.'

She ignored this, and walked to the window. 'Look – snowdrops! Aren't they a delight? Such a promise after a long hard winter.'

'Yes, I noticed them as we came through the wood.'

'I don't suppose you remember, when you were a child, that I once had a good friend, a gentleman who taught medical sorts of stuff.'

'Vaguely.'

'He once told me something very interesting. A child can only have blue eyes if one of its parents has blue eyes.'

'I know. I learned that at school.'

She looked at me in great surprise. 'Really? You never told me. No wonder Penelope went to Oxford if they taught you that sort of stuff.'

'What does that have to do with snowdrops?'

'With snowdrops, nothing. With Granville, everything. Your stepsister Cecilia is the one who favours her mother. What colour eyes does she have?'

'She says hazel.'

'Exactly. Oh perhaps I shouldn't even be saying any of this. It doesn't matter now.'

'You can't stop now. Are you saying that you-know-who isn't . . .'

'Granville isn't Sheldon's child.'

'Does Pa know?'

'I don't know. Not for me to ask, not for me or you to interfere in that way, except to make ourselves agreeable, and make Sheldon's life a long and happy one. Poor dear. Sometimes I thought he did know. You see the first Mrs Thackrey knew that Sheldon loved me. Perhaps that was why she . . . Well, perhaps that was why he had such an odd assortment of feelings towards Granville. Nothing in families is simple. I just want you to know that, in case it helps. If it doesn't now, it may, sometime in the future. Life's peculiar that way. A little thing that you dismiss comes back later and takes a different shape.'

She was right. I didn't know what shape that knowledge might take in the future but in that moment, I felt a kind of grudging pity towards the stupid Granville who never had been cut out for what Pa had in mind.

'Where has he gone?'

'Abroad. Don't worry yourself about where. That Chamber of Commerce chap, what's his name?'

'Mr Broughton.'

'Mr Broughton. He's found Granville an overseas post very far away, where he can do no harm.'

'I wouldn't think there is such a place.'

'Well at least you needn't worry. He won't set foot in England again.'

Sophie

We walked arm in arm by Westminster at night, gazing at the moon's shifting reflection in the Thames. Gas lights glowed. Big Ben's face seemed to smile at the people strolling by.

This was an England I'd never seen before. We visited the British Museum, Buckingham Palace, the art galleries. None of it felt as if it belonged to me. Even after only a year and a half in New York, that was where I belonged, where you could walk Manhattan top to bottom, move through rags and riches and back to rags. Because that was how life had been for me, with nothing certain, except the love of those closest to you. London felt foreign, strange, until we went to the theatre.

It was the time between the matinee and the evening performance. I took Fergal to meet Rosa in her dressing room. She leaped at me, and I thought would never let me go. It's true that I looked different. Like someone who had made a new start. I could see Fergal impressed even her.

'I did see you once before.' He shook her hand. 'You were on quayside, waving to Sophie. She watched you until you were out of sight, and I watched her, watching you.'

'Well you better keep your eyes on the stage tonight,' Rosa warned him. 'I like the full attention of my audience.'

After he left us alone and went to the stalls bar, she made us a cup of tea. 'Look at you, Sophie.' We gazed at each other in her mirror. 'You still haven't learned how to put make-up on.'

'I don't want to. I'm not planning to go on stage.'

'Sophie! You are hopeless. Sit down, let me show you what a difference it can make.'

'Don't plaster me in grease paint.'

The scent and the look of her dressing table, make-up and costumes gave me just the same thrill of excitement as in the Blanchflower Babes's dressing room at The Grand Theatre when she was in the pantomime all those years ago, but I didn't want to look like a performer.

'No! Some of my own make-up. Watch, just see if it doesn't make you feel on top of the world and ready for anything.'

'I already feel that way.'

She stopped and looked at me in surprise. It was then I saw that the pain of all that had happened still haunted her, and I felt guilty that sometimes, just sometimes, I could forget.

She pushed away the make-up. 'Some other time.'

'Yes.'

There were sounds in the corridor. A knock on the door. Soon I would have to go.

'I'm terrible,' she whispered as we sat together in the few more minutes before her call came. 'Don't tell anyone, but I have lessons every morning – diction, dancing, singing. We thought I did everything properly, but I don't.'

So it was a surprise to me to see her on stage, full of confidence and life, her eyes shining, throwing smiles to her leading man. In the story, she was eloping with him to Vienna to avoid an arranged marriage, and it was almost as romantic as her performance in Montague Burton's drama group.

During the interval, I told Fergal how we had all gone to see her in *Humpty-Dumpty* at the Grand Theatre, and sat on the front row. Then walked home together in the cold January night, each of us trying on her new gloves from Mrs Thackrey.

'I can see her,' he said, 'and hear her singing "Me and My Shadow". I can feel the nip in the air, and hear your mother coughing. You'll have to go on telling me things, so that I'll know what it was like for you.'

And as the lights went down for the second act, he kissed my hair.

Afterwards we all went out to supper at a place with red lampshades and white tablecloths.

In real life, her leading man is much older than he looks on stage. I do believe he is in love with Rosa. She said not, when I asked her in the ladies' cloakroom.

We sat on pink velvet chairs in the powder room. Rosa lit a cigarette. 'I didn't have a chance to ask you before. But what about Danny? You said he gave you away, and made

362

a speech at the wedding. Where is he now? How did he take the news about Dad?'

'He took it badly. He's gone to join a silent order of monks in upstate New York.'

'You're kidding?'

'No. He said he'll never be able to atone for what he did to Dad. And also, there were certain people after him. He'd got into a bit of bother.'

'Doesn't he ever learn?'

'Seems not. He's quite sure that the last place these people will look for him is in a monastery.'

'Well yes, I can see that. But silent?'

'He won't be asked any awkward questions, will he? And he's taken the name Brother Sebastian, because he feels shot through with arrows.'

'And what about his share of the bank robbery money? The first bank robbery I mean.'

'Gone.'

'You didn't tell him about ours?'

'No.'

'Thank God for that. It's a pity it's a silent order he's joined.' Rosa flicked ash into the china dish of rose petals. 'He won't be able to do his impersonation of the train.'

One thing did make me nervous, and that was the thought of taking Fergal to May's shop. It's one thing admitting to being poor and quite another expecting to be bitten to death by fleas. But we didn't stay long, just long enough for May to get her coat on and come out to the taxi, so that we could collect the Scholar and go for lunch at the Queen's Hotel.

But first, May directed the driver to take us round the old area of the Bank for one last time. House after house was boarded up and abandoned. Whole streets were reduced to rubble, so the journey over the cobbles felt like a nightmare where you try to find your way to a familiar place and the landmarks have shifted places, grown in size, or disappeared.

'Where's Tab Street?' Fergal asked.

Tab Street was gone.

'They're demolishing 'em all,' May said. 'Part of the slum clearance they say. It's an insult if you ask me. How dare they say we lived in slums? Yours was a little palace, Sophie.'

The Scholar's street was still standing and only two or three houses boarded up. He was watching for the taxi, and came out straight away, his hair plastered down, wearing a good suit that smacked of May's shop.

I introduced Fergal to him and they shook hands awkwardly across the taxi seats.

'I've replaced the clip and packed your Mam's mirror,' the Scholar said, as we left the old neighbourhood of the Bank behind. 'You must collect it on the way back, so it can hang on your wall in New York.'

And I wished he hadn't said that, because then I had to look out of the window very attentively, to keep from crying.

Lydia

'Theo and I have talked about it. We want a quiet wedding.'

'Absolute nonsense!' Ma was sitting on my bed, swatches of bridal material spread on the counterpane.

'You and Pa didn't make a great fuss over your nuptials, and don't say you did, because I was there.'

She gave a great sigh, as if I knew nothing. She explained. It would look bad for the family not to push the boat out. People might imagine Pa didn't value his adopted daughter, which he did, very much.

'Your life might turn out drearily enough, hitched to a penniless architect. You might at least try and get off to a good start.'

'There's nothing dreary about Theo.'

'Yes, yes, he's a fine specimen, I'll grant you . . .'

'Specimen?'

'Stop quibbling with everything I say.' She laid a sheaf of white satin across my arm. 'How about this?'

'I prefer cream to white.'

'So do I.' She tossed the white satin aside. 'White is so stark and uncompromising. Try this.'

I stood in front of the mirror, holding the top-of-the-milk creamy satin material at my throat.

'That's the one,' Ma said. 'Now. Bridesmaids?'

'Penelope I suppose. And I'd like Rosa.'

Ma's face, watching me through the mirror, lit up with her cheeriest smile. 'Rosa Devine, musical comedy star! Brilliant, darling. She'll move us into a different sphere as far as the press are concerned. Of course, you must out-shine her. We'll have the bridesmaids wear little caps of some sort, to cover their hair.'

'Rosa might not be free to come. It'll be a Saturday. She'll have shows.'

'She will be free on your Saturday. Bank on it.'

From the garden, I heard barking. Theo had trained Patience to call to me. I looked from the window. There Theo stood, looking up.

'I'm coming, darling!' I waved to him. Patience wagged her tail. 'I'm off out now, Ma. We're taking Patience for a walk.'

'If you must. At least we've got a lot decided today. I can begin to picture it now, you'll walk across the path through the side gate to St Stephen's on Sheldon's arm, Penelope and Rosa holding your train. Will the other girl come, Rosa's sister?'

'Sophie Corey. Yes. She's over here with her husband, and they've arranged to stay for the wedding.'

'Good. And at least both girls have shed that name of theirs. What was it?'

'Moran.'

Ma sighed. 'Off you go then. I'll be in touch with the dressmaker. When she comes tomorrow, we'll settle on the design.'

I hurried down to Theo. He was waiting for me on the drive. When I ran into his arms he picked me up and whirled me round and round. Patience ran in circles herself, barking with delight.

'I love you, Lydia Bellamy Thackrey,' Theo said. 'I wish we were marrying tomorrow.'

'So do I.'

We set off walking through the fields at the back of the house, Theo carrying the picnic basket. The creamy yellow primroses were out, and tiny blue speedwells. Ma's wedding mania must have been catching. I started to wonder what flowers I would carry on my big day, and who might catch my bouquet.

On the morning of my wedding, Sophie came to the house early, to help me get ready. When the hairdresser left, she and I took a breather. With a robe around my shoulders, and she in her silky summer dress, we stood at the bedroom window and looked at the marquees. On top of each tent, a colourful banner blew in the breeze. By the tennis courts, a group of men were putting the finishing touches to the bandstand, festooning it with ribbons and balloons. Through the open window, the sound of birdsong floated across from the woods. Then the musicians began to tune their instruments.

'There's my Fergal,' Sophie said. 'Look where he's standing.'

He stood on the edge of the wood, pausing to light a cigarette.

'What about it?' I asked.

'It's where we all sat that day, my family, when we came to your garden party. Little Billy laughed his head off when I swung him round. Mam was sitting with her back against that very tree, thinking this was the life, the life of Riley. And Danny, like a daft monkey hanging from the branches.'

'Don't go all morose on me.'

'I'm not. It's just that . . . new things happen in life don't they? Now, when I think of your garden and that wood, there'll be a new scene to overlay the old one. Not just the Moran family on their day out, but Fergal, on the morning of your wedding. Stopping for a smoke at the spot where little Billy laughed for the last time in his life.'

'I wish you wouldn't say things like that.'

'Sorry. I didn't mean to upset you.'

'I've gone all shivery. You're here to help me go through with this.'

'You're not getting cold feet are you?'

'Not a bit, as far as Theo's concerned. It's everything else that goes with it.'

It was the fuss, the Thackrey family, the press and photographers that would descend.

'Forget all that.' Sophie waved away my misgivings. 'After today, it'll be just you and Theo. Here, get your stockings on. I've something that'll be both borrowed and blue. This garter. I bought it at Saks Fifth Avenue, knowing it'd come in handy.'

Slowly and carefully, I drew on my white silk stockings, and then the blue garter.

'I hope you'll enjoy today,' Sophie patted her hair into place. 'I enjoyed my wedding, even though there was only Danny there for me, on my side. The church was packed with Coreys, sitting on both sides, as if that evened it up.'

On my side, at St Stephen's, would be Ma and my two little brothers. Mr Crampton and Ada. There'd be my step-sisters and their steel magnate and concrete mixer husbands, and families, all mentally totting up the cost of the nuptials and wondering how much of the Thackrey fortune would be squandered on the actress's daughter. The thought of them all staring at the back of Theo's and my head seemed to turn my innards to iron.

'The whole thing's a charade, Sophie. I don't think I can do it.'

'You're not going to jilt him?'

'No! He's the love of my life. I can't imagine being without him. I can't wait to be with him all the time. But maybe we could just run away, to Gretna Green or something. It's not too late, is it? Would you go ask him? Would you stay behind and explain if we do?'

'No!'

'I feel such a fraud. Even Theo doesn't know . . .'

Sophie walked across to close the bedroom door which the hairdresser had left ajar.

'No. And neither does Fergal know. And he's not going to.'

'I'm not the person Theo thinks he's marrying. That's why I feel a fraud. If he knew we'd robbed the bank . . . For heaven's sake, he's a clergyman's son.'

Sophie lifted my dress from its hanger. 'No one truly knows another person, and a good thing too. It's not what went before that matters. It's what comes next.'

'We're partners in crime, Sophie. Will we carry that secret to our graves?'

'Now who's being morbid? But yes, we will. That's what a secret is. It's just separate from Fergal, and it'll be separate from Theo. We had to do something, Lydia. And wouldn't you do the same again?'

When she put it that way, and I remembered how things were, I nodded.

'Well then. Are you going to step into this gown, or will it go over your head?'

'Over my head.'

And when I was dressed and ready, in came my bridesmaids, in their blue gowns and small caps, Rosa's cap bulging because of her tucked in copper curls.

Sophie kissed my cheek. 'I'll see you in the church.'

I watched her and Fergal walk arm in arm along the path towards the church, where I would walk in just a few minutes more, on Sheldon Thackrey's arm, with Rosa and Penelope to carry my train.

'I hope you don't mind those little caps,' I said to them. 'It was Ma's idea.'

'Great relief!' Rosa said. 'I don't want my hair to be the star of the show.'

Ma came in, dressed in peach-coloured silk with a straw hat in a matching colour wound with broad ribbons. 'Your bouquet is downstairs. You can pick it up on the way out.' She gave me a kiss. 'You look exquisite. Now I must go. Don't want to weep too soon.'

The walk to the church felt unreal. But Sophie was right. You could overlay a landscape with a new story. I passed by Granville's summerhouse with only the smallest of shudders.

And when Theo heard us clip-clopping into the church and turned to smile, it was as if everyone else melted away.

On our way back down the aisle, Sophie winked at me. I smiled my bride's radiant smile. No matter how I far I travelled with Theo, the love of my life, my husband and soul mate, I would never forget my partner in crime.

Acknowledgements

Thanks to Ian Blakeman; Catherine Fell; Barbara Garden; Jill Hyem; Ann-Mary Inglehearn; Ralph Lindley and Mary Patterson.

Also by Frances Brody

Sisters on Bread Street

Leeds, 1914. Sisters Julia and Margaret Wood are
struggling to rise above devastating poverty, while the
threat of war looms large over their community. Angry
feelings about foreigners have reached boiling point; their
German-Jewish father's search for work proves hopeless,
leaving entrepreneurial Julia to keep the family afloat by
hawking homemade pies on the streets of Leeds.

Her beautiful elder sister Margaret, an apprentice
milliner and new member of the suffragette set, seeks a
faster way out of the daily grind, pinning her hopes on a
rich suffragette's journalist son, Thomas.

But as the war rages on, it is left to Julia to discover the
true meaning of courage and family, as she learns to
look forward to the start of the new day – and the
promise of a better life ahead.

'This beautifully evoked slice of regional experience
offers universal appeal . . . a colourful network of
characters leaps from the pages' *Guardian*

**Available now in paperback and ebook
from Piatkus**

Also by Frances Brody

Sixpence in Her Shoe

In 1920s Leeds, Jess is starting on her journey through life. Growing up in the aftermath of the Great War, she is torn between her downtrodden father and her cantankerous, ambitious mother. After a disastrous spell as housekeeper to the local priest, she works happily in the office of her uncle's shoe factory and falls in love with her childhood sweetheart, Wilf.

But Wilf is determined to be a successful artist, and Jess can't bring herself to stand in the way of his dreams. She also faces a bigger fight: she is consumed by the desire to save her godchild Leila from an orphanage – a battle that eventually threatens to break her heart.

A story of courage, loyalty and enduring love, and how the ties of family bind forever.

'[Frances Brody] has that indefinable talent of the born storyteller' *Daily Mail*

**Available now in paperback and ebook
from Piatkus**